EVERYMAN, I will go with thee,

and be thy guide,

In thy most need to go by thy side

GEORGE BORROW

Born at East Dereham, Norfolk, in 1803. Went
to live in Norwich in 1820 and was articled to a
solicitor. In 1824 he worked in a London publishing firm. In 1826 he started wandering
through England and the Continent. As an
agent to the Bible Society he travelled in Spain
from 1835 to 1839. Married in 1840 and lived at
Oulton Broad until his death in 1881.

GEORGE BORROW

The Romany Rye

INTRODUCTION BY
WALTER STARKIE
C.M.G., C.B.E., M.A., LITT.D.

DENT: LONDON
EVERYMAN'S LIBRARY
DUTTON: NEW YORK

NO. *1*20

64541

SBN: 460 00120 5

PUBLISHER'S NOTE

The Romany Rye forms virtually one book with
Lavengro; the author himself describes it as a
sequel to the latter. Dr Starkie's Introduction
to both works is accordingly printed in *Lavengro*
(Everyman's Library, No. 119).

SELECT BIBLIOGRAPHY

WORKS. *Faustus, His Life and Death* (from the German of F. M. von Klinger), 1825; *Romantic Ballads* (from the Danish of Öhlenschläger, and from the Kiempé Viser), and miscellaneous pieces (from the Danish of Ewald and others), 1826; *Targum, or Metrical Translations from Thirty Languages and Dialects*, 1835; *The Talisman of A. Pushkin, with other pieces* (from Russian and Polish), 1835; *Embéo e Majaró Lucas* . . . El *Evangelio segun S. Lucas, traducido al Romani*, 1837; *The Zincali* (Gypsies of Spain), 2 vols., 1841; *The Bible in Spain*, 3 vols., 1843; *Lavengro: The Scholar—The Gypsy—The Priest*, 3 vols., 1851; *The Romany Rye*, 2 vols., 1857; *The Sleeping Bard*, translated from the Cambrian British, 1860; *Wild Wales*, 3 vols., 1862; *Romano Lavo-Lil: Word-Book of the Romany*, 1874; *Násr Al-Din, Khwájah, The Turkish Jester* (from the Turkish), 1884; *Death of Balder* (from the Danish of Ewald), 1889; *Celtic Bards, Chiefs and Kings*, 1928.

COLLECTED EDITIONS. *The Life, Writings and Correspondence of George Borrow*, in 2 vols., by W. I. Knapp, appeared in 1899. Those who are specially interested in Borrow's philological acquirements, or deficiencies, will do well to consult the editions of *Lavengro* by Knapp (1900), and F. Hindes Groome (2 vols., 1901), and that of *The Romany Rye*, by John Sampson (1903). The Norwich edition, edited by C. Shorter, was issued in 16 vols., 1923–4, while the 'Definitive' edition is that issued by John Murray in seven volumes, including the Life of Borrow by Herbert Jenkins (1912). A complete bibliography was done by T. J. Wise (1914, 1966).

BIOGRAPHY AND CRITICISM. W. A. Dutt, *George Borrow in East Anglia*, 1896; R. A. J. Watling, *George Borrow: the Man and His Work*, 1908; E. Thomas, *George Borrow: the Man and His Books*, 1912; C. K. Shorter, *George Borrow and His Circle*, 1913, and *The Life of George Borrow*, 1920; R. T. Hopkins, *George Borrow, Lord of the Open Road*, 1922; G. A. Stephen, *Borrow House Museum: A Brief Account of the Life of George Borrow and His Norwich Home, with bibliography*, 1927; W. Starkie, *Spanish Raggle-Taggle*, 1934, *Introduction to Romany Rye*, 1948, and *In Saras Tents*, 1953; S. Dearden, *The Gypsy Gentleman*, 1939; E. Bigland, *In the Steps of George Borrow*, 1951; B. Vesey-Fitzgerald, *Gypsy Borrow*, 1953; R. Fréchet, *George Borrow*, 1956; R. R. Meyers, *George Borrow*, 1966.

CONTENTS

Contents

Contents

Contents

Contents

xiv   Contents

APPENDIX

ADVERTISEMENT

It having been frequently stated in print that the book called "Lavengro" was got up expressly against the popish agitation, in the years 1850–51, the author takes this opportunity of saying that the principal part of that book was written in the year '43, that the whole of it was completed before the termination of the year '46, and that it was in the hands of the publisher in the year '48. And here he cannot forbear observing, that it was the duty of that publisher to have rebutted a statement which he knew to be a calumny; and also to have set the public right on another point dealt with in the Appendix to the present work, more especially as he was the proprietor of a review enjoying, however undeservedly, a certain sale and reputation.

> "But take your own part, boy!
> For if you don't, no one will take it for you."

With respect to "Lavengro," the author feels that he has no reason to be ashamed of it. In writing that book he did his duty, by pointing out to his country people the nonsense which, to the greater part of them, is as the breath of their nostrils, and which, if indulged in, as it probably will be, to the same extent as hitherto, will, within a very few years, bring the land which he most loves beneath a foreign yoke: he does not here allude to the yoke of Rome.

Instead of being ashamed, has he not rather cause to be proud of a book which has had the honour of being rancorously abused and execrated by the very people of whom the country has least reason to be proud?

ONE day Cogia Efendy went to a bridal festival. The masters of the feast, observing his old and coarse apparel, paid him no consideration whatever. The Cogia saw that he had no chance of notice; so going out, he hurried to his house, and, putting on a splendid pelisse, returned to the place of festival. No sooner did he enter the door than the masters advanced to meet him, and saying, "Welcome, Cogia Efendy," with all imaginable honour and reverence, placed him at the head of the table, and said, "Please to eat, Lord Cogia." Forthwith the Cogia, taking hold of one of the furs of his pelisse, said, "Welcome, my pelisse; please to eat, my lord." The masters looking at the Cogia with great surprise, said, "What are you about?" Whereupon the Cogia replied, "As it is quite evident that all the honour paid, is paid to my pelisse, I think it ought to have some food too."—PLEASANTRIES OF THE COGIA NASR EDDIN EFENDI.

CHAPTER I

The Making of the Linch-pin—The Sound Sleeper—Breakfast—The
Postillion's Departure.

I AWOKE at the first break of day, and, leaving the
postillion fast asleep, stepped out of the tent. The dingle
was dank and dripping. I lighted a fire of coals, and got
my forge in readiness. I then ascended to the field, where
the chaise was standing as we had left it on the previous
evening. After looking at the cloud-stone near it, now
cold, and split into three pieces, I set about prying narrowly
into the condition of the wheel and axletree—the latter had
sustained no damage of any consequence, and the wheel,
as far as I was able to judge, was sound, being only
slightly injured in the box. The only thing requisite to set
the chaise in a travelling condition appeared to be a linch-
pin, which I determined to make. Going to the companion
wheel, I took out the linch-pin, which I carried down with
me to the dingle, to serve as a model.

I found Belle by this time dressed, and seated near the
forge: with a slight nod to her like that which a person
gives who happens to see an acquaintance when his mind
is occupied with important business, I forthwith set about
my work. Selecting a piece of iron which I thought would
serve my purpose, I placed it in the fire, and plying the
bellows in a furious manner, soon made it hot; then seizing
it with the tongs, I laid it on my anvil, and began to beat
it with my hammer, according to the rules of my art. The
dingle resounded with my strokes. Belle sat still, and occasionally smiled, but suddenly started up, and retreated towards her encampment, on a spark which I purposely sent
in her direction alighting on her knee. I found the making
of a linch-pin no easy matter; it was, however, less difficult
than the fabrication of a pony-shoe; my work, indeed, was
much facilitated by my having another pin to look at. In
about three-quarters of an hour I had succeeded tolerably

well, and had produced a linch-pin which I thought would serve. During all this time, notwithstanding the noise which I was making, the postillion never showed his face. His non-appearance at first alarmed me: I was afraid he might be dead, but, on looking into the tent, I found him still buried in the soundest sleep. "He must surely be descended from one of the seven sleepers," said I, as I turned away, and resumed my work. My work finished, I took a little oil, leather, and sand, and polished the pin as well as I could; then, summoning Belle, we both went to the chaise, where, with her assistance, I put on the wheel. The linch-pin which I had made fitted its place very well, and having replaced the other, I gazed at the chaise for some time with my heart full of that satisfaction which results from the consciousness of having achieved a great action; then, after looking at Belle in the hope of obtaining a compliment from her lips, which did not come, I returned to the dingle, without saying a word, followed by her. Belle set about making preparations for breakfast; and I taking the kettle, went and filled it at the spring. Having hung it over the fire, I went to the tent in which the postillion was still sleeping, and called upon him to arise. He awoke with a start, and stared around him at first with the utmost surprise, not unmixed, I could observe, with a certain degree of fear. At last, looking in my face, he appeared to recollect himself. "I had quite forgot," said he, as he got up, "where I was, and all that happened yesterday. However, I remember now the whole affair, thunder-storm, thunder-bolt, frightened horses, and all your kindness. Come, I must see after my coach and horses; I hope we shall be able to repair the damage." "The damage is already quite repaired," said I, "as you will see, if you come to the field above." "Yo don't say so," said the postillion, coming out of the tent; "well, I am mightily beholden to you. Good morning, young gentle-woman," said he, addressing Belle, who, having finished her preparations, was seated near the fire. "Good morning, young man," said Belle, "I suppose you would be glad of some breakfast; however, you must wait a little, the kettle does not boil." "Come and look at your chaise," said I; "but tell me how it happened that the noise which I have been making did not awake you; for three-quarters of an hour at least I was hammering close at your ear." " I heard you all the time," said the postillion, " but your hammering made me sleep all the sounder; I am used to hear hammering in my morning sleep. There's a forge close by the room where I sleep when I'm at home, at my inn; for we have all kinds of conveniences at my inn—forge, carpenter's shop, and wheelwright's,—so that when I heard you hammering I thought, no doubt, that it was the old noise, and that I was comfortable in my bed at my own inn." We now ascended to the field, where I showed the postillion his chaise. He looked at the pin attentively, rubbed his hands, and gave a loud laugh. " Is it not well done?" said I. " It will do till I get home," he replied. " And that is all you have to say?" I demanded. " And that's a good deal," said he, " considering who made it. But don't be offended," he added, " I shall prize it all the more for its being made by a gentleman, and no blacksmith; and so will my governor, when I show it to him. I shan't let it remain where it is, but will keep it, as a remembrance of you, as long as I live." He then again rubbed his hands with great glee, and said, " I will now go and see after my horses, and then to breakfast, partner, if you please." Suddenly, however, looking at his hands, he said, " Before sitting down to breakfast I am in the habit of washing my hands and face: I suppose you could not furnish me with a little soap and water." " As much water as you please," said I, " but if you want soap, I must go and trouble the young gentlewoman for some." " By no means," said the postillion, " water will do at a pinch." " Follow me," said I, and leading him to the pond of the frogs and newts, I said, " this is my ewer; you are welcome to part of it—the water is so soft that it is scarcely necessary to add soap to it;" then lying down on the bank, I plunged my head into the water, then scrubbed my hands and face, and afterwards wiped them with some long grass which grew on the margin of the pond. " Bravo," said the postillion, " I see you know how to make a shift:" he then followed my example, declared he never felt more refreshed in his life, and, giving a bound, said, " he would go and look after his horses."

We then went to look after the horses, which we found not much the worse for having spent the night in the open air. My companion again inserted their heads in the cornbags, and, leaving the animals to discuss their corn, returned with me to the dingle, where we found the kettle boiling. We sat down, and Belle made tea and did the honours of the meal. The postillion was in high spirits, ate heartily, and, to Belle's evident satisfaction, declared that he had never drank better tea in his life, or indeed any half so good. Breakfast over, he said that he must now go and harness his horses, as it was high time for him to return to his inn. Belle gave him her hand and wished him farewell: the postillion shook her hand warmly, and was advancing close up to her—for what purpose I cannot say—whereupon Belle, withdrawing her hand, drew herself up with an air which caused the postillion to retreat a step or two with an exceedingly sheepish look. Recovering himself, however, he made a low bow, and proceeded up the path. I attended him, and helped to harness his horses and put them to the vehicle; he then shook me by the hand, and taking the reins and whip mounted to his seat; ere he drove away he thus addressed me: "If ever I forget your kindness and that of the young woman below, dash my buttons. If ever either of you should enter my inn you may depend upon a warm welcome, the best that can be set before you, and no expense to either, for I will give both of you the best of characters to the governor, who is the very best fellow upon all the road. As for your linch-pin, I trust it will serve till I get home, when I will take it out and keep it in remembrance of you all the days of my life:" then giving the horses a jerk with his reins, he cracked his whip and drove off.

I returned to the dingle, Belle had removed the breakfast things, and was busy in her own encampment: nothing occurred, worthy of being related, for two hours, at the end of which time Belle departed on a short expedition, and I again found myself alone in the dingle.

CHAPTER II

The Man in Black—The Emperor of Germany—Nepotism—Donna Olympia—Omnipotence—Camillo Astalli—The Five Propositions.

IN the evening I received another visit from the man in black. I had been taking a stroll in the neighbourhood, and was sitting in the dingle in rather a listless manner, scarcely knowing how to employ myself; his coming, therefore, was by no means disagreeable to me. I produced the hollands and glass from my tent, where Isopel Berners had requested me to deposit them, and also some lump sugar, then taking the gotch I fetched water from the spring, and, sitting down, begged the man in black to help himself; he was not slow in complying with my desire, and prepared for himself a glass of hollands and water with a lump of sugar in it. After he had taken two or three sips with evident satisfaction, I, remembering his chuckling exclamation of "Go to Rome for money," when he last left the dingle, took the liberty, after a little conversation, of reminding him of it, whereupon, with a he! he! he! he replied, "Your idea was not quite so original as I supposed. After leaving you the other night, I remembered having read of an Emperor of Germany who conceived the idea of applying to Rome for money, and actually put it into practice.

"Urban the Eighth then occupied the papal chair, of the family of the Barbarini, nicknamed the Mosche, or Flies, from the circumstance of bees being their armorial bearing. The Emperor having exhausted all his money in endeavouring to defend the church against Gustavus Adolphus, the great King of Sweden, who was bent on its destruction, applied in his necessity to the Pope for a loan of money. The Pope, however, and his relations, whose cellars were at that time full of the money of the church, which they had been plundering for years, refused to lend him a scudo; whereupon a pasquinade picture was stuck up at Rome, representing the church lying on a bed, gashed with dreadful wounds, and beset all over with flies, which were sucking her, whilst the Emperor of Germany was kneeling before her with a miserable face, requesting a little money towards carrying on the war against the heretics, to which the poor church was made to say: 'How can I assist you, O my champion, do you not see that the flies have sucked me to the very bones?' Which story," said he, "shows that the idea of going to Rome for money was not quite so original as I imagined the other night, though utterly preposterous.

"This affair," said he, "occurred in what were called the days of nepotism. Certain popes, who wished to make themselves in some degree independent of the cardinals, surrounded themselves with their nephews and the rest of their family, who sucked the church and Christendom as much as they could, none doing so more effectually than the relations of Urban the Eighth, at whose death, according to the book called the ' Nipotismo di Roma,' there were in the Barbarini family two hundred and twenty-seven governments, abbeys and high dignities ; and so much hard cash in their possession, that threescore and ten mules were scarcely sufficient to convey the plunder of one of them to Palestrina." He added, however, that it was probable that Christendom fared better whilst the popes were thus independent, as it was less sucked, whereas before and after that period it was sucked by hundreds instead of tens, by the cardinals and all their relations, instead of by the pope and his nephews only.

Then, after drinking rather copiously of his hollands, he said that it was certainly no bad idea of the popes to surround themselves with nephews, on whom they bestowed great church dignities, as by so doing they were tolerably safe from poison, whereas a pope, if abandoned to the cardinals, might at any time be made away with by them, provided they thought that he lived too long, or that he seemed disposed to do anything which they disliked; adding, that Ganganelli would never have been poisoned provided he had had nephews about him to take care of his life, and to see that nothing unholy was put into his food, or a bustling stirring brother's wife like Donna Olympia. He then with a he ! he ! he ! asked me if I had ever read the book called the " Nipotismo di Roma "; and on my replying in the negative, he told me that it was a very curious and entertaining book, which he occasionally looked at in an idle hour, and proceeded to relate to me anecdotes out of the " Nipotismo di Roma," about the successor of Urban, Innocent the Tenth, and Donna Olympia, showing how fond he was of her, and how she cooked his food, and kept the cardinals away from it, and how she and her creatures plundered Christendom, with the sanction of the Pope, until Christendom, becoming enraged, insisted that he should put her away, which he did for a time, putting a nephew—one Camillo Astalli—in her place, in which, however, he did not continue long; for the Pope, conceiving a pique against him, banished him from his sight, and recalled Donna Olympia, who took care of his food, and plundered Christendom until Pope Innocent died.

I said that I only wondered that between pope and cardinals the whole system of Rome had not long fallen to the ground, and was told, in reply, that its not having fallen was the strongest proof of its vital power, and the absolute necessity for the existence of the system. That the system, notwithstanding its occasional disorders, went on. Popes and cardinals might prey upon its bowels, and sell its interests, but the system survived. The cutting off of this or that member was not able to cause Rome any vital loss; for, as soon as she lost a member, the loss was supplied by her own inherent vitality; though her popes had been poisoned by cardinals, and her cardinals by popes; and though priests occasionally poisoned popes, cardinals, and each other, after all that had been, and might be, she had still, and would ever have, her priests, cardinals, and pope.

Finding the man in black so communicative and reasonable, I determined to make the best of my opportunity, and learn from him all I could with respect to the papal system, and told him that he would particularly oblige me by telling me who the Pope of Rome was; and received for answer, that he was an old man elected by a majority of cardinals to the papal chair; who, immediately after his election, became omnipotent and equal to God on earth. On my begging him not to talk such nonsense, and asking him how a person could be omnipotent who could not always preserve himself from poison, even when fenced round by nephews, or protected by a bustling woman, he, after taking a long sip of hollands and water, told me that I must not expect too much from omnipotence; for example, that as it would be unreasonable to expect that One above could annihilate the past—for instance, the Seven Years' War, or the French Revolution—though any one who believed in Him would acknowledge Him to be omnipotent, so would it be unreasonable for the faithful to expect that the Pope could always guard himself from poison. Then, after looking at me for a moment stedfastly, and taking another sip, he told me that popes had frequently done impossibilities; for example, Innocent the Tenth had created a nephew; for, not liking particularly any of his real nephews, he had created the said Camillo Astalli his nephew; asking me, with a he! he! " What but omnipotence could make a young man nephew to a person to whom he was not in the slightest degree related?" On my observing that of course no one believed that the young fellow was really the Pope's nephew, though the Pope might have adopted him as such, the man in black replied, " that the reality of the nephew-ship of Camillo Astalli had hitherto never become a point of faith; let, however, the present pope, or any other pope, proclaim that it is necessary to believe in the reality of the nephewship of Camillo Astalli, and see whether the faithful would not believe in it. Who can doubt that," he added, " seeing that they believe in the reality of the five proposi-tions of Jansenius? The Jesuits, wishing to ruin the Jan-senists, induced a pope to declare that such and such damn-able opinions, which they called five propositions, were to be found in a book written by Jansen, though, in reality, no such propositions were to be found there; whereupon the existence of these propositions became forthwith a point of faith to the faithful. Do you then think," he de-manded, " that there is one of the faithful who would not swallow, if called upon, the nephewship of Camillo Astalli as easily as the five propositions of Jansenius?" " Surely, then," said I, " the faithful must be a pretty pack of sim-pletons!" Whereupon the man in black exclaimed, " What! a Protestant, and an infringer of the rights of faith! Here's a fellow, who would feel himself insulted if any one were to ask him how he could believe in the miraculous conception, calling people simpletons who swal-low the five propositions of Jansenius, and are disposed, if called upon, to swallow the reality of the nephewship of Camillo Astalli."

I was about to speak, when I was interrupted by the arrival of Belle. After unharnessing her donkey, and ad-justing her person a little, she came and sat down by us. In the meantime I had helped my companion to some more hollands and water, and had plunged with him into yet deeper discourse.

CHAPTER III

Necessity of Religion—The Great Indian One—Image-worship—
Shakespeare—The Pat Answer—Krishna—Amen.

HAVING told the man in black that I should like to know all the truth with regard to the Pope and his system, he assured me he should be delighted to give me all the information in his power; that he had come to the dingle, not so much for the sake of the good cheer which I was in the habit of giving him, as in the hope of inducing me to enlist under the banners of Rome, and to fight in her cause; and that he had no doubt that, by speaking out frankly to me, he ran the best chance of winning me over.

He then proceeded to tell me that the experience of countless ages had proved the necessity of religion; the necessity, he would admit, was only for simpletons; but as nine-tenths of the dwellers upon this earth were simpletons, it would never do for sensible people to run counter to their folly, but, on the contrary, it was their wisest course to encourage them in it, always provided that, by so doing, sensible people would derive advantage; that the truly sensible people of this world were the priests, who, without caring a straw for religion for its own sake, made use of it as a cord by which to draw the simpletons after them; that there were many religions in this world, all of which had been turned to excellent account by the priesthood; but that the one the best adapted for the purposes of priestcraft was the popish, which, he said, was the oldest in the world and the best calculated to endure. On my inquiring what he meant by saying the popish religion was the oldest in the world, whereas there could be no doubt that the Greek and Roman religion had existed long before it, to say nothing of the old Indian religion still in existence and vigour; he said, with a nod, after taking a sip at his glass, that, between me and him, the popish religion, that of Greece and Rome, and the old Indian system were, in reality, one and the same.

"You told me that you intended to be frank," said I; "but, however frank you may be, I think you are rather wild."

"We priests of Rome," said the man in black, "even those amongst us who do not go much abroad, know a great deal about church matters, of which you heretics have very little idea. Those of our brethren of the Propaganda, on their return home from distant missions, not unfrequently tell us very strange things relating to our dear mother; for example, our first missionaries to the East were not slow in discovering and telling to their brethren that our religion and the great Indian one were identical, no more difference between them than between Ram and Rome. Priests, convents, beads, prayers, processions, fastings, penances, all the same, not forgetting anchorites and vermin, he! he! The pope they found under the title of the grand lama, a sucking child surrounded by an immense number of priests. Our good brethren, some two hundred years ago, had a hearty laugh, which their successors have often re-echoed; they said that helpless suckling and its priests put them so much in mind of their own old man, surrounded by his cardinals, he! he! Old age is second childhood."

" Did they find Christ?" said I.

" They found him too," said the man in black, " that is, they saw his image; he is considered in India as a pure kind of being, and on that account, perhaps, is kept there rather in the background, even as he is here."

" All this is very mysterious to me," said I.

" Very likely," said the man in black; " but of this I am tolerably sure, and so are most of those of Rome, that modern Rome had its religion from ancient Rome, which had its religion from the East."

" But how?" I demanded.

" It was brought about, I believe, by the wanderings of nations," said the man in black. " A brother of the Propaganda, a very learned man, once told me—I do not mean Mezzofanti, who has not five ideas—this brother once told me that all we of the Old World, from Calcutta to Dublin, are of the same stock, and were originally of the same language, and——"

" All of one religion," I put in.

" All of one religion," said the man in black; " and now follow different modifications of the same religion."

" We Christians are not image-worshippers," said I.

" You heretics are not, you mean," said the man in black; " but you will be put down, just as you have always been, though others may rise up after you; the true religion is image-worship; people may strive against it, but they will only work themselves to an oil; how did it fare with that Greek Emperor, the Iconoclast, what was his name, Leon the Isaurian? Did not his image-breaking cost him Italy, the fairest province of his empire, and did not ten fresh images start up at home for every one which he demolished? Oh! you little know the craving which the soul sometimes feels after a good bodily image."

" I have indeed no conception of it," said I; " I have

an abhorrence of idolatry—the idea of bowing before a
graven figure!"

"The idea, indeed!" said Belle, who had now joined us.

"Did you never bow before that of Shakespeare?" said
the man in black, addressing himself to me, after a low bow
to Belle.

"I don't remember that I ever did," said I, "but even
suppose I did?"

"Suppose you did," said the man in black; "shame on
you, Mr. Hater of Idolatry; why, the very supposition
brings you to the ground; you must make figures of Shakespeare, must you? then why not of St. Antonio, or Ignacio,
or of a greater personage still! I know what you are
going to say," he cried, interrupting me, as I was about
to speak. "You don't make his image in order to pay it
divine honours, but only to look at it, and think of Shakespeare; but this looking at a thing in order to think of a
person is the very basis of idolatry. Shakespeare's works
are not sufficient for you; no more are the Bible or the
legend of Saint Anthony or Saint Ignacio for us, that is for
those of us who believe in them; I tell you, Zingara, that
no religion can exist long which rejects a good bodily
image."

"Do you think," said I, "that Shakespeare's works
would not exist without his image?"

"I believe," said the man in black, "that Shakespeare's
image is looked at more than his works, and will be looked
at, and perhaps adored, when they are forgotten. I am
surprised that they have not been forgotten long ago; I
am no admirer of them."

"But I can't imagine," said I, "how you will put aside
the authority of Moses. If Moses strove against image-
worship, should not his doing so be conclusive as to the
impropriety of the practice; what higher authority can you
have than that of Moses?"

"The practice of the great majority of the human race,"
said the man in black, "and the recurrence to image-worship where image-worship has been abolished. Do you
know that Moses is considered by the church as no better
than a heretic, and though, for particular reasons, it has
been obliged to adopt his writings, the adoption was merely
a sham one, as it never paid the slightest attention to them?
No, no, the church was never led by Moses, nor by one

mightier than he, whose doctrine it has equally nullified—I allude to Krishna in his second avatar; the church, it is true, governs in his name, but not unfrequently gives him the lie, if he happens to have said anything which it dislikes. Did you never hear the reply which Padre Paolo Segani made to the French Protestant Jean Anthoine Guerin, who had asked him whether it was easier for Christ to have been mistaken in his Gospel, than for the Pope to be mistaken in his decrees?"

" I never heard their names before," said I.

" The answer was pat," said the man in black, " though he who made it was confessedly the most ignorant fellow of the very ignorant order to which he belonged, the Augustine. ' Christ might err as a man,' said he, ' but the Pope can never err, being God.' The whole story is related in the Nipotismo."

" I wonder you should ever have troubled yourself with Christ at all," said I.

" What was to be done?" said the man in black; " the power of that name suddenly came over Europe, like the power of a mighty wind; it was said to have come from Judea, and from Judea it probably came when it first began to agitate minds in these parts; but it seems to have been known in the remote East, more or less, for thousands of years previously. It filled people's minds with madness; it was followed by books which were never much regarded, as they contained little of insanity; but the name! what fury that breathed into people! the books were about peace and gentleness, but the name was the most horrible of war-cries—those who wished to uphold old names at first strove to oppose it, but their efforts were feeble, and they had no good war-cry; what was Mars as a war-cry compared with the name of . . . .? It was said that they persecuted terribly, but who said so? The Christians. The Christians could have given them a lesson in the art of persecution, and eventually did so. None but Christians have ever been good persecutors; well, the old religion succumbed, Christianity prevailed, for the ferocious is sure to prevail over the gentle."

" I thought," said I, " you stated a little time ago that the Popish religion and the ancient Roman are the same?"

" In every point but that name, that Krishna and the fury and love of persecution which it inspired," said the man in black. "A hot blast came from the East, sounding Krishna; it absolutely maddened people's minds, and the people would call themselves his children; we will not belong to Jupiter any longer, we will belong to Krishna, and they did belong to Krishna; that is in name, but in nothing else; for who ever cared for Krishna in the Christian world, or who ever regarded the words attributed to him, or put them in practice?"

"Why, we Protestants regard his words, and endeavour to practise what they enjoin as much as possible."

"But you reject his image," sad the man in black; "better reject his words than his image: no religion can exist long which rejects a good bodily image. Why, the very negro barbarians of High Barbary could give you a lesson on that point; they have their fetish images, to which they look for help in their afflictions; they have like-wise a high priest, whom they call——"

"Mumbo Jumbo," said I; "I know all about him already."

"How came you to know anything about him?" said the man in black, with a look of some surprise.

"Some of us poor Protestants tinkers," said I, "though we live in dingles, are also acquainted with a thing or two."

"I really believe you are," said the man in black, staring at me; "but, in connection with this Mumbo Jumbo, I could relate to you a comical story about a fellow, an English servant, I once met at Rome."

"It would be quite unnecessary," said I; "I would much sooner hear you talk about Krishna, his words and image."

"Spoken like a true heretic," said the man in black; "one of the faithful would have placed his image before his words; for what are all the words in the world com-pared with a good bodily image!"

"I believe you occasionally quote his words?" said I.

"He! he!" said the man in black; "occasionally."

"For example," said I, "upon this rock I will found my church."

"He! he!" said the man in black; "you must really become one of us."

"Yet you must have had some difficulty in getting the rock to Rome?"

"None whatever," said the man in black; "faith can remove mountains, to say nothing of rocks—ho! ho!"

"But I cannot imagine," said I, "what advantage you could derive from perverting those words of Scripture in which the Saviour talks about eating his body."

"I do not know, indeed, why we troubled our heads about the matter at all," said the man in black; "but when you talk about perverting the meaning of the text, you speak ignorantly, Mr. Tinker; when he whom you call the Saviour gave his followers the sop, and bade them eat it, telling them it was his body, he delicately alluded to what it was incumbent upon them to do after his death, namely, to eat his body."

"You do not mean to say that he intended they should actually eat his body?"

"Then you suppose ignorantly," said the man in black; "eating the bodies of the dead was a heathenish custom, practised by the heirs and legatees of people who left property; and this custom is alluded to in the text."

"But what has the New Testament to do with heathen customs," said I, "except to destroy them?"

"More than you suppose," said the man in black. "We priests of Rome, who have long lived at Rome, know much better what the New Testament is made of than the heretics and their theologians, not forgetting their Tinkers; though I confess some of the latter have occasionally surprised us— for example, Bunyan. The New Testament is crowded with allusions to heathen customs, and with words connected with pagan sorcery. Now, with respect to words, I would fain have you, who pretend to be a philologist, tell me the meaning of Amen."

I made no answer.

"We of Rome," said the man in black, "know two or three things of which the heretics are quite ignorant; for example, there are those amongst us—those, too, who do not pretend to be philologists—who know what Amen is, and, moreover, how we got it. We got it from our ancestors, the priests of ancient Rome; and they got the word from their ancestors of the East, the priests of Buddh and Brahma."

"And what is the meaning of the word?" I demanded.

"Amen," said the man in black, "is a modification of the old Hindoo formula, Omani batsikhom, by the almost ceaseless repetition of which the Indians hope to be received finally to the rest or state of forgetfulness of

Buddh or Brahma; a foolish practice you will say, but are you heretics much wiser, who are continually sticking Amen to the end of your prayers, little knowing when you do so, that you are consigning yourselves to the repose of Buddh! Oh, what hearty laughs our missionaries have had when comparing the eternally-sounding Eastern gibberish of Omani batsikhom, Omani batsikhom, and the Ave Maria and Amen Jesus of our own idiotical devotees."

"I have nothing to say about the Ave Marias and Amens of your superstitious devotees," said I; "I dare say that they use them nonsensically enough, but in putting Amen to the end of a prayer, we merely intend to express, 'So let it be.'"

"It means nothing of the kind," said the man in black; "and the Hindoos might just as well put your national oath at the end of their prayers, as perhaps they will after a great many thousand years, when English is forgotten, and only a few words of it remembered by dim tradition without being understood. How strange if, after the lapse of four thousand years, the Hindoos should damn themselves to the blindness so dear to their present masters, even as their masters at present consign themselves to the forgetfulness so dear to the Hindoos; but my glass has been empty for a considerable time; perhaps, Bellissima Biondina," said he, addressing Belle, "you will deign to replenish it?"

"I shall do no such thing," said Belle, "you have drunk quite enough, and talked more than enough, and to tell you the truth I wish you would leave us alone."

"Shame on you, Belle," said I; "consider the obligations of hospitality."

"I am sick of that word," said Belle, "you are so frequently misusing it; were this place not Mumpers' Dingle, and consequently as free to the fellow as ourselves, I would lead him out of it."

"Pray be quiet, Belle," said I. "You had better help yourself," said I, addressing myself to the man in black, "the lady is angry with you."

"I am sorry for it," said the man in black; "if she is angry with me, I am not so with her, and shall be always proud to wait upon her; in the meantime, I will wait upon myself."

CHAPTER IV

The Proposal—The Scotch Novel—Latitude—Miracles—Pestilent
Heretics—Old Fraser—Wonderful Texts—No Armenian.

THE man in black having helped himself to some more of
his favourite beverage, and tasted it, I thus addressed him :
" The evening is getting rather advanced, and I can see
that this lady," pointing to Belle, " is anxious for her tea,
which she prefers to take cosily and comfortably with me
in the dingle : the place, it is true, is as free to you as to ourselves, nevertheless, as we are located here by necessity,
whilst you merely come as a visitor, I must take the liberty
of telling you that we shall be glad to be alone, as soon as
you have said what you have to say, and have finished the
glass of refreshment at present in your hand. I think you
said some time ago that one of your motives for coming
hither was to induce me to enlist under the banner of Rome.
I wish to know whether that was really the case?"

" Decidedly so," said the man in black; " I come here
principally in the hope of enlisting you in our regiment, in
which I have no doubt you could do us excellent service."

" Would you enlist my companion as well?" I demanded.

" We should be only too proud to have her among us,
whether she comes with you or alone," said the man in
black, with a polite bow to Belle.

" Before we give you an answer," I replied, " I would
fain know more about you; perhaps you will declare your
name?"

" That I will never do," said the man in black; " no one
in England knows it but myself, and I will not declare it,
even in a dingle; as for the rest, *Sono un Prete Cattolico
Appostolico*—that is all that many a one of us can say for
himself, and it assuredly means a great deal."

" We will now proceed to business," said I. " You must
be aware that we English are generally considered a self-
interested people."

" And with considerable justice," said the man in black,
drinking. " Well, you are a person of acute perception,
and I will presently make it evident to you that it would
be to your interest to join with us. You are at present,
evidently, in very needy circumstances, and are lost, not
only to yourself, but to the world; but should you enlist

with us, I could find you an occupation not only agreeable, but one in which your talents would have free scope. I would introduce you in the various grand houses here in England, to which I have myself admission, as a surprising young gentleman of infinite learning, who by dint of study has discovered that the Roman is the only true faith. I tell you confidently that our popish females would make a saint, nay, a God of you; they are fools enough for anything. There is one person in particular with whom I would wish to make you acquainted, in the hope that you would be able to help me to perform good service to the holy see. He is a gouty old fellow, of some learning, residing in an old hall, near the great western seaport, and is one of the very few amongst the English Catholics possessing a grain of sense. I think you could help us to govern him, for he is not unfrequently disposed to be restive, asks us strange questions—occasionally threatens us with his crutch; and behaves so that we are often afraid that we shall lose him, or, rather, his property, which he has bequeathed to us, and which is enormous. I am sure that you could help us to deal with him; sometimes with your humour, sometimes with your learning, and perhaps occasionally with your fists.''

"And in what manner would you provide for my companion?" said I.

"We would place her at once," said the man in black, "in the house of two highly respectable Catholic ladies in this neighbourhood, where she would be treated with every care and consideration till her conversion should be accomplished in a regular manner; we would then remove her to a female monastic establishment, where, after undergoing a year's probation, during which time she would be instructed in every elegant accomplishment, she should take the veil. Her advancement would speedily follow, for, with such a face and figure, she would make a capital lady abbess, especially in Italy, to which country she would probably be sent; ladies of her hair and complexion—to say nothing of her height—being a curiosity in the south. With a little care and management she could soon obtain a vast reputation for sanctity; and who knows but after her death she might become a glorified saint—he! he! Sister Maria Theresa, for that is the name I propose you should bear. Holy Mother Maria Theresa—glorified and celestial saint, I have the honour of drinking to your health," and the man in black drank.

" Well, Belle," said I, " what have you to say to the gentleman's proposal?"

" That if he goes on in this way I will break his glass against his mouth."

" You have heard the lady's answer," said I.

" I have," said the man in black, " and shall not press the matter. I can't help, however, repeating that she would make a capital lady abbess; she would keep the nuns in order, I warrant her; no easy matter ! Break the glass against my mouth—he ! he ! How she would send the holy utensils flying at the nuns' heads occasionally, and just the person to wring the nose of Satan, should he venture to appear one night in her cell in the shape of a handsome black man. No offence, madam, no offence, pray retain your seat," said he, observing that Belle had started up; " I mean no offence. Well, if you will not consent to be an abbess, perhaps you will consent to follow this young Zingaro, and to co-operate with him and us. I am a priest, madam, and can join you both in an instant, *connubio stabili*, as I suppose the knot has not been tied already."

" Hold your mumping gibberish," said Belle, " and leave the dingle this moment, for though 'tis free to every one, you have no right to insult me in it."

" Pray be pacified," said I to Belle, getting up, and placing myself between her and the man in black, " he will presently leave, take my word for it—there, sit down again," said I, as I led her to her seat; then, resuming my own, I said to the man in black : " I advise you to leave the dingle as soon as possible."

" I should wish to have your answer to my proposal first," said he.

" Well, then, here you shall have it : I will not entertain your proposal; I detest your schemes : they are both wicked and foolish."

" Wicked," said the man in black, " have they not—he ! he !—the furtherance of religion in view?"

" A religion," said I, " in which you yourself do not believe, and which you contemn."

" Whether I believe in it or not," said the man in black, " it is adapted for the generality of the human race; so I will forward it, and advise you to do the same. It was nearly extirpated in these regions, but it is springing up again, owing to circumstances. Radicalism is a good friend to us; all the liberals laud up our system out of hatred to the Established Church, though our system is ten times less liberal than the Church of England. Some of them have really come over to us. I myself confess a baronet who presided over the first radical meeting ever held in England—he was an atheist when he came over to us, in the hope of mortifying his own church—but he is now—ho! ho!—a real Catholic devotee—quite afraid of my threats; I make him frequently scourge himself before me. Well, Radicalism does us good service, especially amongst the lower classes, for Radicalism chiefly flourishes amongst them; for though a baronet or two may be found amongst the radicals, and perhaps as many lords—fellows who have been discarded by their own order for clownishness, or something they have done—it incontestably flourishes best among the lower orders. Then the love of what is foreign is a great friend to us; this love is chiefly confined to the middle and upper classes. Some admire the French, and imitate them; others must needs be Spaniards, dress themselves up in a zamarra, stick a cigar in their mouth, and say, ' Carajo.' Others would pass for Germans; he! he! the idea of any one wishing to pass for a German! but what has done us more service than anything else in these regions—I mean amidst the middle classes—has been the novel, the Scotch novel. The good folks, since they have read the novels, have become Jacobites; and, because all the Jacobs were Papists, the good folks must become Papists also, or, at least, papistically inclined. The very Scotch Presbyterians, since they have read the novels, are become all but Papists; I speak advisedly, having lately been amongst them. There's a trumpery bit of a half papist sect, called the Scotch Episcopalian Church, which lay dormant and nearly forgotten for upwards of a hundred years, which has of late got wonderfully into fashion in Scotland, because, forsooth, some of the long-haired gentry of the novels were said to belong to it, such as Montrose and Dundee; and to this the Presbyterians are going over in throngs, traducing and vilifying their own forefathers, or denying them altogether, and calling themselves descendants of—ho! ho! ho!—Scottish Cavaliers!!! I have heard

them myself repeating snatches of Jacobite ditties about
' Bonnie Dundee,' and—

> " ' Come, fill up my cup, and fill up my can,
>   And saddle my horse, and call up my man.'

There's stuff for you ! Not that I object to the first part of
the ditty. It is natural enough that a Scotchman should
cry, ' Come, fill up my cup !' more especially if he's drinking at another person's expense—all Scotchmen being fond
of liquor at free cost : but ' Saddle his horse ! ! !'—for what
purpose, I would ask? Where is the use of saddling a
horse, unless you can ride him? and where was there ever
a Scotchman who could ride?"

" Of course you have not a drop of Scotch blood in your
veins," said I, " otherwise you would never have uttered
that last sentence."

" Don't be too sure of that," said the man in black ;
" you know little of Popery if you imagine that it cannot
extinguish love of country, even in a Scotchman. A
thorough-going Papist—and who more thorough-going
than myself?—cares nothing for his country ; and why
should he? he belongs to a system, and not to a country."

" One thing," said I, " connected with you, I cannot
understand ; you call yourself a thorough-going Papist,
yet are continually saying the most pungent things against
Popery, and turning to unbounded ridicule those who show
any inclination to embrace it."

" Rome is a very sensible old body," said the man in
black, " and little cares what her children say, provided
they do her bidding. She knows several things, and
amongst others, that no servants work so hard and faithfully as those who curse their masters at every stroke they
do. She was not fool enough to be angry with the Mique-
lets of Alba, who renounced her, and called her ' puta ' all
the time they were cutting the throats of the Nether-
landers. Now, if she allowed her faithful soldiers the
latitude of renouncing her, and calling her ' puta ' in the
market-place, think not she is so unreasonable as to object
to her faithful priests occasionally calling her ' puta ' in
the dingle."

" But," said I, " suppose some one were to tell the
world some of the disorderly things which her priests say
in the dingle?"

"He would have the fate of Cassandra," said the man in black; "no one would believe him—yes, the priests would: but they would make no sign of belief. They believe in the Alcoran des Cordeliers—that is, those who have read it; but they make no sign."

"A pretty system," said I, "which extinguishes love of country and of everything noble, and brings the minds of its ministers to a parity with those of devils, who delight in nothing but mischief."

"The system," said the man in black, "is a grand one, with unbounded vitality. Compare it with your Protestantism, and you will see the difference. Popery is ever at work, whilst Protestantism is supine. A pretty church, indeed, the Protestant! Why, it can't even work a miracle."

"Can your church work miracles?" I demanded.

"That was the very question," said the man in black, "which the ancient British clergy asked of Austin Monk, after they had been fools enough to acknowledge their own inability. 'We don't pretend to work miracles; do you?' 'Oh! dear me, yes,' said Austin; 'we find no difficulty in the matter. We can raise the dead, we can make the blind see; and to convince you, I will give sight to the blind. Here is this blind Saxon, whom you cannot cure, but on whose eyes I will manifest my power, in order to show the difference between the true and the false church;' and forthwith, with the assistance of a handkerchief and a little hot water, he opened the eyes of the barbarian. So we manage matters! A pretty church, that old British church, which could not work miracles—quite as helpless as the modern one. The fools! was birdlime so scarce a thing amongst them?—and were the properties of warm water so unknown to them, that they could not close a pair of eyes and open them?"

"It's a pity," said I, "that the British clergy at that interview with Austin, did not bring forward a blind Welshman, and ask the monk to operate upon him."

"Clearly," said the man in black; "that's what they ought to have done; but they were fools without a single resource." Here he took a sip at his glass.

"But they did not believe in the miracle?" said I.

"And what did their not believing avail them?" said the man in black. "Austin remained master of the field,

and they went away holding their heads down, and muttering to themselves. What a fine subject for a painting
would be Austin's opening the eyes of the Saxon barbarian, and the discomfiture of the British clergy! I
wonder it has not been painted!—he! he!"

"I suppose your church still performs miracles occasionally!" said I.

"It does," said the man in black. "The Rev. ——
has lately been performing miracles in Ireland, destroying
devils that had got possession of people; he has been
eminently successful. In two instances he not only
destroyed the devils, but the lives of the people possessed
—he! he! Oh! there is so much energy in our system;
we are always at work, whilst Protestantism is supine."

"You must not imagine," said I, "that all Protestants
are supine; some of them appear to be filled with unbounded zeal. They deal, it is true, not in lying miracles,
but they propagate God's Word. I remember only a few
months ago, having occasion for a Bible, going to an
establishment, the object of which was to send Bibles all
over the world. The supporters of that establishment
could have no self-interested views; for I was supplied
by them with a noble-sized Bible at a price so small as to
preclude the idea that it could bring any profit to the
vendors."

The countenance of the man in black slightly fell. "I
know the people to whom you allude," said he; "indeed,
unknown to them, I have frequently been to see them,
and observed their ways. I tell you frankly that there is
not a set of people in this kingdom who have caused our
church so much trouble and uneasiness. I should rather
say that they alone cause us any; for as for the rest, what
with their drowsiness, their plethora, their folly and their
vanity, they are doing us anything but mischief. These
fellows are a pestilent set of heretics, whom we would
gladly see burnt; they are, with the most untiring perseverance, and in spite of divers minatory declarations of
the holy father, scattering their books abroad through all
Europe, and have caused many people in Catholic countries
to think that hitherto their priesthood have endeavoured,
as much as possible, to keep them blinded. There is one
fellow amongst them for whom we entertain a particular
aversion; a big, burly parson, with the face of a lion, the

voice of a buffalo, and a fist like a sledge-hammer. The last time I was there, I observed that his eye was upon me, and I did not like the glance he gave me at all; I observed him clench his fist, and I took my departure as fast as I conveniently could. Whether he suspected who I was, I know not; but I did not like his look at all, and do not intend to go again."

"Well, then," said I, "you confess that you have redoubtable enemies to your plans in these regions, and that even amongst the ecclesiastics there are some widely different from those of the plethoric and Platitude schools?"

"It is but too true," said the man in black; "and if the rest of your church were like them we should quickly bid adieu to all hope of converting these regions, but we are thankful to be able to say that such folks are not numerous; there are, moreover, causes at work quite sufficient to undermine even their zeal. Their sons return at the vacations, from Oxford and Cambridge, puppies, full of the nonsense which they have imbibed from Platitude professors; and this nonsense they retail at home, where it fails not to make some impression, whilst the daughters scream—I beg their pardons—warble about Scotland's Montrose, and Bonny Dundee, and all the Jacobs; so we have no doubt that their papas' zeal about the propagation of such a vulgar book as the Bible will in a very little time be terribly diminished. Old Rome will win, so you had better join her."

And the man in black drained the last drop in his glass.

"Never," said I, "will I become the slave of Rome."

"She will allow you latitude," said the man in black; "do but serve her, and she will allow you to call her 'puta' at a decent time and place, her popes occasionally call her 'puta.' A pope has been known to start from his bed at midnight and rush out into the corridor, and call out 'puta' three times in a voice which pierced the Vatican; that pope was——"

"Alexander the Sixth, I dare say," said I; "the greatest monster that ever existed, though the worthiest head which the pope system ever had—so his conscience was not always still. I thought it had been seared with a brand of iron."

"I did not allude to him, but to a much more modern pope," said the man in black; "it is true he brought the word, which is Spanish, from Spain, his native country, to Rome. He was very fond of calling the church by that name, and other popes have taken it up. She will allow you to call her by it, if you belong to her."

"I shall call her so," said I, "without belonging to her, or asking her permission."

"She will allow you to treat her as such, if you belong to her," said the man in black; "there is a chapel in Rome, where there is a wondrously fair statue—the son of a cardinal—I mean his nephew—once——Well, she did not cut off his head, but slightly boxed his cheek and bade him go."

"I have read all about that in 'Keysler's Travels,'" said I; "do you tell her that I would not touch her with a pair of tongs, unless to seize her nose."

"She is fond of lucre," said the man in black; "but does not grudge a faithful priest a little private perquisite," and he took out a very handsome gold repeater.

"Are you not afraid," said I, "to flash that watch before the eyes of a poor tinker in a dingle?"

"Not before the eyes of one like you," said the man in black.

"It is getting late," said I; "I care not for perquisites."

"So you will not join us?" said the man in black.

"You have had my answer," said I.

"If I belong to Rome," said the man in black, "why should not you?"

"I may be a poor tinker," said I; "but I may never have undergone what you have. You remember, perhaps, the fable of the fox who had lost his tail?"

The man in black winced, but almost immediately recovering himself, he said, "Well, we can do without you, we are sure of winning."

"It is not the part of wise people," said I, "to make sure of the battle before it is fought: there's the landlord of the public-house, who made sure that his cocks would win, yet the cocks lost the main, and the landlord is little better than a bankrupt."

"People very different from the landlord," said the man in black, "both in intellect and station, think we shall

surely win; there are clever machinators among us who
have no doubt of our success."

"Well," said I, "I will set the landlord aside, and will
adduce one who was in every point a very different person
from the landlord, both in understanding and station; he
was very fond of laying schemes, and, indeed, many of
them turned out successful. His last and darling one,
however, miscarried, notwithstanding that by his calculations he had persuaded himself that there was no possibility of its failing—the person that I allude to was old
Fraser——"

"Who?" said the man in black, giving a start, and
letting his glass fall.

"Old Fraser, of Lovat," said I, "the prince of all con-
spirators and machinators; he made sure of placing the
Pretender on the throne of these realms. 'I can bring
into the field so many men,' said he; 'my son-in-law Cluny,
so many, and likewise my cousin, and my good friend;'
then speaking of those on whom the government reckoned
for support, he would say, 'So and so are lukewarm, this
person is ruled by his wife, who is with us, the clergy are
anything but hostile to us, and as for the soldiers and
sailors, half are disaffected to King George, and the rest
cowards.' Yet when things came to a trial, this person
whom he had calculated upon to join the Pretender did not
stir from his home, another joined the hostile ranks, the
presumed cowards turned out heroes, and those whom he
thought heroes ran away like lusty fellows at Culloden;
in a word, he found himself utterly mistaken, and in nothing more than in himself; he thought he was a hero, and
proved himself nothing more than an old fox; he got up a
hollow tree, didn't he, just like a fox?

"'L'opere sue non furon leonine, ma di volpe.'"

The man in black sat silent for a considerable time, and
at length answered in rather a faltering voice, "I was not
prepared for this; you have frequently surprised me by
your knowledge of things which I should never have
expected any person of your appearance to be acquainted
with, but that you should be aware of my name is a
circumstance utterly incomprehensible to me. I had
imagined that no person in England was acquainted with
it; indeed, I don't see how any person should be, I have

revealed it to no one, not being particularly proud of it. Yes, I acknowledge that my name is Fraser, and that I am of the blood of that family or clan, of which the rector of our college once said, that he was firmly of opinion that every individual member was either rogue or fool. I was born at Madrid, of pure, *oimè,* Fraser blood. My parents, at an early age, took me to ——, where they shortly died, not, however, before they had placed me in the service of a cardinal, with whom I continued for some years, and who, when he had no further occasion for me, sent me to the college, in the left-hand cloister of which, as you enter, rest the bones of Sir John ——; there, in studying logic and humane letters, I lost whatever of humanity I had retained when discarded by the cardinal. Let me not, however, forget two points,—I am a Fraser, it is true, but not a Flannagan; I may bear the vilest name of Britain, but not of Ireland; I was bred up at the English house, and there is at —— a house for the education of bog-trotters; I was not bred up at that; beneath the lowest gulf, there is one yet lower; whatever my blood may be, it is at least not Irish; whatever my education may have been, I was not bred at the Irish seminary—on those accounts I am thankful—yes, *per dio!* I am thankful. After some years at college—but why should I tell you my history? you know it already perfectly well, probably much better than myself. I am now a missionary priest, labouring in heretic England, like Parsons and Garnet of old, save and except that, unlike them, I run no danger, for the times are changed. As I told you before, I shall cleave to Rome—I must; *no hay remedio,* as they say at Madrid, and I will do my best to further her holy plans —he! he!—but I confess I begin to doubt of their being successful here—you put me out; old Fraser, of Lovat! I have heard my father talk of him; he had a gold-headed cane, with which he once knocked my grandfather down —he was an astute one, but, as you say, mistaken, particularly in himself. I have read his life by Arbuthnot, it is in the library of our college. Farewell! I shall come no more to this dingle—to come would be of no utility; I shall go and labour elsewhere, though——how you came to know my name, is a fact quite inexplicable—farewell! to you both."

He then arose; and without further salutation departed

from the dingle, in which I never saw him again. "How, in the name of wonder, came you to know that man's name?" said Belle, after he had been gone some time.

"I, Belle? I knew nothing of the fellow's name, I assure you."

"But you mentioned his name."

"If I did, it was merely casually, by way of illustration. I was saying how frequently cunning people were mistaken in their calculations, and I adduced the case of old Fraser, of Lovat, as one in point; I brought forward his name, because I was well acquainted with his history, from having compiled and inserted it in a wonderful work, which I edited some months ago, entitled 'Newgate Lives and Trials,' but without the slightest idea that it was the name of him who was sitting with us; he, however, thought that I was aware of his name. Belle! Belle! for a long time I doubted the truth of Scripture, owing to certain conceited individuals, but now I begin to believe firmly; what wonderful texts are in Scripture, Belle; 'The wicked trembleth where—where——'"

"'They were afraid where no fear was; thou hast put them to confusion, because God hath despised them,'" said Belle; "I have frequently read it before the clergyman in the great house of Long Melford. But if you did not know the man's name, why let him go away supposing that you did?"

"Oh, if he was fool enough to make such a mistake, I was not going to undeceive him—no, no! Let the enemies of old England make the most of all their blunders and mistakes, they will have no help from me; but enough of the fellow, Belle; let us now have tea, and after that——"

"No Armenian," said Belle; "but I want to ask a question: pray are all people of that man's name either rogues or fools?"

"It is impossible for me to say, Belle, this person being the only one of the name I have ever personally known. I suppose there are good and bad, clever and foolish, amongst them, as amongst all large bodies of people; however, after the tribe had been governed for upwards of thirty years, by such a person as old Fraser, it were no wonder if the greater part had become either rogues or fools: he was a ruthless tyrant, Belle, over his own people,

and by his cruelty and rapaciousness must either have
stunned them into an apathy approaching to idiotcy, or made
them artful knaves in their own defence. The qualities of
parents are generally transmitted to their descendants—
the progeny of trained pointers are almost sure to point,
even without being taught : if, therefore, all Frasers are
either rogues or fools, as this person seems to insinuate,
it is little to be wondered at, their parents or grandparents
having been in the training-school of old Fraser ! But
enough of the old tyrant and his slaves. Belle, prepare
tea this moment, or dread my anger. I have not a gold-
headed cane like old Fraser of Lovat, but I have, what
some people would dread much more, an Armenian rune-
stick.''

CHAPTER V

Fresh Arrivals—Pitching the Tent—Certificated Wife—High-flying
Notions.

ON the following morning, as I was about to leave my
tent, I heard the voice of Belle at the door, exclaiming,
'' Sleepest thou, or wakest thou?'' '' I was never more
awake in my life,'' said I, going out. '' What is the
matter?'' '' He of the horse-shoe,'' said she, '' Jasper, of
whom I have heard you talk, is above there on the field
with all his people; I went out about a quarter of an hour
ago to fill the kettle at the spring, and saw them arriving.'' '' It is well,'' said I ; '' have you any objection to
asking him and his wife to breakfast?'' '' You can do as
you please,'' said she; '' I have cups enough, and have
no objection to their company.'' '' We are the first
occupiers of the ground,'' said I, '' and, being so, should
consider ourselves in the light of hosts, and do our best
to practise the duties of hospitality.'' '' How fond you
are of using that word,'' said Belle; '' if you wish to invite
the man and his wife, do so, without more ado; remember,
however, that I have not cups enough, nor indeed tea
enough, for the whole company.'' Thereupon hurrying
up the ascent, I presently found myself outside the dingle.
It was as usual a brilliant morning, the dewy blades of the

rye-grass which covered the plain sparkled brightly in the beams of the sun, which had probably been about two hours above the horizon. A rather numerous body of my ancient friends and allies occupied the ground in the vicinity of the mouth of the dingle. About five yards on the right I perceived Mr. Petulengro busily employed in erecting his tent; he held in his hand an iron bar, sharp at the bottom, with a kind of arm projecting from the top for the purpose of supporting a kettle or cauldron over the fire, and which is called in the Romanian language " Kekauviskoe saster." With the sharp end of this Mr. Petulengro was making holes in the earth, at about twenty inches distant from each other, into which he inserted certain long rods with a considerable bend towards the top, which constituted no less than the timber of the tent, and the supporters of the canvas. Mrs. Petulengro, and a female with a crutch in her hand, whom I recognised as Mrs. Chikno, sat near him on the ground, whilst two or three children, from six to ten years old, who composed the young family of Mr. and Mrs. Petulengro, were playing about.

" Here we are, brother," said Mr. Petulengro, as he drove the sharp end of the bar into the ground; " here we are, and plenty of us—Bute dosta Romany chals."

" I am glad to see you all," said I; " and particularly you, madam," said I, making a bow to Mrs. Petulengro; " and you also, madam," taking off my hat to Mrs. Chikno.

" Good-day to you, sir," said Mrs. Petulengro; " you look, as usual, charmingly, and speak so, too; you have not forgot your manners."

" It is not all gold that glitters," said Mrs. Chikno. " However, good-morrow to you, young rye."

" I do not see Tawno," said I, looking around; " where is he?"

" Where, indeed!" said Mrs. Chikno; " I don't know; he who countenances him in the roving line can best answer."

" He will be here anon," said Mr. Petulengro; " he has merely ridden down a by-road to show a farmer a two-year-old colt; she heard me give him directions, but she can't be satisfied."

" I can't indeed," said Mrs. Chikno.

" And why not, sister?"

" Because I place no confidence in your words, brother ; as I said before, you countenances him."

" Well," said I, " I know nothing of your private concerns ; I am come on an errand. Isopel Berners, down in the dell there, requests the pleasure of Mr. and Mrs. Petulengro's company at breakfast. She will be happy also to see you, madam," said I, addressing Mrs. Chikno.

" Is that young female your wife, young man?" said Mrs. Chikno.

" My wife?" said I.

" Yes, young man ; your wife, your lawful certificated wife?"

" No," said I ; " she is not my wife."

" Then I will not visit with her," said Mrs. Chikno ; " I countenance nothing in the roving line."

" What do you mean by the roving line?" I demanded.

" What do I mean by the roving line? Why, by it I mean such conduct as is not tatcheno. When ryes and rawnies live together in dingles, without being certificated, I call such behaviour being tolerably deep in the roving line, everything savouring of which I am determined not to sanctify. I have suffered too much by my own certificated husband's outbreaks in that line to afford anything of the kind the slightest shadow of countenance."

" It is hard that people may not live in dingles together without being suspected of doing wrong," said I.

" So it is," said Mrs. Petulengro, interposing ; " and, to tell you the truth, I am altogether surprised at the illiberality of my sister's remarks. I have often heard say, that it is in good company—and I have kept good company in my time—that suspicion is king's evidence of a narrow and uncultivated mind ; on which account I am suspicious of nobody, not even of my own husband, whom some people would think I have a right to be suspicious of, seeing that on his account I once refused a lord ; but I ask him whether I am suspicious of him, and whether I seek to keep him close tied to my apron-string ; he will tell you nothing of the kind ; but that, on the contrary, I always allows him an agreeable latitude, permitting him to go where he pleases, and to converse with any one to whose manner of speaking he may take a fancy. But I have had the advantage of keeping good company, and therefore——"

"Meklis," said Mrs. Chikno, "pray drop all that, sister; I believe I have kept as good company as yourself; and with respect to that offer with which you frequently fatigue those who keeps company with you, I believe, after all, it was something in the roving and uncertificated line."

"In whatever line it was," said Mrs. Petulengro, "the offer was a good one. The young duke—for he was not only a lord, but a duke too—offered to keep me a fine carriage, and to make me his second wife; for it is true that he had another who was old and stout, though mighty rich, and highly good-natured; so much so, indeed, that the young lord assured me that she would have no manner of objection to the arrangement; more especially if I would consent to live in the same house with her, being fond of young and cheerful society. So you see——"

"Yes, yes," said Mrs. Chikno, "I see, what I before thought, that it was altogether in the uncertificated line."

"Meklis," said Mrs. Petulengro; "I use your own word, madam, which is Romany: for my own part, I am not fond of using Romany words, unless I can hope to pass them off for French, which I cannot in the present company. I heartily wish that there was no such language, and do my best to keep it away from my children, lest the frequent use of it should altogether confirm them in low and vulgar habits. I have four children, madam, but——"

"I suppose by talking of your four children you wish to check me for having none," said Mrs. Chikno, bursting into tears; "if I have no children, sister, it is no fault of mine, it is—but why do I call you sister?" said she, angrily; "you are no sister of mine, you are a grasni, a regular mare—a pretty sister, indeed, ashamed of your own language. I remember well that by your high-flying notions you drove your own mother——"

"We will drop it," said Mrs. Petulengro; "I do not wish to raise my voice, and to make myself ridiculous. Young gentleman," said she, "pray present my compliments to Miss Isopel Berners, and inform her that I am very sorry that I cannot accept her polite invitation. I am just arrived, and have some slight domestic matters to see to—amongst others, to wash my children's faces; but that in the course of the forenoon, when I have attended to what I have to do, and have dressed myself, I hope to do myself the honour of paying her a regular visit; you will tell her that, with my compliments. With respect to my husband he can answer for himself, as I, not being of a jealous disposition, never interferes with his matters."

"And tell Miss Berners," said Mr. Petulengro, "that I shall be happy to wait upon her in company with my wife as soon as we are regularly settled: at present I have much on my hands, having not only to pitch my own tent, but this here jealous woman's, whose husband is absent on my business."

Thereupon I returned to the dingle, and, without saying anything about Mrs. Chikno's observations, communicated to Isopel the messages of Mr. and Mrs. Petulengro; Isopel made no other reply than by replacing in her coffer two additional cups and saucers, which, in expectation of company, she had placed upon the board. The kettle was by this time boiling. We sat down, and, as we breakfasted, I gave Isopel Berners another lesson in the Armenian language.

CHAPTER VI

The Promised Visit—Roman Fashion—Wizard and Witch—Catching at Words—The Two Females—Dressing of Hair—The New Roads—Belle's Altered Appearance—Herself Again.

ABOUT mid-day Mr. and Mrs. Petulengro came to the dingle to pay the promised visit. Belle, at the time of their arrival, was in her tent, but I was at the fire-place, engaged in hammering part of the outer-tire, or defence, which had come off from one of the wheels of my vehicle. On perceiving them I forthwith went to receive them. Mr. Petulengro was dressed in Roman fashion, with a somewhat smartly-cut sporting-coat, the buttons of which were half-crowns—and a waistcoat, scarlet and black, the buttons of which were spaded half-guineas; his breeches were of a stuff half velveteen, half corduroy, the cords exceedingly broad. He had leggings of buff cloth, furred at the bottom; and upon his feet were highlows. Under his left arm was a long black whalebone riding-whip, with a red lash, and an immense silver knob. Upon his head was a hat with a high peak, somewhat of the kind which the Spaniards call *calané,* so much in favour with the bravos of Seville and Madrid. Now, when I have added that Mr. Petulengro had on a very fine white holland shirt, I think I have described his array. Mrs. Petulengro—I beg pardon for not having spoken of her first—was also arrayed very much in the Roman fashion. Her hair, which was exceedingly black and lustrous, fell in braids on either side of her head. In her ears were rings, with long drops of gold. Round her neck was a string of what seemed very much like very large pearls, somewhat tarnished, however, and apparently of considerable antiquity. " Here we are, brother," said Mr. Petulengro; " here we are, come to see you—wizard and witch, witch and wizard :—

> " ' There's a chovahanee, and a chovahano,
>   The nav se len is Petulengro.' "

" Hold your tongue, sir," said Mrs. Petulengro; " you make me ashamed of you with your vulgar ditties. We are come a visiting now, and everything low should be left behind."

" True," said Mr. Petulengro; " why bring what's low to the dingle, which is low enough already?"

" What, are you a catcher at words?" said I. " I thought that catching at words had been confined to the pothouse farmers and village witty bodies."

" All fools," said Mrs. Petulengro, " catch at words, and very naturally, as by so doing they hope to prevent the possibility of rational conversation. Catching at words confined to pothouse farmers, and village witty bodies ! No, not to Jasper Petulengro. Listen for an hour or two to the discourse of a set they call newspaper editors, and if you don't go out and eat grass, as a dog does when he is sick, I am no female woman. The young lord whose hand I refused when I took up with wise Jasper, once brought two of them to my mother's tan, when hankering after my company; they did nothing but carp at each other's words, and a pretty hand they made of it. Ill-favoured dogs they were; and their attempts at what they called wit almost as unfortunate as their countenances."

" Well," said I, " madam, we will drop all catchings and carpings for the present. Pray take your seat on this stool, whilst I go and announce to Miss Isopel Berners your arrival."

Thereupon I went to Belle's habitation, and informed her that Mr. and Mrs. Petulengro had paid us a visit of ceremony, and were awaiting her at the fire-place. "Pray go and tell them that I am busy," said Belle, who was engaged with her needle. "I do not feel disposed to take part in any such nonsense." "I shall do no such thing," said I; "and I insist upon your coming forthwith, and showing proper courtesy to your visitors. If you do not, their feelings will be hurt, and you are aware that I cannot bear that people's feelings should be outraged. Come this moment, or——" "Or what?" said Belle, half smiling. "I was about to say something in Armenian," said I. "Well," said Belle, laying down her work, "I will come." "Stay," said I; "your hair is hanging about your ears, and your dress is in disorder; you had better stay a minute or two to prepare yourself to appear before your visitors, who have come in their very best attire." "No," said Belle, "I will make no alteration in my appearance; you told me to come this moment, and you shall be obeyed." So Belle and I advanced towards our guests. As we drew nigh Mr. Petulengro took off his hat, and made a profound obeisance to Belle, whilst Mrs. Petulengro rose from the stool, and made a profound curtsey. Belle, who had flung her hair back over her shoulders, returned their salutations by bending her head, and after slightly glancing at Mr. Petulengro, fixed her large blue eyes full upon his wife. Both these females were very handsome—but how unlike! Belle fair, with blue eyes and flaxen hair; Mrs. Petulengro with olive complexion, eyes black, and hair dark—as dark as could be. Belle, in demeanour calm and proud; the gypsy graceful, but full of movement and agitation. And then how different were those two in stature! The head of the Romany rawnie scarcely ascended to the breast of Isopel Berners. I could see that Mrs. Petulengro gazed on Belle with unmixed admiration; so did her husband. "Well," said the latter, "one thing I will say, which is, that there is only one on earth worthy to stand up in front of this she, and that is the beauty of the world, as far as man flesh is concerned, Tawno Chikno; what a pity ne did not come down!"

"Tawno Chikno," said Mrs. Petulengro, flaring up;

" a pretty fellow he to stand up in front of this gentle-woman, a pity he didn't come, quotha? not at all, the fellow is a sneak, afraid of his wife. He stand up against this rawnie! why, the look she has given me would knock the fellow down."

" It is easier to knock him down with a look than with a fist," said Mr. Petulengro; " that is, if the look comes from a woman: not that I am disposed to doubt that this female gentlewoman is able to knock him down either one way or the other. I have heard of her often enough, and have seen her once or twice, though not so near as now. Well, ma'am, my wife and I are come to pay our respects to you; we are both glad to find that you have left off keeping company with Flaming Bosville, and have taken up with my pal; he is not very handsome, but a better——"

" I take up with your pal, as you call him! you had better mind what you say," said Isopel Berners, " I take up with nobody."

" I merely mean taking up your quarters with him," said Mr. Petulengro; " and I was only about to say a better fellow-lodger you cannot have, or a more instructive, especially if you have a desire to be inoculated with tongues, as he calls them. I wonder whether you and he have had any tongue-work already."

" Have you and your wife anything particular to say? if you have nothing but this kind of conversation I must leave you, as I am going to make a journey this afternoon, and should be getting ready."

" You must excuse my husband, madam," said Mrs. Petulengro, " he is not overburdened with understanding, and has said but one word of sense since he has been here, which was that we came to pay our respects to you. We have dressed ourselves in our best Roman way, in order to do honour to you; perhaps you do not like it; if so, I am sorry. I have no French clothes, madam; if I had any, madam, I would have come in them, in order to do you more honour."

" I like to see you much better as you are," said Belle; " people should keep to their own fashions, and yours is very pretty."

" I am glad you are pleased to think it so, madam; it has been admired in the great city; it created what they call a sensation; and some of the great ladies, the court ladies, imitated it, else I should not appear in it so often as I am accustomed; for I am not very fond of what is Roman, having an imagination that what is Roman is ungenteel; in fact, I once heard the wife of a rich citizen say that gypsies were vulgar creatures. I should have taken her saying very much to heart, but for her improper pronunciation; she could not pronounce her words, madam, which we gypsies, as they call us, usually can, so I thought she was no very high purchase. You are very beautiful, madam, though you are not dressed as I could wish to see you, and your hair is hanging down in sad confusion; allow me to assist you in arranging your hair, madam; I will dress it for you in our fashion; I would fain see how your hair would look in our poor gypsy fashion; pray allow me, madam?" and she took Belle by the hand.

"I really can do no such thing," said Belle, withdrawing her hand; "I thank you for coming to see me, but——"

"Do allow me to officiate upon your hair, madam," said Mrs. Petulengro. "I should esteem your allowing me a great mark of condescension. You are very beautiful, madam, and I think you doubly so, because you are so fair; I have a great esteem for persons with fair complexions and hair; I have a less regard for people with dark hair and complexions, madam."

"Then why did you turn off the lord, and take up with me?" said Mr. Petulengro; "that same lord was fair enough all about him."

"People do when they are young and silly what they sometimes repent of when they are of riper years and understandings. I sometimes think that had I not been something of a simpleton, I might at this time be a great court lady. Now, madam," said she, again taking Belle by the hand, "do oblige me by allowing me to plait your hair a little?"

"I have really a good mind to be angry with you," said Belle, giving Mrs. Petulengro a peculiar glance.

"Do allow her to arrange your hair," said I; "she means no harm, and wishes to do you honour; do oblige her and me too, for I should like to see how your hair would look dressed in her fashion."

"You hear what the young rye says?" said Mrs. Petulengro. "I am sure you will oblige the young rye, if not

myself. Many people would be willing to oblige the young
rye, if he would but ask them; but he is not in the habit
of asking favours. He has a nose of his own, which he
keeps tolerably exalted; he does not think small-beer of
himself, madam; and all the time I have been with him,
I never heard him ask a favour before; therefore, madam,
I am sure you will oblige him. My sister Ursula would be
very willing to oblige him in many things, but he will not
ask for anything, except for such a favour as a word,
which is a poor favour after all. I don't mean for her
word; perhaps he will some day ask you for your word.
If so——"

"Why, here you are, after railing at me for catching
at words, catching at a word yourself," said Mr. Petulengro.

"Hold your tongue, sir," said Mrs. Petulengro.
"Don't interrupt me in my discourse; if I caught at a
word now, I am not in the habit of doing so. I am no
conceited body; no newspaper Neddy; no pothouse witty
person. I was about to say, madam, that if the young
rye asks you at any time for your word, you will do as
you deem convenient; but I am sure you will oblige him
by allowing me to braid your hair."

"I shall not do it to oblige him," said Belle; "the
young rye, as you call him, is nothing to me."

"Well, then, to oblige me," said Mrs. Petulengro; "do
allow me to become your poor tire-woman."

"It is great nonsense," said Belle, reddening; "however, as you came to see me, and ask the matter as a particular favour to yourself——"

"Thank you, madam," said Mrs. Petulengro, leading
Belle to the stool; "please to sit down here. Thank you;
your hair is very beautiful, madam," she continued, as she
proceeded to braid Belle's hair; "so is your countenance.
Should you ever go to the great city, among the grand
folks, you would make a sensation, madam. I have made
one myself, who am dark; the chi she is kauley, which last
word signifies black, which I am not, though rather dark.
There is no colour like white, madam; it's so lasting, so
genteel. Gentility will carry the day, madam, even with the
young rye. He will ask words of the black lass, but beg
the word of the fair."

In the meantime Mr. Petulengro and myself entered into

conversation. "Any news stirring, Mr. Petulengro?" said I. "Have you heard anything of the great religious movements?"

"Plenty," said Mr. Petulengro; "all the religious people, more especially the Evangelicals—those that go about distributing tracts—are very angry about the fight between Gentleman Cooper and White-headed Bob, which they say ought not to have been permitted to take place; and then they are trying all they can to prevent the fight between the lion and the dogs, which they say is a disgrace to a Christian country. Now I can't say that I have any quarrel with the religious party and the Evangelicals; they are always civil to me and mine, and frequently give us tracts, as they call them, which neither I nor mine can read; but I cannot say that I approve of any movements, religious or not, which have in aim to put down all life and manly sport in this here country."

"Anything else?" said I.

"People are becoming vastly sharp," said Mr. Petulengro; "and I am told that all the old-fashioned good-tempered constables are going to be set aside, and a paid body of men to be established, who are not to permit a tramper or vagabond on the roads of England;—and talking of roads, puts me in mind of a strange story I heard two nights ago, whilst drinking some beer at a public-house in company with my cousin Sylvester. I had asked Tawno to go, but his wife would not let him. Just opposite me, smoking their pipes, were a couple of men, something like engineers, and they were talking of a wonderful invention which was to make a wonderful alteration in England; inasmuch as it would set aside all the old roads, which in a little time would be ploughed up, and sowed with corn, and cause all England to be laid down with iron roads, on which people would go thundering along in vehicles, pushed forward by fire and smoke. Now, brother, when I heard this, I did not feel very comfortable; for I thought to myself, what a queer place such a road would be to pitch one's tent upon, and how impossible it would be for one's cattle to find a bite of grass upon it; and I thought likewise of the danger to which one's family would be exposed in being run over and severely scorched by these same flying fiery vehicles; so I made bold to say, that I hoped such an invention would never be countenanced, because it was likely to do a great deal of harm. Whereupon, one of the men, giving me a glance, said, without taking the pipe out of his mouth, that for his part, he sincerely hoped that it would take effect; and if it did no other good than stopping the rambles of gypsies, and other like scamps, it ought to be encouraged. Well, brother, feeling myself insulted, I put my hand into my pocket, in order to pull out money, intending to challenge him to fight for a five-shilling stake, but merely found sixpence, having left all my other money at the tent; which sixpence was just sufficient to pay for the beer which Sylvester and myself were drinking, of whom I couldn't hope to borrow anything—' poor as Sylvester ' being a by-word amongst us. So, not being able to back myself, I held my peace, and let the Gorgio have it all his own way, who, after turning up his nose at me, went on discoursing about the said invention, saying what a fund of profit it would be to those who knew how to make use of it, and should have the laying down of the new roads, and the shoeing of England with iron. And after he had said this, and much more of the same kind, which I cannot remember, he and his companion got up and walked away; and presently I and Sylvester got up and walked to our camp; and there I lay down in my tent by the side of my wife, where I had an ugly dream of having camped upon an iron road; my tent being overturned by a flying vehicle; my wife's leg injured; and all my affairs put into great confusion."

" Now, madam," said Mrs. Petulengro, " I have braided your hair in our fashion : you look very beautiful, madam; more beautiful, if possible, than before." Belle now rose, and came forward with her tire-woman. Mr. Petulengro was loud in his applause, but I said nothing, for I did not think Belle was improved in appearance by having submitted to the ministry of Mrs. Petulengro's hand. Nature never intended Belle to appear as a gypsy; she had made her too proud and serious. A more proper part for her was that of a heroine, a queenly heroine,—that of Theresa of Hungary, for example; or, better still, that of Brynhilda the Valkyrie, the beloved of Sigurd, the serpent-killer, who incurred the curse of Odin, because, in the tumult of spears, she sided with the young king, and doomed the old warrior to die, to whom Odin had promised victory.

Belle looked at me for a moment in silence; then turning to Mrs. Petulengro, she said, " You have had your will with me; are you satisfied?" "Quite so, madam," said Mrs. Petulengro, "and I hope you will be so too, as soon as you have looked in the glass." "I have looked in one already," said Belle; "and the glass does not flatter." "You mean the face of the young rye," said Mrs. Petulengro; "never mind him, madam; the young rye, though he knows a thing or two, is not a university, nor a person of universal wisdom. I assure you, that you never looked so well before; and I hope that, from this moment, you will wear your hair in this way." "And who is to braid it in this way?" said Belle, smiling. "I, madam," said Mrs. Petulengro; "I will braid it for you every morning, if you will but be persuaded to join us. Do so, madam, and I think, if you did, the young rye would do so too." "The young rye is nothing to me, nor I to him," said Belle; "we have stayed some time together; but our paths will soon be apart. Now, farewell, for I am about to take a journey." "And you will go out with your hair as I have braided it," said Mrs. Petulengro; "if you do, everybody will be in love with you." "No," said Belle; "hitherto I have allowed you to do what you please, but henceforth I shall have my own way. Come, come," said she, observing that the gypsy was about to speak, "we have had enough of nonsense; whenever I leave this hollow, it will be wearing my hair in my own fashion." "Come, wife," said Mr. Petulengro; "we will no longer intrude upon the rye and rawnie; there is such a thing as being troublesome." Thereupon Mr. Petulengro and his wife took their leave, with many salutations. "Then you are going?" said I, when Belle and I were left alone. "Yes," said Belle; "I am going on a journey; my affairs compel me." "But you will return again?" said I. "Yes," said Belle, "I shall return once more." "Once more," said I; "what do you mean by once more? The Petulengros will soon be gone, and will you abandon me in this place?" "You were alone here," said Belle, "before I came, and I suppose, found it agreeable, or you would not have stayed in it." "Yes," said I, "that was before I knew you; but having lived with you here, I should be very loth to live here without you." "Indeed," said Belle; "I did not know that I was of so much consequence to you. Well, the day is wearing away—I must go and harness Traveller to the cart." "I will do that," said I, "or anything else

you may wish me. Go and prepare yourself; I will see
after Traveller and the cart." Belle departed to her tent,
and I set about performing the task I had undertaken. In
about half-an-hour Belle again made her appearance—she
was dressed neatly and plainly. Her hair was no longer in
the Roman fashion, in which Pakomovna had plaited it,
but was secured by a comb; she held a bonnet in her hand.
" Is there anything else I can do for you?" I demanded.
" There are two or three bundles by my tent, which you
can put into the cart," said Belle. I put the bundles into
the cart, and then led Traveller and the cart up the winding
path to the mouth of the dingle, near which was Mr. Petulengro's encampment. Belle followed. At the top, I delivered the reins into her hands; we looked at each other
stedfastly for some time. Belle then departed, and I returned to the dingle, where, seating myself on my stone,
I remained for upwards of an hour in thought.

CHAPTER VII

The Festival—The Gypsy Song—Piramus of Rome—The Scotchman—
Gypsy Names.

ON the following day there was much feasting amongst
the Romany chals of Mr. Petulengro's party. Throughout
the forenoon the Romany chies did scarcely anything but
cook flesh, and the flesh which they cooked was swine's
flesh. About two o'clock, the chals dividing themselves
into various parties, sat down and partook of the fare,
which was partly roasted, partly sodden. I dined that day
with Mr. Petulengro and his wife and family, Ursula, Mr.
and Mrs. Chikno, and Sylvester and his two children.
Sylvester, it will be as well to say, was a widower, and had
consequently no one to cook his victuals for him, supposing
he had any, which was not always the case, Sylvester's
affairs being seldom in a prosperous state. He was noted
for his bad success in trafficking, notwithstanding the many
hints which he received from Jasper, under whose protection
he had placed himself, even as Tawno Chikno had done,
who himself, as the reader has heard on a former occasion,

was anything but a wealthy subject, though he was at all times better off than Sylvester, the Lazarus of the Romany tribe.

All our party ate with a good appetite, except myself, who, feeling rather melancholy that day, had little desire to eat. I did not, like the others, partake of the pork, but got my dinner entirely off the body of a squirrel which had been shot the day before by a chal of the name of Piramus, who, besides being a good shot, was celebrated for his skill in playing on the fiddle. During the dinner a horn filled with ale passed frequently around; I drank of it more than once, and felt inspirited by the draughts. The repast concluded, Sylvester and his children departed to their tent, and Mr. Petulengro, Tawno, and myself, getting up, went and lay down under a shady hedge, where Mr. Petulengro, lighting his pipe, began to smoke, and where Tawno presently fell asleep. I was about to fall asleep also, when I heard the sound of music and song. Piramus was playing on the fiddle, whilst Mrs. Chikno, who had a voice of her own, was singing in tones sharp enough, but of great power, a gypsy song :—

POISONING THE PORKER.

By Mrs. Chikno.

To mande shoon ye Romany chals
Who besh in the pus about the yag,
I'll pen how we drab the baulo,
I'll pen how we drab the baulo.

We jaws to the drab-engro ker,
Trin horsworth there of drab we lels,
And when to the swety back we wels
We pens we'll drab the baulo,
We'll have a drab at a baulo.

And then we kairs the drab opré,
And then we jaws to the farming ker,
To mang a beti habben,
A beti poggado habben.

A rinkeno baulo there we dick,
And then we pens in Romano jib;
Wust lis odoi opré ye chick,
And the baulo he will lel lis,
The baulo he will lel lis.

Coliko, coliko saulo we
Apopli to the farming ker
Will wel and mang him mullo,
Will wel and mang his truppo.

And so we kairs, and so we kairs;
The baulo in the rarde mers;
We mang him on the saulo,
And rig to the tan the baulo.

And then we toves the wendror well
Till sore the wendror iuziou se,
Till kekkeno drab's adrey lis,
Till drab there's kek adrey lis.

And then his truppo well we hatch,
Kin levinor at the kitchema,
And have a kosko habben,
A kosko Romano habben.

The boshom engro kils, he kils,
The tawnie juva gils, she gils
A puro Romano gillie,
Now shoon the Romano gillie.

Which song I had translated in the following manner, in my younger days, for a lady's album :

Listen to me ye Romanlads, who are seated in the straw about the fire, and I will tell how we poison the porker, I will tell how we poison the porker.

We go to the house of the poison-monger,[1] where we buy three pennies' worth of bane, and when we return to our people we say, we will poison the porker; we will try and poison the porker.

We then make up the poison, and then we take our way to the house of the farmer, as if to beg a bit of victuals, a little broken victuals.

We see a jolly porker, and then we say in Roman language, "Fling the bane yonder amongst the dirt, and the porker soon will find it, the porker soon will find it."

Early on the morrow, we will return to the farm-house, and beg the dead porker, the body of the dead porker.

And so we do, even so we do; the porker dieth during the night; on the morrow we beg the porker, and carry to the tent the porker.

And then we wash the inside well, till all the inside is perfectly clean, till there's no bane within it, not a poison grain within it.

And then we roast the body well, send for ale to the alehouse, and have a merry banquet, a merry Roman banquet.

The fellow with the fiddle plays, he plays; the little lassie sings, she sings an ancient Roman ditty; now hear the Roman ditty.

---

[1] The apothecary.

SONG OF THE BROKEN CHASTITY.

By Ursula.

Penn'd the Romany chi ké laki dye
" Miry dearie dye mi shom cambri!''
" And coin kerdo tute cambri,
  Miry dearie chi, miry Romany chi?''
" O miry dye a boro rye,
  A bovalo rye, a gorgiko rye,
  Sos kistur pré a pellengo grye,
  'Twas yov sos kerdo man cambri.''
" Tu tawnie vassavie lubbeny,
  Tu chal from miry tan abri;
  Had a Romany chal kair'd tute cambri,
  Then I had penn'd ke tute chie,
  But tu shan a vassavie lubbeny
  With gorgikie rat to be cambri.''

" There's some kernel in those songs, brother,'' said Mr. Petulengro, when the songs and music were over.

" Yes,'' said I; " they are certainly very remarkable songs. I say, Jasper, I hope you have not been drabbing baulor lately.''

" And suppose we have, brother, what then?''

" Why, it is a very dangerous practice, to say nothing of the wickedness of it.''

" Necessity has no law, brother.''

" That is true,'' said I; " I have always said so, but you are not necessitous, and should not drab baulor.''

" And who told you we had been drabbing baulor?''

" Why, you have had a banquet of pork, and after the banquet, Mrs. Chikno sang a song about drabbing baulor, so I naturally thought you might have lately been engaged in such a thing.''

" Brother, you occasionally utter a word or two of common sense. It was natural for you to suppose, after seeing that dinner of pork, and hearing that song, that we had been drabbing baulor; I will now tell you that we have not been doing so. What have you to say to that?''

" That I am very glad of it.''

" Had you tasted that pork, brother, you would have found that it was sweet and tasty, which balluva that is drabbed can hardly be expected to be. We have no reason to drab baulor at present, we have money and credit; but necessity has no law. Our forefathers occasionally drabbed baulor; some of our people may still do such a thing, but only from compulsion.''

" I see," said I; " and at your merry meetings you sing
songs upon the compulsatory deeds of your people, alias,
their villainous actions; and, after all, what would the
stirring poetry of any nation be, but for its compulsatory
deeds? Look at the poetry of Scotland, the heroic part,
founded almost entirely on the villainous deeds of the
Scotch nation; cow-stealing, for example, which is very
little better than drabbing baulor; whilst the softer part is
mostly about the slips of its females among the broom, so
that no upholder of Scotch poetry could censure Ursula's
song as indelicate, even if he understood it. What do you
think, Jasper?"

" I think, brother, as I before said, that occasionally you
utter a word of common sense; you were talking of the
Scotch, brother; what do you think of a Scotchman finding
fault with Romany!"

" A Scotchman finding fault with Romany, Jasper! Oh
dear, but you joke, the thing could never be."

" Yes, and at Piramus's fiddle; what do you think of a
Scotchman turning up his nose at Piramus's fiddle?"

" A Scotchman turning up his nose at Piramus's fiddle!
nonsense, Jasper."

" Do you know what I most dislike, brother?"

" I do not, unless it be the constable, Jasper."

" It is not the constable; it's a beggar on horseback,
brother."

" What do you mean by a beggar on horseback?"

" Why, a scamp, brother, raised above his proper place,
who takes every opportunity of giving himself fine airs.
About a week ago, my people and myself camped on a green
by a plantation in the neighbourhood of a great house. In
the evening we were making merry, the girls were dancing,
while Piramus was playing on the fiddle a tune of his own
composing, to which he has given his own name, Piramus
of Rome, and which is much celebrated amongst our people,
and from which I have been told that one of the grand
gorgio composers, who once heard it, has taken several
hints. So, as we were making merry, a great many grand
people, lords and ladies, I believe, came from the great
house, and looked on, as the girls danced to the tune of
Piramus of Rome, and seemed much pleased; and when
the girls had left off dancing, and Piramus playing, the
ladies wanted to have their fortunes told; so I bade Mikailia

Chikno, who can tell a fortune when she pleases better than any one else, tell them a fortune, and she, being in a good mind, told them a fortune which pleased them very much. So, after they had heard their fortunes, one of them asked if any of our women could sing; and I told them several could, more particularly Leviathan—you know Leviathan, she is not here now, but some miles distant, she is our best singer, Ursula coming next. So the lady said she should like to hear Leviathan sing, whereupon Leviathan sang the Gudlo pesham, and Piramus played the tune of the same name, which as you know, means the honeycomb, the song and the tune being well entitled to the name, being wonderfully sweet. Well, everybody present seemed mighty well pleased with the song and music, with the exception of one person, a carroty-haired Scotch body; how he came there I don't know, but there he was; and, coming forward, he began in Scotch as broad as a barn-door to find fault with the music and the song, saying, that he had never heard viler stuff than either. Well, brother, out of consideration for the civil gentry with whom the fellow had come, I held my peace for a long time, and in order to get the subject changed, I said to Mikailia in Romany, You have told the ladies their fortunes, now tell the gentlemen theirs, quick, quick,—pen lende dukkerin. Well, brother, the Scotchman, I suppose, thinking I was speaking ill of him, fell into a greater passion than before, and catching hold of the word dukkerin—' Dukkerin,' said he, ' what's dukkerin?' ' Dukkerin,' said I, ' is fortune, a man or woman's destiny; don't you like the word?' ' Word! d'ye ca' that a word? a bonnie word,' said he. ' Perhaps, you'll tell us what it is in Scotch,' said I, ' in order that we may improve our language by a Scotch word; a pal of mine has told me that we have taken a great many words from foreign lingos.' ' Why, then, if that be the case, fellow, I will tell you; it is e'en "spaeing,"' said he, very seriously. ' Well, then,' said I, ' I'll keep my own word, which is much the prettiest—spaeing! spaeing! why, I should be ashamed to make use of the word, it sounds so much like a certain other word;' and then I made a face as if I were unwell. ' Perhaps it's Scotch also for that?' ' What do ye mean by speaking in that guise to a gentleman?' said he; ' you insolent vagabond, without a name or a country.' ' There you are mistaken,' said I; ' my country is Egypt, but we 'Gyptians, like you Scotch, are rather fond of travelling; and as for name—my name is Jasper Petulengro, perhaps you have a better; what is it?' ' Sandy Macraw.' At that, brother, the gentlemen burst into a roar of laughter, and all the ladies tittered.''

" You were rather severe on the Scotchman, Jasper.''

" Not at all, brother, and suppose I were, he began first; I am the civilest man in the world, and never interfere with anybody, who lets me and mine alone. He finds fault with Romany, forsooth! why, L—d A'mighty, what's Scotch? He doesn't like our songs; what are his own? I understand them as little as he mine; I have heard one or two of them, and pretty rubbish they seemed. But the best of the joke is, the fellow's finding fault with Piramus's fiddle— a chap from the land of bagpipes finding fault with Piramus's fiddle! Why, I'll back that fiddle against all the bagpipes in Scotland, and Piramus against all the bagpipers; for though Piramus weighs but ten stone, he shall flog a Scotchman of twenty.''

" Scotchmen are never so fat as that," said I, " unless indeed, they have been a long time pensioners of England. I say, Jasper, what remarkable names your people have!''

" And what pretty names, brother; there's my own, for example, Jasper; then there's Ambrose and Sylvester; then there's Culvato, which signifies Claude; then there's Piramus—that's a nice name, brother.''

" Then there's your wife's name, Pakomovna; then there's Ursula and Morella.''

" Then, brother, there's Ercilla.''

" Ercilla! the name of the great poet of Spain, how wonderful; then Leviathan.''

" The name of a ship, brother; Leviathan was named after a ship, so don't make a wonder out of her. But there's Sanpriel and Synfye.''

" Ay, and Clementina and Lavinia, Camillia and Lydia, Curlanda and Orlanda; wherever did they get those names?''

" Where did my wife get her necklace, brother?''

" She knows best, Jasper. I hope——''

" Come, no hoping! She got it from her grandmother, who died at the age of a hundred and three, and sleeps in Coggeshall churchyard. She got it from her mother, who

also died very old, and who could give no other account of
it than that it had been in the family time out of mind."

" Whence could they have got it?"

" Why, perhaps where they got their names, brother.
A gentleman, who had travelled much, once told me that
he had seen the sister of it about the neck of an Indian
queen."

" Some of your names, Jasper, appear to be church
names; your own, for example, and Ambrose, and Sylvester; perhaps you got them from the Papists, in the times
of Popery; but where did you get such a name as Piramus,
a name of Grecian romance? Then some of them appear to
be Slavonian; for example, Mikailia and Pakomovna. I
don't know much of Slavonian; but——"

" What is Slavonian, brother?"

" The family name of certain nations, the principal of
which is the Russian, and from which the word slave is
originally derived. You have heard of the Russians,
Jasper?"

" Yes, brother; and seen some. I saw their crallis at the
time of the peace; he was not a bad-looking man for a
Russian."

" By the bye, Jasper, I'm half inclined to think that crallis
is a Slavish word. I saw something like it in a lil called
' Voltaire's Life of Charles.' How you should have come
by such names and words is to me incomprehensible."

" You seem posed, brother."

" I really know very little about you, Jasper."

" Very little indeed, brother. We know very little about
ourselves; and you know nothing, save what we have told
you; and we have now and then told you things about us
which are not exactly true, simply to make a fool of you,
brother. You will say that was wrong; perhaps it was.
Well, Sunday will be here in a day or two, when we will
go to church, where possibly we shall hear a sermon on the
disastrous consequences of lying."

CHAPTER VIII

The Church—The Aristocratical Pew—Days of Yore—The Clergyman
—" In What Would a Man be Profited?"

WHEN two days had passed, Sunday came; I breakfasted
by myself in the solitary dingle; and then, having set
things a little to rights, I ascended to Mr. Petulengro's
encampment. I could hear church-bells ringing around in
the distance, appearing to say, " Come to church, come to
church," as clearly as it was possible for church-bells to
say. I found Mr. Petulengro seated by the door of his
tent, smoking his pipe, in rather an ungenteel undress.
" Well, Jasper," said I, " are you ready to go to church?
for if you are, I am ready to accompany you." " I am not
ready, brother," said Mr. Petulengro, " nor is my wife; the
church, too, to which we shall go is three miles off; so it
is of no use to think of going there this morning, as the
service would be three-quarters over before we got there;
if, however, you are disposed to go in the afternoon, we are
your people." Thereupon I returned to my dingle, where
I passed several hours in conning the Welsh Bible, which
the preacher, Peter Williams, had given me.

At last I gave over reading, took a slight refreshment,
and was about to emerge from the dingle, when I heard
the voice of Mr. Petulengro calling me. I went up again
to the encampment, where I found Mr. Petulengro, his
wife, and Tawno Chikno, ready to proceed to church. Mr.
and Mrs. Petulengro were dressed in Roman fashion,
though not in the full-blown manner in which they had paid
their visit to Isopel and myself. Tawno had on a clean
white slop, with a nearly new black beaver, with very broad
rims, and the nap exceedingly long. As for myself, I was
dressed in much the same manner as that in which I departed from London, having on, in honour of the day, a
shirt perfectly clean, having washed one on purpose for the
occasion, with my own hands, the day before, in the pond
of tepid water in which the newts and defts were in the habit
of taking their pleasure. We proceeded for upwards of a
mile, by footpaths through meadows and corn-fields; we
crossed various stiles; at last, passing over one, we found
ourselves in a road, wending along which for a considerable
distance, we at last came in sight of a church, the bells of

which had been tolling distinctly in our ears for some time; before, however, we reached the church-yard, the bells had ceased their melody. It was surrounded by lofty beech-trees of brilliant green foliage. We entered the gate, Mrs. Petulengro leading the way, and proceeded to a small door near the east end of the church. As we advanced, the sound of singing within the church rose upon our ears. Arrived at the small door, Mrs. Petulengro opened it and entered, followed by Tawno Chikno. I myself went last of all, following Mr. Petulengro, who, before I entered, turned round, and, with a significant nod, advised me to take care how I behaved. The part of the church which we had entered was the chancel; on one side stood a number of venerable old men—probably the neighbouring poor—and on the other a number of poor girls belonging to the village school, dressed in white gowns and straw bonnets, whom two elegant but simply dressed young women were superintending. Every voice seemed to be united in singing a certain anthem, which, notwithstanding it was written neither by Tate nor Brady, contains some of the sublimest words which were ever put together, not the worst of which are those which burst on our ears as we entered:

> " Every eye shall now behold Him,
>   Robed in dreadful majesty;
> Those who set at nought and sold Him,
>   Pierced and nailed Him to the tree,
>   Deeply wailing,
>   Shall the true Messiah see."

Still following Mrs. Petulengro, we proceeded down the chancel and along the aisle; notwithstanding the singing, I could distinctly hear as we passed many a voice whispering, " Here come the gypsies! here come the gypsies!" I felt rather embarrassed, with a somewhat awkward doubt as to where we were to sit; none of the occupiers of the pews, who appeared to consist almost entirely of farmers, with their wives, sons, and daughters, opened a door to admit us. Mrs. Petulengro, however, appeared to feel not the least embarrassment, but tripped along the aisle with the greatest nonchalance. We passed under the pulpit, in which stood the clergyman in his white surplice, and reached the middle of the church, where we were confronted by the sexton dressed in long blue coat, and holding in his hand a wand. This functionary motioned towards the lower end

of the church, where were certain benches, partly occupied
by poor people and boys. Mrs. Petulengro, however, with
a toss of her head, directed her course to a magnifi-
cent pew, which was unoccupied, which she opened and
entered, followed closely by Tawno Chikno, Mr. Petulengro, and myself. The sexton did not appear by any
means to approve of the arrangement, and as I stood next
the door, laid his finger on my arm, as if to intimate that
myself and companions must quit our aristocratical loca-
tion. I said nothing, but directed my eyes to the clergyman, who uttered a short and expressive cough; the sexton
looked at him for a moment, and then, bowing his head,
closed the door—in a moment more the music ceased. I
took up a prayer-book, on which was engraved an earl's
coronet. The clergyman uttered, " I will arise, and go to
my father." England's sublime liturgy had commenced.

Oh, what feelings came over me on finding myself again
in an edifice devoted to the religion of my country! I had
not been in such a place I cannot tell for how long—certainly not for years; and now I had found my way there
again, it appeared as if I had fallen asleep in the pew of the
old church of pretty D——. I had occasionally done so
when a child, and had suddenly woke up. Yes, surely I
had been asleep and had woke up; but no! alas, no! I
had not been asleep—at least not in the old church—if I had
been asleep I had been walking in my sleep, struggling,
striving, learning, and unlearning in my sleep. Years had
rolled away whilst I had been asleep—ripe fruit had fallen,
green fruit had come on whilst I had been asleep—how
circumstances had altered, and above all myself, whilst I
had been asleep. No, I had not been asleep in the old
church! I was in a pew, it is true, but not the pew of
black leather, in which I sometimes fell asleep in days of
yore, but in a strange pew; and then my companions, they
were no longer those of days of yore. I was no longer with
my respectable father and mother, and my dear brother,
but with the gypsy cral and his wife, and the gigantic
Tawno, the Antinous of the dusky people. And what was
I myself? No longer an innocent child, but a moody man,
bearing in my face, as I knew well, the marks of my striv-
ings and strugglings, of what I had learnt and unlearnt;
nevertheless, the general aspect of things brought to my
mind what I had felt and seen of yore. There was differ-

ence enough, it is true, but still there was a similarity—at least I thought so—the church, the clergyman, and the clerk, differing in many respects from those of prettyD——, put me strangely in mind of them; and then the words !— by the bye, was it not the magic of the words which brought the dear enchanting past so powerfully before the mind of Lavengro? for the words were the same sonorous words of high import which had first made an impression on his childish ear in the old church of pretty D——.

The liturgy was now over, during the reading of which my companions behaved in a most unexceptionable manner, sitting down and rising up when other people sat down and rose, and holding in their hands prayer-books which they found in the pew, into which they stared intently, though I observed that, with the exception of Mrs. Petulengro, who knew how to read a little, they held the books by the top, and not the bottom, as is the usual way. The clergyman now ascended the pulpit, arrayed in his black gown. The congregation composed themselves to attention, as did also my companions, who fixed their eyes upon the clergyman with a certain strange immovable stare, which I believe to be peculiar to their race. The clergyman gave out his text, and began to preach. He was a tall, gentlemanly man, seemingly between fifty and sixty, with greyish hair; his features were very handsome, but with a somewhat melancholy cast : the tones of his voice were rich and noble, but also with somewhat of melancholy in them. The text which he gave out was the following one, " In what would a man be profited, provided he gained the whole world, and lost his own soul?"

And on this text the clergyman preached long and well : he did not read his sermon, but spoke it extempore; his doing so rather surprised and offended me at first; I was not used to such a style of preaching in a church devoted to the religion of my country. I compared it within my mind with the style of preaching used by the high-church rector in the old church of pretty D——, and I thought to myself it was very different, and being very different I did not like it, and I thought to myself how scandalized the people of D—— would have been had they heard it, and I figured to myself how indignant the high-church clerk would have been had any clergyman got up in the church of D—— and preached in such a manner. Did it not

savour strongly of dissent, methodism, and similar low
stuff? Surely it did; why, the Methodist I had heard
preach on the heath above the old city, preached in the
same manner—at least he preached extempore; ay, and
something like the present clergyman; for the Methodist
spoke very zealously and with great feeling, and so did the
present clergyman; so I, of course, felt rather offended
with the clergyman for speaking with zeal and feeling.
However, long before the sermon was over I forgot the
offence which I had taken, and listened to the sermon with
much admiration, for the eloquence and powerful reasoning
with which it abounded.

Oh, how eloquent he was, when he talked of the inestim-
able value of a man's soul, which he said endured for ever,
whilst his body, as every one knew, lasted at most for a
very contemptible period of time; and how forcibly he
reasoned on the folly of a man, who, for the sake of gaining
the whole world—a thing, he said, which provided he gained
he could only possess for a part of the time, during which
his perishable body existed—should lose his soul, that is,
cause that precious deathless portion of him to suffer indescribable misery time without end.

There was one part of his sermon which struck me in a
very particular manner: he said, "That there were some
people who gained something in return for their souls; if
they did not get the whole world, they got a part of it—
lands, wealth, honour, or renown; mere trifles, he allowed,
in comparison with the value of a man's soul, which is
destined either to enjoy delight, or suffer tribulation time
without end; but which, in the eyes of the worldly, had a
certain value, and which afforded a certain pleasure and
satisfaction. But there were also others who lost their
souls, and got nothing for them—neither lands, wealth,
renown, nor consideration, who were poor outcasts, and
despised by everybody. My friends," he added, "if the
man is a fool who barters his soul for the whole world,
what a fool he must be who barters his soul for nothing."

The eyes of the clergyman, as he uttered these words,
wandered around the whole congregation; and when he
had concluded them, the eyes of the whole congregation
were turned upon my companions and myself.

CHAPTER IX

Return from Church—The Cuckoo and Gypsy—Spiritual Discourse.

THE service over, my companions and myself returned towards the encampment, by the way we came. Some of the humble part of the congregation laughed and joked at us as we passed. Mr. Petulengro and his wife, however, returned their laughs and jokes with interest. As for Tawno and myself, we said nothing : Tawno, like most handsome fellows, having very little to say for himself at any time; and myself, though not handsome, not being particularly skilful at repartee. Some boys followed us for a considerable time, making all kinds of observations about gypsies; but as we walked at a great pace, we gradually left them behind, and at last lost sight of them. Mrs. Petulengro and Tawno Chikno walked together, even as they had come; whilst Mr. Petulengro and myself followed at a little distance.

"That was a very fine preacher we heard," said I to Mr. Petulengro, after we had crossed the stile into the fields.

"Very fine indeed, brother," said Mr. Petulengro; "he is talked of, far and wide, for his sermons; folks say that there is scarcely another like him in the whole of England."

"He looks rather melancholy, Jasper."

"He lost his wife several years ago, who, they say, was one of the most beautiful women ever seen. They say that it was grief for her loss that made him come out mighty strong as a preacher; for, though he was a clergyman, he was never heard of in the pulpit before he lost his wife; since then, the whole country has rung with the preaching of the clergyman of M—— as they call him. Those two nice young gentlewomen, whom you saw with the female childer, are his daughters."

"You seem to know all about him, Jasper. Did you ever hear him preach before?"

"Never, brother; but he has frequently been to our tent, and his daughters too, and given us tracts; for he is one of the people they call Evangelicals, who give folks tracts which they cannot read."

"You should learn to read, Jasper."

" We have no time, brother."

" Are you not frequently idle?"

" Never, brother; when we are not engaged in our traffic, we are engaged in taking our relaxation: so we have no time to learn."

" You really should make an effort. If you were disposed to learn to read, I would endeavour to assist you. You would be all the better for knowing how to read."

" In what way, brother?"

" Why, you could read the Scriptures, and, by so doing, learn your duty towards your fellow-creatures."

" We know that already, brother; the constables and justices have contrived to knock that tolerably into our heads."

" Yet you frequently break the laws."

" So, I believe, do now and then those who know how to read, brother."

" Very true, Jasper; but you really ought to learn to read, as, by so doing, you might learn your duty towards yourselves: and your chief duty is to take care of your own souls; did not the preacher say, ' In what is a man profited provided he gain the whole world?' "

" We have not much of the world, brother."

" Very little indeed, Jasper. Did you not observe how the eyes of the whole congregation were turned towards our pew, when the preacher said, ' There are some people who lose their souls, and get nothing in exchange; who are outcast, despised, and miserable?' Now was not what he said quite applicable to the gypsies?"

" We are not miserable, brother."

" Well, then, you ought to be, Jasper. Have you an inch of ground of your own? Are you of the least use? Are you not spoken ill of by everybody? What's a gypsy?"

" What's the bird noising yonder, brother?"

" The bird! oh, that's the cuckoo tolling; but what has the cuckoo to do with the matter?"

" We'll see, brother; what's the cuckoo?"

" What is it? you know as much about it as myself, Jasper."

" Isn't it a kind of roguish, chaffing bird, brother?"

" I believe it is, Jasper."

" Nobody knows whence it comes, brother?"

" I believe not, Jasper."

" Very poor, brother, not a nest of its own?"

" So they say, Jasper."

" With every person's bad word, brother?"

" Yes, Jasper, every person is mocking it."

" Tolerably merry, brother?"

" Yes, tolerably merry, Jasper."

" Of no use at all, brother?"

" None whatever, Jasper."

" You would be glad to get rid of the cuckoos, brother?"

" Why, not exactly, Jasper; the cuckoo is a pleasant, funny bird, and its presence and voice give a great charm to the green trees and fields; no, I can't say I wish exactly to get rid of the cuckoo."

" Well, brother, what's a Romany chal?"

" You must answer that question yourself, Jasper."

" A roguish, chaffing fellow, a'n't he, brother?"

" Ay, ay, Jasper."

" Of no use at all, brother?"

" Just so, Jasper; I see——"

" Something very much like a cuckoo, brother?"

" I see what you are after, Jasper."

" You would like to get rid of us, wouldn't you?"

" Why no, not exactly."

" We are no ornament to the green lanes in spring and summer time, are we, brother? and the voices of our chies, with their cukkerin and dukkerin, don't help to make them pleasant?"

" I see what you are at, Jasper."

" You would wish to turn the cuckoos into barn-door fowls, wouldn't you?"

" Can't say I should, Jasper, whatever some people might wish."

" And the chals and chies into radical weavers and factory wenches, hey, brother?"

" Can't say that I should, Jasper. You are certainly a picturesque people, and in many respects an ornament both to town and country; painting and lil writing too are under great obligations to you. What pretty pictures are made out of your campings and groupings, and what pretty books have been written in which gypsies, or at least creatures intended to represent gypsies, have been the principal figures. I think if we were without you, we should begin to miss you."

" Just as you would the cuckoos, if they were all converted into barn-door fowls. I tell you what, brother; frequently, as I have sat under a hedge in spring or summer
time, and heard the cuckoo, I have thought that we chals
and cuckoos are alike in many respects, but especially in
character. Everybody speaks ill of us both, and everybody
is glad to see both of us again."

" Yes, Jasper, but there is some difference between men
and cuckoos; men have souls, Jasper!"

" And why not cuckoos, brother?"

" You should not talk so, Jasper; what you say is little
short of blasphemy. How should a bird have a soul?"

" And how should a man?"

" Oh, we know very well that a man has a soul."

" How do you know it?"

" We know very well."

" Would you take your oath of it, brother—your bodily
oath?"

" Why, I think I might, Jasper!"

" Did you ever see the soul, brother?"

" No, I never saw it."

" Then how could you swear to it? A pretty figure you
would make in a court of justice, to swear to a thing which
you never saw. Hold up your head, fellow. When and
where did you see it? Now upon your oath, fellow, do you
mean to say that this Roman stole the donkey's foal? Oh,
there's no one for cross-questioning like Counsellor P——.
Our people when they are in a hobble always like to employ
him, though he is somewhat dear. Now, brother, how can
you get over the ' upon your oath, fellow, will you say that
you have a soul?' "

" Well, we will take no oaths on the subject; but you
yourself believe in the soul. I have heard you say that
you believe in dukkerin; now what is dukkerin but the
soul science?"

" When did I say that I believed in it?"

" Why, after that fight, when you pointed to the bloody
mark in the cloud, whilst he you wot of was galloping in the
barouche to the old town, amidst the rain-cataracts, the
thunder, and flame of heaven."

" I have some kind of remembrance of it, brother."

" Then, again, I heard you say that the dook of Abershaw
rode every night on horseback down the wooded hill."

" I say, brother, what a wonderful memory you have!"

" I wish I had not, Jasper; but I can't help it, it is my misfortune."

" Misfortune! well, perhaps it is; at any rate it is very ungenteel to have such a memory. I have heard my wife say that to show you have a long memory looks very vulgar; and that you can't give a greater proof of gentility than by forgetting a thing as soon as possible—more especially a promise, or an acquaintance when he happens to be shabby. Well, brother, I don't deny that I may have said that I believe in dukkerin, and in Abershaw's dook, which you say is his soul; but what I believe one moment, or say I believe, don't be certain that I shall believe the next, or say I do."

" Indeed, Jasper, I heard you say on a previous occasion, on quoting a piece of a song, that when a man dies he is cast into the earth, and there's an end of him."

" I did, did I? Lor' what a memory you have, brother. But you are not sure that I hold that opinion now."

" Certainly not, Jasper. Indeed, after such a sermon as we have been hearing, I should be very shocked if you held such an opinion."

" However, brother, don't be sure I do not, however shocking such an opinion may be to you."

" What an incomprehensible people you are, Jasper."

" We are rather so, brother; indeed, we have posed wiser heads than yours before now."

" You seem to care for so little, and yet you rove about a distinct race."

" I say, brother!"

" Yes, Jasper."

" What do you think of our women?"

" They have certainly very singular names, Jasper."

" Names! Lavengro! However, brother, if you had been as fond of things as of names, you would never have been a pal of ours."

" What do you mean, Jasper?"

" A'n't they rum animals?"

" They have tongues of their own, Jasper."

" Did you ever feel their teeth and nails, brother?"

" Never, Jasper, save Mrs. Herne's. I have always been very civil to them, so——"

" They let you alone. I say, brother, some part of the secret is in them."

" They seem rather flighty, Jasper."

" Ay, ay, brother !"

" Rather fond of loose discourse !"

" Rather so, brother."

" Can you always trust them, Jasper?"

" We never watch them, brother."

" Can they always trust you?"

" Not quite so well as we can them. However, we get on very well together, except Mikailia and her husband; but Mikailia is a cripple, and is married to the beauty of the world, so she may be expected to be jealous—though he would not part with her for a duchess, no more than I would part with my rawnie, nor any other chal with his."

" Ay, but would not the chi part with the chal for a duke, Jasper?"

" My Pakomovna gave up the duke for me, brother."

" But she occasionally talks of him, Jasper."

" Yes, brother, but Pakomovna was born on a common not far from the sign of the gammon."

" Gammon of bacon, I suppose."

" Yes, brother; but gammon likewise means——"

" I know it does, Jasper; it means fun, ridicule, jest; it is an ancient Norse word, and is found in the Edda."

" Lor', brother ! how learned in lils you are !"

" Many words of Norse are to be found in our vulgar sayings, Jasper; for example—in that particularly vulgar saying of ours, ' Your mother is up,' there's a noble Norse word; mother, there, meaning not the female who bore us, but rage and choler, as I discovered by reading the Sagas, Jasper."

" Lor', brother ! how book-learned you be."

" Indifferently so, Jasper. Then you think you might trust your wife with the duke?"

" I think I could, brother, or even with yourself."

" Myself, Jasper ! Oh, I never troubled my head about your wife; but I suppose there have been love affairs between gorgios and Romany chies. Why, novels are stuffed with such matters; and then even one of your own songs says so—the song which Ursula was singing the other afternoon."

" That is somewhat of an old song, brother, and is sung by the chies as a warning at our solemn festivals."

" Well ! but there's your sister-in-law, Ursula, herself, Jasper."

" Ursula, herself, brother?"

" You were talking of my having her, Jasper."

" Well, brother, why didn't you have her?"

" Would she have had me?"

" Of course, brother. You are so much of a Roman, and speak Romany so remarkably well."

" Poor thing! she looks very innocent!"

" Remarkably so, brother! however, though not born on the same common with my wife, she knows a thing or two of Roman matters."

" I should like to ask her a question or two, Jasper, in connection with that song."

" You can do no better, brother. Here we are at the camp. After tea, take Ursula under a hedge, and ask her a question or two in connection with that song."

CHAPTER X

Sunday Evening—Ursula—Action at Law—Meridiana—Married Already.

I TOOK tea that evening with Mr. and Mrs. Petulengro and Ursula, outside of their tent. Tawno was not present, being engaged with his wife in his own tabernacle; Sylvester was there, however, lolling listlessly upon the ground. As I looked upon this man, I thought him one of the most disagreeable fellows I had ever seen. His features were ugly, and, moreover, as dark as pepper; and, besides being dark, his skin was dirty. As for his dress, it was torn and sordid. His chest was broad, and his arms seemed powerful; but, upon the whole, he looked a very caitiff. " I am sorry that man has lost his wife," thought I; " for I am sure he will never get another." What surprises me is, that he ever found a woman disposed to unite her lot with his!

After tea I got up and strolled about the field. My thoughts were upon Isopel Berners. I wondered where she was, and how long she would stay away. At length becoming tired and listless, I determined to return to the dingle, and resume the reading of the Bible at the place where I had left off. "What better could I do," methought, "on a Sunday evening?" I was then near the wood which surrounded the dingle, but at that side which was farthest from the encampment, which stood near the entrance. Suddenly, on turning round the southern corner of the copse, which surrounded the dingle, I perceived Ursula seated under a thornbush. I thought I never saw her look prettier than then, dressed as she was, in her Sunday's best.

"Good evening, Ursula," said I; "I little thought to have the pleasure of seeing you here."

"Nor would you, brother," said Ursula, "had not Jasper told me that you had been talking about me, and wanted to speak to me under a hedge; so, hearing that, I watched your motions, and came here and sat down."

"I was thinking of going to my quarters in the dingle, to read the Bible, Ursula, but——"

"Oh, pray then, go to your quarters, brother, and read the Miduveleskoe lil; you can speak to me under a hedge some other time."

"I think I will sit down with you, Ursula; for, after all, reading godly books in dingles at eve, is rather sombre work. Yes, I think I will sit down with you;" and I sat down by her side.

"Well, brother, now you have sat down with me under the hedge, what have you to say to me?"

"Why, I hardly know, Ursula."

"Not know, brother; a pretty fellow you to ask young women to come and sit with you under hedges, and, when they come, not know what to say to them."

"Oh! ah! I remember; do you know, Ursula, that I take a great interest in you?"

"Thank ye, brother; kind of you, at any rate."

"You must be exposed to a great many temptations, Ursula."

"A great many indeed, brother. It is hard to see fine things, such as shawls, gold watches, and chains in the shops, behind the big glasses, and to know that they are not intended for one. Many's the time I have been tempted to make a dash at them; but I bethought myself that by so doing I should cut my hands, besides being almost certain of being grabbed and sent across the gull's bath to the foreign country."

"Then you think gold and fine things temptations, Ursula?"

"Of course, brother, very great temptations; don't you think them so?"

"Can't say I do, Ursula."

"Then more fool you, brother; but have the kindness to tell me what you would call a temptation?"

"Why, for example, the hope of honour and renown, Ursula."

"The hope of honour and renown! very good, brother; but I tell you one thing, that unless you have money in your pocket, and good broad-cloth on your back, you are not likely to obtain much honour and—what do you call it? amongst the gorgios, to say nothing of the Romany chals."

"I should have thought, Ursula, that the Romany chals, roaming about the world as they do, free and independent, were above being led by such trifles."

"Then you know nothing of the gypsies, brother; no people on earth are fonder of those trifles, as you call them, than the Romany chals, and more disposed to respect those who have them."

"Then money and fine clothes would induce you to do anything, Ursula?"

"Ay, ay, brother, anything."

"To chore, Ursula?"

"Like enough, brother; gypsies have been transported before now for choring."

"To hokkawar?"

"Ay, ay; I was telling dukkerin only yesterday, brother."

"In fact, to break the law in everything?"

"Who knows, brother, who knows? as I said before, gold and fine clothes are great temptations."

"Well, Ursula, I am sorry for it, I should never have thought you so depraved."

"Indeed, brother."

"To think that I am seated by one who is willing to— to——"

"Go on, brother."

"To play the thief."

"Go on, brother."

"The liar."

" Go on, brother."

" The—the——"

" Go on, brother."

" The—the lubbeny."

" The what, brother?" said Ursula, starting from her seat.

" Why, the lubbeny; don't you——"

" I tell you what, brother," said Ursula, looking some-what pale, and speaking very low, " if I had only some-thing in my hand, I would do you a mischief."

" Why, what is the matter, Ursula?" said I; " how have I offended you?"

" How have you offended me? Why, didn't you in-sinivate just now that I was ready to play the—the——"

" Go on, Ursula."

" The—the—— I'll not say it; but I only wish I had something in my hand."

" If I have offended, Ursula, I am very sorry for it; any offence I may have given you was from want of understanding you. Come, pray be seated, I have much to question you about—to talk to you about."

" Seated, not I! It was only just now that you gave me to understand that you was ashamed to be seated by me, a thief, a liar."

" Well, did you not almost give me to understand that you were both, Ursula?"

" I don't much care being called a thief and a liar," said Ursula; " a person may be a liar and thief, and yet a very honest woman, but——"

" Well, Ursula."

" I tell you what, brother, if you ever sinivate again that I could be the third thing, so help me duvel! I'll do you a mischief. By my God I will!"

" Well, Ursula, I assure you that I shall sinivate, as you call it, nothing of the kind about you. I have no doubt, from what you have said, that you are a very paragon of virtue—a perfect Lucretia; but——"

" My name is Ursula, brother, and not Lucretia: Lucretia is not of our family, but one of the Bucklands; she travels about Oxfordshire; yet I am as good as she any day."

" Lucretia; how odd! Where could she have got that name? Well, I make no doubt, Ursula, that you are quite as good as she, and she as her namesake of ancient Rome; but there is a mystery in this same virtue, Ursula, which I cannot fathom; how a thief and a liar should be able, or indeed willing, to preserve her virtue is what I don't understand. You confess that you are very fond of gold. Now, how is it that you don't barter your virtue for gold sometimes? I am a philosopher, Ursula, and like to know everything. You must be every now and then exposed to great temptation, Ursula; for you are of a beauty calculated to captivate all hearts. Come, sit down and tell me how you are enabled to resist such a temptation as gold and fine clothes?"

"Well, brother," said Ursula, "as you say you mean no harm, I will sit down beside you, and enter into discourse with you; but I will uphold that you are the coolest hand that I ever came nigh, and say the coolest things."

And thereupon Ursula sat down by my side.

"Well, Ursula, we will, if you please, discourse on the subject of your temptations. I suppose that you travel very much about, and show yourself in all kinds of places?"

"In all kinds, brother; I travels, as you say, very much about, attends fairs and races, and enters booths and public-houses, where I tells fortunes, and sometimes dances and sings."

"And do not people often address you in a very free manner?"

"Frequently, brother; and I give them tolerably free answers."

"Do people ever offer to make you presents? I mean presents of value, such as——"

"Silk handkerchiefs, shawls, and trinkets; very frequently, brother."

"And what do you do, Ursula?"

"I takes what people offers me, brother, and stows it away as soon as I can."

"Well, but don't people expect something for their presents? I don't mean dukkerin, dancing, and the like; but such a moderate and innocent thing as a choomer, Ursula?"

"Innocent thing, do you call it, brother?"

"The world calls it so, Ursula. Well, do the people

who give you the fine things never expect a choomer in return?"

" Very frequently, brother."

" And do you ever grant it?"

" Never, brother."

" How do you avoid it?"

" I gets away as soon as possible, brother. If they follows me, I tries to baffle them, by means of jests and laughter; and if they persist, I uses bad and terrible language, of which I have plenty in store."

" But if your terrible language has no effect?"

" Then I screams for the constable, and if he comes not, I uses my teeth and nails."

" And are they always sufficient?"

" I have only had to use them twice, brother; but then I found them sufficient."

" But suppose the person who followed you was highly agreeable, Ursula? A handsome young officer of local militia, for example, all dressed in Lincoln green, would you still refuse him the choomer?"

" We makes no difference, brother; the daughters of the gypsy-father makes no difference; and what's more, sees none."

" Well, Ursula, the world will hardly give you credit for such indifference."

" What cares we for the world, brother! we are not of the world."

" But your fathers, brothers, and uncles, give you credit, I suppose, Ursula."

" Ay, ay, brother, our fathers, brothers, and cokos gives us all manner of credit; for example, I am telling lies and dukkerin in a public-house where my batu or coko—perhaps both—are playing on the fiddle; well, my batu and my coko beholds me amongst the public-house crew, talking nonsense and hearing nonsense; but they are under no apprehension; and presently they sees the good-looking officer of militia, in his greens and Lincolns, get up and give me a wink, and I go out with him abroad, into the dark night perhaps; well, my batu and my coko goes on fiddling just as if I were six miles off asleep in the tent, and not out in the dark street with the local officer, with his Lincolns and his greens."

" They know they can trust you, Ursula?"

"Ay, ay, brother; and, what's more, I knows I can trust myself."

"So you would merely go out to make a fool of him, Ursula?"

"Merely go out to make a fool of him, brother, I assure you."

"But such proceedings really have an odd look, Ursula."

"Amongst gorgios, very so, brother."

"Well, it must be rather unpleasant to lose one's character even amongst gorgios, Ursula; and suppose the officer, out of revenge for being tricked and duped by you, were to say of you the thing that is not, were to meet you on the race-course the next day, and boast of receiving favours which he never had, amidst a knot of jeering militia-men, how would you proceed, Ursula? would you not be abashed?"

"By no means, brother; I should bring my action of law against him."

"Your action at law, Ursula?"

"Yes, brother, I should give a whistle, whereupon all one's cokos and batus, and all my near and distant relations, would leave their fiddling, dukkerin, and horse-dealing, and come flocking about me. 'What's the matter, Ursula?' says my coko. 'Nothing at all,' I replies, 'save and except that gorgio, in his greens and his Lincolns, says that I have played the —— with him.' 'Oho, he does, Ursula,' says my coko, 'try your action of law against him, my lamb,' and he puts something privily into my hands; whereupon I goes close up to the grinning gorgio, and staring him in the face, with my head pushed forward, I cries out: 'You say I did what was wrong with you last night when I was out with you abroad?' 'Yes,' says the local officer, 'I says you did,' looking down all the time. 'You are a liar,' says I, and forthwith I breaks his head with the stick which I holds behind me, and which my coko has conveyed privily into my hand."

"And this is your action at law, Ursula?"

"Yes, brother, this is my action at club-law."

"And would your breaking the fellow's head quite clear you of all suspicion in the eyes of your batus, cokos, and what not?"

" They would never suspect me at all, brother, because they would know that I would never condescend to be over-intimate with a gorgio; the breaking the head would be merely intended to justify Ursula in the eyes of the gorgios."

" And would it clear you in their eyes?"

" Would it not, brother? when they saw the blood running down from the fellow's cracked poll on his greens and Lincolns, they would be quite satisfied; why, the fellow would not be able to show his face at fair or merry-making for a year and three-quarters."

" Did you ever try it, Ursula?"

" Can't say I ever did, brother, but it would do."

" And how did you ever learn such a method of proceeding?"

" Why, 't is advised by gypsy liri, brother. It 's part of our way of settling difficulties amongst ourselves; for example, if a young Roman were to say the thing which is not respecting Ursula and himself, Ursula would call a great meeting of the people, who would all sit down in a ring, the young fellow amongst them; a coko would then put a stick in Ursula's hand, who would then get up and go to the young fellow, and say, ' Did I play the —— with you?' and were he to say ' Yes,' she would crack his head before the eyes of all."

" Well," said I, " Ursula, I was bred an apprentice to gorgio law, and of course ought to stand up for it, whenever I conscientiously can, but I must say the gypsy manner of bringing an action for defamation is much less tedious, and far more satisfactory, than the gorgiko one. I wish you now to clear up a certain point which is rather mysterious to me. You say that for a Romany chi to do what is unseemly with a gorgio is quite out of the question, yet only the other day I heard you singing a song in which a Romany chi confesses herself to be cambri by a grand gorgious gentleman."

" A sad let down," said Ursula.

" Well," said I, " sad or not, there's the song that speaks of the thing, which you give me to understand is not."

" Well, if the thing ever was," said Ursula, " it was a long time ago, and perhaps, after all, not true."

" Then why do you sing the song?"

" I'll tell you, brother, we sings the song now and then to be a warning to ourselves to have as little to do as possible in the way of acquaintance with the gorgios; and a warning it is; you see how the young woman in the song was driven out of her tent by her mother, with all kind of disgrace and bad language; but you don't know that she was afterwards buried alive by her cokos and pals, in an uninhabited place; the song doesn't say it, but the story says it, for there is a story about it, though, as I said before, it was a long time ago, and perhaps, after all, wasn't true."

" But if such a thing were to happen at present, would the cokos and pals bury the girl alive?"

" I can't say what they would do," said Ursula; " I suppose they are not so strict as they were long ago; at any rate, she would be driven from the tan, and avoided by all her family and relations as a gorgio's acquaintance; so that, perhaps, at last, she would be glad if they would bury her alive."

" Well, I can conceive that there would be an objection on the part of the cokos and batus that a Romany chi should form an improper acquaintance with a gorgio, but I should think that the batus and cokos could hardly object to the chi's entering into the honourable estate of wedlock with a gorgio."

Ursula was silent.

" Marriage is an honourable estate, Ursula."

" Well, brother, suppose it be?"

" I don't see why a Romany chi should object to enter into the honourable estate of wedlock with a gorgio."

" You don't, brother; don't you?"

" No," said I; " and, moreover, I am aware, notwithstanding your evasion, Ursula, that marriages and connections now and then occur between gorgios and Romany chies; the result of which is the mixed breed, called half and half, which is at present travelling about England, and to which the Flaming Tinman belongs, otherwise called Anselo Herne."

" As for the half and halfs," said Ursula, " they are a bad set; and there is not a worse blackguard in England than Anselo Herne."

" All that you say may be very true, Ursula, but you admit that there are half and halfs."

" The more's the pity, brother."

" Pity, or not, you admit the fact; but how do you account for it?"

" How do I account for it? why, I will tell you, by the break up of a Roman family, brother—the father of a small family dies, and, perhaps, the mother; and the poor children are left behind; sometimes, they are gathered up by their relations, and sometimes, if they have none, by charitable Romans, who bring them up in the observance of gypsy law; but sometimes they are not so lucky, and falls into the company of gorgios, trampers, and basket-makers, who live in caravans, with whom they take up, and so—— I hate to talk of the matter, brother; but so comes this race of the half and halfs."

" Then you mean to say, Ursula, that no Romany chi, unless compelled by hard necessity, would have anything to do with a gorgio?"

" We are not over-fond of gorgios, brother, and we hates basket-makers, and folks that live in caravans."

" Well," said I, " suppose a gorgio who is not a basket-maker, a fine, handsome gorgious gentleman, who lives in a fine house——"

" We are not fond of houses, brother; I never slept in a house in my life."

" But would not plenty of money induce you?"

" I hate houses, brother, and those who live in them."

" Well, suppose such a person were willing to resign his fine house; and, for love of you, to adopt gypsy law, speak Romany, and live in a tan, would you have nothing to say to him?"

" Bringing plenty of money with him, brother?"

" Well, bringing plenty of money with him, Ursula."

" Well, brother, suppose you produce your man; where is he?"

" I was merely supposing such a person, Ursula."

" Then you don't know of such a person, brother?"

" Why, no, Ursula; why do you ask?"

" Because, brother, I was almost beginning to think that you meant yourself."

" Myself! Ursula; I have no fine house to resign; nor have I money. Moreover, Ursula, though I have a great regard for you, and though I consider you very handsome, quite as handsome, indeed, as Meridiana in——"

"Meridiana! where did you meet with her?" said Ursula, with a toss of her head.

"Why, in old Pulci's——"

"At old Fulcher's! that's not true, brother. Meridiana is a Borzlam, and travels with her own people, and not with old Fulcher, who is a gorgio, and a basket-maker."

"I was not speaking of old Fulcher, but Pulci, a great Italian writer, who lived many hundred years ago, and who, in his poem called 'Morgante Maggiore,' speaks of Meridiana, the daughter of——"

"Old Carus Borzlam," said Ursula; "but if the fellow you mention lived so many hundred years ago, how, in the name of wonder, could he know anything of Meridiana?"

"The wonder, Ursula, is, how your people could ever have got hold of that name, and similar ones. The Meridiana of Pulci was not the daughter of old Carus Borzlam, but of Caradoro, a great pagan king of the East, who, being besieged in his capital by Manfredonio, another mighty pagan king, who wished to obtain possession of his daughter, who had refused him, was relieved in his distress by certain paladins of Charlemagne, with one of whom, Oliver, his daughter Meridiana fell in love."

"I see," said Ursula, "that it must have been altogether a different person, for I am sure that Meridiana Borzlam would never have fallen in love with Oliver. Oliver! why, that is the name of the curo-mengro, who lost the fight near the chong gav, the day of the great tempest, when I got wet through. No, no! Meridiana Borzlam would never have so far forgot her blood as to take up with Tom Oliver."

"I was not talking of that Oliver, Ursula, but of Oliver, peer of France, and paladin of Charlemagne, with whom Meridiana, daughter of Caradoro, fell in love, and for whose sake she renounced her religion and became a Christian, and finally ingravidata, or cambri, by him:—

'E nacquene un figliuol, dice la storia,
    Che dette a Carlo-man poi gran vittoria;'

which means——"

"I don't want to know what it means," said Ursula; "no good, I'm sure. Well, if the Meridiana of Charles's wain's pal was no handsomer than Meridiana Borzlam, she was no great catch, brother; for though I am by no means given to vanity, I think myself better to look at than she, though I will say she is no lubbeny, and would scorn——"

"I make no doubt she would, Ursula, and I make no doubt that you are much handsomer than she, or even the Meridiana of Oliver. What I was about to say, before you interrupted me, is this, that though I have a great regard for you, and highly admire you, it is only in a brotherly way, and——"

"And you had nothing better to say to me," said Ursula, "when you wanted to talk to me beneath a hedge, than that you liked me in a brotherly way! well, I declare——"

"You seem disappointed, Ursula."

"Disappointed, brother! not I."

"You were just now saying that you disliked gorgios, so, of course, could only wish that I, who am a gorgio, should like you in a brotherly way: I wished to have a conversation with you beneath a hedge, but only with the view of procuring from you some information respecting the song which you sung the other day, and the conduct of Roman females, which has always struck me as being highly unaccountable; so, if you thought anything else——"

"What else should I expect from a picker-up of old words, brother? Bah! I dislike a picker-up of old words worse than a picker-up of old rags."

"Don't be angry, Ursula, I feel a great interest in you; you are very handsome, and very clever; indeed, with your beauty and cleverness, I only wonder that you have not long since been married."

"You do, do you, brother?"

"Yes. However, keep up your spirits, Ursula, you are not much past the prime of youth, so——"

"Not much past the prime of youth! Don't be uncivil, brother, I was only twenty-two last month."

"Don't be offended, Ursula, but twenty-two is twenty-two, or, I should rather say, that twenty-two in a woman is more than twenty-six in a man. You are still very beautiful, but I advise you to accept the first offer that's made to you."

"Thank you, brother, but your advice comes rather late; I accepted the first offer that was made me five years ago."

" You married five years ago, Ursula ! is it possible?"

" Quite possible, brother, I assure you."

" And how came I to know nothing about it?"

" How comes it that you don't know many thousand things about the Romans, brother? Do you think they tell you all their affairs?"

" Married, Ursula, married ! well, I declare !"

" You seem disappointed, brother."

" Disappointed ! Oh ! no, not at all ; but Jasper, only a few weeks ago, told me that you were not married ; and, indeed, almost gave me to understand that you would be very glad to get a husband."

" And you believed him? I'll tell you, brother, for your instruction, that there is not in the whole world a greater liar than Jasper Petulengro."

" I am sorry to hear it, Ursula ; but with respect to him you married—who might he be? A gorgio, or a Romany chal?"

" Gorgio, or Romany chal ! Do you think I would ever condescend to a gorgio ! It was a Camomescro, brother, a Lovell, a distant relation of my own."

" And where is he? and what became of him ! Have you any family?"

" Don't think I am going to tell you all my history, brother ; and, to tell you the truth, I am tired of sitting under hedges with you, talking nonsense. I shall go to my house."

" Do sit a little longer, sister Ursula. I most heartily congratulate you on your marriage. But where is this same Lovell? I have never seen him : I wish to congratulate him too. You are quite as handsome as the Meridiana of Pulci, Ursula, ay, or the Despina of Riciardetto. Riciardetto, Ursula, is a poem written by one Fortiguerra, about ninety years ago, in imitation of the Morgante of Pulci. It treats of the wars of Charlemagne and his Paladins with various barbarous nations, who came to besiege Paris. Despina was the daughter and heiress of Scricca, King of Cafria ; she was the beloved of Riciardetto, and was beautiful as an angel ; but I make no doubt you are quite as handsome as she."

" Brother," said Ursula—but the reply of Ursula I reserve for another chapter, the present having attained to rather an uncommon length, for which, however, the importance of the matter discussed is a sufficient apology.

CHAPTER XI

Ursula's Tale—The Patteran—The Deep Water—Second Husband.

" Brother," said Ursula, plucking a dandelion which
grew at her feet, " I have always said that a more civil and
pleasant-spoken person than yourself can't be found.   I
have a great regard for you and your learning, and am
willing to do you any pleasure in the way of words or
conversation.   Mine is not a very happy story, but as
you wish to hear it, it is quite at your service.   Launcelot
Lovell made me an offer, as you call it, and we were
married in Roman fashion; that is, we gave each other
our right hands, and promised to be true to each other.
We lived together two years, travelling sometimes by
ourselves, sometimes with our relations; I bore him two
children, both of which were still-born, partly, I believe,
from the fatigue I underwent in running about the country
telling dukkerin when I was not exactly in a state to do
so, and partly from the kicks and blows which my husband
Launcelot was in the habit of giving me every night,
provided I came home with less than five shillings, which
it is sometimes impossible to make in the country, provided no fair or merry-making is going on.   At the end of
two years my husband, Launcelot, whistled a horse from
a farmer's field, and sold it for forty-pounds; and for
that horse he was taken, put in prison, tried, and condemned to be sent to the other country for life.   Two
days before he was to be sent away, I got leave to see
him in the prison, and in the presence of the turnkey I
gave him a thin cake of gingerbread, in which there was
a dainty saw which could cut through iron.   I then took
on wonderfully, turned my eyes inside out, fell down in a
seeming fit, and was carried out of the prison.   That same
night my husband sawed his irons off, cut through the
bars of his window, and dropping down a height of fifty
feet, lighted on his legs, and came and joined me on a
heath where I was camped alone.   We were just getting
things ready to be off, when we heard people coming,
and sure enough they were runners after my husband,
Launcelot Lovell; for his escape had been discovered
within a quarter of an hour after he had got away.   My

husband, without bidding me farewell, set off at full speed, and they after him, but they could not take him, and so they came back and took me, and shook me, and threatened me, and had me before the poknees, who shook his head at me, and threatened me in order to make me discover where my husband was, but I said I did not know, which was true enough; not that I would have told him if I had. So at last the poknees and the runners, not being able to make anything out of me, were obliged to let me go, and I went in search of my husband. I wandered about with my cart for several days in the direction in which I saw him run off, with my eyes bent on the ground, but could see no marks of him; at last, coming to four cross roads, I saw my husband's patteran."

" You saw your husband's patteran?"

" Yes, brother. Do you know what patteran means?"

" Of course, Ursula; the gypsy trail, the handful of grass which the gypsies strew in the roads as they travel, to give information to any of their companions who may be behind, as to the route they have taken. The gypsy patteran has always had a strange interest for me, Ursula."

" Like enough, brother; but what does patteran mean?"

" Why, the gypsy trail, formed as I told you before."

" And you know nothing more about patteran, brother?"

" Nothing at all, Ursula; do you?"

" What's the name for the leaf of a tree, brother?"

" I don't know," said I; " it's odd enough that I have asked that question of a dozen Romany chals and chies, and they always told me that they did not know."

" No more they did, brother; there's only one person in England that knows, and that's myself—the name for a leaf is patteran. Now there are two that knows it—the other is yourself."

" Dear me, Ursula, how very strange! I am much obliged to you. I think I never saw you look so pretty as you do now; but who told you?"

" My mother, Mrs. Herne, told it me one day, brother, when she was in a good humour, which she very seldom was, as no one has a better right to know than yourself, as she hated you mortally: it was one day when you had been asking our company what was the word for a leaf, and nobody could tell you, that she took me aside and told me, for she was in a good humour, and triumphed in seeing you balked. She told me the word for leaf was patteran, which our people use now for trail, having forgotten the true meaning. She said that the trail was called patteran, because the gypsies of old were in the habit of making the marks with the leaves and branches of trees, placed in a certain manner. She said that nobody knew it but herself, who was one of the old sort, and begged me never to tell the word to any one but him I should marry; and to be particularly cautious never to let you know it, whom she hated. Well, brother, perhaps I have done wrong to tell you; but, as I said before, I likes you, and am always ready to do your pleasure in words and conversation; my mother, more-over, is dead and gone, and, poor thing, will never know anything about the matter. So, when I married, I told my husband about the patteran, and we were in the habit of making our private trails with leaves and branches of trees, which none of the other gypsy people did; so, when I saw my husband's patteran, I knew it at once, and I followed it upwards of two hundred miles towards the north; and then I came to a deep, awful-looking water, with an overhanging bank, and on the bank I found the patteran, which directed me to proceed along the bank towards the east, and I followed my husband's patteran towards the east; and before I had gone half a mile, I came to a place where I saw the bank had given way, and fallen into the deep water. Without paying much heed, I passed on, and presently came to a public-house, not far from the water, and I entered the public-house to get a little beer, and perhaps to tell a dukkerin, for I saw a great many people about the door; and, when I entered, I found there was what they calls an inquest being held upon a body in that house, and the jury had just risen to go and look at the body; and being a woman, and having a curiosity, I thought I would go with them, and so I did; and no sooner did I see the body, than I knew it to be my husband's; it was much swelled and altered, but I knew it partly by the clothes, and partly by a mark on the forehead, and I cried out, 'It is my husband's body,' and I fell down in a fit, and the fit that time, brother, was not a seeming one."

"Dear me," said I, "how terrible! but tell me, Ursula, how did your husband come by his death?"

"The bank, overhanging the deep water, gave way under him, brother, and he was drowned; for, like most of our people, he could not swim, or only a little. The body, after it had been in the water a long time, came up of itself, and was found floating. Well, brother, when the people of the neighbourhood found that I was the wife of the drowned man, they were very kind to me, and made a subscription for me, with which, after having seen my husband buried, I returned the way I had come, till I met Jasper and his people, and with them I have travelled ever since: I was very melancholy for a long time, I assure you, brother; for the death of my husband preyed very much upon my mind."

"His death was certainly a very shocking one, Ursula; but, really, if he had died a natural one, you could scarcely have regretted it, for he appears to have treated you barbarously."

"Women must bear, brother; and, barring that he kicked and beat me, and drove me out to tell dukkerin when I could scarcely stand, he was not a bad husband. A man, by gypsy law, brother, is allowed to kick and beat his wife, and to bury her alive, if he thinks proper. I am a gypsy, and have nothing to say against the law."

"But what has Mikailia Chikno to say about it?"

"She is a cripple, brother, the only cripple amongst the Roman people: so she is allowed to do and say as she pleases. Moreover, her husband does not think fit to kick or beat her, though it is my opinion she would like him all the better if he were occasionally to do so, and threaten to bury her alive; at any rate, she would treat him better, and respect him more."

"Your sister does not seem to stand much in awe of Jasper Petulengro, Ursula."

"Let the matters of my sister and Jasper Petulengro alone, brother; you must travel in their company some time before you can understand them; they are a strange two, up to all kind of chaffing: but two more regular Romans don't breathe, and I'll tell you, for your instruction, that there isn't a better mare-breaker in England than Jasper Petulengro, if you can manage Miss Isope¹ Berners as well as——"

" Isopel Berners," said I, " how came you to think of her?"

" How should I but think of her, brother, living as she does with you in Mumper's dingle, and travelling about with you; you will have, brother, more difficulty to manage her, than Jasper has to manage my sister Pakomovna. I should have mentioned her before, only I wanted to know what you had to say to me; and when we got into discourse, I forgot her. I say, brother, let me tell you your dukkerin, with respect to her, you will never——"

" I want to hear no dukkerin, Ursula."

" Do let me tell you your dukkerin, brother, you will never manage——"

" I want to hear no dukkerin, Ursula, in connection with Isopel Berners. Moreover, it is Sunday, we will change the subject; it is surprising to me that, after all you have undergone, you should look so beautiful. I suppose you do not think of marrying again, Ursula?"

" No, brother, one husband at a time is quite enough for any reasonable mort; especially such a good husband as I have got."

" Such a good husband! why, I thought you told me your husband was drowned?"

" Yes, brother, my first husband was."

" And have you a second?"

" To be sure, brother."

" And who is he? in the name of wonder."

" Who is he? why Sylvester, to be sure."

" I do assure you, Ursula, that I feel disposed to be angry with you; such a handsome young woman as yourself to take up with such a nasty pepper-faced good for nothing——"

" I won't hear my husband abused, brother; so you had better say no more."

" Why, is he not the Lazarus of the gypsies? has he a penny of his own, Ursula?"

" Then the more his want, brother, of a clever chi like me to take care of him and his childer. I tell you what, brother, I will chore, if necessary, and tell dukkerin for Sylvester, if even so heavy as scarcely to be able to stand. You call him lazy; you would not think him lazy if you were in a ring with him: he is a proper man with his hands; Jasper is going to back him for twenty pounds against Slammocks of the Chong gav, the brother of Roarer and Bell-metal, he says he has no doubt that he will win."

"Well, if you like him, I, of course, can have no objection. Have you been long married?"

"About a fortnight, brother; that dinner, the other day, when I sang the song, was given in celebration of the wedding."

"Were you married in a church, Ursula?"

"We were not, brother; none but gorgios, cripples, and lubbenys are ever married in a church : we took each other's words. Brother, I have been with you near three hours beneath this hedge. I will go to my husband."

"Does he know that you are here?"

"He does, brother."

"And is he satisfied?"

"Satisfied! of course. Lor', you gorgies! Brother, I go to my husband and my house." And, thereupon, Ursula rose and departed.

After waiting a little time I also arose; it was now dark, and I thought I could do no better than betake myself to the dingle; at the entrance of it I found Mr. Petulengro. "Well, brother," said he, "what kind of conversation have you and Ursula had beneath the hedge?"

"If you wished to hear what we were talking about, you should have come and sat down beside us; you knew where we were."

"Well, brother, I did much the same, for I went and sat down behind you."

"Behind the hedge, Jasper?"

"Behind the hedge, brother."

"And heard all our conversation."

"Every word, brother; and a rum conversation it was."

"'Tis an old saying, Jasper, that listeners never hear any good of themselves; perhaps you heard the epithet that Ursula bestowed upon you."

"If, by epitaph, you mean that she called me a liar, I did, brother, and she was not much wrong, for I certainly do not always stick exactly to truth; you, however, have not much to complain of me."

"You deceived me about Ursula, giving me to understand she was not married."

"She was not married when I told you so, brother; that

is, not to Sylvester; nor was I aware that she was going to marry him. I once thought you had a kind of regard for her, and I am sure she had as much for you as a Romany chi can have for a gorgio. I half expected to have heard you make love to her behind the hedge, but I begin to think you care for nothing in this world but old words and strange stories. Lor' to take a young woman under a hedge, and talk to her as you did to Ursula; and yet you got everything out of her that you wanted, with your gammon about old Fulcher and Meridiana. You are a cunning one, brother."

"There you are mistaken, Jasper. I am not cunning. If people think I am, it is because, being made up of art themselves, simplicity of character is a puzzle to them. Your women are certainly extraordinary creatures, Jasper."

"Didn't I say they were rum animals? Brother, we Romans shall always stick together as long as they stick fast to us."

"Do you think they always will, Jasper?"

"Can't say, brother; nothing lasts for ever. Romany chies are Romany chies still, though not exactly what they were sixty years ago. My wife, though a rum one, is not Mrs. Herne, brother. I think she is rather fond of Frenchmen and French discourse. I tell you what, brother, if ever gypsyism breaks up, it will be owing to our chies having been bitten by that mad puppy they calls gentility."

CHAPTER XII

The Dingle at Night—The Two Sides of the Question—Roman Females—Filling the Kettle—The Dream—The Tall Figure.

I DESCENDED to the bottom of the dingle. It was nearly involved in obscurity. To dissipate the feeling of melancholy which came over my mind, I resolved to kindle a fire; and having heaped dry sticks upon my hearth, and added a billet or two, I struck a light, and soon produced a blaze. Sitting down, I fixed my eyes upon the blaze, and soon fell into a deep meditation. I thought of the events of the day, the scene at church, and what I had heard at church, the danger of losing one's soul, the doubts of

Jasper Petulengro as to whether one had a soul. I thought
over the various arguments which I had either heard, or
which had come spontaneously to my mind, for or against
the probability of a state of future existence. They
appeared to me to be tolerably evenly balanced. I then
thought that it was at all events taking the safest part to
conclude that there was a soul. It would be a terrible
thing, after having passed one's life in the disbelief of the
existence of a soul, to wake up after death a soul, and to
find one's self a lost soul. Yes, methought I would come
to the conclusion that one has a soul. Choosing the safe
side, however, appeared to me to be playing a rather dastardly part. I had never been an admirer of people who
chose the safe side in everything; indeed I had always
entertained a thorough contempt for them. Surely it
would be showing more manhood to adopt the dangerous
side, that of disbelief; I almost resolved to do so—but yet
in a question of so much importance, I ought not to be
guided by vanity. The question was not which was the
safe, but the true side? yet how was I to know which was
the true side? Then I thought of the Bible—which I had
been reading in the morning—that spoke of the soul and a
future state; but was the Bible true? I had heard learned
and moral men say that it was true, but I had also heard
learned and moral men say that it was not: how was I to
decide? Still that balance of probabilities! If I could but
see the way of truth, I would follow it, if necessary, upon
hands and knees; on that I was determined; but I could
not see it. Feeling my brain begin to turn round, I resolved to think of something else; and forthwith began to
think of what had passed between Ursula and myself in
our discourse beneath the hedge.

I mused deeply on what she had told me as to the virtue
of the females of her race. How singular that virtue must
be which was kept pure and immaculate by the possessor,
whilst indulging in habits of falsehood and dishonesty! I
had always thought the gypsy females extraordinary
beings. I had often wondered at them, their dress, their
manner of speaking, and, not least, at their names; but,
until the present day, I had been unacquainted with the most
extraordinary point connected with them. How came they
possessed of this extraordinary virtue? was it because they
were thievish? I remembered that an ancient thief-taker,

who had retired from his useful calling, and who frequently
visited the office of my master at law, the respectable
S——, who had the management of his property—I remembered to have heard this worthy, with whom I occasionally held discourse, philosophic and profound, when he and
I chanced to be alone together in the office, say that all
first-rate thieves were sober, and of well-regulated morals,
their bodily passions being kept in abeyance by their love
of gain; but this axiom could scarcely hold good with
respect to these women—however thievish they might be,
they did care for something besides gain : they cared for
their husbands. If they did thieve, they merely thieved for
their husbands; and though, perhaps, some of them were
vain, they merely prized their beauty because it gave them
favour in the eyes of their husbands. Whatever the husbands were—and Jasper had almost insinuated that the
males occasionally allowed themselves some latitude—they
appeared to be as faithful to their husbands as the ancient
Roman matrons were to theirs. Roman matrons ! and,
after all, might not these be in reality Roman matrons?
They called themselves Romans; might not they be the
descendants of the old Roman matrons? Might not they
be of the same blood as Lucretia? And were not many
of their strange names—Lucretia amongst the rest—
handed down to them from old Rome? It is true their language was not that of old Rome; it was not, however,
altogether different from it. After all, the ancient Romans
might be a tribe of these people, who settled down and
founded a village with the tilts of carts, which, by degrees,
and the influx of other people, became the grand city of
the world. I liked the idea of the grand city of the world
owing its origin to a people who had been in the habit of
carrying their houses in their carts. Why, after all, should
not the Romans of history be a branch of these Romans?
There were several points of similarity between them; if
Roman matrons were chaste, both men and women were
thieves. Old Rome was the thief of the world; yet still
there were difficulties to be removed before I could persuade myself that the old Romans and my Romans were
identical; and in trying to remove these difficulties, I felt
my brain once more beginning to turn, and in haste took
up another subject of meditation, and that was the patteran, and what Ursula had told me about it.

I had always entertained a strange interest for that sign by which in their wanderings the Romanese gave to those of their people who came behind intimation as to the direction which they took; but it now inspired me with greater interest than ever,—now that I had learnt that the proper meaning of it was the leaves of trees. I had, as I had said in my dialogue with Ursula, been very eager to learn the word for leaf in the Romanian language, but had never learnt it till this day; so patteran signified leaf of a tree; and no one at present knew that but myself and Ursula, who had learnt it from Mrs. Herne, the last, it was said, of the old stock; and then I thought what strange people the gypsies must have been in the old time. They were sufficiently strange at present, but they must have been far stranger of old; they must have been a more peculiar people—their language must have been more perfect—and they must have had a greater stock of strange secrets. I almost wished that I had lived some two or three hundred years ago, that I might have observed these people when they were yet stranger than at present. I wondered whether I could have introduced myself to their company at that period, whether I should have been so fortunate as to meet such a strange, half-malicious, half good-humoured being as Jasper, who would have instructed me in the language, then more deserving of note than at present. What might I not have done with that language, had I known it in its purity? Why, I might have written books in it; yet those who spoke it would hardly have admitted me to their society at that period, when they kept more to themselves. Yet I thought that I might possibly have gained their confidence, and have wandered about with them, and learnt their language, and all their strange ways, and then—and then—and a sigh rose from the depth of my breast; for I began to think, "Supposing I had accomplished all this, what would have been the profit of it; and in what would all this wild gypsy dream have terminated?"

Then rose another sigh, yet more profound, for I began to think, "What was likely to be the profit of my present way of life; the living in dingles, making pony and donkey shoes, conversing with gypsy-women under hedges, and extracting from them their odd secrets?" What was likely to be the profit of such a kind of life, even should it continue for a length of time?—a supposition not very probable, for I was earning nothing to support me, and the funds with which I had entered upon this life were gradually disappearing. I was living, it is true, not unpleasantly, enjoying the healthy air of heaven; but, upon the whole, was I not sadly misspending my time? Surely I was; and, as I looked back, it appeared to me that I had always been doing so. What had been the profit of the tongues which I had learnt? had they ever assisted me in the day of hunger? No, no! it appeared to me that I had always misspent my time, save in one instance, when by a desperate effort I had collected all the powers of my imagination, and written the "Life of Joseph Sell;" but even when I wrote the Life of Sell, was I not in a false position? Provided I had not misspent my time, would it have been necessary to make that effort, which, after all, had only enabled me to leave London, and wander about the country for a time? But could I, taking all circumstances into consideration, have done better than I had? With my peculiar temperament and ideas, could I have pursued with advantage the profession to which my respectable parents had endeavoured to bring me up? It appeared to me that I could not, and that the hand of necessity had guided me from my earliest years, until the present night, in which I found myself seated in the dingle, staring on the brands of the fire. But ceasing to think of the past which, as irrecoverably gone, it was useless to regret, even were there cause to regret it, what should I do in future? Should I write another book like the Life of Joseph Sell; take it to London, and offer it to a publisher? But when I reflected on the grisly sufferings which I had undergone whilst engaged in writing the Life of Sell, I shrank from the idea of a similar attempt; moreover, I doubted whether I possessed the power to write a similar work—whether the materials for the life of another Sell lurked within the recesses of my brain? Had I not better become in reality what I had hitherto been merely playing at—a tinker or a gypsy? But I soon saw that I was not fitted to become either in reality. It was much more agreeable to play the gypsy or the tinker than to become either in reality. I had seen enough of gypsying and tinkering to be convinced of that. All of a sudden the idea of tilling the soil came into my head; tilling the soil was a healthful and noble pursuit! but my idea of tilling the soil had no connection with Britain; for I could only expect to till the soil in Britain as a serf. I thought of tilling it in America, in which it was said there was plenty of wild, unclaimed land, of which any one, who chose to clear it of its trees, might take possession. I figured myself in America, in an immense forest, clearing the land destined, by my exertions, to become a fruitful and smiling plain. Methought I heard the crash of the huge trees as they fell beneath my axe; and then I bethought me that a man was intended to marry—I ought to marry; and if I married, where was I likely to be more happy as a husband and a father than in America, engaged in tilling the ground? I fancied myself in America, engaged in tilling the ground, assisted by an enormous progeny. Well, why not marry, and go and till the ground in America? I was young, and youth was the time to marry in, and to labour in. I had the use of all my faculties; my eyes, it is true, were rather dull from early study, and from writing the Life of Joseph Sell; but I could see tolerably well with them, and they were not bleared. I felt my arms, and thighs, and teeth—they were strong and sound enough; so now was the time to labour, to marry, eat strong flesh, and beget strong children—the power of doing all this would pass away with youth, which was terribly transitory. I bethought me that a time would come when my eyes would be bleared, and, perhaps, sightless; my arms and thighs strengthless and sapless; when my teeth would shake in my jaws, even supposing they did not drop out. No going a wooing then—no labouring—no eating strong flesh, and begetting lusty children then; and I bethought me how, when all this should be, I should bewail the days of my youth as misspent, provided I had not in them founded for myself a home, and begotten strong children to take care of me in the days when I could not take care of myself; and thinking of these things, I became sadder and sadder, and stared vacantly upon the fire till my eyes closed in a doze.

I continued dozing over the fire, until rousing myself I perceived that the brands were nearly consumed, and I thought of retiring for the night. I arose, and was about to enter my tent, when a thought struck me. "Suppose," thought I, "that Isopel Berners should return in the midst of the night, how dark and dreary would the dingle appear without a fire! truly, I will keep up the fire, and I will do more; I have no board to spread for her, but I will fill the kettle, and heat it, so that, if she comes, I may be able to welcome her with a cup of tea, for I know she loves tea.'' Thereupon, I piled more wood upon the fire, and soon succeeded in procuring a better blaze than before; then, taking the kettle, I set out for the spring. On arriving at the mouth of the dingle, which fronted the east, I perceived that Charles's wain was nearly opposite to it, high above in the heavens, by which I knew that the night was tolerably well advanced. The gypsy encampment lay before me; all was hushed and still within it, and its inmates appeared to be locked in slumber; as I advanced, however, the dogs, which were fastened outside the tents, growled and barked; but presently recognising me, they were again silent, some of them wagging their tails. As I drew near a particular tent, I heard a female voice say—'' Some one is coming!'' and, as I was about to pass it, the cloth which formed the door was suddenly lifted up, and a black head and part of a huge naked body protruded. It was the head and upper part of the giant Tawno, who, according to the fashion of gypsy men, lay next the door wrapped in his blanket; the blanket had, however, fallen off, and the starlight shone clear on his athletic tawny body, and was reflected from his large staring eyes.

'' It is only I, Tawno,'' said I, '' going to fill the kettle, as it is possible that Miss Berners may arrive this night.'' '' Kos-ko,'' drawled out Tawno, and replaced the curtain. '' Good, do you call it?'' said the sharp voice of his wife; '' there is no good in the matter! if that young chap were not living with the rawnee in the illegal and uncertificated line, he would not be getting up in the middle of the night to fill her kettles.'' Passing on, I proceeded to the spring, where I filled the kettle, and then returned to the dingle.

Placing the kettle upon the fire, I watched it till it began to boil; then removing it from the top of the brands, I placed it close beside the fire, and leaving it simmering, I retired to my tent; where, having taken off my shoes, and a few of my garments, I lay down on my palliasse, and was not long in falling asleep. I believe I slept soundly for some time, thinking and dreaming of nothing; suddenly, however, my sleep became disturbed, and the subject of the patterans began to occupy my brain. I imagined that I saw Ursula tracing her husband, Launcelot Lovel, by means of his patterans; I imagined that she had considerable difficulty in doing so; that she was occasionally interrupted by parish beadles and constables, who asked her whither she was travelling, to whom she gave various answers. Presently methought that, as she was passing by a farm-yard, two fierce and savage dogs flew at her; I was in great trouble, I remember, and wished to assist her, but could not, for though I seemed to see her, I was still at a distance: and now it appeared that she had escaped from the dogs, and was proceeding with her cart along a gravelly path which traversed a wild moor; I could hear the wheels grating amidst sand and gravel. The next moment I was awake, and found myself sitting up in my tent; there was a glimmer of light through the canvas caused by the fire; a feeling of dread came over me, which was perhaps natural, on starting suddenly from one's sleep in that wild lone place; I half imagined that some one was nigh the tent; the idea made me rather uncomfortable, and, to dissipate it, I lifted up the canvas of the door and peeped out, and, lo! I had a distinct view of a tall figure standing by the tent. "Who is that?" said I, whilst I felt my blood rush to my heart. "It is I," said the voice of Isopel Berners; "you little expected me, I dare say; well, sleep on, I do not wish to disturb you." "But I was expecting you," said I, recovering myself, "as you may see by the fire and kettle. I will be with you in a moment."

Putting on in haste the articles of dress which I had flung off, I came out of the tent, and addressing myself to Isopel, who was standing beside her cart, I said—"Just as I was about to retire to rest I thought it possible that you might come to-night, and got everything in readiness for you. Now, sit down by the fire whilst I lead the donkey and cart to the place where you stay; I will unharness the animal, and presently come and join you." "I need not trouble you," said Isopel; "I will go myself and see after my things." "We will go together," said I, "and then return and have some tea." Isopel made no objection, and in about half-an-hour we had arranged everything at her quarters, I then hastened and prepared tea.

Presently Isopel rejoined me, bringing her stool; she had divested herself of her bonnet, and her hair fell over her shoulders; she sat down, and I poured out the beverage, handing her a cup. "Have you made a long journey to-night?" said I. "A very long one," replied Belle. "I have come nearly twenty miles since six o'clock." "I believe I heard you coming in my sleep," said I; "did the dogs above bark at you?" "Yes," said Isopel, "very violently; did you think of me in your sleep?" "No," said I, "I was thinking of Ursula and something she had told me." "When and where was that?" said Isopel. "Yesterday evening," said I, "beneath the dingle hedge." "Then you were talking with her beneath the hedge?" "I was," said I, "but only upon gypsy matters. Do you know, Belle, that she has just been married to Sylvester, so that you need not think that she and I——" "She and you are quite at liberty to sit where you please," said Isopel. "However, young man," she continued, dropping her tone, which she had slightly raised, "I believe what you said, that you were merely talking about gypsy matters, and also what you were going to say, if it was, as I suppose, that she and you had no particular acquaintance." Isopel was now silent for some time. "What are you thinking of?" said I. "I was thinking," said Belle, "how exceedingly kind it was of you to get everything in readiness for me, though you did not know that I should come." "I had a presentiment that you would come," said I; "but you forget that I have prepared the kettle for you before, though it was true that I was then certain that you would come." "I had not forgotten your doing so, young man," said Belle; "but I was beginning to think that you were utterly selfish, caring for nothing but the gratification of your own selfish whims." "I am very fond of having my own way," said I, "but utterly selfish I am not, as I dare say I shall frequently prove to you. You will often find the kettle boiling when you come home." "Not heated by you," said Isopel, with a sigh. "By whom else?" said I; "surely you are not thinking of driving me away?" "You have as much right here as myself," said Isopel, "as I have told you before; but I must be going myself." "Well," said I, "we can go together; to tell you the truth, I am rather tired of this place." "Our paths must be separate," said Belle.

" Separate," said I, " what do you mean? I shan't let
you go alone, I shall go with you; and you know the road
is as free to me as to you; besides, you can't think of
parting company with me, considering how much you
would lose by doing so; remember that you know scarcely
anything of the Armenian language; now, to learn
Armenian from me would take you twenty years."

Belle faintly smiled. " Come," said I, " take another
cup of tea." Belle took another cup of tea, and yet another;
we had some indifferent conversation, after which I arose
and gave her donkey a considerable feed of corn. Belle
thanked me, shook me by the hand, and then went to her
own tabernacle, and I returned to mine.

CHAPTER XIII

Visit to the Landlord—His Mortifications—Hunter and his Clan—
Resolution.

ON the following morning, after breakfasting with Belle,
who was silent and melancholy, I left her in the dingle,
and took a stroll amongst the neighbouring lanes. After
some time I thought I would pay a visit to the landlord of
the public-house, whom I had not seen since the day when
he communicated to me his intention of changing his
religion. I therefore directed my steps to the house, and
on entering it found the landlord standing in the kitchen.
Just then two mean-looking fellows, who had been drinking at one of the tables, and who appeared to be the only
customers in the house, got up, brushed past the landlord, and saying in a surly tone, we shall pay you some
time or other, took their departure. " That's the way
they serve me now," said the landlord, with a sigh. " Do
you know those fellows," I demanded, " since you let them
go away in your debt?" " I know nothing about them,"
said the landlord, " save that they are a couple of scamps."
" Then why did you let them go away without paying
you?" said I. " I had not the heart to stop them," said
the landlord; " and, to tell you the truth, everybody
serves me so now, and I suppose they are right, for a

child could flog me." "Nonsense," said I, "behave more like a man, and with respect to those two fellows run after them, I will go with you, and if they refuse to pay the reckoning I will help you to shake some money out of their clothes." "Thank you," said the landlord; "but as they are gone, let them go on. What they have drank is not of much consequence." "What is the matter with you?" said I, staring at the landlord, who appeared strangely altered; his features were wild and haggard, his formerly bluff cheeks were considerably sunken in, and his figure had lost much of its plumpness. "Have you changed your religion already, and has the fellow in black commanded you to fast?" "I have not changed my religion yet," said the landlord, with a kind of shudder; "I am to change it publicly this day fortnight, and the idea of doing so—I do not mind telling you—preys much upon my mind; moreover, the noise of the thing has got abroad, and everybody is laughing at me, and what's more, coming and drinking my beer, and going away without paying for it, whilst I feel myself like one bewitched, wishing but not daring to take my own part. Confound the fellow in black, I wish I had never seen him! yet what can I do without him? The brewer swears that unless I pay him fifty pounds within a fortnight he'll send a distress warrant into the house, and take all I have. My poor niece is crying in the room above; and I am thinking of going into the stable and hanging myself; and perhaps it's the best thing I can do, for it's better to hang myself before selling my soul than afterwards, as I'm sure I should, like Judas Iscariot, whom my poor niece, who is somewhat religiously inclined, has been talking to me about." "I wish I could assist you," said I, "with money, but that is quite out of my power. However, I can give you a piece of advice. Don't change your religion by any means; you can't hope to prosper if you do; and if the brewer chooses to deal hardly with you, let him. Everybody would respect you ten times more provided you allowed yourself to be turned into the roads rather than change your religion, than if you got fifty pounds for renouncing it." "I am half inclined to take your advice," said the landlord, "only, to tell you the truth, I feel quite low, without any heart in me." "Come into the bar," said I, "and let us have something together

—you need not be afraid of my not paying for what I order."

We went into the bar-room, where the landlord and I discussed between us two bottles of strong ale, which he said were part of the last six which he had in his possession. At first he wished to drink sherry, but I begged him to do no such thing, telling him that sherry would do him no good under the present circumstances; nor, indeed, to the best of my belief, under any, it being of all wines the one for which I entertained the most contempt. The landlord allowed himself to be dissuaded, and, after a glass or two of ale, confessed that sherry was a sickly, disagreeable drink, and that he had merely been in the habit of taking it from an idea he had that it was genteel. Whilst quaffing our beverage, he gave me an account of the various mortifications to which he had of late been subject, dwelling with particular bitterness on the conduct of Hunter, who he said came every night and mouthed him, and afterwards went away without paying for what he had drank or smoked, in which conduct he was closely imitated by a clan of fellows who constantly attended him. After spending several hours at the public-house I departed, not forgetting to pay for the two bottles of ale. The landlord, before I went, shaking me by the hand, declared that he had now made up his mind to stick to his religion at all hazards, the more especially as he was convinced he should derive no good by giving it up.

CHAPTER XIV

Preparations for the Fair—The Last Lesson—The Verb Siriel

IT might be about five in the evening, when I reached the gypsy encampment. Here I found Mr. Petulengro, Tawno Chikno, Sylvester, and others in a great bustle, clipping and trimming certain ponies and old horses which they had brought with them. On inquiring of Jasper the reason of their being so engaged, he informed me that they were getting the horses ready for a fair, which was to be held on the morrow, at a place some miles distant, at which they should endeavour to dispose of them, adding—" Perhaps, brother, you will go with us, provided you have nothing better to do?" Not having any particular engagement, I assured him that I should have great pleasure in being of the party. It was agreed that we should start early on the following morning. Thereupon I descended into the dingle. Belle was sitting before the fire, at which the kettle was boiling. " Were you waiting for me?" I inquired. " Yes," said Belle, " I thought that you would come, and I waited for you." " That was very kind," said I. " Not half so kind," said she, " as it was of you to get everything ready for me in the dead of last night, when there was scarcely a chance of my coming." The teathings were brought forward, and we sat down. " Have you been far?" said Belle. " Merely to that publichouse," said I, " to which you directed me on the second day of our acquaintance." " Young men should not make a habit of visiting public-houses," said Belle, " they are bad places." " They may be so to some people," said I, " but I do not think the worst public-house in England could do me any harm." " Perhaps you are so bad already," said Belle, with a smile, " that it would be impossible to spoil you." " How dare you catch at my words?" said I; " come, I will make you pay for doing so—you shall have this evening the longest lesson in Armenian which I have yet inflicted upon you." " You may well say inflicted," said Belle, " but pray spare me. I do not wish to hear anything about Armenian, especially this evening." " Why this evening?" said I. Belle made no answer. " I will not spare you," said I; " this evening I intend to make you conjugate an Armenian verb." " Well, be it so," said Belle; " for this evening you shall command." " To command is hramahyel," said I. " Ram her ill, indeed," said Belle; " I do not wish to begin with that." " No," said I, " as we have come to the verbs, we will begin regularly; hramahyel is a verb of the second conjugation. We will begin with the first." " First of all tell me," said Belle, " what a verb is?" " A part of speech," said I, " which, according to the dictionary, signifies some action or passion; for example, I command you, or I hate you." " I have given you no cause to hate me," said Belle, looking me sorrowfully in the face.

"I was merely giving two examples," said I, "and neither was directed at you. In those examples, to command and hate are verbs. Belle, in Armenian there are four conjugations of verbs; the first ends in al, the second in yel, the third in oul, and the fourth in il. Now, have you understood me?"

"I am afraid, indeed, it will all end ill," said Belle. "Hold your tongue," said I, "or you will make me lose my patience." "You have already made me nearly lose mine," said Belle. "Let us have no unprofitable interruptions," said I; "the conjugations of the Armenian verbs are neither so numerous nor so difficult as the declensions of the nouns; hear that, and rejoice. Come, we will begin with the verb hntal, a verb of the first conjugation, which signifies to rejoice. Come along; hntam, I rejoice; hntas, thou rejoicest; why don't you follow, Belle?"

"I am sure I don't rejoice, whatever you may do," said Belle. "The chief difficulty, Belle," said I, "that I find in teaching you the Armenian grammar, proceeds from your applying to yourself and me every example I give. Rejoice, in this instance, is merely an example of an Armenian verb of the first conjugation, and has no more to do with your rejoicing than lal, which is also a verb of the first conjugation, and which signifies to weep, would have to do with your weeping, provided I made you conjugate it. Come along; hntam, I rejoice; hntas, thou rejoicest; hntà, he rejoices; hntamk, we rejoice : now, repeat those words."

"I can't," said Belle, "they sound more like the language of horses than human beings. Do you take me for——?" "For what?" said I. Belle was silent. "Were you going to say mare?" said I. "Mare! mare! by the bye, do you know, Belle, that mare in old English stands for woman; and that when we call a female an evil mare, the strict meaning of the term is merely a bad woman. So if I were to call you a mare without prefixing bad, you must not be offended." "But I should though," said Belle. "I was merely attempting to make you acquainted with a philological fact," said I. "If mare, which in old English, and likewise in vulgar English, signifies a woman, sounds the same as mare, which in modern and polite English signifies a female horse, I

can't help it. There is no such confusion of sounds in
Armenian, not, at least, in the same instance. Belle, in
Armenian, woman is ghin, the same word, by the by, as
our queen, whereas mare is madagh tzi, which signifies a
female horse; and perhaps you will permit me to add, that
a hard-mouthed jade is, in Armenian, madagh tzi
hsdierah.''

"I can't bear this much longer," said Belle. "Keep
yourself quiet," said I; "I wish to be gentle with you; and
to convince you, we will skip hntal, and also for the present
verbs of the first conjugation and proceed to the second.
Belle, I will now select for you to conjugate the prettiest
verb in Armenian; not only of the second, but also of all
the four conjugations; that verb is siriel. Here is the
present tense:—siriem, siries, sirè, siriemk, sirèk, sirien.
You observe that it runs on just in the same manner as
hntal, save and except that the e is substituted for a; and
it will be as well to tell you that almost the only difference
between the second, third, and fourth conjugation, and the
first, is the substituting in the present, preterite and other
tenses e or ou, or i for a; so you see that the Armenian
verbs are by no means difficult. Come on, Belle, and say
siriem." Belle hesitated. "Pray oblige me, Belle, by
saying siriem!" Belle still appeared to hesitate. "You
must admit, Belle, that it is much softer than hntam." "It
is so," said Belle; "and to oblige you I will say siriem."
"Very well indeed, Belle," said I. "No vartabied, or
doctor, could have pronounced it better; and now, to show
you how verbs act upon pronouns in Armenian, I will say
siriem zkiez. Please to repeat siriem zkiez!" "Siriem
zkiez!" said Belle; "that last word is very hard to say."
"Sorry that you think so, Belle," said I. "Now please to
say sirià zis." Belle did so. "Exceedingly well," said I.
"Now say, yerani thè sirèir zis." "Yerani thè sirèir zis,"
said Belle. "Capital!" said I; "you have now said, I love
you—love me—ah! would that you would love me!"

"And I have said all these things?" said Belle. "Yes,"
said I; "you have said them in Armenian." "I would
have said them in no language that I understood," said
Belle; "and it was very wrong of you to take advantage of
my ignorance, and make me say such things." "Why
so?" said I; "if you said them, I said them too." "You
did so," said Belle; "but I believe you were merely banter-

ing and jeering." "As I told you before, Belle," said I, "the chief difficulty which I find in teaching you Armenian proceeds from your persisting in applying to yourself and me every example I give." "Then you meant nothing after all," said Belle, raising her voice. "Let us proceed," said I; "sirietsi, I loved." "You never loved any one but yourself," said Belle; "and what's more——" "Sirietsits, I will love," said I; "sirietsies, thou wilt love." "Never one so thoroughly heartless," said Belle. "I tell you what, Belle, you are becoming intolerable, but we will change the verb; or rather I will now proceed to tell you here, that some of the Armenian conjugations have their anomalies; one species of these I wish to bring before your notice. As old Villotte says—from whose work I first contrived to pick up the rudiments of Armenian—' Est verborum transitivorum, quorum infinitivus——' but I forgot, you don't understand Latin. He says there are certain transitive verbs, whose infinitive is in outsaniel; the preterite in outsi; the imperative in oue; for example—parghatsoutsaniem, I irritate——"

"You do, you do," said Belle; "and it will be better for both of us, if you leave off doing so."

"You would hardly believe, Belle," said I, "that the Armenian is in some respects closely connected with the Irish, but so it is; for example, that word parghatsoutsaniem is evidently derived from the same root as feargaim, which, in Irish, is as much as to say I vex."

"You do, indeed," said Belle, sobbing.

"But how do you account for it?"

"O man, man!" said Belle, bursting into tears, "for what purpose do you ask a poor ignorant girl such a question, unless it be to vex and irritate her? If you wish to display your learning, do so to the wise and instructed, and not to me, who can scarcely read or write. Oh, leave off your nonsense; yet I know you will not do so, for it is the breath of your nostrils! I could have wished we should have parted in kindness, but you will not permit it. I have deserved better at your hands than such treatment. The whole time we have kept company together in this place, I have scarcely had one kind word from you, but the strangest——" and here the voice of Belle was drowned in her sobs.

"I am sorry to see you take on so, dear Belle," said I.

" I really have given you no cause to be so unhappy; surely teaching you a little Armenian was a very innocent kind of diversion."

" Yes, but you went on so long, and in such a strange way, and made me repeat such strange examples, as you call them, that I could not bear it."

" Why, to tell you the truth, Belle, it's just my way; and I have dealt with you just as I would with——"

" A hard-mouthed jade," said Belle, " and you practising your horse-witchery upon her. I have been of an unsubdued spirit, I acknowledge, but I was always kind to you; and if you have made me cry, it's a poor thing to boast of."

" Boast of !" said I; " a pretty thing indeed to boast of; I had no idea of making you cry. Come, I beg your pardon; what more can I do? Come, cheer up, Belle. You were talking of parting; don't let us part, but depart, and that together."

" Our ways lie different," said Belle.

" I don't see why they should," said I. " Come, let us be off to America together."

" To America together?" said Belle, looking full at me.

" Yes," said I; " where we will settle down in some forest, and conjugate the verb siriel conjugally."

" Conjugally?" said Belle.

" Yes," said I; " as man and wife in America, air yew ghin."

" You are jesting, as usual," said Belle.

" Not I, indeed. Come, Belle, make up your mind, and let us be off to America; and leave priests, humbug, learning, and languages behind us."

" I don't think you are jesting," said Belle; " but I can hardly entertain your offers; however, young man, I thank you."

" You had better make up your mind at once," said I, " and let us be off. I shan't make a bad husband, I assure you. Perhaps you think I am not worthy of you? To convince you, Belle, that I am, I am ready to try a fall with you this moment upon the grass. Brynhilda, the valkyrie, swore that no one should ever marry her who could not fling her down. Perhaps you have done the same. The man who eventually married her, got a friend of his, who was called Sygurd, the serpent-killer, to wrestle with her, disguising him in his own armour.

Sygurd flung her down, and won her for his friend, though he loved her himself. I shall not use a similar deceit, nor employ Jasper Petulengro to personate me—so get up, Belle, and I will do my best to fling you down."

"I require no such thing of you, or anybody," said Belle; "you are beginning to look rather wild."

"I every now and then do," said I; "come, Belle, what do you say?"

"I will say nothing at present on the subject," said Belle, "I must have time to consider."

"Just as you please," said I, "to-morrow I go to a fair with Mr. Petulengro, perhaps you will consider whilst I am away. Come, Belle, let us have some more tea. I wonder whether we shall be able to procure tea as good as this in the American forest."

CHAPTER XV

The Dawn of Day—The Last Farewell—Departure for the Fair—
The Fine Horse—Return to the Dingle—No Isopel.

IT was about the dawn of day when I was awakened by the voice of Mr. Petulengro shouting from the top of the dingle, and bidding me get up. I arose instantly, and dressed myself for the expedition to the fair. On leaving my tent, I was surprised to observe Belle, entirely dressed, standing close to her own little encampment. "Dear me," said I, "I little expected to find you up so early. I suppose Jasper's call awakened you, as it did me." "I merely lay down in my things," said Belle, "and have not slept during the night." "And why did you not take off your things and go to sleep?" said I. "I did not undress," said Belle, "because I wished to be in readiness to bid you farewell when you departed; and as for sleeping, I could not." "Well, God bless you!" said I, taking Belle by the hand. Belle made no answer, and I observed that her hand was very cold. "What is the matter with you?" said I, looking her in the face. Belle looked at me for a moment in the eyes—and then cast down her own—her features were very pale. "You are really unwell," said I, "I had better

not go to the fair, but stay here, and take care of you."
"No," said Belle, "pray go, I am not unwell." "Then
go to your tent," said I, "and do not endanger your
health by standing abroad in the raw morning air. God
bless you, Belle. I shall be home to-night, by which time
I expect you will have made up your mind; if not, another
lesson in Armenian, however late the hour be." I then
wrung Belle's hand, and ascended to the plain above.

I found the Romany party waiting for me, and everything
in readiness for departing. Mr. Petulengro and Tawno
Chikno were mounted on two old horses. The rest, who
intended to go to the fair, amongst whom were two or three
women, were on foot. On arriving at the extremity of the
plain, I looked towards the dingle. Isopel Berners stood
at the mouth, the beams of the early morning sun shone
full on her noble face and figure. I waved my hand towards
her. She slowly lifted up her right arm. I turned away,
and never saw Isopel Berners again.

My companions and myself proceeded on our way. In
about two hours we reached the place where the fair was to
be held. After breakfasting on bread and cheese and ale
behind a broken stone wall, we drove our animals to the
fair. The fair was a common cattle and horse fair: there
was little merriment going on, but there was no lack of
business. By about two o'clock in the afternoon, Mr.
Petulengro and his people had disposed of their animals at
what they conceived very fair prices—they were all in high
spirits, and Jasper proposed to adjourn to a public-house.
As we were proceeding to one, a very fine horse, led by a
jockey, made its appearance on the ground. Mr. Petulengro
stopped short, and looked at it stedfastly: "Fino covar
dove odoy sas miro—a fine thing were that if it were but
mine!" he exclaimed. "If you covet it," said I, "why
do you not purchase it?" "We low 'Gyptians never buy
animals of that description; if we did we could never sell
them, and most likely should be had up as horse-stealers."
"Then why did you say just now, ' It were a fine thing if
it were but yours?'" said I. "We 'Gyptians always say so
when we see anything that we admire. An animal like
that is not intended for a little hare like me, but for some
grand gentleman like yourself. I say, brother, do you
buy that horse!" "How should I buy the horse, you
foolish person?" said I. "Buy the horse, brother," said

Mr. Petulengro, "if you have not the money I can lend it you, though I be of lower Egypt." "You talk nonsense," said I; "however, I wish you would ask the man the price of it." Mr. Petulengro, going up to the jockey, inquired the price of the horse—the man, looking at him scornfully, made no reply. "Young man," said I, going up to the jockey, "do me the favour to tell me the price of that horse, as I suppose it is to sell." The jockey, who was a surly-looking man, of about fifty, looked at me for a moment, then, after some hesitation, said, laconically, "Seventy." "Thank you," said I, and turned away. "Buy that horse," said Mr. Petulengro, coming after me; "the dook tells me that in less than three months he will be sold for twice seventy." "I will have nothing to do with him," said I; "besides, Jasper, I don't like his tail. Did you observe what a mean scrubby tail he has?" "What a fool you are, brother," said Mr. Petulengro; "that very tail of his shows his breeding. No good bred horse ever yet carried a fine tail—'tis your scrubby-tailed horses that are your out-and-outers. Did you ever hear of Syntax, brother? That tail of his puts me in mind of Syntax. Well, I say nothing more, have your own way—all I wonder at is, that a horse like him was ever brought to such a fair of dog cattle as this."

We then made the best of our way to a public-house, where we had some refreshment. I then proposed returning to the encampment, but Mr. Petulengro declined, and remained drinking with his companions till about six o'clock in the evening, when various jockeys from the fair came in. After some conversation a jockey proposed a game of cards; and in a little time, Mr. Petulengro and another gypsy sat down to play a game of cards with two of the jockeys.

Though not much acquainted with cards, I soon conceived a suspicion that the jockeys were cheating Mr. Petulengro and his companion, I therefore called Mr. Petulengro aside, and gave him a hint to that effect. Mr. Petulengro, however, instead of thanking me, told me to mind my own bread and butter, and forthwith returned to his game. I continued watching the players for some hours. The gypsies lost considerably, and I saw clearly that the jockeys were cheating them most confoundedly. I therefore once more called Mr. Petulengro aside, and told him that the jockeys were cheating him, conjuring him to return to the encampment. Mr. Petulengro, who was by this time somewhat the worse for liquor, now fell into a passion, swore several oaths, and asking me who had made me a Moses over him and his brethren, told me to return to the encampment by myself. Incensed at the unworthy return which my well-meant words had received, I forthwith left the house, and having purchased a few articles of provision, I set out for the dingle alone. It was a dark night when I reached it, and descending I saw the glimmer of a fire from the depths of the dingle; my heart beat with fond anticipation of a welcome. "Isopel Berners is waiting for me," said I, "and the first words that I shall hear from her lips is that she has made up her mind. We shall go to America, and be so happy together." On reaching the bottom of the dingle, however, I saw seated near the fire, beside which stood the kettle simmering, not Isopel Berners, but a gypsy girl, who told me that Miss Berners when she went away had charged her to keep up the fire, and have the kettle boiling against my arrival. Startled at these words, I inquired at what hour Isopel had left, and whither she was gone, and was told that she had left the dingle, with her cart, about two hours after I departed; but where she was gone she, the girl, did not know. I then asked whether she had left no message, and the girl replied that she had left none, but had merely given directions about the kettle and fire, putting, at the same time, sixpence into her hand. "Very strange," thought I; then dismissing the gypsy girl I sat down by the fire. I had no wish for tea, but sat looking on the embers, wondering what could be the motive of the sudden departure of Isopel. "Does she mean to return?" thought I to myself. "Surely she means to return," Hope replied, "or she would not have gone away without leaving any message"—"and yet she could scarcely mean to return," muttered Foreboding, "or she assuredly would have left some message with the girl." I then thought to myself what a hard thing it would be, if, after having made up my mind to assume the yoke of matrimony, I should be disappointed of the woman of my choice. "Well, after all," thought I, "I can scarcely be disappointed; if such an ugly scoundrel as Sylvester had no difficulty in getting such a nice wife as Ursula, surely I, who am not a tenth part so ugly, cannot fail to obtain the hand of Isopel Berners, uncommonly fine damsel though she be. Husbands do not grow upon hedgerows; she is merely gone after a little business and will return to-morrow."

Comforted in some degree by these hopeful imaginings, I retired to my tent, and went to sleep.

CHAPTER XVI

Gloomy Forebodings—The Postman's Mother—The Letter—Bears and Barons—The Best of Advice.

NOTHING occurred to me of any particular moment during the following day. Isopel Berners did not return; but Mr. Petulengro and his companions came home from the fair early in the morning. When I saw him, which was about midday, I found him with his face bruised and swelled. It appeared that, some time after I had left him, he himself perceived that the jockeys with whom he was playing cards were cheating him and his companion; a quarrel ensued, which terminated in a fight between Mr. Petulengro and one of the jockeys, which lasted some time, and in which Mr. Petulengro, though he eventually came off victor, was considerably beaten. His bruises, in conjunction with his pecuniary loss, which amounted to about seven pounds, were the cause of his being much out of humour; before night, however, he had returned to his usual philosophic frame of mind, and, coming up to me as I was walking about, apologized for his behaviour on the preceding day, and assured me that he was determined, from that time forward, never to quarrel with a friend for giving him good advice.

Two more days passed, and still Isopel Berners did not return. Gloomy thoughts and forebodings filled my mind. During the day I wandered about the neighbouring roads in the hopes of catching an early glimpse of her and her returning vehicle; and at night lay awake, tossing about on my hard couch, listening to the rustle of every leaf, and occasionally thinking that I heard the sound of her wheels upon the distant road. Once at midnight, just as I was

about to fall into unconsciousness, I suddenly started up,
for I was convinced that I heard the sound of wheels. I
listened most anxiously, and the sound of wheels striking
against stones was certainly plain enough. " She comes
at last," thought I, and for a few moments I felt as if a
mountain had been removed from my breast ;—" here she
comes at last, now, how shall I receive her? Oh," thought
I, " I will receive her rather coolly, just as if I was not
particularly anxious about her—that's the way to manage
these women." The next moment the sound became very
loud, rather too loud, I thought, to proceed from her
wheels, and then by degrees became fainter. Rushing out
of my tent, I hurried up the path to the top of the dingle,
where I heard the sound distinctly enough, but it was going
from me, and evidently proceeded from something much
larger than the cart of Isopel. I could, moreover, hear the
stamping of a horse's hoof at a lumbering trot. Those only
whose hopes have been wrought up to a high pitch, and
then suddenly cast down, can imagine what I felt at that
moment; and yet when I returned to my lonely tent, and
lay down on my hard pallet, the voice of conscience told me
that the misery I was then undergoing I had fully merited,
for the unkind manner in which I had intended to receive
her, when for a brief moment I supposed that she had
returned.

It was on the morning after this affair, and the fourth,
if I forget not, from the time of Isopel's departure, that,
as I was seated on my stone at the bottom of the dingle,
getting my breakfast, I heard an unknown voice from the
path above—apparently that of a person descending—exclaim, " Here's a strange place to bring a letter to;" and
presently an old woman, with a belt round her middle, to
which was attached a leathern bag, made her appearance,
and stood before me.

" Well, if I ever !" said she, as she looked about her.
" My good gentlewoman," said I, " pray what may you
please to want?" " Gentlewoman !" said the old dame,
" please to want—well, I call that speaking civilly, at any
rate. It is true, civil words cost nothing; nevertheless, we
do not always get them. What I please to want is to deliver
a letter to a young man in this place; perhaps you be he?"
" What's the name on the letter?" said I, getting up, and
going to her. " There's no name upon it," said she, taking

a letter out of her scrip, and looking at it. "It is directed to the young man in Mumper's Dingle." "Then it is for me, I make no doubt," said I, stretching out my hand to take it. "Please to pay me ninepence first," said the old woman. "However," said she, after a moment's thought, "civility is civility, and, being rather a scarce article, should meet with some return. Here's the letter, young man, and I hope you will pay for it; for if you do not I must pay the postage myself." "You are the postwoman, I suppose," said I, as I took the letter. "I am the postman's mother," said the old woman; "but as he has a wide beat, I help him as much as I can, and I generally carry letters to places like this, to which he is afraid to come himself." "You say the postage is ninepence," said I, "here's a shilling." "Well, I call that honourable," said the old woman, taking the shilling, and putting it into her pocket—"here's your change, young man," said she, offering me threepence. "Pray keep that for yourself," said I; "you deserve it for your trouble." "Well, I call that genteel," said the old woman; "and as one good turn deserves another, since you look as if you couldn't read, I will read your letter for you. Let's see it; it's from some young woman or other, I dare say." "Thank you," said I, "but I can read." "All the better for you," said the old woman; "your being able to read will frequently save you a penny, for that's the charge I generally make for reading letters; though, as you behaved so genteelly to me, I should have charged you nothing. Well, if you can read, why don't you open the letter, instead of keeping it hanging between your finger and thumb?" "I am in no hurry to open it," said I, with a sigh. The old woman looked at me for a moment—"Well, young man," said she, "there are some—especially those who can read—who don't like to open their letters when anybody is by, more especially when they come from young women. Well, I won't intrude upon you, but leave you alone with your letter. I wish it may contain something pleasant. God bless you," and with these words she departed.

I sat down on my stone, with my letter in my hand. I knew perfectly well that it could have come from no other person than Isopel Berners; but what did the letter contain? I guessed tolerably well what its purport was—an eternal farewell! yet I was afraid to open the letter, lest my expectation should be confirmed. There I sat with the letter, putting off the evil moment as long as possible. At length I glanced at the direction, which was written in a fine bold hand, and was directed, as the old woman had said, to the young man in " Mumpers' Dingle," with the addition, near ——, in the county of —— Suddenly the idea occurred to me, that, after all, the letter might not contain an eternal farewell; and that Isopel might have written, requesting me to join her. Could it be so? " Alas! no," presently said Foreboding. At last I became ashamed of my weakness. The letter must be opened sooner or later. Why not at once? So as the bather who, for a considerable time, has stood shivering on the bank, afraid to take the decisive plunge, suddenly takes it, I tore open the letter almost before I was aware. I had no sooner done so than a paper fell out. I examined it; it contained a lock of bright flaxen hair. " This is no good sign," said I, as I thrust the lock and paper into my bosom, and proceeded to read the letter, which ran as follows :—

" TO THE YOUNG MAN IN MUMPERS' DINGLE.

" SIR,—I send these lines, with the hope and trust that they will find you well, even as I am myself at this moment, and in much better spirits, for my own are not such as I could wish they were, being sometimes rather hysterical and vapourish, and at other times, and most often, very low. I am at a sea-port, and am just going on shipboard; and when you get these I shall be on the salt waters, on my way to a distant country, and leaving my own behind me, which I do not expect ever to see again.

" And now, young man, I will, in the first place, say something about the manner in which I quitted you. It must have seemed somewhat singular to you that I went away without taking any leave, or giving you the slightest hint that I was going; but I did not do so without considerable reflection. I was afraid that I should not be able to support a leave-taking; and as you had said that you were determined to go wherever I did, I thought it best not to tell you at all; for I did not think it advisable that you should go with me, and I wished to have no dispute.

" In the second place, I wish to say something about an offer of wedlock which you made me; perhaps, young man, had you made it at the first period of our acquaintance, I should have accepted it, but you did not, and kept putting off and putting off, and behaving in a very strange manner, till I could stand your conduct no longer, but determined upon leaving you and Old England, which last step I had been long thinking about; so when you made your offer at last, everything was arranged—my cart and donkey engaged to be sold—and the greater part of my things disposed of. However, young man, when you did make it, I frankly tell you that I had half a mind to accept it; at last, however, after very much consideration, I thought it best to leave you for ever, because, for some time past, I had become almost convinced, that though with a wonderful deal of learning, and exceedingly shrewd in some things, you were—pray don't be offended—at the root mad! and though mad people, I have been told, sometimes make very good husbands, I was unwilling that your friends, if you had any, should say that Belle Berners, the workhouse girl, took advantage of your infirmity; for there is no concealing that I was born and bred up in a workhouse; notwithstanding that, my blood is better than your own, and as good as the best; you having yourself told me that my name is a noble name, and once, if I mistake not, that it was the same word as baron, which is the same thing as bear; and that to be called in old times a bear was considered a great compliment—the bear being a mighty strong animal, on which account our forefathers called all their great fighting-men barons, which is the same as bears.

" However, setting matters of blood and family entirely aside, many thanks to you, young man, from poor Belle, for the honour you did her in making that same offer; for, after all, it is an honour to receive an honourable offer, which she could see clearly yours was, with no floriness nor chaff in it; but, on the contrary, entire sincerity. She assures you that she shall always bear it and yourself in mind, whether on land or water; and as a proof of the goodwill she bears to you, she sends you a lock of the hair which she wears on her head, which you were often looking at, and were pleased to call flax, which word she supposes you meant as a compliment, even as the old people meant to pass a compliment to their great folks, when they called them bears; though she cannot help thinking that they might have found an animal as strong as a bear, and somewhat less uncouth, to call their great folks after: even as she thinks yourself, amongst your great store of words, might have found something a little more genteel to call her hair after than flax, which, though strong and useful, is rather a coarse and common kind of article.

"And as another proof of the good-will she bears to you, she sends you, along with the lock, a piece of advice, which is worth all the hair in the world, to say nothing of the flax.

"*Fear God*, and take your own part. There's Bible in that, young man: see how Moses feared God, and how he took his own part against everybody who meddled with him. And see how David feared God, and took his own part against all the bloody enemies which surrounded him —so fear God, young man, and never give in! The world can bully, and is fond, provided it sees a man in a kind of difficulty, of getting about him, calling him coarse names, and even going so far as to hustle him: but the world, like all bullies, carries a white feather in its tail, and no sooner sees the man taking off his coat, and offering to fight its best, than it scatters here and there, and is always civil to him afterwards. So when folks are disposed to ill-treat you, young man, say, 'Lord have mercy upon me!' and then tip them to Long Melford, which, as the saying goes, there is nothing comparable for shortness all the world over; and these last words, young man, are the last you will ever have from her who is nevertheless,

"Your affectionate female servant,
"ISOPEL BERNERS."

After reading the letter I sat for some time motionless, holding it in my hand. The daydream in which I had been a little time before indulging, of marrying Isopel Berners, of going with her to America, and having by her a large progeny, who were to assist me in felling trees, cultivating the soil, and who would take care of me when I was old, was now thoroughly dispelled. Isopel had deserted me, and was gone to America by herself, where, perhaps, she would marry some other person, and would bear him a progeny, who would do for him what in my dream I had hoped my progeny by her would do for me. Then the thought came into my head that though she was gone, I might follow her to America, but then I thought that if I did I might not find her; America was a very large place, and I did not know the port to which she was bound; but I could follow her to the port from which she had sailed, and there possibly discover the port to which she was bound; but I did not even know the port from which she had set out, for Isopel had not dated her letter from any place. Suddenly it occurred to me that the post-mark on the letter would tell me from whence it came, so I forthwith looked at the back of the letter, and in the post-mark read the name of a well-known and not very distant sea-port. I then knew with tolerable certainty the port where she had embarked, and I almost determined to follow her, but I almost instantly determined to do no such thing. Isopel Berners had abandoned me, and I would not follow her; "Perhaps," whispered Pride," if I overtook her, she would only despise me for running after her;" and it also told me pretty roundly, provided I ran after her, whether I overtook her or not, I should heartily despise myself. So I determined not to follow Isopel Berners; I took her lock of hair, and looked at it, then put it in her letter, which I folded up and carefully stowed away, resolved to keep both for ever, but I determined not to follow her. Two or three times, however, during the day, I wavered in my determination, and was again and again almost tempted to follow her, but every succeeding time the temptation was fainter. In the evening I left the dingle, and sat down with Mr. Petulengro and his family by the door of his tent; Mr. Petulengro soon began talking of the letter which I had received in the morning. "Is it not from Miss Berners, brother?" said he. I told him it was. "Is she coming back, brother?" "Never," said I; "she is gone to America, and has deserted me." "I always knew that you two were never destined for each other," said he. "How did you know that?" I inquired. "The dook told me so, brother; you are born to be a great traveller." "Well," said I, "if I had gone with her to America, as I was thinking of doing, I should have been a great traveller." "You are to travel in another direction, brother," said he. "I wish you would tell me all about my future wanderings," said I. "I can't, brother," said Mr. Petulengro, "there's a power of clouds before my eye." "You are a poor seer, after all," said I; and getting up, I retired to my dingle and my tent, where I betook myself to my bed, and there, knowing the worst, and being no longer agitated by apprehension, nor agonized by expectation, I was soon buried in a deep slumber, the first which I had fallen into for several nights.

CHAPTER XVII

The Public-house—Landlord on His Legs Again—A Blow in Season —The Way of the World—The Grateful Mind—The Horse's Neigh.

IT was rather late on the following morning when I awoke. At first I was almost unconscious of what had occurred on the preceding day; recollection, however, by degrees returned, and I felt a deep melancholy coming over me, but perfectly aware that no advantage could be derived from the indulgence of such a feeling, I sprang up, prepared my breakfast, which I ate with a tolerable appetite, and then left the dingle, and betook myself to the gypsy encampment, where I entered into discourse with various Romanies, both male and female. After some time, feeling myself in better spirits, I determined to pay another visit to the landlord of the public-house. From the position of his affairs when I had last visited him I entertained rather gloomy ideas with respect to his present circumstances. I imagined that I should either find him alone in his kitchen smoking a wretched pipe, or in company with some surly bailiff or his follower, whom his friend the brewer had sent into the house in order to take possession of his effects.

Nothing more entirely differing from either of these anticipations could have presented itself to my view than what I saw about one o'clock in the afternoon, when I entered the house. I had come, though somewhat in want of consolation myself, to offer any consolation which was at my command to my acquaintance Catchpole, and perhaps like many other people who go to a house with " drops of compassion trembling on their eyelids," I felt rather disappointed at finding that no compassion was necessary. The house was thronged with company, and cries for ale and porter, hot brandy and water, cold gin and water, were numerous; moreover, no desire to receive and not to pay for the landlord's liquids was manifested—on the contrary, everybody seemed disposed to play the most honourable part: "Landlord, here's the money for this glass of brandy and water—do me the favour to take it; all right, remember I have paid you." "Landlord, here's the money for the pint of half-and-half—fourpence halfpenny, ain't it?—here's sixpence; keep the change—confound the change!" The landlord, assisted by his niece, bustled about; his brow erect, his cheeks plumped out, and all his features exhibiting a kind of surly satisfaction. Wherever he moved, marks of the most cordial amity were shown him, hands were thrust out to grasp his, nor were looks of respect, admiration, nay, almost of adoration, wanting. I observed one fellow, as the landlord advanced, take the pipe out of his mouth, and gaze upon him with a kind of grin of wonder, probably much the same as his ancestor, the Saxon lout of old, put on when he saw his idol Thur, dressed in a new kirtle. To avoid the press, I got into a corner, where on a couple of chairs sat two respectable-looking individuals, whether farmers or sow-gelders, I know not, but highly respectable-looking, who were discoursing about the landlord. "Such another," said one, "you will not find in a summer's day." "No, nor in the whole of England," said the other. "Tom of Hopton," said the first: "ah! Tom of Hopton," echoed the other; "the man who could beat Tom of Hopton could beat the world." "I glory in him," said the first. "So do I," said the second, "I'll back him against the world. Let me hear any one say anything against him, and if I don't——" then, looking at me, he added, "have you anything to say against him, young man?" "Not a word," said I, "save that he regularly puts me out." "He'll put any one out," said the man, "any one out of conceit with himself;" then, lifting a mug to his mouth, he added, with a hiccough," I drink his health." Presently the landlord, as he moved about, observing me, stopped short: "Ah!" said he, "are you here? I am glad to see you, come this way. Stand back," said he to his company, as I followed him to the bar, "stand back for me and this gentleman." Two or three young fellows were in the bar, seemingly sporting yokels, drinking sherry and smoking. "Come, gentlemen," said the landlord, "clear the bar, I must have a clear bar for me and my friend here." "Landlord, what will you take," said one, "a glass of sherry? I know you like it." "—— sherry and you too," said the landlord, " I want neither sherry nor yourself; didn't you hear what I told you?" "All right, old fellow," said the other, shaking the landlord by the hand, "all right, don't wish to intrude—but I suppose when you and your friend have done, I may come in again;" then, with a " sarvant, sir," to me, he took himself into the kitchen, followed by the rest of the sporting yokels.

Thereupon the landlord, taking a bottle of ale from a basket, uncorked it, and pouring the contents into two large glasses, handed me one, and motioning me to sit down, placed himself by me; then, emptying his own glass at a draught, he gave a kind of grunt of satisfaction, and fixing his eyes upon the opposite side of the bar, remained motionless, without saying a word, buried apparently in important cogitations. With respect to myself, I swallowed my ale more leisurely, and was about to address my friend, when his niece, coming into the bar, said that more and more customers were arriving, and how she should supply their wants she did not know, unless her uncle would get up and help her.

" The customers!" said the landlord, " let the scoundrels wait till you have time to serve them, or till I have leisure to see after them." " The kitchen won't contain half of them," said his niece. " Then let them sit out abroad," said the landlord. " " But there are not benches enough, uncle," said the niece. " Then let them stand or sit on the ground," said the uncle, "what care I; I'll let them know that the man who beat Tom of Hopton stands as well again on his legs as ever." Then opening a side door which led from the bar into the back yard, he beckoned me to follow him. " You treat your customers in rather a cavalier manner," said I, when we were alone together in the yard.

"Don't I?" said the landlord; "and I'll treat them more so yet; now I have got the whiphand of the rascals I intend to keep it. I dare say you are a bit surprised with regard to the change which has come over things since you were last here. I'll tell you how it happened. You remember in what a desperate condition you found me, thinking of changing my religion, selling my soul to the man in black, and then going and hanging myself like Pontius Pilate; and I dare say you can't have forgotten how you gave me good advice, made me drink ale, and give up sherry. Well, after you were gone, I felt all the better for your talk, and what you had made me drink, and it was a mercy that I did feel better; for my niece was gone out, poor thing, and I was left alone in the house, without a soul to look at, or to keep me from doing myself a mischief in case I was so inclined. Well, things wore on in this way till it grew dusk, when in came that blackguard Hunter with his train to drink at my expense, and to insult me as usual; there were more than a dozen of them, and a pretty set they looked. Well, they ordered about in a very free and easy manner for upwards of an hour and a half, occasionally sneering and jeering at me, as they had been in the habit of doing for some time past; so, as I said before, things wore on, and other customers came in, who, though they did not belong to Hunter's gang, also passed off their jokes upon me; for, as you perhaps know, we English are a set of low hounds, who will always take part with the many by way of making ourselves safe, and currying favour with the stronger side. I said little or nothing, for my spirits had again become very low, and I was verily scared and afraid. All of a sudden I thought of the ale which I had drank in the morning, and of the good it did me then, so I went into the bar, opened another bottle, took a glass, and felt better; so I took another, and feeling better still, I went back into the kitchen, just as Hunter and his crew were about leaving. 'Mr. Hunter,' said I, 'you and your people will please to pay me for what you have had?' 'What do you mean by my people?' said he, with an oath. 'Ah, what do you mean by calling us his people?' said the clan. 'We are nobody's people;' and then there was a pretty load of abuse, and threatening to serve me out. 'Well,' said I, 'I was perhaps wrong to call them your people, and beg your pardon and theirs. And now you will please to pay me for what you have had yourself, and afterwards I can settle with them.' 'I shall pay you when I think fit,' said Hunter. 'Yes,' said the rest, 'and so shall we. We shall pay you when we think fit.' 'I tell you what,' said Hunter, 'I conceives I do such an old fool as you an honour when I comes into his house and drinks his beer, and goes away without paying for it;' and then there was a roar of laughter from everybody, and almost all said the same thing. 'Now do you please to pay me, Mr. Hunter?'

said I. ' Pay you !' said Hunter; ' pay you ! Yes, here's the pay;' and thereupon he held out his thumb, twirling it round till it just touched my nose. I can't tell you what I felt that moment; a kind of madhouse thrill came upon me, and all I know is, that I bent back as far as I could, then lunging out, struck him under the ear, sending him reeling two or three yards, when he fell on the floor. I wish you had but seen how my company looked at me and at each other. One or two of the clan went to raise Hunter, and get him to fight, but it was no go; though he was not killed, he had had enough for that evening. Oh, I wish you had seen my customers; those who did not belong to the clan, but who had taken part with them, and helped to jeer and flout me, now came and shook me by the hand, wishing me joy, and saying as how ' I was a brave fellow, and had served the bully right !' As for the clan, they all said Hunter was bound to do me justice; so they made him pay me what he owed for himself, and the reckoning of those among them who said they had no money. Two or three of them then led him away, while the rest stayed behind, and flattered me, and worshipped me, and called Hunter all kinds of dogs' names. What do you think of that?"

"Why," said I, " it makes good what I read in a letter which I received yesterday. It is just the way of the world."

"A'n't it," said the landlord. " Well, that a'n't all; let me go on. Good fortune never yet came alone. In about an hour comes home my poor niece, almost in high sterricks with joy, smiling and sobbing. She had been to the clergyman of M———, the great preacher, to whose church she was in the habit of going, and to whose daughters she was well known; and to him she told a lamentable tale about my distresses, and about the snares which had been laid for my soul; and so well did she plead my cause, and so strong did the young ladies back all she said, that the good clergyman promised to stand my friend, and to lend me sufficient money to satisfy the brewer, and to get my soul out of the snares of the man in black; and sure enough the next morning the two young ladies brought me the fifty pounds, which I forthwith carried to the brewer, who was monstrously civil, saying that he hoped any little misunderstanding we had

had would not prevent our being good friends in future. That a'n't all; the people of the neighbouring county hearing as if by art witchcraft that I had licked Hunter, and was on good terms with the brewer, forthwith began to come in crowds to look at me, pay me homage, and be my customers. Moreover, fifty scoundrels who owed me money, and would have seen me starve rather than help me as long as they considered me a down pin, remembered their debts, and came and paid me more than they owed. That a'n't all; the brewer being about to establish a stage-coach and three, to run across the country, says it shall stop and change horses at my house, and the passengers breakfast and sup as it goes and returns. He wishes me—whom he calls the best man in England— to give his son lessons in boxing, which he says he considers a fine manly English art, and a great defence against Popery—notwithstanding that only a month ago, when he considered me a down pin, he was in the habit of railing against it as a blackguard practice, and against me as a blackguard for following it; so I am going to commence with young hopeful to-morrow."

"I really cannot help congratulating you on your good fortune," said I.

"That a'n't all," said the landlord. "This very morning the folks of our parish made me churchwarden, which they would no more have done a month ago, when they considered me a down pin, than they——"

"Mercy upon us!" said I, "if fortune pours in upon you in this manner, who knows but that within a year they may make you a justice of the peace?"

"Who knows, indeed!" said the landlord. "Well, I will prove myself worthy of my good luck by showing the grateful mind—not to those who would be kind to me now, but to those who were, when the days were rather gloomy. My customers shall have abundance of rough language, but I'll knock any one down who says anything against the clergyman who lent me the fifty pounds, or against the Church of England, of which he is parson and I am churchwarden. I am also ready to do anything in reason for him who paid me for the ale he drank, when I shouldn't have had the heart to collar him for the money had he refused to pay; who never jeered or flouted me like the rest of my customers when I was a down pin—

and though he refused to fight cross *for* me was never cross
with me, but listened to all I had to say, and gave me all
kinds of good advice. Now who do you think I mean by
this last? why, who but yourself—who on earth but yourself? The parson is a good man and a great preacher,
and I'll knock anybody down who says to the contrary;
and I mention him first, because why; he's a gentleman,
and you a tinker. But I am by no means sure you are
not the best friend of the two; for I doubt, do you see,
whether I should have had the fifty pounds but for you.
You persuaded me to give up that silly drink they call
sherry, and drink ale; and what was it but drinking ale
which gave me courage to knock down that fellow Hunter
—and knocking him down was, I verily believe, the turning point of my disorder. God don't love them who won't
strike out for themselves; and as far as I can calculate
with respect to time, it was just the moment after I had
knocked down Hunter, that the parson consented to lend
me the money, and everything began to grow civil to me.
So, dash my buttons if I show the ungrateful mind to you!
I don't offer to knock anybody down for you, because why
—I dare say you can knock a body down yourself; but
I'll offer something more to the purpose; as my business
is wonderfully on the increase, I shall want somebody to
help me in serving my customers, and keeping them in
order. If you choose to come and serve for your board,
and what they'll give you, give me your fist; or if you
like ten shillings a week better than their sixpences and
ha'pence, only say so—though, to be open with you, I
believe you would make twice ten shillings out of them—
the sneaking, fawning, curry-favouring humbugs!"

"I am much obliged to you," said I, "for your handsome offer, which, however, I am obliged to decline."

"Why so?" said the landlord.

"I am not fit for service," said I; "moreover, I am
about to leave this part of the country." As I spoke a
horse neighed in the stable. "What horse is that?"
said I.

"It belongs to a cousin of mine, who put it into my
hands yesterday in the hopes that I might get rid of it
for him, though he would no more have done so a week
ago, when he considered me a down pin, than he would
have given the horse away. Are you fond of horses?"

"Very much," said I.

"Then come and look at it." He led me into the stable, where, in a stall, stood a noble-looking animal.

"Dear me," said I, "I saw this horse at —— fair."

"Like enough," said the landlord; "he was there and was offered for seventy pounds, but didn't find a bidder at any price. What do you think of him?"

"He's a splendid creature."

"I am no judge of horses," said the landlord; "but I am told he's a firstrate trotter, good leaper, and has some of the blood of Syntax. What does all that signify? —the game is against his master, who is a down pin, is thinking of emigrating, and wants money confoundedly. He asked seventy pounds at the fair; but, between ourselves, he would be glad to take fifty here."

"I almost wish," said I, "that I were a rich squire."

"You would buy him then," said the landlord. Here he mused for some time, with a very profound look. "It would be a rum thing," said he, "if, some time or other, that horse should come into your hands. Didn't you hear how he neighed when you talked about leaving the country? My granny was a wise woman, and was up to all kinds of signs and wonders, sounds and noises, the interpretation of the language of birds and animals, crowing and lowing, neighing and braying. If she had been here, she would have said at once that that horse was fated to carry you away. On that point, however, I can say nothing, for under fifty pounds no one can have him. Are you taking that money out of your pocket to pay me for the ale? That won't do; nothing to pay; I invited you this time. Now if you are going, you had best get into the road through the yard-gate. I won't trouble you to make your way through the kitchen and my fine-weather company—confound them!"

CHAPTER XVIII

Mr. Petulengro's Device—The Leathern Purse—Consent to Purchase a Horse.

As I returned along the road I met Mr. Petulengro and one of his companions, who told me that they were bound for the public-house; whereupon I informed Jasper how I had seen in the stable the horse which we had admired at the fair. "I shouldn't wonder if you buy that horse after all, brother," said Mr. Petulengro. With a smile at the absurdity of such a supposition, I left him and his companion, and betook myself to the dingle. In the evening I received a visit from Mr. Petulengro, who forthwith commenced talking about the horse, which he had again seen, the landlord having shown it to him on learning that he was a friend of mine. He told me that the horse pleased him more than ever, he having examined his points with more accuracy than he had an opportunity of doing on the first occasion, concluding by pressing me to buy him. I begged him to desist from such foolish importunity, assuring him that I had never so much money in all my life as would enable me to purchase the horse. Whilst this discourse was going on, Mr. Petulengro and myself were standing together in the midst of the dingle. Suddenly he began to move round me in a very singular manner, making strange motions with his hands, and frightful contortions with his features, till I became alarmed, and asked him whether he had not lost his senses? Whereupon, ceasing his movements and contortions, he assured me that he had not, but had merely been seized with a slight dizziness, and then once more returned to the subject of the horse. Feeling myself very angry, I told him that if he continued persecuting me in that manner, I should be obliged to quarrel with him; adding, that I believed his only motive for asking me to buy the animal was to insult my poverty. "Pretty poverty," said he, "with fifty pounds in your pocket; however, I have heard say that it is always the custom of your rich people to talk of their poverty, more especially when they wish to avoid laying out money." Surprised at his saying that I had fifty pounds in my pocket, I asked him what he meant; whereupon he told me that he was very sure that I had fifty pounds in my pocket, offering to lay me five shillings to that effect. "Done!" said I; "I have scarcely more than the fifth part of what you say." "I know better, brother," said Mr. Petulengro; "if you only pull out what you have in the pocket of your slop, I am sure you will have lost your wager." Putting my hand into the pocket, I felt something which

I had never felt there before, and pulling it out, perceived that it was a clumsy leathern purse, which I found on opening contained four ten-pound-notes, and several pieces of gold. "Didn't I tell you so, brother?" said Mr. Petulengro. "Now, in the first place, please to pay me the five shillings you have lost." "This is only a foolish piece of pleasantry," said I; "you put it into my pocket whilst you were moving about me, making faces like a distracted person. Here, take your purse back." "I?" said Mr. Petulengro, "not I, indeed! don't think I am such a fool. I have won my wager, so pay me the five shillings, brother." "Do drop this folly," said I, "and take your purse;" and I flung it on the ground. "Brother," said Mr. Petulengro, "you were talking of quarrelling with me just now. I tell you now one thing, which is, that if you do not take back the purse I will quarrel with you; and it shall be for good and all. I'll drop your acquaintance, no longer call you my pal, and not even say sarshan to you when I meet you by the roadside. Hir mi diblis I never will." I saw by Jasper's look and tone that he was in earnest, and, as I had really a regard for the strange being, I scarcely knew what to do. "Now, be persuaded, brother," said Mr. Petulengro, taking up the purse, and handing it to me; "be persuaded; put the purse into your pocket, and buy the horse." "Well," said I, "if I did so, would you acknowledge the horse to be yours, and receive the money again as soon as I should be able to repay you?"

"I would, brother, I would," said he; "return me the money as soon as you please, provided you buy the horse." "What motive have you for wishing me to buy that horse?" said I. "He's to be sold for fifty pounds," said Jasper, "and is worth four times that sum; though, like many a splendid bargain, he is now going a begging; buy him, and I'm confident that, in a little time, a grand gentleman of your appearance may have anything he asks for him, and found a fortune by his means. Moreover, brother, I want to dispose of this fifty pounds in a safe manner. If you don't take it, I shall fool it away in no time, perhaps at card-playing, for you saw how I was cheated by those blackguard jockeys the other day—we gyptians don't know how to take care of money: our best plan when we have got a handful of guineas is to make buttons with them; but I have plenty of golden buttons, and don't wish to be troubled with more, so you can do me no greater favour than vesting the money in this speculation, by which my mind will be relieved of considerable care and trouble for some time at least."

Perceiving that I still hesitated, he said, "Perhaps, brother, you think I did not come honestly by the money: by the honestest manner in the world, for it is the money I earnt by fighting in the ring: I did not steal it, brother, nor did I get it by disposing of spavined donkeys, or glandered ponies—nor is it, brother, the profits of my wife's witchcraft and dukkerin."

"But," said I, "you had better employ it in your traffic." "I have plenty of money for my traffic, independent of this capital," said Mr. Petulengro; "ay, brother, and enough besides to back the husband of my wife's sister, Sylvester, against Slammocks of the Chong gav for twenty pounds, which I am thinking of doing."

"But," said I, "after all, the horse may have found another purchaser by this time." "Not he," said Mr. Petulengro, "there is nobody in this neighbourhood to purchase a horse like that, unless it be your lordship—so take the money, brother," and he thrust the purse into my hand. Allowing myself to be persuaded, I kept possession of the purse. "Are you satisfied now?" said I. "By no means, brother," said Mr. Petulengro, "you will please to pay me the five shillings which you lost to me." "Why," said I, "the fifty pounds which I found in my pocket were not mine, but put in by yourself." "That's nothing to do with the matter, brother," said Mr. Petulengro, "I betted you five shillings that you had fifty pounds in your pocket, which sum you had: I did not say that they were your own, but merely that you had fifty pounds; you will therefore pay me, brother, or I shall not consider you an honourable man." Not wishing to have any dispute about such a matter, I took five shillings out of my under pocket, and gave them to him. Mr. Petulengro took the money with great glee, observing— "These five shillings I will take to the public-house forthwith, and spend in drinking with four of my brethren, and doing so will give me an opportunity of telling the landlord that I have found a customer for his horse, and that you are the man. It will be as well to secure the horse as soon as possible; for though the dook tells me that the horse is intended for you, I have now and then found that the dook is, like myself, somewhat given to lying."

He then departed, and I remained alone in the dingle. I thought at first that I had committed a great piece of folly in consenting to purchase this horse; I might find no desirable purchaser for him, until the money in my possession should be totally exhausted, and then I might be compelled to sell him for half the price I had given for him, or be even glad to find a person who would receive him at a gift; I should then remain sans horse, and in-debted to Mr. Petulengro. Nevertheless, it was possible that I might sell the horse very advantageously, and by so doing obtain a fund sufficient to enable me to execute some grand enterprise or other. My present way of life afforded no prospect of support, whereas the purchase of the horse did afford a possibility of bettering my condition, so, after all, had I not done right in consenting to purchase the horse? the purchase was to be made with another person's property, it is true, and I did not exactly like the idea of speculating with another person's property, but Mr. Petul-engro had thrust his money upon me, and if I lost his money, he could have no one but himself to blame; so I persuaded myself that I had, upon the whole, done right, and having come to that persuasion, I soon began to enjoy the idea of finding myself on horseback again, and figured to myself all kinds of strange adventures which I should meet with on the roads before the horse and I should part company.

CHAPTER XIX

Trying the Horse—The Feats of Tawno—Man with the Red Waist-coat—Disposal of Property.

I saw nothing more of Mr. Petulengro that evening—on the morrow, however, he came and informed me that he had secured the horse for me, and that I was to go and pay for it at noon. At the hour appointed, therefore, I went with Mr. Petulengro and Tawno to the public, where, as

before, there was a crowd of company. The landlord
received us in the bar with marks of much satisfaction and
esteem, made us sit down, and treated us with some excellent mild draught ale. "Who do you think has been
here this morning?" he said to me, "why, that fellow in
black, who came to carry me off to a house of Popish
devotion, where I was to pass seven days and nights in
meditation, as I think he called it, before I publicly renounced the religion of my country. I read him a pretty
lecture, calling him several unhandsome names, and asking
him what he meant by attempting to seduce a churchwarden of the Church of England. I tell you what, he
ran some danger; for some of my customers, learning his
errand, laid hold on him, and were about to toss him in
a blanket, and then duck him in the horse-pond. I, however, interfered, and said, 'that what he came about was
between me and him, and that it was no business of theirs.'
To tell you the truth, I felt pity for the poor devil, more
especially when I considered that they merely sided against
him because they thought him the weakest, and that they
would have wanted to serve me in the same manner had
they considered me a down pin; so I rescued him from their
hands, told him not to be afraid, for that nobody should
touch him, and offered to treat him to some cold gin and
water with a lump of sugar in it; and on his refusing,
told him that he had better make himself scarce, which he
did, and I hope I shall never see him again. So I suppose
you are come for the horse; mercy upon us! who would
have thought you would have become the purchaser? The
horse, however, seemed to know it by his neighing. How
did you ever come by the money? however, that's no matter
of mine. I suppose you are strongly backed by certain
friends you have."

I informed the landlord that he was right in supposing
that I came for the horse, but that, before I paid for him,
I should wish to prove his capabilities. "With all my
heart," said the landlord. "You shall mount him this
moment." Then going into the stable, he saddled and
bridled the horse, and presently brought him out before
the door. I mounted him, Mr. Petulengro putting a heavy
whip into my hand, and saying a few words to me in his
own mysterious language. "The horse wants no whip,"
said the landlord. "Hold your tongue, daddy," said Mr.

Petulengro. "My pal knows quite well what to do with
the whip, he's not going to beat the horse with it." About
four hundred yards from the house there was a hill, to the
foot of which the road ran almost on a perfect level; towards the foot of this hill I trotted the horse, who set off
at a long, swift pace, seemingly at the rate of about sixteen
miles an hour. On reaching the foot of the hill, I wheeled
the animal round, and trotted him towards the house—the
horse sped faster than before. Ere he had advanced a
hundred yards, I took off my hat, in obedience to the advice
which Mr. Petulengro had given me, in his own language,
and holding it over the horse's head commenced drumming
on the crown with the knob of the whip; the horse gave
a slight start, but instantly recovering himself, continued
his trot till he arrived at the door of the public-house,
amidst the acclamations of the company, who had all
rushed out of the house to be spectators of what was going
on. "I see now what you wanted the whip for," said
the landlord, "and sure enough, that drumming on your
hat was no bad way of learning whether the horse was
quiet or not. Well, did you ever see a more quiet horse,
or a better trotter?" "My cob shall trot against him,"
said a fellow, dressed in velveteen, mounted on a low
powerful-looking animal. "My cob shall trot against him
to the hill and back again—come on!" We both started;
the cob kept up gallantly against the horse for about half
way to the hill, when he began to lose ground; at the foot
of the hill he was about fifteen yards behind. Whereupon
I turned slowly and waited for him. We then set off
towards the house, but now the cob had no chance, being
at least twenty yards behind when I reached the door.
This running of the horse, the wild uncouth forms around
me, and the ale and beer which were being guzzled from
pots and flagons, put me wonderfully in mind of the ancient
horse-races of the heathen north. I almost imagined myself Gunnar of Hlitharend at the race of——

"Are you satisfied?" said the landlord. "Didn't you
tell me that he could leap?" I demanded. "I am told
he can," said the landlord; "but I can't consent that he
should be tried in that way, as he might be damaged."
"That's right!" said Mr. Petulengro, "don't trust my
pal to leap that horse, he'll merely fling him down, and
break his neck and his own. There's a better man than

he close by; let him get on his back and leap him." "You mean yourself, I suppose," said the landlord. "Well, I call that talking modestly, and nothing becomes a young man more than modesty." "It a'n't I, daddy," said Mr. Petulengro. "Here's the man," said he, pointing to Tawno. "Here's the horse-leaper of the world!" "You mean the horse-back breaker," said the landlord. "That big fellow would break down my cousin's horse." "Why, he weighs only sixteen stone," said Mr. Petulengro. "And his sixteen stone, with his way of handling a horse, does not press so much as any other one's thirteen. Only let him get on the horse's back, and you'll see what he can do!" "No," said the landlord, "it won't do." Whereupon Mr. Petulengro became very much excited; and pulling out a handful of money, said, "I'll tell you what, I'll forfeit these guineas, if my black pal there does the horse any kind of damage; duck me in the horse-pond if I don't." "Well," said the landlord, "for the sport of the thing I consent, so let your white pal get down, and your black pal mount as soon as he pleases." I felt rather mortified at Mr. Petulengro's interference; and showed no disposition to quit my seat; whereupon he came up to me and said, "Now, brother, do get out of the saddle—you are no bad hand at trotting, I am willing to acknowledge that; but at leaping a horse there is no one like Tawno. Let every dog be praised for his own gift. You have been showing off in your line for the last half-hour; now do give Tawno a chance of exhibiting a little; poor fellow, he hasn't often a chance of exhibiting, as his wife keeps him so much out of sight." Not wishing to appear desirous of engrossing the public attention, and feeling rather desirous to see how Tawno, of whose exploits in leaping horses I had frequently heard, would acquit himself in the affair, I at length dismounted, and Tawno, at a bound, leaped into the saddle, where he really looked like Gunnar of Hlitharend, save and except the complexion of Gunnar was florid, whereas that of Tawno was of nearly Mulatto darkness; and that all Tawno's features were cast in the Grecian model, whereas Gunnar had a snub nose. "There's a leaping-bar behind the house," said the landlord. "Leaping-bar!" said Mr. Petulengro, scornfully. "Do you think my black pal ever rides at a leaping-bar? No more than a windle-straw. Leap over that meadow-wall,

Tawno." Just past the house, in the direction in which I had been trotting, was a wall about four feet high, beyond which was a small meadow. Tawno rode the horse gently up to the wall, permitted him to look over, then backed him for about ten yards, and pressing his calves against the horse's sides, he loosed the rein, and the horse launching forward, took the leap in gallant style. "Well done, man and horse!" said Mr. Petulengro, "now come back, Tawno." The leap from the side of the meadow was, however, somewhat higher; and the horse, when pushed at it, at first turned away; whereupon Tawno backed him to a greater distance, pushed the horse to a full gallop, giving a wild cry; whereupon the horse again took the wall, slightly grazing one of his legs against it. "A near thing," said the landlord; "but a good leap. Now, no more leaping, so long as I have control over the animal." The horse was then led back to the stable; and the landlord, myself and companions going into the bar, I paid down the money for the horse.

Scarcely was the bargain concluded, when two or three of the company began to envy me the possession of the horse, and forcing their way into the bar, with much noise and clamour, said that the horse had been sold too cheap. One fellow, in particular, with a red waistcoat, the son of a wealthy farmer, said that if he had but known that the horse had been so good a one, he would have bought it at the first price asked for it, which he was now willing to pay, that is to-morrow, supposing—"supposing your father will let you have the money," said the landlord, "which, after all, might not be the case; but, however that may be, it is too late now. I think myself the horse has been sold for too little money, but if so all the better for the young man, who came forward when no other body did with his money in his hand. There, take yourselves out of my bar," he said to the fellows; "and a pretty scoundrel you," said he to the man of the red waistcoat, "to say the horse has been sold too cheap; why, it was only yesterday you said he was good for nothing, and were passing all kinds of jokes at him. Take yourself out of my bar, I say, you and all of you," and he turned the fellows out. I then asked the landlord whether he would permit the horse to remain in the stable for a short time, provided I paid for his entertainment; and on his willingly consenting, I treated my friends with ale, and then returned with them to the encampment.

That evening I informed Mr. Petulengro and his party that on the morrow I intended to mount my horse, and leave that part of the country in quest of adventures; inquiring of Jasper where, in the event of my selling the horse advantageously, I might meet with him, and repay the money I had borrowed of him; whereupon Mr. Petulengro informed me that in about ten weeks I might find him at a certain place at the Chong gav. I then stated that as I could not well carry with me the property which I possessed in the dingle, which after all was of no considerable value, I had resolved to bestow the said property, namely, the pony, tent, tinker-tools, etc., on Ursula and her husband, partly because they were poor, and partly on account of the great kindness which I bore to Ursula, from whom I had, on various occasions, experienced all manner of civility, particularly in regard to crabbed words. On hearing this intelligence, Ursula returned many thanks to her gentle brother, as she called me, and Sylvester was so overjoyed that, casting aside his usual phlegm, he said I was the best friend he had ever had in the world, and in testimony of his gratitude swore that he would permit his wife to give me a choomer in the presence of the whole company, which offer, however, met with a very mortifying reception, the company frowning disapprobation, Ursula protesting against anything of the kind, and I myself showing no forwardness to avail myself of it, having inherited from nature a considerable fund of modesty, to which was added no slight store acquired in the course of my Irish education. I passed that night alone in the dingle in a very melancholy manner, with little or no sleep, thinking of Isopel Berners; and in the morning when I quitted it I shed several tears, as I reflected that I should probably never again see the spot where I had passed so many hours in her company.

CHAPTER XX

Farewell to the Romans—The Landlord and His Niece—Set Out as a Traveller.

On reaching the plain above, I found my Romany friends breakfasting, and on being asked by Mr. Petulengro to join them, I accepted the invitation. No sooner was breakfast over than I informed Ursula and her husband that they would find the property, which I had promised them, in the dingle, commending the little pony Ambrol to their best care. I took leave of the whole company, which was itself about to break up camp and to depart in the direction of London, and made the best of my way to the public-house. I had a small bundle in my hand, and was dressed in the same manner as when I departed from London, having left my waggoner's slop with the other effects in the dingle. On arriving at the public-house, I informed the landlord that I was come for my horse, inquiring, at the same time, whether he could not accommodate me with a bridle and saddle. He told me that the bridle and saddle, with which I had ridden the horse on the preceding day, were at my service for a trifle; that he had received them some time since in payment for a debt, and that he had himself no use for them. The leathers of the bridle were rather shabby, and the bit rusty, and the saddle was old fashioned; but I was happy to purchase them for seven shillings, more especially as the landlord added a small valise, which he said could be strapped to the saddle, and which I should find very convenient for carrying my things in. I then proceeded to the stable, told the horse we were bound on an expedition, and giving him a feed of corn, left him to discuss it, and returned to the bar-room to have a little farewell chat with the landlord, and at the same time to drink with him a farewell glass of ale. Whilst we were talking and drinking, the niece came and joined us: she was a decent, sensible young woman, who appeared to take a great interest in her uncle, whom she regarded with a singular mixture of pride and disapprobation—pride for the renown which he had acquired by his feats of old, and disapprobation for his late imprudences. She said that she hoped that his misfortunes would be a warning to him to turn more to his God than he had hitherto done, and to give up cock-fighting and other low-life practices. To which the landlord replied, that with respect to cock-fighting he intended to give it up entirely, being determined no longer to risk his capital upon birds, and with respect to his religious duties, he should attend the church of which he was churchwarden at least once a quarter, adding, however, that he did not intend to become either canter or driveller, neither of which characters would befit a publican surrounded by such customers as he was, and that to the last day of his life he hoped to be able to make use of his fists. After a stay of about two hours I settled accounts, and having bridled and saddled my horse, and strapped on my valise, I mounted, shook hands with the landlord and his niece, and departed, notwithstanding that they both entreated me to tarry until the evening, it being then the heat of the day.

CHAPTER XXI

An Adventure on the Roads—The Six Flint Stones—A Rural Scene—
Mead—The Old Man and His Bees.

I BENT my course in the direction of the north, more induced by chance than any particular motive; all quarters of the world having about equal attractions for me. I was in high spirits at finding myself once more on horseback, and trotted gaily on, until the heat of the weather induced me to slacken my pace, more out of pity for my horse than because I felt any particular inconvenience from it—heat and cold being then, and still, matters of great indifference to me. What I thought of I scarcely know, save and except that I have a glimmering recollection that I felt some desire to meet with one of those adventures which upon the roads of England are generally as plentiful as blackberries in autumn; and Fortune, who has generally been ready to gratify my inclinations, provided it cost her very little by so doing, was not slow in furnishing me with an adventure, perhaps as characteristic of the English roads as anything which could have happened.

I might have travelled about six miles amongst cross roads and lanes, when suddenly I found myself upon a broad and very dusty road which seemed to lead due north. As I wended along this I saw a man upon a donkey riding towards me. The man was commonly dressed, with a broad felt hat on his head, and a kind of satchel on his back; he seemed to be in a mighty hurry, and was every now and then belabouring the donkey with a cudgel. The donkey, however, which was a fine large creature of the silver-grey species, did not appear to sympathize at all with its rider in his desire to get on, but kept its head turned back as much as possible, moving from one side of the road to the other, and not making much forward way. As I passed, being naturally of a very polite disposition, I gave the man the sele of the day, asking him, at the same time, why he beat the donkey; whereupon the fellow eyeing me askance, told me to mind my own business, with the addition of something which I need not repeat. I had not proceeded a furlong before I saw seated on the dust by the wayside, close by a heap of stones, and with several flints before him, a respectable-looking old man, with a straw hat and a white smock, who was weeping bitterly.

"What are you crying for, father?" said I. "Have you come to any hurt?" "Hurt enough," sobbed the old man, "I have just been tricked out of the best ass in England by a villain, who gave me nothing but these trash in return," pointing to the stones before him. "I really scarcely understand you," said I, "I wish you would explain yourself more clearly." "I was riding on my ass from market," said the old man, "when I met here a fellow with a sack on his back, who, after staring at the ass and me a moment or two, asked me if I would sell her. I told him that I could not think of selling her, as she was very useful to me, and though an animal, my true companion, whom I loved as much as if she were my wife and daughter. I then attempted to pass on, but the fellow stood before me, begging me to sell her, saying that he would give me anything for her; well, seeing that he persisted, I said at last that if I sold her, I must have six pounds for her, and I said so to get rid of him, for I saw that he was a shabby fellow, who had probably not six shillings in the world; but I had better have held my tongue," said the old man, crying more bitterly than before, "for the words were scarcely out of my mouth, when he said he would give me what I asked, and taking the sack from his back, he pulled out a steelyard, and going to the heap of stones there, he took up several of them and weighed them, then flinging them down before me, he said, ' There are six pounds, neighbour; now, get off the ass, and hand her over to me.' Well, I sat like one dumbfoundered for a time, till at last I asked him what he meant? ' What do I mean?' said he, ' you old rascal, why, I mean to claim my purchase,' and then he swore so awfully, that scarcely knowing what I did I got down, and he jumped on the animal and rode off as fast as he could." "I suppose he was the fellow," said I, " whom I just now met upon a fine gray ass, which he was beating with a cudgel." " I dare say he was," said the old man, " I saw him beating her as he rode away, and I thought I should have died." " I never heard such a story," said I; " well, do you mean to submit to such a piece of roguery quietly?" " Oh, dear," said the old man, " what can I do? I am seventy-nine years of age; I am bad on my feet, and dar'n't go after him." " Shall I go?" said I; " the fellow is a thief, and any one has a right to stop him." " Oh, if you could but bring her again to me," said the old man, " I would bless you till my dying day; but have a care; I don't know but after all the law may say that she is his lawful purchase. I asked six pounds for her, and he gave me six pounds." " Six flints, you mean," said I, " no, no, the law is not quite so bad as that either; I know something about her, and am sure that she will never sanction such a quibble. At all events, I'll ride after the fellow." Thereupon turning my horse round, I put him to his very best trot; I rode nearly a mile without obtaining a glimpse of the fellow, and was becoming apprehensive that he had escaped me by turning down some by-path, two or three of which I had passed. Suddenly, however, on the road making a slight turning, I perceived him right before me, moving at a tolerably swift pace, having by this time probably overcome the resistance of the animal. Putting my horse to a full gallop, I shouted at the top of my voice, " Get off that donkey, you rascal, and give her up to me, or I'll ride you down." The fellow hearing the thunder of the horse's hoofs behind him, drew up on one side of the road. "What do you want?" said he, as I stopped my charger, now almost covered with sweat and foam close beside him. "Do you want to rob me?" "To rob you?" said I. "No! but to take from you that ass, of which you have just robbed its owner." "I have robbed no man," said the fellow; "I just now purchased it fairly of its master, and the law will give it to me; he asked six pounds for it, and I gave him six pounds." "Six stones, you mean, you rascal," said I; "get down, or my horse shall be upon you in a moment;" then with a motion of my reins, I caused the horse to rear, pressing his sides with my heels as if I intended to make him leap. "Stop," said the man, "I'll get down, and then try if I can't serve you out." He then got down, and confronted me with his cudgel; he was a horrible-looking fellow, and seemed prepared for anything. Scarcely, however, had he dismounted, when the donkey jerked the bridle out of his hand, and probably in revenge for the usage she had received, gave him a pair of tremendous kicks on the hip with her hinder legs, which overturned him, and then scampered down the road the way she had come. "Pretty treatment this," said the fellow, getting up without his cudgel, and holding his hand to his side, "I wish I may not be lamed for life." "And if you be," said I, "it will merely serve you right, you rascal, for trying to cheat a poor old man out of his property by quibbling at words." "Rascal!" said the fellow, "you lie, I am no rascal; and as for quibbling with words— suppose I did! What then? All the first people does it! The newspapers does it! the gentlefolks that calls themselves the guides of the popular mind does it! I'm no ignoramus. I read the newspapers, and knows what's what." "You read them to some purpose," said I. "Well, if you are lamed for life, and unfitted for any active line—turn newspaper editor; I should say you are perfectly qualified, and this day's adventure may be the foundation of your fortune," thereupon I turned round and rode off. The fellow followed me with a torrent of abuse. "Confound you," said he—yet that was not the expression either—"I know you; you are one of the horse-patrol come down into the country on leave to see your relations. Confound you, you and the like of you have knocked my business on the head near Lunnon, and I suppose we shall have you shortly in the country." "To the newspaper office," said I, "and fabricate false-hoods out of flint stones;" then touching the horse with my heels, I trotted off, and coming to the place where I had seen the old man, I found him there, risen from the ground, and embracing his ass.

I told him that I was travelling down the road, and said, that if his way lay in the same direction as mine he could do no better than accompany me for some distance, lest the fellow who, for aught I knew, might be hovering nigh, might catch him alone, and again get his ass from him. After thanking me for my offer, which he said he would accept, he got upon his ass, and we proceeded together down the road. My new acquaintance said very little of his own accord; and when I asked him a question, answered rather incoherently. I heard him every now and then say, "Villain!" to himself, after which he would pat the donkey's neck, from which circumstance I concluded that his mind was occupied with his late adventure. After travelling about two miles, we reached a place where a drift-way on the right led from the great road; here my companion stopped, and on my asking him whether he was going any farther, he told me that the path to the right was the way to his home.

I was bidding him farewell, when he hemmed once or twice, and said, that as he did not live far off, he hoped that I would go with him and taste some of his mead. As I had never tasted mead, of which I had frequently read in the compositions of the Welsh bards, and, moreover, felt rather thirsty from the heat of the day, I told him that I should have great pleasure in attending him. Whereupon, turning off together, we proceeded about half a mile, sometimes between stone walls, and at other times hedges, till we reached a small hamlet, through which we passed, and presently came to a very pretty cottage, delightfully situated within a garden, surrounded by a hedge of wood-bines. Opening a gate at one corner of the garden he led the way to a large shed, which stood partly behind the cottage, which he said was his stable; thereupon he dismounted and led his donkey into the shed, which was without stalls, but had a long rack and manger. On one side he tied his donkey, after taking off her caparisons, and I followed his example, tying my horse at the other side with a rope halter which he gave me; he then asked me to come in and taste his mead, but I told him that I must attend to the comfort of my horse first, and forthwith, taking a wisp of straw, rubbed him carefully down. Then taking a pailful of clear water which stood in the shed, I allowed the horse to drink about half a pint; and then turning to the old man, who all the time had stood by looking at my proceedings, I asked him whether he had any oats? "I have all kinds of grain," he replied; and, going out, he presently returned with two measures, one a large and the other a small one, both filled with oats, mixed with a few beans, and handing the large one to me for the horse, he emptied the other before the donkey, who, before she began to despatch it, turned her nose to her master's face, and fairly kissed him. Having given my horse his portion, I told the old man that I was ready to taste his mead as soon as he pleased, whereupon he ushered me into his cottage, where, making me sit down by a deal table in a neatly sanded kitchen, he produced from an old-fashioned closet a bottle, holding about a quart, and a couple of cups, which might each contain about half a pint, then opening the bottle and filling the cups with a brown-coloured liquor, he handed one to me, and taking a seat opposite to me, he lifted the other, nodded, and saying to me—" Health and welcome," placed it to his lips and drank.

" Health and thanks," I replied; and being very thirsty, emptied my cup at a draught; I had scarcely done so, however, when I half repented. The mead was deliciously sweet and mellow, but appeared strong as brandy; my eyes reeled in my head, and my brain became slightly dizzy. " Mead is a strong drink," said the old man, as he looked at me, with a half smile on his countenance. " This is at any rate," said I, " so strong, indeed, that I would not drink another cup for any consideration." " And I would not ask you," said the old man; " for, if you did, you would most probably be stupid all day, and wake the next morning with a headache. Mead is a good drink, but woundily strong, especially to those who be not used to it, as I suppose you are not." " Where do you get it?" said I. " I make it myself," said the old man, "from the honey which my bees make." "Have you many bees?" I inquired. "A great many," said the old man. "And do you keep them," said I, "for the sake of making mead with their honey?" "I keep them," he replied, "partly because I am fond of them, and partly for what they bring me in; they make me a great deal of honey, some of which I sell, and with a little I make some mead to warm my poor heart with, or occasionally to treat a friend with like yourself." "And do you support yourself entirely by means of your bees?" "No," said the old man; "I have a little bit of ground behind my house, which is my principal means of support." "And do you live alone?" "Yes," said he; "with the exception of the bees and the donkey, I live quite alone." "And have you always lived alone?" The old man emptied his cup, and his heart being warmed with the mead, he told me his history, which was simplicity itself. His father was a small yeoman, who, at his death, had left him, his only child, the cottage, with a small piece of ground behind it, and on this little property he had lived ever since. About the age of twenty-five he had married an industrious young woman, by whom he had one daughter, who died before reaching years of womanhood. His wife, however, had survived her daughter many years, and had been a great comfort to him, assisting him in his rural occupations; but, about four years before the present period, he had lost her, since which time he had lived alone, making himself as comfortable as he could; cultivating his ground, with the help of a lad from the neighbouring village, attending to his bees, and occasionally riding his donkey to market, and hearing the word of God, which he said he was sorry he could not read, twice a week regularly at the parish church. Such was the old man's tale.

When he had finished speaking, he led me behind his house, and showed me his little domain. It consisted of about two acres in admirable cultivation; a small portion of it formed a kitchen garden, while the rest was sown with four kinds of grain, wheat, barley, peas, and beans. The air was full of ambrosial sweets, resembling those proceeding from an orange grove; a place which though I had never seen at that time, I since have. In the garden was the habitation of the bees, a long box, supported upon three oaken stumps. It was full of small round glass windows, and appeared to be divided into a great many compartments, much resembling drawers placed sideways. He told me that, as one compartment was filled, the bees left it for another; so that, whenever he wanted honey, he could procure some without injury to the insects. Through the little round windows I could see several of the bees at work; hundreds were going in and out of the doors; hundreds were buzzing about on the flowers, the woodbines, and beans. As I looked around on the well-cultivated field, the garden, and the bees, I thought I had never before seen so rural and peaceful a scene.

When we returned to the cottage we again sat down, and I asked the old man whether he was not afraid to live alone. He told me that he was not, for that, upon the whole, his neighbours were very kind to him. I mentioned the fellow who had swindled him of his donkey upon the road. "That was no neighbour of mine," said the old man, "and, perhaps, I shall never see him again, or his like." "It's a dreadful thing," said I, "to have no other resource, when injured, than to shed tears on the road." "It is so," said the old man; "but God saw the tears of the old, and sent a helper." "Why did you not help yourself?" said I. "Instead of getting off your ass, why did you not punch at the fellow, or at any rate use dreadful language, call him villain, and shout robbery?" "Punch!" said the old man, "shout! what, with these hands, and this voice—Lord, how you run on! I am old, young chap, I am old!" "Well," said I, "it is a shameful thing to cry even when old." "You think so now," said the old man, "because you are young and strong; perhaps when you are as old as I, you will not be ashamed to cry."

Upon the whole I was rather pleased with the old man, and much with all about him. As evening drew nigh, I told him that I must proceed on my journey; whereupon he invited me to tarry with him during the night, telling me that he had a nice room and bed above at my service. I, however, declined; and bidding him farewell, mounted my horse, and departed. Regaining the road, I proceeded once more in the direction of the north; and, after a few hours, coming to a comfortable public-house, I stopped, and put up for the night.

CHAPTER XXII

The Singular Noise—Sleeping in a Meadow—The Book—Cure for
Wakefulness—Literary Tea Party—Poor Byron.

I DID not awake till rather late the next morning; and when
I did, I felt considerable drowsiness, with a slight headache, which I was uncharitable enough to attribute to the
mead which I had drunk on the preceding day. After
feeding my horse, and breakfasting, I proceeded on my
wanderings. Nothing occurred worthy of relating till
mid-day was considerably past, when I came to a pleasant
valley, between two gentle hills. I had dismounted, in
order to ease my horse, and was leading him along by the
bridle, when, on my right, behind a bank in which some
umbrageous ashes were growing, I heard a singular noise.
I stopped short and listened, and presently said to myself,
"Surely this is snoring, perhaps that of a hedgehog." On
further consideration, however, I was convinced that the
noise which I heard, and which certainly seemed to be
snoring, could not possibly proceed from the nostrils of so
small an animal, but must rather come from those of a
giant, so loud and sonorous was it. About two or three
yards farther was a gate, partly open, to which I went,
and peeping into the field, saw a man lying on some rich
grass, under the shade of one of the ashes; he was snoring
away at a great rate. Impelled by curiosity, I fastened
the bridle of my horse to the gate, and went up to the
man. He was a genteelly-dressed individual; rather cor-
pulent, with dark features, and seemingly about forty-five.
He lay on his back, his hat slightly over his brow, and at
his right hand lay an open book. So strenuously did he
snore that the wind from his nostrils agitated, perceptibly,
a fine cambric frill which he wore at his bosom. I gazed
upon him for some time, expecting that he might awake;
but he did not, but kept on snoring, his breast heaving
convulsively. At last, the noise he made became so terrible, that I felt alarmed for his safety, imagining that a
fit might seize him, and he lose his life while fast asleep.
I therefore exclaimed, "Sir, sir, awake! you sleep over-
much." But my voice failed to rouse him, and he continued snoring as before; whereupon I touched him slightly
with my riding wand, but failing to wake him, I touched

him again more vigorously; whereupon he opened his eyes, and, probably imagining himself in a dream, closed them again. But I was determined to arouse him, and cried as loud as I could, " Sir, sir, pray sleep no more !" He heard what I said, opened his eyes again, stared at me with a look of some consciousness, and, half raising himself upon his elbows, asked me what was the matter. " I beg your pardon," said I, " but I took the liberty of awaking you, because you appeared to be much disturbed in your sleep—I was fearful, too, that you might catch a fever from sleeping under a tree." " I run no risk," said the man, " I often come and sleep here; and as for being disturbed in my sleep, I felt very comfortable; I wish you had not awoke me." " Well," said I, " I beg your pardon once more. I assure you that what I did was with the best intention." " Oh ! pray make no further apology," said the individual, " I make no doubt that what you did was done kindly; but there's an old proverb, to the effect, ' that you should let sleeping dogs lie,' " he added with a smile. Then, getting up, and stretching himself with a yawn, he took up his book and said, " I have slept quite long enough, and it's quite time for me to be going home." " Excuse my curiosity," said I, " if I inquire what may induce you to come and sleep in this meadow?" " To tell you the truth," answered he, " I am a bad sleeper." " Pray pardon me," said I, " if I tell you that I never saw one sleep more heartily." " If I did so," said the individual, " I am beholden to this meadow and this book; but I am talking riddles, and will explain myself. I am the owner of a very pretty property, of which this valley forms part. Some years ago, however, up started a person who said the property was his; a lawsuit ensued, and I was on the brink of losing my all, when, most unexpectedly, the suit was determined in my favour. Owing, however, to the anxiety to which my mind had been subjected for several years, my nerves had become terribly shaken; and no sooner was the trial terminated than sleep forsook my pillow. I sometimes passed nights without closing an eye; I took opiates, but they rather increased than alleviated my malady. About three weeks ago a friend of mine put this book into my hand, and advised me to take it every day to some pleasant part of my estate, and try and read a page or two, assuring me, if I did, that

I should infallibly fall asleep. I took his advice, and selecting this place, which I considered the pleasantest part of my property, I came, and lying down, commenced reading the book, and before finishing a page was in a dead slumber. Every day since then I have repeated the experiment, and every time with equal success. I am a single man, without any children; and yesterday I made my will, in which, in the event of my friend's surviving me, I have left him all my fortune, in gratitude for his having procured for me the most invaluable of all blessings—sleep."

"Dear me," said I, "how very extraordinary! Do you think that your going to sleep is caused by the meadow or the book?" "I suppose by both," said my new acquaintance, "acting in co-operation." "It may be so," said I; "the magic influence does certainly not proceed from the meadow alone; for since I have been here, I have not felt the slightest inclination to sleep. Does the book consist of prose or poetry?" "It consists of poetry," said the individual. "Not Byron's?" said I. "Byron's!" repeated the individual, with a smile of contempt; "no, no; there is nothing narcotic in Byron's poetry. I don't like it. I used to read it, but it thrilled, agitated, and kept me awake. No; this is not Byron's poetry, but the inimitable ——'s "—mentioning a name which I had never heard till then. "Will you permit me to look at it?" said I. "With pleasure," he answered, politely handing me the book. I took the volume, and glanced over the contents. It was written in blank verse, and appeared to abound in descriptions of scenery; there was much mention of mountains, valleys, streams, and waterfalls, harebells and daffodils. These descriptions were interspersed with dialogues, which, though they proceeded from the mouths of pedlars and rustics, were of the most edifying description; mostly on subjects moral or metaphysical, and couched in the most gentlemanly and unexceptionable language, without the slightest mixture of vulgarity, coarseness, or pie-bald grammar. Such appeared to me to be the contents of the book; but before I could form a very clear idea of them, I found myself nodding, and a surprising desire to sleep coming over me. Rousing myself, however, by a strong effort, I closed the book, and, returning it to the owner, inquired of him, "Whether he had any motive in coming and lying down in the meadow, besides the wish of enjoying sleep?" "None whatever," he replied; "indeed, I should be very glad not to be compelled to do so, always provided I could enjoy the blessing of sleep; for by lying down under trees, I may possibly catch the rheumatism, or be stung by serpents; and, moreover, in the rainy season and winter the thing will be impossible, unless I erect a tent, which will possibly destroy the charm." "Well," said I, "you need give yourself no further trouble about coming here, as I am fully convinced that with this book in your hand, you may go to sleep anywhere, as your friend was doubtless aware, though he wished to interest your imagination for a time by persuading you to lie abroad; therefore, in future, whenever you feel disposed to sleep, try to read the book, and you will be sound asleep in a minute; the narcotic influence lies in the book, and not in the field." "I will follow your advice," said the individual; "and this very night take it with me to bed; though I hope in time to be able to sleep without it, my nerves being already much quieted from the slumbers I have enjoyed in this field." He then moved towards the gate, where we parted; he going one way, and I and my horse the other.

More than twenty years subsequent to this period, after much wandering about the world, returning to my native country, I was invited to a literary tea-party, where, the discourse turning upon poetry, I, in order to show that I was not more ignorant than my neighbours, began to talk about Byron, for whose writings I really entertained considerable admiration, though I had no particular esteem for the man himself. At first, I received no answer to what I said—the company merely surveying me with a kind of sleepy stare. At length a lady, about the age of forty, with a large wart on her face, observed, in a drawling tone, "That she had not read Byron—at least, since her girlhood—and then only a few passages; but that the impression on her mind was, that his writings were of a highly objectionable character." "I also read a little of him in my boyhood," said a gentleman about sixty, but who evidently, from his dress and demeanour, wished to appear about thirty, "but I highly disapproved of him; for, notwithstanding he was a nobleman, he is frequently very coarse, and very fond of raising emotion. Now emotion is what I dislike;" drawling out the last syllable of the word dislike. "There is only one poet for me—the divine ——" and then he mentioned a name which I had only once heard, and afterwards quite forgotten; the same mentioned by the snorer in the field. "Ah! there is no one like him!" murmured some more of the company; "the poet of nature—of nature without its vulgarity." I wished very much to ask these people whether they were ever bad sleepers, and whether they had read the poet, so called, from a desire of being set to sleep. Within a few days, however, I learnt that it had of late become very fashionable and genteel to appear half asleep, and that one could exhibit no better mark of superfine breeding than by occasionally in company setting one's rhomal organ in action. I then ceased to wonder at the popularity, which I found nearly universal, of ——'s poetry; for, certainly in order to make one's self appear sleepy in company, or occasionally to induce sleep, nothing could be more efficacious than a slight prelection of his poems. So poor Byron, with his fire and emotion—to say nothing of his mouthings and coxcombry—was dethroned, as I prophesied he would be more than twenty years before, on the day of his funeral, though I had little idea that his humiliation would have been brought about by one, whose sole strength consists in setting people to sleep. Well, all things are doomed to terminate in sleep. Before that termination, however, I will venture to prophesy that people will become a little more awake—snoring and yawning be a little less in fashion—and poor Byron be once more reinstated on his throne, though his rival will always stand a good chance of being worshipped by those whose ruined nerves are insensible to the narcotic powers of opium and morphine.

CHAPTER XXIII

Drivers and Front Outside Passengers—Fatigue of Body and Mind—
Unexpected Greeting—My Inn—The Governor—Engagement.

I CONTINUED my journey, passing through one or two villages. The day was exceedingly hot, and the roads dusty. In order to cause my horse as little fatigue as possible, and not to chafe his back, I led him by the bridle, my doing which brought upon me a shower of remarks, jests, and would-be witticisms from the drivers and front outside passengers of sundry stage-coaches which passed me in one direction or the other. In this way I proceeded till considerably past noon, when I felt myself very fatigued, and my horse appeared no less so; and it is probable that the lazy and listless manner in which we were moving on, tired us both much more effectually than hurrying along at a swift trot would have done, for I have observed that when the energies of the body are not exerted a languor frequently comes over it. At length arriving at a very large building with an archway, near the entrance of a town, I sat down on what appeared to be a stepping-block, and presently experienced a great depression of spirits. I began to ask myself whither I was going, and what I should do with myself and the horse which I held by the bridle? It appeared to me that I was alone in the world with the poor animal, who looked for support to me, who knew not how to support myself. Then the image of Isopel Berners came into my mind, and when I thought how I had lost her for ever, and how happy I might have been with her in the New World had she not deserted me, I became yet more miserable.

As I sat in this state of mind, I suddenly felt some one clap me on the shoulder, and heard a voice say, "Ha! comrade of the dingle, what chance has brought you into these parts?" I turned round, and beheld a man in the dress of a postillion, whom I instantly recognized as he to whom I had rendered assistance on the night of the storm.

"Ah!" said I, "is it you? I am glad to see you, for I was feeling very lonely and melancholy."

"Lonely and melancholy," he replied, "how is that? how can any one be lonely and melancholy with such a noble horse as that you hold by the bridle?"

"The horse," said I, "is one cause of my melancholy, for I know not in the world what to do with it."

"It is your own?"

"Yes," said I, "I may call it my own, though I borrowed the money to purchase it."

"Well, why don't you sell it?"

" It is not always easy to find a purchaser for a horse like this," said I; " can you recommend me one?"

" I? Why no, not exactly; but you'll find a purchaser shortly—pooh! if you have no other cause for disquiet than that horse, cheer up, man, don't be cast down. Have you nothing else on your mind? By the bye, what's become of the young woman you were keeping company with in that queer lodging place of yours?"

" She has left me," said I.

" You quarrelled, I suppose?"

" No," said I, " we did not exactly quarrel, but we are parted."

" Well," replied he, " but you will soon come together again."

" No," said I, " we are parted for ever."

" For ever! Pooh! you little know how people some-times come together again who think they are parted for ever. Here's something on that point relating to myself. You remember, when I told you my story in that dingle of yours, that I mentioned a young woman, my fellow-servant when I lived with the English family in Mumbo Jumbo's town, and how she and I, when our foolish governors were thinking of changing their religion, agreed to stand by each other, and be true to old Church of England, and to give our governors warning, provided they tried to make us renegades. Well, she and I parted soon after that, and never thought to meet again, yet we met the other day in the fields, for she lately came to live with a great family not far from here, and we have since agreed to marry, to take a little farm, for we have both a trifle of money, and live together till ' death us do part.' So much for parting for ever! But what do I mean by keep-ing you broiling in the sun with your horse's bridle in your hand, and you on my own ground? Do you know where you are? Why, that great house is my inn, that is, it's my master's, the best fellow in ——. Come along, you and your horse both will find a welcome at my inn."

Thereupon he led the way into a large court in which there were coaches, chaises, and a great many people; taking my horse from me, he led it into a nice cool stall, and fastened it to the rack—he then conducted me into a postillion's keeping-room, which at that time chanced to be empty, and he then fetched a pot of beer and sat down by me.

After a little conversation he asked me what I intended to do, and I told him frankly that I did not know; whereupon he observed that, provided I had no objection, he had little doubt that I could be accommodated for some time at his inn. "Our upper ostler," said he, "died about a week ago; he was a clever fellow, and, besides his trade, understood reading and accounts."

"Dear me," said I, interrupting him, "I am not fitted for the place of ostler—moreover, I refused the place of ostler at a public-house, which was offered to me only a few days ago." The postillion burst into a laugh. "Ostler at a public-house, indeed! why, you would not compare a berth at a place like that with the situation of ostler at my inn, the first road-house in England! However, I was not thinking of the place of ostler for you; you are, as you say, not fitted for it, at any rate, not at a house like this. We have, moreover, the best under-ostler in all England—old Bill, with the drawback that he is rather fond of drink. We could make shift with him very well, provided we could fall in with a man of writing and figures, who could give an account of the hay and corn which comes in and goes out, and wouldn't object to give a look occasionally at the yard. Now it appears to me that you are just such a kind of man, and, if you will allow me to speak to the governor, I don't doubt that he will gladly take you, as he feels kindly disposed towards you from what he has heard me say concerning you."

"And what should I do with my horse?" said I.

"The horse need give you no uneasiness," said the postillion; "I know he will be welcome here both for bed and manger, and, perhaps, in a little time you may find a purchaser, as a vast number of sporting people frequent this house." I offered two or three more objections, which the postillion overcame with great force of argument, and the pot being nearly empty, he drained it to the bottom drop, and then starting up, left me alone.

In about twenty minutes he returned, accompanied by a highly intelligent-looking individual, dressed in blue and black, with a particularly white cravat, and without a hat on his head: this individual, whom I should have mistaken for a gentleman but for the intelligence depicted in his face, he introduced to me as the master of the inn. The master of the inn shook me warmly by the hand, told me that he was happy to see me in his house, and thanked me in the handsomest terms for the kindness I had shown to his servant in the affair of the thunderstorm. Then saying that he was informed I was out of employ, he assured me that he should be most happy to engage me to keep his hay and corn account, and as general superintendent of the yard, and that with respect to the horse, which he was told I had, he begged to inform me that I was perfectly at liberty to keep it at the inn upon the very best, until I could find a purchaser,—that with regard to wages —but he had no sooner mentioned wages than I cut him short, saying, that provided I stayed I should be most happy to serve him for bed and board, and requested that he would allow me until the next morning to consider of his offer; he willingly consented to my request, and, begging that I would call for anything I pleased, left me alone with the postillion.

I passed that night until about ten o'clock with the postillion, when he left me, having to drive a family about ten miles across the country; before his departure, however, I told him that I had determined to accept the offer of his governor, as he called him. At the bottom of my heart I was most happy that an offer had been made, which secured to myself and the animal a comfortable retreat at a moment when I knew not whither in the world to take myself and him.

CHAPTER XXIV

An Inn of Times gone by—A First-rate Publican—Hay and Corn—
Old-fashioned Ostler—Highwaymen—Mounted Police—Grooming.

THE inn, of which I had become an inhabitant, was a place of infinite life and bustle. Travellers of all descriptions, from all the cardinal points, were continually stopping at it; and to attend to their wants, and minister to their convenience, an army of servants, of one description or other, was kept; waiters, chambermaids, grooms, postillions, shoe-blacks, cooks, scullions, and what not, for there was a barber and hair-dresser, who had been at Paris, and talked French with a cockney accent; the French sounding all the better, as no accent is so melodious as the cockney. Jacks creaked in the kitchens turning round spits, on which large joints of meat piped and smoked before great big fires. There was running up and down stairs, and along galleries, slamming of doors, cries of "Coming, sir," and "Please to step this way, ma'am," during eighteen hours of the four-and-twenty. Truly a very great place for life and bustle was this inn. And often in after life, when lonely and melancholy, I have called up the time I spent there, and never failed to become cheerful from the recollection.

I found the master of the house a very kind and civil person. Before being an inn-keeper he had been in some other line of business; but on the death of the former proprietor of the inn had married his widow, who was still alive, but, being somewhat infirm, lived in a retired part of the house. I have said that he was kind and civil; he was, however, not one of those people who suffer themselves to be made fools of by anybody; he knew his customers, and had a calm, clear eye, which would look through a man without seeming to do so. The accommodation of his house was of the very best description; his wines were good, his viands equally so, and his charges not immoderate; though he very properly took care of himself. He was no vulgar inn-keper, had a host of friends, and deserved them all. During the time I lived with him, he was presented by a large assemblage of his friends and customers with a dinner at his own house, which was very costly, and at which the best of wines were sported, and after the dinner with a piece of plate estimated at fifty guineas. He received the plate, made a neat speech of thanks, and when the bill was called for, made another neat speech, in which he refused to receive one farthing for the entertainment, ordering in at the same time two dozen more of the best champagne, and sitting down amidst uproarious applause, and cries of "You shall be no loser by it!" Nothing very wonderful in such conduct, some people will say; I don't say there is, nor have I any intention to endeavour to persuade the reader that the landlord was a Carlo Boromeo; he merely gave a quid pro quo; but it is not every person who will give you a quid pro quo. Had he been a vulgar publican, he would have sent in a swinging bill after receiving the plate; "but then no vulgar publican would have been presented with plate;" perhaps not, but many a vulgar public character has been presented with plate, whose admirers never received a quid pro quo, except in the shape of a swinging bill.

I found my duties of distributing hay and corn, and keeping an account thereof, anything but disagreeable, particularly after I had acquired the good-will of the old ostler, who at first looked upon me with rather an evil eye, considering me somewhat in the light of one who had usurped an office which belonged to himself by the right of succession; but there was little gall in the old fellow, and, by speaking kindly to him, never giving myself any airs of assumption; but, above all, by frequently reading the newspapers to him—for though passionately fond of news and politics, he was unable to read—I soon succeeded in placing myself on excellent terms with him. A regular character was that old ostler; he was a Yorkshireman by birth, but had seen a great deal of life in the vicinity of London, to which, on the death of his parents, who were very poor people, he went at a very early age. Amongst other places where he had served as ostler was a small inn at Hounslow, much frequented by highwaymen, whose exploits he was fond of narrating, especially those of Jerry Abershaw, who, he said, was a capital rider; and on hearing his accounts of that worthy, I half regretted that the old fellow had not been in London, and I had not formed his acquaintance about the time I was thinking of writing the life of the said Abershaw, not doubting that with his assistance, I could have produced a book at least as remarkable as the life and adventures of that entirely imaginary personage Joseph Sell; perhaps, however, I was mistaken; and whenever Abershaw's life shall appear before the public—and my publisher credibly informs me that it has not yet appeared—I beg and entreat the public to state which it likes best, the life of Abershaw, or that of Sell, for which latter work I am informed that during the last few months there has been a prodigious demand. My old friend, however, after talking of Abershaw, would frequently add, that, good rider as Abershaw certainly was, he was decidedly inferior to Richard Ferguson, generally called Galloping Dick, who was a pal of Abershaw's, and had enjoyed a career as long, and nearly as remarkable as his own. I learned from him that both were capital customers at the Hounslow inn, and that he had frequently drank with them in the corn-room. He said that no man could desire more jolly or entertaining companions over a glass of " summut;" but that upon the road it was anything but desirable to meet them; there they were terrible, cursing and swearing, and thrusting the muzzles of their pistols into people's mouths; and at this part of his locution the old man winked, and said, in a somewhat lower voice, that upon the whole they were right in doing so, and that when a person had once made up his mind to become a highwayman, his best policy was to go the whole hog, fearing nothing, but making everybody afraid of him; that people never thought of resisting a savage-faced, foul-mouthed highwayman, and if he were taken, were afraid to bear witness against him, lest he should get off and cut their throats some time or other upon the roads; whereas people would resist being robbed by a sneaking, pale-visaged rascal, and would swear bodily against him on the first opportunity,—adding, that Abershaw and Ferguson, two most awful fellows, had enjoyed a long career, whereas two disbanded officers of the army, who wished to rob a coach like gentlemen, had begged the passengers' pardon, and talked of hard necessity, had been set upon by the passengers themselves, amongst whom were three women, pulled from their horses, conducted to Maidstone, and hanged with as little pity as such contemptible fellows deserved. " There is nothing like going the whole hog," he repeated, " and if ever I had been a highwayman, I would have done so; I should have thought myself all the more safe; and, moreover, shouldn't have despised myself. To curry favour with those you are robbing, sometimes at the expense of your own comrades, as I have known fellows do, why, it is the greatest——"

" So it is," interposed my friend the postillion, who chanced to be present at a considerable part of the old ostler's discourse; " it is, as you say, the greatest of humbug, and merely, after all, gets a fellow into trouble; but no regular bred highwayman would do it. I say, George, catch the Pope of Rome trying to curry favour with anybody he robs; catch old Mumbo Jumbo currying favour with the Archbishop of Canterbury and the Dean and Chapter, should he meet them in a stage-coach; it would be with him, Bricconi Abbasso, as he knocked their teeth out with the butt of his trombone; and the old regular-built ruffian would be all the safer for it, as Bill would say, as ten to one the Archbishop and Chapter, after such a spice of his quality, would be afraid to swear against him, and to hang him, even if he were in their power, though that would be the proper way; for, if it is the greatest of all humbug for a highwayman to curry favour with those he robs, the next greatest is to try to curry favour with a highwayman when you have got him, by letting him off."

Finding the old man so well acquainted with the history of highwaymen, and taking considerable interest in the subject, having myself edited a book containing the lives of many remarkable people who had figured on the highway, I forthwith asked him how it was that the trade of highwaymen had become extinct in England, as at present we never heard of any one following it. Whereupon he told me that many causes had contributed to bring about that result; the principal of which were the following:—the refusal to license houses which were known to afford shelter to highwaymen, which, amongst many others, had caused the inn at Hounslow to be closed; the inclosure of many a wild heath in the country, on which they were in the habit of lurking, and particularly the establishing in the neighbourhood of London of a well-armed mounted patrol, who rode the highwaymen down, and delivered them up to justice, which hanged them without ceremony.

"And that would be the way to deal with Mumbo Jumbo and his gang," said the postillion, "should they show their visages in these realms; and I hear by the newspapers that they are becoming every day more desperate. Take away the license from their public-houses, cut down the rookeries and shadowy old avenues in which they are fond of lying in wait, in order to sally out upon people as they pass in the roads; but, above all, establish a good mounted police to ride after the ruffians and drag them by the scruff of the neck to the next clink, where they might lie till they could be properly dealt with by law; instead of which, the Government are repealing the wise old laws enacted against such characters, giving fresh licenses every day to their public-houses, and saying that it would be a pity to cut down their rookeries and thickets because they look so very picturesque; and, in fact, giving them all kind of encouragement; why, if such behaviour is not enough to drive an honest man mad, I know not what is. It is of no use talking, I only wish the power were in my hands, and if I did not make short work of them, might I be a mere jackass postillion all the remainder of my life."

Besides acquiring from the ancient ostler a great deal of curious information respecting the ways and habits of the heroes of the road, with whom he had come in contact in the early portion of his life, I picked up from him many excellent hints relating to the art of grooming horses. Whilst at the inn, I frequently groomed the stage and post-horses, and those driven up by travellers in their gigs: I was not compelled, nor indeed expected, to do so; but I took pleasure in the occupation; and I remember at that period one of the principal objects of my ambition was to be a first-rate groom, and to make the skins of the creatures I took in hand look sleek and glossy like those of moles. I have said that I derived valuable hints from the old man, and, indeed, became a very tolerable groom, but there was a certain finishing touch which I could never learn from him, though he possessed it himself, and which I could never attain to by my own endeavours; though my want of success certainly did not proceed from want of application, for I have rubbed the horses down, purring and buzzing all the time, after the genuine ostler fashion, until the perspiration fell in heavy drops upon my shoes, and when I had done my best and asked the old fellow what he thought of my work, I could never extract from him more than a kind of grunt, which might be translated, "Not so very bad, but I have seen a horse groomed much better," which leads me to suppose that a person, in order to be a first-rate groom, must have something in him when he is born which I had not, and, indeed, which many other people have not who pretend to be grooms. What does the reader think?

CHAPTER XXV

Stable Hartshorn—How to Manage a Horse on a Journey—Your Best Friend.

OF one thing I am certain, that the reader must be much delighted with the wholesome smell of the stable, with which many of these pages are redolent; what a contrast to the sickly odours exhaled from those of some of my contemporaries, especially of those who pretend to be of the highly fashionable class, and who treat of reception-rooms, well may they be styled so, in which dukes, duchesses, earls, countesses, archbishops, bishops, mayors, mayoresses—not forgetting the writers themselves, both male and female—congregate and press upon one another; how cheering, how refreshing, after having been nearly knocked down with such an atmosphere, to come in contact with genuine stable hartshorn. Oh! the reader shall have yet more of the stable, and of that old ostler, for which he or she will doubtless exclaim, " Much obliged !"—and, lest I should forget to perform my promise, the reader shall have it now.

I shall never forget an harangue from the mouth of the old man, which I listened to one warm evening as he and I sat on the threshold of the stable, after having attended to some of the wants of a batch of coach-horses. It related to the manner in which a gentleman should take care of his horse and self, whilst engaged in a journey on horseback, and was addressed to myself, on the supposition of my one day coming to an estate, and of course becoming a gentleman.

" When you are a gentleman," said he, " should you ever wish to take a journey on a horse of your own, and you could not have a much better than the one you have here eating its fill in the box yonder—I wonder, by the bye, how you ever came by it—you can't do better than follow the advice I am about to give you, both with respect to your animal and yourself. Before you start, merely give your horse a couple of handfuls of corn and a little water, somewhat under a quart, and if you drink a pint of water yourself out of the pail, you will feel all the better during the whole day; then you may walk and trot your animal for about ten miles, till you come to some nice inn, where you may get down and see your horse led into a nice stall, telling the ostler not to feed him till you come. If the ostler happens to be a dog-fancier, and has an English terrier-dog like that of mine there, say what a nice dog it is, and praise its black and tawn; and if he does not happen to be a dog-fancier, ask him how he's getting on, and whether he ever knew worse times; that kind of thing will please the ostler, and he will

let you do just what you please with your own horse, and
when your back is turned, he'll say to his comrades what a
nice gentleman you are, and how he thinks he has seen you
before; then go and sit down to breakfast, and, before you
have finished breakfast, get up and go and give your horse
a feed of corn; chat with the ostler two or three minutes till
your horse has taken the shine out of his corn, which will
prevent the ostler taking any of it away when your back
is turned, for such things are sometimes done—not that
I ever did such a thing myself when I was at the inn at
Hounslow. Oh, dear me, no! Then go and finish your
breakfast, and when you have finished your breakfast and
called for the newspaper, go and water your horse, letting
him have one pailful, then give him another feed of corn,
and enter into discourse with the ostler about bull-baiting,
the prime minister, and the like; and when your horse has
once more taken the shine out of his corn, go back to your
room and your newspaper—and I hope for your sake it may
be the *Globe,* for that's the best paper going—then pull the
bell-rope and order in your bill, which you will pay without
counting it up—supposing you to be a gentleman. Give
the waiter sixpence, and order out your horse, and when
your horse is out, pay for the corn, and give the ostler a
shilling, then mount your horse and walk him gently for five
miles; and whilst you are walking him in this manner, it
may be as well to tell you to take care that you do not let
him down and smash his knees, more especially if the road
be a particularly good one, for it is not at a desperate hiver-
man pace, and over very bad roads, that a horse tumbles
and smashes his knees, but on your particularly nice road,
when the horse is going gently and lazily, and is half
asleep, like the gemman on his back; well, at the end of the
five miles, when the horse has digested his food, and is all
right, you may begin to push your horse on, trotting him a
mile at a heat, and then walking him a quarter of a one,
that his wind may be not distressed; and you may go on in
that way for thirty miles, never galloping, of course, for
none but fools or hivermen ever gallop horses on roads; and
at the end of that distance you may stop at some other nice
inn to dinner. I say, when your horse is led into the stable,
after that same thirty miles' trotting and walking, don't let
the saddle be whisked off at once, for if you do your horse
will have such a sore back as will frighten you, but let

your saddle remain on your horse's back, with the girths loosened, till after his next feed of corn, and be sure that he has no corn, much less water, till after a long hour and more; after he is fed he may be watered to the tune of half a pail, and then the ostler can give him a regular rub down; you may then sit down to dinner, and when you have dined get up and see to your horse as you did after breakfast, in fact, you must do much after the same fashion you did at t'other inn; see to your horse, and by no means disoblige the ostler. So when you have seen to your horse a second time, you will sit down to your bottle of wine—supposing you to be a gentleman—and after you have finished it, and your argument about the corn-laws with any commercial gentleman who happens to be in the room, you may mount your horse again—not forgetting to do the proper thing to the waiter and ostler; you may mount your horse again and ride him, as you did before, for about five and twenty miles, at the end of which you may put up for the night after a very fair day's journey, for no gentleman—supposing he weighs sixteen stone, as I suppose you will by the time you become a gentleman—ought to ride a horse more than sixty-five miles in one day, provided he has any regard for his horse's back, or his own either. See to your horse at night, and have him well rubbed down. The next day you may ride your horse forty miles, just as you please, but never foolishly, and those forty miles will bring you to your journey's end, unless your journey be a plaguy long one, and if so, never ride your horse more than five and thirty miles a day, always, however, seeing him well fed, and taking more care of him than yourself; which is but right and reasonable, seeing as how the horse is the best animal of the two."

"When you are a gentleman," said he, after a pause, "the first thing you must think about is to provide yourself with a good horse for your own particular riding; you will, perhaps, keep a coach and pair, but they will be less your own than your lady's, should you have one, and your young gentry, should you have any; or, if you have neither, for madam, your housekeeper, and the upper female servants; so you need trouble your head less about them, though, of course, you would not like to pay away your money for screws; but be sure you get a good horse for your own riding; and that you may have a good chance of having a good one, buy one that's young and has plenty of belly—a little more than the one has which you now have, though you are not yet a gentleman; you will, of course, look to his head, his withers, legs and other points, but never buy a horse at any price that has not plenty of belly; no horse that has not belly is ever a good feeder, and a horse that a'n't a good feeder can't be a good horse; never buy a horse that is drawn up in the belly behind; a horse of that description can't feed, and can never carry sixteen stone.

" So when you have got such a horse be proud of it—as I daresay you are of the one you have now—and wherever you go swear there a'n't another to match it in the country, and if anybody gives you the lie, take him by the nose and tweak it off, just as you would do if anybody were to speak ill of your lady, or, for want of her, of your housekeeper. Take care of your horse, as you would of the apple of your eye— I am sure I would, if I were a gentleman, which I don't ever expect to be, and hardly wish, seeing as how I am sixty-nine, and am rather too old to ride—yes, cherish and take care of your horse as perhaps the best friend you have in the world; for, after all, who will carry you through thick and thin as your horse will? not your gentlemen friends, I warrant, nor your upper servants, male or female; perhaps your lady would, that is, if she is a whopper, and one of the right sort; the others would be more likely to take up mud and pelt you with it, provided they saw you in trouble, than to help you. So take care of your horse, and feed him every day with your own hands; give him three quarters of a peck of corn each day, mixed up with a little hay-chaff, and allow him besides one hundredweight of hay in the course of the week; some say that the hay should be hardland hay, because it is the wholesomest, but I say, let it be clover hay, because the horse likes it best; give him through summer and winter, once a week, a pailful of bran mash, cold in summer and in winter hot; ride him gently about the neighbourhood every day, by which means you will give exercise to yourself and horse, and, moreover, have the satisfaction of exhibiting yourself and your horse to advantage, and hearing, perhaps, the men say what a fine horse, and the ladies saying what a fine man : never let your groom mount your horse, as it is ten to one, if you do, your groom will be wishing to show off before company, and will fling your horse down. I was groom to a gemman before I went to the inn at Hounslow, and flung him a horse down worth ninety guineas, by endeavouring to show off before some ladies that I met on the road. Turn your horse out to grass throughout May and the first part of June, for then the grass is sweetest, and the flies don't sting so bad as they do later in summer; afterwards merely turn him out occasionally in the swale of the morn and the evening; after September the grass is good for little, lash and sour at best; every horse should go out to grass, if not his blood becomes full of greasy humours, and his wind is apt to become affected, but he ought to be kept as much as possible from the heat and flies, always got up at night, and never turned out late in the year—Lord! if I had always such a nice attentive person to listen to me as you are, I could go on talking about 'orses to the end of time.''

CHAPTER XXVI

The Stage-Coachmen of England—A Bully Served Out—Broughton's Guard—The Brazen Head.

I LIVED on very good terms, not only with the master and the old ostler, but with all the domestics and hangers on at the inn; waiters, chambermaids, cooks, and scullions, not forgetting the " boots,'' of which there were three. As for the postillions, I was sworn brother with them all, and some of them went so far as to swear that I was the best fellow in the world; for which high opinion entertained by them of me, I believe I was principally indebted to the good account their comrade gave of me, whom I had so hospitably received in the dingle. I repeat that I lived on good terms with all the people connected with the inn, and was noticed and spoken kindly to by some of the guests—especially by that class termed commercial travellers—all of whom were great friends and patronizers of the landlord, and were the principal promoters of the dinner, and subscribers to the gift of plate, which I have already spoken of, the whole fraternity striking me as the jolliest set of fellows imaginable, the best customers to an inn, and the most liberal to servants; there was one description of persons, however, frequenting the inn, which I did not like at all, and which I did not get on well with, and these people were the stage-coach-men.

The stage-coachmen of England, at the time of which I am speaking, considered themselves mighty fine gentry, nay, I verily believe the most important personages of the realm, and their entertaining this high opinion of themselves can scarcely be wondered at; they were low fellows, but masters at driving; driving was in fashion, and sprigs of nobility used to dress as coachmen and imitate the slang and behaviour of the coachmen, from whom occasionally they would take lessons in driving as they sat beside them on the box, which post of honour any sprig of nobility who happened to take a place on a coach claimed as his unques-tionable right; and these sprigs would smoke cigars and drink sherry with the coachmen in bar-rooms, and on the road; and, when bidding them farewell, would give them a guinea or a half-guinea, and shake them by the hand, so that these fellows, being low fellows, very naturally thought no small liquor of themselves, but would talk familiarly of their friends lords so and so, the honourable misters so and so, and Sir Harry and Sir Charles, and be wonderfully saucy to any one who was not a lord, or something of the kind; and this high opinion of themselves received daily augmentation from the servile homage paid them by the generality of the untitled male passengers, especially those on the fore part of the coach, who used to contend for the honour of sitting on the box with the coachman when no sprig was nigh to put in his claim. Oh! what servile homage these craven creatures did pay these same coach fellows, more especially after witnessing this or t' other act of brutality practised upon the weak and unoffending—upon some poor friendless woman travelling with but little money, and perhaps a brace of hungry children with her, or upon some thin and half-starved man travelling on the hind part of the coach from London to Liverpool with only eighteen pence in his pocket after his fare was paid, to defray his expenses on the road; for as the insolence of these knights was vast, so was their rapacity enormous; they had been so long accustomed to have crowns and half-crowns rained upon them by their admirers and flatterers, that they would look at a shilling, for which many an honest labourer was happy to toil for ten hours under a broiling sun, with the utmost contempt; would blow upon it derisively, or fillip it into the air before they pocketed it; but when nothing was given them, as would occasionally happen—for how could they receive from those who had nothing? and nobody was bound to give them anything, as they had certain wages from their employers—then what a scene would ensue! Truly the brutality and rapacious insolence of English coachmen had reached a climax; it was time that these fellows should be disenchanted, and the time—thank Heaven!—was not far distant. Let the craven dastards who used to curry favour with them, and applaud their brutality, lament their loss now that they and their vehicles have disappeared from the roads; I, who have ever been an enemy to insolence, cruelty, and tyranny, loathe their memory, and, what is more, am not afraid to say so, well aware of the storm of vituperation, partly learnt from them, which I may expect from those who used to fall down and worship them.

Amongst the coachmen who frequented the inn was one who was called " the bang-up coachman." He drove to our inn, in the fore part of every day, one of what were called the fast coaches, and afterwards took back the corresponding vehicle. He stayed at our house about twenty minutes, during which time the passengers of the coach which he was to return with dined; those at least who were inclined for dinner, and could pay for it. He derived his sobriquet of " the bang-up coachman " partly from his being dressed in the extremity of coach dandyism, and partly from the peculiar insolence of his manner, and the unmerciful fashion in which he was in the habit of lashing on the poor horses committed to his charge. He was a large tall fellow, of about thirty, with a face which, had it not been bloated by excess, and insolence and cruelty stamped most visibly upon it, might have been called good-looking. His insolence indeed was so great, that he was hated by all the minor fry connected with coaches along the road upon which he drove, especially the ostlers, whom he was continually abusing or finding fault with. Many was the hearty curse which he received when his back was turned; but the generality of people were much afraid of him, for he was a swinging strong fellow, and had the reputation of being a fighter, and in one or two instances had beaten in a barbarous manner individuals who had quarrelled with him.

I was nearly having a fracas with this worthy. One day, after he had been drinking sherry with a sprig, he swaggered into the yard where I happened to be standing; just then a waiter came by carrying upon a tray part of a splendid Cheshire cheese, with a knife, plate, and napkin. Stopping the waiter, the coachman cut with the knife a tolerably large lump out of the very middle of the cheese, stuck it on the end of the knife, and putting it to his mouth nibbled a slight piece off it, and then, tossing the rest away with disdain, flung the knife down upon the tray, motioning the waiter to proceed; "I wish," said I, "you may not want before you die what you have just flung away," whereupon the fellow turned furiously towards me; just then, however, his coach being standing at the door, there was a cry for coachman, so that he was forced to depart, contenting himself for the present with shaking his fist at me, and threatening to serve me out on the first opportunity; before, however, the opportunity occurred he himself got served out in a most unexpected manner.

The day after this incident he drove his coach to the inn, and after having dismounted and received the contributions of the generality of the passengers, he strutted up, with a cigar in his mouth, to an individual who had come with him, and who had just asked me a question with respect to the direction of a village about three miles off, to which he was going. "Remember the coachman," said the knight of the box to this individual, who was a thin person of about sixty, with a white hat, rather shabby black coat, and buff-coloured trousers, and who held an umbrella and a small bundle in his hand. "If you expect me to give you anything," said he to the coachman, "you are mistaken; I will give you nothing. You have been very insolent to me as I rode behind you on the coach, and have encouraged two or three trumpery fellows, who rode along with you, to cut scurvy jokes at my expense, and now you come to me for money; I am not so poor, but I could have given you a shilling had you been civil; as it is, I will give you nothing." "Oh! you won't, won't you?" said the coachman; "dear me! I hope I shan't starve because you won't give me anything—a shilling! why, I could afford to give you twenty if I thought fit, you pauper! civil to you, indeed! things are come to a fine pass if I need be civil to you! Do you know who you are speaking to? why, the best lords in the country are proud to speak to me. Why, it was only the other day that the Marquis of —— said to me ——" and then he went on to say what the Marquis said to him; after which, flinging down his cigar, he strutted up the road, swearing to himself about paupers.

"You say it is three miles to ——," said the individual to me; "I think I shall light my pipe, and smoke it as I go along." Thereupon he took out from a side-pocket a tobacco-box and short meerschaum pipe, and implements for striking a light, filled his pipe, lighted it, and commenced smoking. Presently the coachman drew near. I saw at once that there was mischief in his eye; the man smoking was standing with his back towards him, and he came so nigh to him, seemingly purposely, that as he passed a puff of smoke came of necessity against his face. "What do you mean by smoking in my face?" said he, striking the pipe of the elderly individual out of his mouth. The other, without manifesting much surprise, said, "I thank you; and if you will wait a minute, I will give you a receipt for that favour;" then gathering up his pipe, and taking off his coat and hat, he laid them on a stepping-block which stood near, and rubbing his hands together, he advanced towards the coachman in an attitude of offence, holding his hands crossed very near to his face. The coachman, who probably expected anything but such a movement from a person of the age and appearance of the individual whom he had insulted, stood for a moment motionless with surprise; but, recollecting himself, he pointed at him derisively with his finger; the next moment, however, the other was close upon him, had struck aside the extended hand with his left fist, and given him a severe blow on the nose with his right, which he immediately followed by a left-hand blow in the eye; then drawing his body slightly backward, with the velocity of lightning he struck the coachman full in the mouth, and the last blow was the severest of all, for it cut the coachman's lips nearly through; blows so quickly and sharply dealt I had never seen. The coachman reeled like a fir-tree in a gale, and seemed nearly unsensed. "Ho! what's this? a fight! a fight!" sounded from a dozen voices, and people came running from all directions to see what was going on. The coachman, coming somewhat to himself, disencumbered himself of his coat and hat; and, encouraged by two or three of his brothers of the whip, showed some symptoms of fighting, endeavouring to close with his foe, but the attempt was vain, for his foe was not to be closed with; he did not shift or dodge about, but warded off the blows of his opponent with the greatest sang-froid, always using the guard which I have already described, and putting in, in return, short chopping blows with the swiftness of lightning. In a very few minutes the countenance of the coachman was literally cut to pieces, and several of his teeth were dislodged; at length he gave in; stung with mortification, however, he repented, and asked for another round; it was granted, to his own complete demolition. The coachman did not drive his coach back that day, he did not appear on the box again for a week; but he never held up his head afterwards. Before I quitted the inn, he had disappeared from the road, going no one knew where.

The coachman, as I have said before, was very much disliked upon the road, but there was an esprit de corps amongst the coachmen, and those who stood by did not like to see their brother chastised in such tremendous fashion. "I never saw such a fight before," said one. "Fight! why, I don't call it a fight at all; this chap here ha'n't got a scratch, whereas Tom is cut to pieces; it is all along of that guard of his; if Tom could have got within his guard he would have soon served the old chap out." "So he would," said another, "it was all owing to that guard. However, I think I see into it, and if I had not to drive this afternoon, I would have a turn with the old fellow and soon serve him out." "I will fight him now for a guinea," said the other coachman, half taking off his coat; observing, however, that the elderly individual made a motion towards him, he hitched it upon his shoulder again, and added, "that is, if he had not been fighting already, but as it is, I am above taking an advantage, especially of such a poor old creature as that." And when he had said this, he looked around him, and there was a feeble titter of approbation from two or three of the craven crew, who were in the habit of currying favour with the coachmen. The elderly individual looked for a moment at these last, and then said, "To such fellows as you I have nothing to say;" then turning to the coachmen, "and as for you," he said, "ye cowardly bullies, I have but one word, which is, that your reign upon the roads is nearly over, and that a time is coming when ye will no longer be wanted or employed in your present capacity, when ye will either have to drive dung-carts, assist as ostlers at village ale-houses, or rot in the workhouse." Then putting on his coat and hat, and taking up his bundle, not forgetting his meerschaum, and the rest of his smoking apparatus, he departed on his way. Filled with curiosity, I followed him.

"I am quite astonished that you should be able to use your hands in the way you have done," said I, as I walked with this individual in the direction in which he was bound.

"I will tell you how I became able to do so," said the elderly individual, proceeding to fill and light his pipe as he walked along. "My father was a journeyman engraver, who lived in a very riotous neighbourhood in the outskirts of London. Wishing to give me something of an education, he sent me to a day-school, two or three streets distant from where we lived, and there, being rather a puny boy, I suffered much persecution from my schoolfellows, who were a very blackguard set. One day, as I was running home, with one of my tormentors pursuing me, old Sergeant Broughton, the retired fighting-man, seized me by the arm——"

"Dear me," said I, "has it ever been your luck to be acquainted with Sergeant Broughton?"

"You may well call it luck," said the elderly individual; "but for him I should never have been able to make my way through the world. He lived only four doors from our house; so, as I was running along the street, with my tyrant behind me, Sergeant Broughton seized me by the arm. 'Stop, my boy,' said he; 'I have frequently seen that scamp ill-treating you; now I will teach you how to send him home with a bloody nose; down with your bag of books; and now, my game chick,' whispered he to me, placing himself between me and my adversary, so that he could not observe his motions; 'clench your fist in this manner, and hold your arms in this, and when he strikes at you, move them as I now show you, and he can't hurt you; now, don't be afraid, but go at him.' I confess that I was somewhat afraid, but I considered myself in some degree under the protection of the famous Sergeant, and, clenching my fist, I went at my foe, using the guard which my ally recommended. The result corresponded to a certain degree with the predictions of the Sergeant; I gave my foe a bloody nose and a black eye, though, notwith-standing my recent lesson in the art of self-defence, he con-trived to give me two or three clumsy blows. From that moment I was the especial favourite of the Sergeant, who gave me further lessons, so that in a little time I became a very fair boxer, beating everybody of my own size who attacked me. The old gentleman, however, made me pro-mise never to be quarrelsome, nor to turn his instructions to account, except in self-defence. I have always borne in mind my promise, and have made it a point of conscience never to fight unless absolutely compelled. Folks may rail against boxing if they please, but being able to box may sometimes stand a quiet man in good stead. How should I have fared to-day, but for the instructions of Ser-geant Broughton? But for them, the brutal ruffian who insulted me must have passed unpunished. He will not soon forget the lesson which I have just given him—the only lesson he could understand. What would have been the use of reasoning with a fellow of that description? Brave old Broughton! I owe him much."

"And your manner of fighting," said I, "was the manner employed by Sergeant Broughton?"

"Yes," said my new acquaintance; "it was the manner in which he beat every one who attempted to contend with him, till, in an evil hour, he entered the ring with Slack, without any training or preparation, and by a chance blow lost the battle to a man who had been beaten with ease by those who, in the hands of Broughton, appeared like so many children. It was the way of fighting of him who first taught Englishmen to box scientifically, who was the head and father of the fighters of what is now called the old school, the last of which were Johnson and Big Ben."

"A wonderful man, that Big Ben," said I.

"He was so," said the elderly individual; "but had it not been for Broughton, I question whether Ben would have ever been the fighter he was. Oh! there was no one like old Broughton; but for him I should at the present moment be sneaking along the road, pursued by the hiss-ings and hootings of the dirty flatterers of that blackguard coachman."

"What did you mean," said I, "by those words of yours, that the coachmen would speedily disappear from the roads?"

"I meant," said he, "that a new method of travelling is about to be established, which will supersede the old. I am a poor engraver, as my father was before me; but engraving is an intellectual trade, and by following it, I have been brought in contact with some of the cleverest men in England. It has even made me acquainted with the projector of the scheme, which he has told me many of the wisest heads of England have been dreaming of during a period of six hundred years, and which it seems was alluded to by a certain Brazen Head in the story-book of Friar Bacon, who is generally supposed to have been a wizard, but in reality was a great philosopher. Young man, in less than twenty years, by which time I shall be dead and gone, England will be surrounded with roads of metal, on which armies may travel with mighty velocity, and of which the walls of brass and iron by which the friar proposed to defend his native land are the types." He then, shaking me by the hand, proceeded on his way, whilst I returned to the inn.

CHAPTER XXVII

Francis Ardry—His Misfortunes—Dog and Lion Fight—Great Men of the World.

A FEW days after the circumstance which I have last commemorated, it chanced that, as I was standing at the door of the inn, one of the numerous stage-coaches which were in the habit of stopping there, drove up, and several passengers got down. I had assisted a woman with a couple of children to dismount, and had just delivered to her a band-box, which appeared to be her only property, which she had begged me to fetch down from the roof, when I felt a hand laid upon my shoulder, and heard a voice exclaim, "Is it possible, old fellow, that I find you in this place?" I turned round, and, wrapped in a large blue cloak, I beheld my good friend Francis Ardry. I shook him most warmly by the hand, and said, "If you are surprised to see me, I am no less so to see you; where are you bound to?"

"I am bound for L——; at any rate, I am booked for that sea-port," said my friend in reply.

"I am sorry for it," said I, "for in that case we shall have to part in a quarter of an hour, the coach by which you came stopping no longer."

"And whither are you bound?" demanded my friend.

"I am stopping at present in this house, quite undetermined as to what to do."

"Then come along with me," said Francis Ardry.

"That I can scarcely do," said I; "I have a horse in the stall which I cannot afford to ruin by racing to L—— by the side of your coach."

My friend mused for a moment: "I have no particular business at L——," said he; "I was merely going thither to pass a day or two, till an affair, in which I am deeply interested, at C—— shall come off. I think I shall stay with you for four-and-twenty hours at least; I have been rather melancholy of late, and cannot afford to part with a friend like you at the present moment; it is an unexpected piece of good fortune to have met you; and I have not been very fortunate of late," he added, sighing.

"Well," said I, "I am glad to see you once more, whether fortunate, or not; where is your baggage?"

"Yon trunk is mine," said Francis, pointing to a trunk of black Russian leather upon the coach.

"We will soon have it down," said I; and at a word which I gave to one of the hangers-on of the inn, the trunk was taken from the top of the coach. "Now," said I to Francis Ardry, "follow me, I am a person of some authority in this house;" thereupon I led Francis Ardry into the house, and a word which I said to a waiter forthwith installed Francis Ardry in a comfortable private sitting-room, and his trunk in the very best sleeping-room of our extensive establishment.

It was now about one o'clock: Francis Ardry ordered dinner for two, to be ready at four, and a pint of sherry to be brought forthwith, which I requested my friend the waiter might be the very best, and which in effect turned out as I requested; we sat down, and when we had drunk to each other's health, Frank requested me to make known to him how I had contrived to free myself from my embarrassments in London, what I had been about since I quitted that city, and the present posture of my affairs.

I related to Francis Ardry how I had composed the Life of Joseph Sell, and how the sale of it to the bookseller had enabled me to quit London with money in my pocket, which had supported me during a long course of ramble in the country, into the particulars of which I, however, did not enter with any considerable degree of fulness. I summed up my account by saying that " I was at present a kind of overlooker in the stables of the inn, had still some pounds in my purse, and, moreover, a capital horse in the stall."

" No very agreeable posture of affairs," said Francis Ardry, looking rather seriously at me.

" I make no complaints," said I, " my prospects are not very bright, it is true, but sometimes I have visions both waking and sleeping, which, though always strange, are invariably agreeable. Last night, in my chamber near the hayloft, I dreamt that I had passed over an almost interminable wilderness—an enormous wall rose before me, the wall, methought, was the great wall of China :— strange figures appeared to be beckoning to me from the top of the wall; such visions are not exactly to be sneered at. Not that such phantasmagoria," said I, raising my voice, " are to be compared for a moment with such desirable things as fashion, fine clothes, cheques from uncles, parliamentary interest, the love of splendid females. Ah! woman's love," said I, and sighed.

" What's the matter with the fellow?" said Francis Ardry.

" There is nothing like it," said I.

" Like what?"

" Love, divine love," said I.

" Confound love," said Francis Ardry, " I hate the very name; I have made myself a pretty fool by it, but trust me for ever being at such folly again. In an evil hour I abandoned my former pursuits and amusements for it; in one morning spent at Joey's there was more real pleasure than in ——"

" Surely," said I, " you are not hankering after dog-fighting again, a sport which none but the gross and un-refined care anything for? No, one's thoughts should be occupied by something higher and more rational than dog-fighting; and what better than love—divine love? Oh, there's nothing like it!"

" Pray, don't talk nonsense," said Francis Ardry.

"Nonsense," said I; "why I was repeating, to the best of my recollection, what I heard you say on a former occasion."

"If ever I talked such stuff," said Francis Ardry, "I was a fool; and indeed I cannot deny that I have been one: no, there's no denying that I have been a fool. What do you think? that false Annette has cruelly abandoned me."

"Well," said I, "perhaps you have yourself to thank for her having done so; did you never treat her with coldness, and repay her marks of affectionate interest with strange fits of eccentric humour?"

"Lord! how little you know of women," said Francis Ardry; "had I done as you suppose, I should probably have possessed her at the present moment. I treated her in a manner diametrically opposite to that. I loaded her with presents, was always most assiduous to her, always at her feet, as I may say, yet she nevertheless abandoned me—and for whom? I am almost ashamed to say—for a fiddler."

I took a glass of wine, Francis Ardry followed my example, and then proceeded to detail to me the treatment which he had experienced from Annette, and from what he said, it appeared that her conduct to him had been in the highest degree reprehensible; notwithstanding he had indulged her in everything, she was never civil to him, but loaded him continually with taunts and insults, and had finally, on his being unable to supply her with a sum of money which she had demanded, decamped from the lodgings which he had taken for her, carrying with her all the presents which at various times he had bestowed upon her, and had put herself under the protection of a gentleman who played the bassoon at the Italian Opera, at which place it appeared that her sister had lately been engaged as a danseuse. My friend informed me that at first he had experienced great agony at the ingratitude of Annette, but at last had made up his mind to forget her, and, in order more effectually to do so, had left London with the intention of witnessing a fight, which was shortly coming off at a town in these parts, between some dogs and a lion; which combat, he informed me, had for some time past been looked forward to with intense eagerness by the gentlemen of the sporting world.

I commended him for his resolution, at the same time

advising him not to give up his mind entirely to dog-fighting, as he had formerly done, but, when the present combat should be over, to return to his rhetorical studies, and above all to marry some rich and handsome lady on the first opportunity, as, with his person and expectations, he had only to sue for the hand of the daughter of a marquis to be successful, telling him, with a sigh, that all women were not Annettes, and that, upon the whole, there was nothing like them. To which advice he answered, that he intended to return to rhetoric as soon as the lion fight should be over, but that he never intended to marry, having had enough of women; adding that he was glad he had no sister, as, with the feelings which he entertained with respect to her sex, he should be unable to treat her with common affection, and concluded by repeating a proverb which he had learnt from an Arab whom he had met at Venice, to the effect, that, "one who has been stung by a snake, shivers at the sight of a sting."

After a little more conversation, we strolled to the stable, where my horse was standing; my friend, who was a connoisseur in horseflesh, surveyed the animal with attention, and after inquiring where and how I had obtained him, asked what I intended to do with him; on my telling him that I was undetermined, and that I was afraid the horse was likely to prove a burden to me, he said, " It is a noble animal, and if you mind what you are about, you may make a small fortune by him. I do not want such an animal myself, nor do I know any one who does; but a great horse-fair will be held shortly at a place where, it is true, I have never been, but of which I have heard a great deal from my acquaintances, where it is said a first-rate horse is always sure to fetch its value; that place is Horncastle, in Lincolnshire, you should take him thither."

Francis Ardry and myself dined together, and after dinner partook of a bottle of the best port which the inn afforded. After a few glasses, we had a great deal of conversation; I again brought the subject of marriage and love, divine love, upon the carpet, but Francis almost immediately begged me to drop it; and on my having the delicacy to comply, he reverted to dog-fighting, on which he talked well and learnedly; amongst other things, he said it was a princely sport of great antiquity, and quoted from Quintus Curtius to prove that the princes of India must have been of the fancy, they having, according to that author, treated Alexander to a fight between certain dogs and a lion. Becoming, notwithstanding my friend's eloquence and learning, somewhat tired of the subject, I began to talk about Alexander. Francis Ardry said he was one of the two great men whom the world has produced, the other being Napoleon; I replied that I believed Tamerlane was a greater man than either; but Francis Ardry knew nothing of Tamerlane, save what he had gathered from the play of Timour the Tartar. "No," said he, "Alexander and Napoleon are the great men of the world, their names are known everywhere. Alexander has been dead upwards of two thousand years, but the very English bumpkins sometimes christen their boys by the name of Alexander—can there be a greater evidence of his greatness? As for Napoleon, there are some parts of India in which his bust is worshipped." Wishing to make up a triumvirate, I mentioned the name of Wellington, to which Francis Ardry merely said, "bah!" and resumed the subject of dog-fighting.

Francis Ardry remained at the inn during that day and the next, and then departed to the dog and lion fight; I never saw him afterwards, and merely heard of him once after a lapse of some years, and what I then heard was not exactly what I could have wished to hear. He did not make much of the advantages which he possessed, a pity, for how great were those advantages—person, intellect, eloquence, connection, riches! yet, with all these advantages, one thing highly needful seems to have been wanting in Francis. A desire, a craving, to perform something great and good. Oh! what a vast deal may be done with intellect, courage, riches, accompanied by the desire of doing something great and good! Why, a person may carry the blessings of civilization and religion to barbarous, yet at the same time beautiful and romantic lands; and what a triumph there is for him who does so! what a crown of glory! of far greater value than those surrounding the brows of your mere conquerors. Yet who has done so in these times? Not many; not three, not two, something seems to have been always wanting; there is, however, one instance, in which the various requisites have been united, and the crown, the most desirable in the world—at least which I consider to be the most desirable—achieved, and only one, that of Brooke of Borneo.

CHAPTER XXVIII

Mr. Platitude and the Man in Black—The Postillion's Adventures—
The Lone House—A Goodly Assemblage.

It never rains, but it pours. I was destined to see at this inn more acquaintances than one. On the day of Francis Ardry's departure, shortly after he had taken leave of me, as I was standing in the corn-chamber, at a kind of writing-table or desk, fastened to the wall, with a book before me, in which I was making out an account of the corn and hay lately received and distributed, my friend the postillion came running in out of breath. "Here they both are," he gasped out; "pray do come and look at them."

"Whom do you mean?" said I.

"Why, that red-haired Jack Priest, and that idiotic parson, Platitude; they have just been set down by one of the coaches, and want a postchaise to go across the country in; and what do you think? I am to have the driving of them. I have no time to lose, for I must get myself ready; so do come and look at them."

I hastened into the yard of the inn; two or three of the helpers of our establishment were employed in drawing forward a postchaise out of the chaise-house, which occupied one side of the yard, and which was spacious enough to contain nearly twenty of these vehicles, though it was never full, several of them being always out upon the roads, as the demand upon us for postchaises across the country was very great. "There they are," said the postillion, softly, nodding towards two individuals, in one of whom I recognized the man in black, and in the other Mr. Platitude; "there they are; have a good look at them, while I go and get ready." The man in black and Mr. Platitude were walking up and down the yard, Mr. Platitude was doing his best to make himself appear ridiculous, talking very loudly in exceedingly bad Italian, evidently for the purpose of attracting the notice of the bystanders, in which he succeeded, all the stable-boys and hangers-on about the yard, attracted by his vociferation, grinning at his ridiculous figure as he limped up and down. The man in black said little or nothing, but from the glances which he cast sideways appeared to be thoroughly ashamed of his companion; the worthy couple presently arrived close to where I was standing, and the man in black, who was nearest to me, perceiving me, stood still as if hesitating, but recovering himself in a moment, he moved on without taking any farther notice; Mr. Platitude exclaimed as they passed in broken lingo, " I hope we shall find the holy doctors all assembled," and as they returned, " I make no doubt that they will all be rejoiced to see me." Not wishing to be standing an idle gazer, I went to the chaise and assisted in attaching the horses, which had now been brought out, to the pole. The postillion presently arrived, and finding all ready took the reins and mounted the box, whilst I very politely opened the door for the two travellers; Mr. Platitude got in first, and, without taking any notice of me, seated himself on the farther side. In got the man in black, and seated himself nearest to me. "All is right," said I, as I shut the door, whereupon the postillion cracked his whip, and the chaise drove out of the yard. Just as I shut the door, however, and just as Mr. Platitude had recommenced talking in jergo, at the top of his voice, the man in black turned his face partly towards me, and gave me a wink with his left eye.

I did not see my friend the postillion till the next morning, when he gave me an account of the adventures he had met with on his expedition. It appeared that he had driven the man in black and the Reverend Platitude across the country by roads and lanes which he had some difficulty in threading. At length, when he had reached a part of the country where he had never been before, the man in black pointed out to him a house near the corner of a wood, to which he informed him they were bound. The postillion said it was a strange-looking house, with a wall round it; and, upon the whole, bore something of the look of a madhouse. There was already a postchaise at the gate, from which three individuals had alighted— one of them the postillion said was a mean-looking scoundrel, with a regular petty-larceny expression in his countenance. He was dressed very much like the man in black, and the postillion said that he could almost have taken his Bible oath that they were both of the same profession. The other two he said were parsons, he could swear that, though he had never seen them before; there could be no mistake about them. Church of England parsons the postillion swore they were, with their black coats, white cravats, and airs, in which clumsiness and conceit were most funnily blended—Church of England parsons of the Platitude description, who had been in Italy, and seen the Pope, and kissed his toe, and picked up a little broken Italian, and come home greater fools than they went forth. It appeared that they were all acquaintances of Mr. Platitude, for when the postillion had alighted and let Mr. Platitude and his companion out of the chaise, Mr. Platitude shook the whole three by the hand, conversed with his two brothers in a little broken jergo, and addressed the petty-larceny looking individual by the title of Reverend Doctor. In the midst of these greetings, however, the postillion said the man in black came up to him, and proceeded to settle with him for the chaise; he had shaken hands with nobody, and had merely nodded to the others; "and now," said the postillion, "he evidently wished to get rid of me, fearing, probably, that I should see too much of the nonsense that was going on. It was whilst settling with me that he seemed to recognize me for the first time, for he stared hard at me, and at last asked whether I had not been in Italy; to which question, with a nod and a laugh, I replied that I had. I was then going to ask him about the health of the image of Holy Mary, and to say that I hoped it had recovered from its horsewhipping; but he interrupted me, paid me the money for the fare, and gave me a crown for myself, saying he would not detain me any longer. I say, partner, I am a poor postillion, but when he gave me the crown I had a good mind to fling it in his face. I reflected, however, that it was not mere gift-money, but coin which I had earned, and hardly too, so I put it in my pocket, and I bethought me, moreover, that, knave as I knew him to be, he had always treated me with civility; so I nodded to him, and he said something which, perhaps, he meant for Latin, but which sounded very much like 'vails,' and by which he doubtless alluded to the money which he had given me. He then went into the house with the rest, the coach drove away which had brought the others, and I was about to get on the box and follow; observing, however, two more chaises driving up, I thought I would be in no hurry, so I just led my horses and chaise a little out of the way, and pretending to be occupied about the harness, I kept a tolerably sharp look-out at the new arrivals. Well, partner, the next vehicle that drove up was a gentleman's carriage which I knew very well, as well as those within it, who were a father and son, the father a good kind old gentleman, and a justice of the peace, therefore not very wise, as you may suppose; the son a puppy who has been abroad, where he contrived to forget his own language, though only nine months absent, and now rules the roast over his father and mother, whose only child he is, and by whom he is thought wondrous clever. So this foreigneering chap brings his poor old father to this out-of-the-way house to meet these Platitudes and petty-larceny villains, and perhaps would have brought his mother too, only, simple thing, by good fortune she happens to be laid up with the rheumatiz. Well, the father and son, I beg pardon, I mean the son and father, got down and went in, and then after their carriage was gone, the chaise behind drove up, in which was a huge fat fellow, weighing twenty stone at least, but with something of a foreign look, and with him—who do you think? Why, a rascally Unitarian minister, that is, a fellow who had been such a minister, but who, some years ago leaving his own people, who had bred him up and sent him to their college at York, went over to the High Church, and is now, I suppose, going over to some other church, for he was talking, as he got down, wondrous fast in Latin, or what sounded something like Latin, to the fat fellow, who appeared to take things wonderfully easy, and merely grunted to the dog Latin which the scoundrel had learnt at the expense of the poor Unitarians at York. So they went into the house, and presently arrived another chaise, but ere I could make any further observations, the porter of the out-of-the-way house came up to me, asking what I was stopping there for? bidding me go away, and not pry into other people's business. 'Pretty business,' said I to him, 'that is being transacted in a place like this,' and then I was going to say something uncivil, but he went to attend to the new comers, and I took myself away on my own business as he bade me, not, however, before observing that these two last were a couple of blackcoats.''

The postillion then proceeded to relate how he made the

best of his way to a small public-house, about a mile off, where he had intended to bait, and how he met on the way a landau and pair, belonging to a Scotch coxcomb whom he had known in London, about whom he related some curious particulars, and then continued: "Well, after I had passed him and his turn-out, I drove straight to the public-house, where I baited my horses, and where I found some of the chaises and drivers who had driven the folks to the lunatic-looking mansion, and were now waiting to take them up again. Whilst my horses were eating their bait, I sat me down, as the weather was warm, at a table outside, and smoked a pipe, and drank some ale, in company with the coachman of the old gentleman who had gone to the house with his son, and the coachman then told me that the house was a Papist house, and that the present was a grand meeting of all the fools and rascals in the country, who came to bow down to images, and to concert schemes—pretty schemes no doubt—for overturning the religion of the country, and that for his part he did not approve of being concerned with such doings, and that he was going to give his master warning next day. So, as we were drinking and discoursing, up drove the chariot of the Scotchman, and down got his valet and the driver, and whilst the driver was seeing after the horses, the valet came and sat down at the table where the gentleman's coachman and I were drinking. I knew the fellow well, a Scotchman like his master, and just of the same kidney, with white kid gloves, red hair frizzled, a patch of paint on his face, and his hands covered with rings. This very fellow, I must tell you, was one of those most busy in endeavouring to get me turned out of the servants' club in Park Lane, because I happened to serve a literary man; so he sat down, and in a kind of affected tone cried out, 'Landlord, bring me a glass of cold negus.' The landlord, however, told him that there was no negus, but that if he pleased, he could have a jug of as good beer as any in the country. 'Confound the beer,' said the valet, 'do you think that I am accustomed to such vulgar beverage?' However, as he found there was nothing better to be had, he let the man bring him some beer, and when he had got it, soon showed that he could drink it easily enough; so, when he had drunk two or three draughts, he turned his eyes in a contemptuous manner, first, on the coachman, and then on me: I saw the scamp recollected me, for after staring at me and my dress for about half a minute, he put on a broad grin, and flinging his head back, he uttered a loud laugh. Well, I did not like this, as you may well believe, and taking the pipe out of my mouth, I asked him if he meant anything personal, to which he answered, that he had said nothing to me, and that he had a right to look where he pleased, and laugh when he pleased. Well, as to a certain extent he was right, as to looking and laughing; and as I have occasionally looked at a fool and laughed, though I was not the fool in this instance, I put my pipe into my mouth and said no more. This quiet and well-regulated behaviour of mine, however, the fellow interpreted into fear; so, after drinking a little more, he suddenly started up, and striding once or twice before the table, he asked me what I meant by that impertinent question of mine, saying that he had a good mind to wring my nose for my presumption. 'You have?' said I, getting up, and laying down my pipe. 'Well, I'll now give you an opportunity.' So I put myself in an attitude, and went up to him, saying, 'I have an old score to settle with you, you scamp; you wanted to get me turned out of the club, didn't you?' And thereupon, remembering that he had threatened to wring my nose, I gave him a snorter upon his own. I wish you could have seen the fellow when he felt the smart; so far from trying to defend himself, he turned round, and with his hand to his face, attempted to run away; but I was now in a regular passion, and following him up, got before him, and was going to pummel away at him, when he burst into tears, and begged me not to hurt him, saying that he was sorry if he had offended me, and that, if I pleased, he would go down on his knees, or do anything else I wanted. Well, when I heard him talk in this manner, I, of course, let him be; I could hardly help laughing at the figure he cut; his face all blubbered with tears, and blood and paint; but I did not laugh at the poor creature either, but went to the table and took up my pipe, and smoked and drank as if nothing had happened; and the fellow, after having been to the pump, came and sat down, crying, and trying to curry favour with me and the coachman; presently, however, putting on a confidential look, he began to talk of the Popish house, and of the doings there, and said he supposed as how we were of the party, and that it was all right; and then he began to talk of the Pope of Rome, and what a nice man he was, and what a fine thing it was to be of his religion, especially if folks went over to him; and how it advanced them in the world, and gave them consideration; and how his master, who had been abroad and seen the Pope, and kissed his toe, was going over to the Popish religion, and had persuaded him to consent to do so, and to forsake his own, which I think the scoundrel called the 'Piscopal Church of Scotland, and how many others of that church were going over, thinking to better their condition in life by so doing, and to be more thought on; and how many of the English Church were thinking of going over too—and that he had no doubt that it would all end right and comfortably. Well, as he was going on in this way, the old coachman began to spit, and getting up, flung all the beer that was in his jug upon the ground, and going away, ordered another jug of beer, and sat down at another table, saying that he would not drink in such company; and I too got up, and flung what beer remained in my jug, there wasn't more than a drop, in the fellow's face, saying, I would scorn to drink any more in such company; and then I went to my horses, put them to, paid my reckoning, and drove home."

The postillion having related his story, to which I listened with all due attention, mused for a moment, and then said, " I dare say you remember how, some time since, when old Bill had been telling us how the Government a long time ago, had done away with robbing on the highway, by putting down the public-houses and places which the highwaymen frequented, and by sending a good mounted police to hunt them down, I said that it was a shame that the present Government did not employ somewhat the same means in order to stop the proceedings of Mumbo Jumbo and his gang now-a-days in England. Howsomever, since I have driven a fare to a Popish rendezvous, and seen something of what is going on there, I should conceive that the Government are justified in allowing the gang the free exercise of their calling. Anybody is welcome to stoop and pick up nothing, or worse than nothing, and if Mumbo Jumbo's people, after their expeditions, return to their haunts with no better plunder in the shape of converts than what I saw going into yonder place of call, I should say they are welcome to what they get; for if that's the kind of rubbish they steal out of the Church of England, or any other church, who in his senses but would say a good riddance, and many thanks for your trouble : at any rate, that is my opinion of the matter."

CHAPTER XXIX

Deliberations with Self—Resolution—Invitation to Dinner—The Commercial Traveller—The Landlord's Offer—The Comet Wine.

It was now that I had frequent deliberations with myself. Should I continue at the inn in my present position? I was not very much captivated with it; there was little poetry in keeping an account of the corn, hay, and straw which came in, and was given out, and I was fond of poetry; moreover, there was no glory at all to be expected in doing so, and I was fond of glory. Should I give up that situation, and remaining at the inn, become ostler under old Bill? There was more poetry in rubbing down horses than in keeping an account of straw, hay, and corn; there was also some prospect of glory attached to the situation of ostler, for the grooms and stable-boys occasionally talked of an ostler, a great way down the road, who had been presented by some sporting people, not with a silver vase, as our governor had been, but with a silver currycomb, in testimony of their admiration for his skill; but I confess that the poetry of rubbing down had become, as all other poetry becomes, rather prosy by frequent repetition, and with respect to the chance of deriving glory from the employment, I entertained, in the event of my determining to stay, very slight hope of ever attaining skill in the ostler art sufficient to induce sporting people to bestow upon me a silver currycomb. I was not half so good an ostler as old Bill, who had never been presented with a silver currycomb, and I never expected to become so, therefore what chance had I? It was true, there was a prospect of some pecuniary emolument to be derived by remaining in either situation. It was very probable that, provided I continued to keep an account of the hay and corn coming in and expended, the landlord

would consent to allow me a pound a week, which at the
end of a dozen years, provided I kept myself sober, would
amount to a considerable sum. I might, on the retirement
of old Bill, by taking his place, save up a decent sum of
money, provided, unlike him, I kept myself sober, and laid
by all the shillings and sixpences I got; but the prospect
of laying up a decent sum of money was not of sufficient
importance to induce me to continue either at my wooden
desk, or in the inn-yard. The reader will remember what
difficulty I had to make up my mind to become a merchant
under the Armenian's auspices, even with the prospect of
making two or three hundred thousand pounds by following
the Armenian way of doing business, so it was not probable
that I should feel disposed to be a book-keeper or ostler all
my life with no other prospect than being able to make a
tidy sum of money. If indeed, besides the prospect of
making a tidy sum at the end of perhaps forty years'
ostlering, I had been certain of being presented with a
silver currycomb with my name engraved upon it, which
I might have left to my descendants, or, in default thereof,
to the parish church destined to contain my bones, with
directions that it might be soldered into the wall above the
arch leading from the body of the church into the chancel
—I will not say with such a certainty of immortality, com-
bined with such a prospect of moderate pecuniary advantage,—I might not have thought it worth my while
to stay, but I entertained no such certainty, and, taking
everything into consideration, I determined to mount my
horse and leave the inn.

This horse had caused me for some time past no little
perplexity; I had frequently repented of having purchased
him, more especially as the purchase had been made with
another person's money, and had more than once shown
him to people who, I imagined, were likely to purchase
him; but, though they were profuse in his praise, as people
generally are in the praise of what they don't intend to
purchase, they never made me an offer, and now that I
had determined to mount on his back and ride away, what
was I to do with him in the sequel? I could not maintain
him long. Suddenly I bethought me of Horncastle, which
Francis Ardry had mentioned as a place where the horse
was likely to find a purchaser, and not having determined
upon any particular place to which to repair, I thought

that I could do no better than betake myself to Horncastle in the first instance, and there endeavour to dispose of my horse.

On making inquiries with respect to the situation of Horncastle, and the time when the fair would be held, I learned that the town was situated in Lincolnshire, about a hundred and fifty miles from the inn at which I was at present sojourning, and that the fair would be held nominally within about a month, but that it was always requisite to be on the spot some days before the nominal day of the fair, as all the best horses were generally sold before that time, and the people who came to purchase gone away with what they had bought.

The people of the inn were very sorry on being informed of my determination to depart. Old Bill told me that he had hoped as how I had intended to settle down there, and to take his place as ostler when he was fit for no more work, adding, that though I did not know much of the business, yet he had no doubt but that I might improve. My friend the postillion was particularly sorry, and taking me with him to the tap-room called for two pints of beer, to one of which he treated me; and whilst we were drinking told me how particularly sorry he was at the thought of my going, but that he hoped I should think better of the matter. On my telling him that I must go, he said that he trusted I should put off my departure for three weeks, in order that I might be present at his marriage, the banns of which were just about to be published. He said that nothing would give him greater pleasure than to see me dance a minuet with his wife after the marriage dinner; but I told him it was impossible that I should stay, my affairs imperatively calling me elsewhere; and that with respect to my dancing a minuet, such a thing was out of the question, as I had never learned to dance. At which he said that he was exceedingly sorry, and finding me determined to go, wished me success in all my undertakings.

The master of the house, to whom, as in duty bound, I communicated my intention before I spoke of it to the servants, was, I make no doubt, very sorry, though he did not exactly tell me so. What he said was, that he had never expected that I should remain long there, as such a situation never appeared to him quite suitable to me, though I had been very diligent, and had given him perfect satisfaction. On his inquiring when I intended to depart, I informed him next day, whereupon he begged that I would defer my departure till the next day but one, and do him the favour of dining with him on the morrow. I informed him that I should be only too happy.

On the following day at four o'clock I dined with the landlord, in company with a commercial traveller. The dinner was good, though plain, consisting of boiled mackerel—rather a rarity in those parts at that time— with fennel sauce, a prime baron of roast beef after the mackerel, then a tart and noble Cheshire cheese; we had prime sherry at dinner, and whilst eating the cheese prime porter, that of Barclay, the only good porter in the world. After the cloth was removed we had a bottle of very good port; and whilst partaking of the port I had an argument with the commercial traveller on the subject of the corn-laws.

The commercial traveller, having worsted me in the argument on the subject of the corn-laws, got up in great glee, saying that he must order his gig, as business must be attended to. Before leaving the room, however, he shook me patronizingly by the hand, and said something to the master of the house, but in so low a tone that it escaped my ear.

No sooner had he departed than the master of the house told me that his friend the traveller had just said that I was a confounded sensible young fellow, and not at all opinionated, a sentiment in which he himself perfectly agreed—then hemming once or twice, he said that as I was going on a journey he hoped I was tolerably well provided with money, adding that travelling was rather expensive, especially on horseback, the manner in which he supposed, as I had a horse in the stable, I intended to travel. I told him that though I was not particularly well supplied with money, I had sufficient for the expenses of my journey, at the end of which I hoped to procure more. He then hemmed again, and said that since I had been at the inn I had rendered him a great deal of service in more ways than one, and that he should not think of permitting me to depart without making me some remuneration; then putting his hand into his waistcoat pocket, he handed me a cheque for ten pounds, which he had prepared beforehand, the value of which he said I could receive at the next town, or that, if I wished it, any waiter in the house would cash it for me. I thanked him for his generosity in the best terms I could select, but, handing him back the cheque, I told him that I could not accept it, saying that, so far from his being my debtor, I believed myself to be indebted to him, as not only myself but my horse had been living at his house for several weeks. He replied, that as for my board at a house like his it amounted to nothing, and as for the little corn and hay which the horse had consumed it was of no consequence, and that he must insist upon my taking the cheque. But I again declined, telling him that doing so would be a violation of a rule which I had determined to follow, and which nothing but the greatest necessity would ever compel me to break through—never to incur obligations. " But," said he, " receiving this money will not be incurring an obligation, it is your due." " I do not think so," said I; " I did not engage to serve you for money, nor will I take any from you." " Perhaps you will take it as a loan?" said he. " No," I replied, " I never borrow." " Well," said the landlord, smiling, " you are different from all others that I am acquainted with. I never yet knew any one else who scrupled to borrow and receive obligations; why, there are two baronets in the neighbourhood who have borrowed money of me, ay, and who have never repaid what they borrowed; and there are a dozen squires who are under considerable obligations to me, who I dare say will never return them. Come, you need not be more scrupulous than your superiors—I mean in station." " Every vessel must stand on its own bottom," said I; " they take pleasure in receiving obligations, I take pleasure in being independent. Perhaps they are wise, and I am a fool, I know not, but one thing I am certain of, which is, that were I not independent I should be very unhappy: I should have no visions then." " Have you any relations?" said the landlord, looking at me compassionately; " excuse me, but I don't think you are exactly fit to take care of yourself." " There you are mistaken," said I, " I can take precious good care of myself; ay, and can drive a precious hard bargain when I have occasion, but driving bargains is a widely different thing from receiving gifts. I am going to take my horse to Horncastle, and when there I shall endeavour to obtain his full value—ay to the last penny."

"Horncastle!" said the landlord, "I have heard of that place; you mustn't be dreaming visions when you get there, or they'll steal the horse from under you. Well," said he, rising, "I shall not press you further on the subject of the cheque. I intend, however, to put you under an obligation to me." He then rang the bell, and having ordered two fresh glasses to be brought, he went out and presently returned with a small pint bottle, which he uncorked with his own hand; then sitting down, he said, "The wine that I bring here, is port of eighteen hundred and eleven, the year of the comet, the best vintage on record; the wine which we have been drinking," he added, "is good, but not to be compared with this, which I never sell, and which I am chary of. When you have drunk some of it, I think you will own that I have conferred an obligation upon you;" he then filled the glasses, the wine which he poured out diffusing an aroma through the room; then motioning me to drink, he raised his own glass to his lips, saying, "Come, friend, I drink to your success at Horncastle."

CHAPTER XXX

Triumphal Departure—No Season like Youth—Extreme Old Age—
Beautiful England—The Ratcatcher—A Misadventure.

I DEPARTED from the inn much in the same fashion as I had come to it, mounted on a splendid horse indifferently well caparisoned, with the small valise attached to my crupper, in which, besides the few things I had brought with me, was a small book of roads with a map, which had been presented to me by the landlord. I must not forget to state that I did not ride out of the yard, but that my horse was brought to me at the front door by old Bill, who insisted upon doing so, and who refused a five-shilling piece which I offered him; and it will be as well to let the reader know that the landlord shook me by the hand as I mounted, and that the people attached to the inn, male and female—my friend the postillion at the head —assembled before the house to see me off, and gave me three cheers as I rode away. Perhaps no person ever departed from an inn with more éclat or better wishes; nobody looked at me askance, except two stage-coachmen who were loitering about, one of whom said to his companion, "I say, Jim! twig his portmanteau! a regular Newmarket turn-out, by—— !"

It was in the cool of the evening of a bright day—all the days of that summer were bright—that I departed. I felt at first rather melancholy at finding myself again launched into the wide world, and leaving the friends whom I had lately made behind me; but by occasionally trotting the horse, and occasionally singing a song of Romanvile, I had dispelled the feeling of melancholy by the time I had proceeded three miles down the main road. It was at the end of these three miles, just opposite a milestone, that I struck into a cross road. After riding about seven miles, threading what are called, in postillion parlance, cross-country roads, I reached another high road, tending to the east, along which I proceeded for a mile or two, when coming to a small inn, about nine o'clock, I halted and put up for the night.

Early on the following morning I proceeded on my journey, but fearing to gall the horse, I no longer rode him, but led him by the bridle, until I came to a town at the distance of about ten miles from the place where I had passed the night. Here I stayed during the heat of the day, more on the horse's account than my own, and towards evening resumed my journey, leading the animal by the bridle as before; and in this manner I proceeded for several days, travelling on an average from twenty to twenty-five miles a day, always leading the animal, except perhaps now and then of an evening, when, if I saw a good piece of road before me, I would mount and put the horse into a trot, which the creature seemed to enjoy as much as myself, showing his satisfaction by snorting and neighing, whilst I gave utterance to my own exhilaration by shouts, or by "the chi she is kaulo she soves pré lakie dumo," or by something else of the same kind in Romanvile.

On the whole, I journeyed along very pleasantly, certainly quite as pleasantly as I do at present, now that I am become a gentleman and weigh sixteen stone, though some people would say that my present manner of travelling is much the most preferable, riding as I now do, instead of leading my horse; receiving the homage of ostlers instead of their familiar nods; sitting down to dinner in the parlour of the best inn I can find, instead of passing the brightest part of the day in the kitchen of a village alehouse; carrying on my argument after dinner on the subject of the corn-laws, with the best commercial gentlemen on the road, instead of being glad, whilst sipping a pint of beer, to get into conversation with blind trampers, or maimed Abraham sailors, regaling themselves on half-pints at the said village hostelries. Many people will doubtless say that things have altered wonderfully with me for the better, and they would say right, provided I possessed now what I then carried about with me in my journeys—the spirit of youth. Youth is the only season for enjoyment, and the first twenty-five years of one's life are worth all the rest of the longest life of man, even though those five-and-twenty be spent in penury and contempt, and the rest in the possession of wealth, honours, respectability, ay, and many of them in strength and health, such as will enable one to ride forty miles before dinner, and over one's pint of port—for the best gentleman in the land should not drink a bottle—carry on one's argument, with gravity and decorum, with any commercial gentleman who, responsive to one's challenge, takes the part of humanity and common sense against " protection " and the lord of the land.

Ah! there is nothing like youth—not that after-life is valueless. Even in extreme old age one may get on very well, provided we will but accept of the bounties of God. I met the other day an old man, who asked me to drink. " I am not thirsty," said I, " and will not drink with you." " Yes, you will," said the old man, " for I am this day one hundred years old; and you will never again have an opportunity of drinking the health of a man on his hundredth birthday." So I broke my word, and drank. " Yours is a wonderful age," said I. " It is a long time to look back to the beginning of it," said the old man; " yet, upon the whole, I am not sorry to have lived it all." " How have you passed your time?" said I. " As well as I could," said the old man; " always enjoying a good thing when it came honestly within my reach; not forgetting to praise God for putting it there." "I suppose you were fond of a glass of good ale when you were young?" "Yes," said the old man, "I was; and so, thank God, I am still." And he drank off a glass of ale.

On I went in my journey, traversing England from west to east—ascending and descending hills—crossing rivers by bridge and ferry—and passing over extensive plains. What a beautiful country is England! People run abroad to see beautiful countries, and leave their own behind unknown, unnoticed—their own the most beautiful! And then, again, what a country for adventures! especially to those who travel on foot, or on horseback. People run abroad in quest of adventures, and traverse Spain or Portugal on mule or on horseback; whereas there are ten times more adventures to be met with in England than in Spain, Portugal, or stupid Germany to boot. Witness the number of adventures narrated in the present book—a book entirely devoted to England. Why, there is not a chapter in the present book which is not full of adventures, with the exception of the present one, and this is not yet terminated.

After traversing two or three counties, I reached the confines of Lincolnshire. During one particularly hot day I put up at a public-house, to which, in the evening, came a party of harvesters to make merry, who, finding me wandering about the house a stranger, invited me to partake of their ale; so I drank with the harvesters, who sang me songs about rural life, such as—

" Sitting in the swale; and listening to the swindle of the flail, as it sounds dub-a-dub on the corn, from the neighbouring barn."

In requital for which I treated them with a song, not of Romanvile, but the song of " Sivory and the horse Grayman." I remained with them till it was dark, having, after sunset, entered into deep discourse with a celebrated ratcatcher, who communicated to me the secrets of his trade, saying, amongst other things, " When you see the rats pouring out of their holes, and running up my hands and arms, it's not after me they comes, but after the oils I carries about me they comes;" and who subsequently spoke in the most enthusiastic manner of his trade, saying

that it was the best trade in the world, and most diverting, and that it was likely to last for ever; for whereas
all other kinds of vermin were fast disappearing from
England, rats were every day becoming more abundant.
I had quitted this good company, and having mounted my
horse, was making my way towards a town at about six
miles' distance, at a swinging trot, my thoughts deeply
engaged on what I had gathered from the ratcatcher,
when all on a sudden a light glared upon the horse's face,
who purled round in great terror, and flung me out of
the saddle, as from a sling, or with as much violence as
the horse Grayman, in the ballad, flings Sivord the Snares-
wayne. I fell upon the ground—felt a kind of crashing
about my neck—and forthwith became senseless.

CHAPTER XXXI

A Novel Situation—The Elderly Individual—The Surgeon—A Kind
Offer—Chimerical Ideas—Strange Dream.

How long I remained senseless I cannot say, for a considerable time, I believe; at length, opening my eyes, I
found myself lying on a bed in a middle-sized chamber,
lighted by a candle, which stood on a table—an elderly
man stood near me, and a yet more elderly female was
holding a phial of very pungent salts to my olfactory
organ. I attempted to move, but felt very stiff—my right
arm appeared nearly paralyzed, and there was a strange
dull sensation in my head. " You had better remain still,
young man," said the elderly individual, " the surgeon
will be here presently; I have sent a message for him to
the neighbouring village." " Where am I?" said I,
" and what has happened?" " You are in my house,"
said the old man, " and you have been flung from a horse.
I am sorry to say that I was the cause. As I was driving
home, the lights in my gig frightened the animal."
" Where is the horse?" said I. " Below, in my stable,"
said the elderly individual. " I saw you fall, but knowing
that on account of my age I could be of little use to you,
I instantly hurried home, the accident did not occur more

than a furlong off, and procuring the assistance of my lad, and two or three neighbouring cottagers, I returned to the spot where you were lying senseless. We raised you up, and brought you here. My lad then went in quest of the horse, who had run away as we drew nigh. When we saw him first he was standing near you; he caught him with some difficulty, and brought him home. What are you about?" said the old man, as I strove to get off the bed. "I want to see the horse," said I. "I entreat you to be still," said the old man; "the horse is safe, I assure you." "I am thinking about his knees," said I. "Instead of thinking about your horse's knees," said the old man, "be thankful that you have not broke your own neck." "You do not talk wisely," said I; "when a man's neck is broke, he is provided for; but when his horse's knees are broke, he is a lost jockey, that is, if he has nothing but his horse to depend upon. A pretty figure I should cut at Horncastle, mounted on a horse blood-raw at the knees." "Oh, you are going to Horncastle," said the old man, seriously, "then I can sympathize with you in your anxiety about your horse, being a Lincolnshire man, and the son of one who bred horses. I will myself go down into the stable, and examine into the condition of your horse, so pray remain quiet till I return; it would certainly be a terrible thing to appear at Horncastle on a broken-kneed horse."

He left the room and returned in about ten minutes, followed by another person. "Your horse is safe," said he, "and his knees are unblemished; not a hair ruffled. He is a fine animal, and will do credit to Horncastle; but here is the surgeon come to examine into your own condition." The surgeon was a man about thirty-five, thin, and rather tall; his face was long and pale, and his hair, which was light, was carefully combed back as much as possible from his forehead. He was dressed very neatly, and spoke in a very precise tone. "Allow me to feel your pulse, friend?" said he, taking me by the right wrist. I uttered a cry, for at the motion which he caused a thrill of agony darted through my arm. "I hope your arm is not broke, my friend," said the surgeon, "allow me to see; first of all, we must divest you of this cumbrous frock."

The frock was removed with some difficulty, and then

the upper vestments of my frame, with more difficulty still. The surgeon felt my arm, moving it up and down, causing me unspeakable pain. " There is no fracture," said he, at last, " but a contusion—a violent contusion. I am told you were going to Horncastle; I am afraid you will be hardly able to ride your horse thither in time to dispose of him; however, we shall see—your arm must be bandaged, friend; after which I shall bleed you, and administer a composing draught."

To be short, the surgeon did as he proposed, and when he had administered the composing draught, he said, " Be of good cheer; I should not be surprised if you are yet in time for Horncastle." He then departed with the master of the house, and the woman, leaving me to my repose. I soon began to feel drowsy, and was just composing myself to slumber, lying on my back, as the surgeon had advised me, when I heard steps ascending the stairs, and in a moment more the surgeon entered again, followed by the master of the house. " I hope I don't disturb you," said the former; " my reason for returning is to relieve your mind from any anxiety with respect to your horse. I am by no means sure that you will be able, owing to your accident, to reach Horncastle in time: to quiet you, however, I will buy your horse for any reasonable sum. I have been down to the stable, and approve of his figure. What do you ask for him?" " This is a strange time of night," said I, " to come to me about purchasing my horse, and I am hardly in a fitting situation to be applied to about such a matter. What do you want him for?" " For my own use," said the surgeon; " I am a professional man, and am obliged to be continually driving about; I cover at least one hundred and fifty miles every week." " He will never answer your purpose," said I, " he is not a driving horse, and was never between shafts in his life; he is for riding, more especially for trotting, at which he has few equals." " It matters not to me whether he is for riding or driving," said the surgeon, " sometimes I ride, sometimes drive; so, if we can come to terms, I will buy him, though remember it is chiefly to remove any anxiety from your mind about him." " This is no time for bargaining," said I, " if you wish to have the horse for a hundred guineas, you may; if not——" " A hundred guineas!" said the surgeon, " my good friend, you must surely be light-headed; allow me to feel your pulse," and he attempted to feel my left wrist. " I am not light-headed," said I, " and I require no one to feel my pulse; but I should be light-headed if I were to sell my horse for less than I have demanded; but I have a curiosity to know what you would be willing to offer." " Thirty pounds," said the surgeon, " is all I can afford to give; and that is a great deal for a country surgeon to offer for a horse." " Thirty pounds!" said I, " why, he cost me nearly double that sum. To tell you the truth, I am afraid that you want to take advantage of my situation." " Not in the least, friend," said the surgeon, " not in the least; I only wished to set your mind at rest about your horse; but as you think he is worth more than I can afford to offer, take him to Horncastle by all means; I will do my best to cure you in time. Good night, I will see you again on the morrow." Thereupon he once more departed with the master of the house. " A sharp one," I heard him say, with a laugh, as the door closed upon him.

Left to myself, I again essayed to compose myself to rest, but for some time in vain. I had been terribly shaken by my fall, and had subsequently, owing to the incision of the surgeon's lancet, been deprived of much of the vital fluid; it is when the body is in such a state that the merest trifles affect and agitate the mind; no wonder, then, that the return of the surgeon and the master of the house for the purpose of inquiring whether I would sell my horse, struck me as being highly extraordinary, considering the hour of the night, and the situation in which they knew me to be. What could they mean by such conduct— did they wish to cheat me of the animal? " Well, well," said I, " if they did, what matters, they found their match; yes, yes," said I, " but I am in their power, perhaps "— but I instantly dismissed the apprehension which came into my mind, with a pooh, nonsense! In a little time, however, a far more foolish and chimerical idea began to disturb me—the idea of being flung from my horse; was I not disgraced for ever as a horseman by being flung from my horse? Assuredly, I thought; and the idea of being disgraced as a horseman, operating on my nervous system, caused me very acute misery. " After all," said I to my-self, " it was perhaps the contemptible opinion which the surgeon must have formed of my equestrian powers, which induced him to offer to take my horse off my hands; he perhaps thought I was unable to manage a horse, and therefore in pity returned in the dead of night to offer to purchase the animal which had flung me;" and then the thought that the surgeon had conceived a contemptible opinion of my equestrian powers, caused me the acutest misery, and continued tormenting me until some other idea (I have forgot what it was, but doubtless equally foolish) took possession of my mind. At length, brought on by the agitation of my spirits, there came over me the same feeling of horror that I had experienced of old when I was a boy, and likewise of late within the dingle; it was, however, not so violent as it had been on those occasions, and I struggled manfully against it, until by degrees it passed away, and then I fell asleep; and in my sleep I had an ugly dream. I dreamt that I had died of the injuries I had received from my fall, and that no sooner had my soul departed from my body than it entered that of a quadruped, even my own horse in the stable—in a word, I was, to all intents and purposes, my own steed; and as I stood in the stable chewing hay (and I remember that the hay was exceedingly tough), the door opened, and the surgeon who had attended me came in. "My good animal," said he, "as your late master has scarcely left enough to pay for the expenses of his funeral, and nothing to remunerate me for my trouble, I shall make bold to take possession of you. If your paces are good, I shall keep you for my own riding; if not, I shall take you to Horn-castle, your original destination." He then bridled and saddled me, and, leading me out, mounted, and then trotted me up and down before the house, at the door of which the old man, who now appeared to be dressed in regular jockey fashion, was standing. "I like his paces well," said the surgeon; "I think I shall take him for my own use." "And what am I to have for all the trouble his master caused me?" said my late enter-tainer, on whose countenance I now observed, for the first time, a diabolical squint. "The consciousness of having done your duty to a fellow-creature in succouring him in a time of distress, must be your reward," said the surgeon. "Pretty gammon, truly," said my late enter-tainer; "what would you say if I were to talk in that way to you? Come, unless you choose to behave jonnock, I shall take the bridle and lead the horse back into the stable." "Well," said the surgeon, "we are old friends, and I don't wish to dispute with you, so I'll tell you what I will do; I will ride the animal to Horncastle, and we will share what he fetches like brothers." "Good," said the old man, "but if you say that you have sold him for less than a hundred, I shan't consider you jonnock; remember what the young fellow said—that young fellow——" I heard no more, for the next moment I found myself on a broad road leading, as I supposed, in the direction of Horncastle, the surgeon still in the saddle, and my legs moving at a rapid trot. "Get on," said the surgeon, jerking my mouth with the bit; whereupon, full of rage, I instantly set off at a full gallop, determined, if possible, to dash my rider to the earth. The surgeon, however, kept his seat, and, so far from attempting to abate my speed, urged me on to greater efforts with a stout stick, which methought he held in his hand. In vain did I rear and kick, attempting to get rid of my foe; but the surgeon remained as saddle-fast as ever the Maugrabin sorcerer in the Arabian tale what time he rode the young prince transformed into a steed to his enchanted palace in the wilderness. At last, as I was still madly dashing on, panting and blowing, and had almost given up all hope, I saw at a distance before me a heap of stones by the side of the road, probably placed there for the purpose of repairing it; a thought appeared to strike me—I will shy at those stones, and, if I can't get rid of him so, resign myself to my fate. So I increased my speed, till arriving within about ten yards of the heap, I made a desperate start, turning half round with nearly the velocity of a mill-stone. Oh, the joy I experienced when I felt my enemy canted over my neck, and saw him lying senseless in the road. "I have you now in my power," I said, or rather neighed, as, going up to my prostrate foe, I stood over him. "Suppose I were to rear now, and let my fore feet fall upon you, what would your life be worth? that is, supposing you are not killed already; but lie there, I will do you no further harm, but trot to Horncastle without a rider, and when there——" and without further reflection off I trotted in the direction of Horncastle, but had not gone far before my bridle, falling from my neck, got entangled with my off fore foot.

I felt myself falling, a thrill of agony shot through me—my knees would be broken, and what should I do at Horncastle with a pair of broken knees? I struggled, but I could not disengage my off fore foot, and downward I fell, but before I had reached the ground I awoke, and found myself half out of bed, my bandaged arm in considerable pain, and my left hand just touching the floor.

With some difficulty I readjusted myself in bed. It was now early morning, and the first rays of the sun were beginning to penetrate the white curtains of a window on my left, which probably looked into the garden, as I caught a glimpse or two of the leaves of trees through a small uncovered part at the side. For some time I felt uneasy and anxious, my spirits being in a strange fluttering state. At last my eyes fell upon a small row of teacups, seemingly of china, which stood on a mantelpiece exactly fronting the bottom of the bed. The sight of these objects, I know not why, soothed and pacified me; I kept my eyes fixed upon them, as I lay on my back on the bed, with my head upon the pillow, till at last I fell into a calm and refreshing sleep.

CHAPTER XXXII

The Morning after a Fall—The Teapot—Unpretending Hospitality—
The Chinese Student.

IT might be about eight o'clock in the morning when I was awakened by the entrance of the old man. "How have you rested?" said he, coming up to the bedside, and looking me in the face. "Well," said I, "and I feel much better, but I am still very sore." I surveyed him now for the first time with attention. He was dressed in a sober-coloured suit, and was apparently between sixty and seventy. In stature he was rather above the middle height, but with a slight stoop; his features were placid, and expressive of much benevolence, but, as it appeared to me, with rather a melancholy cast—as I gazed upon them, I felt ashamed that I should ever have conceived in my brain a vision like that of the preceding night, in which he appeared in so disadvantageous a light. At length he said, " It is now time for you to take some refreshment. I hear my old servant coming up with your breakfast." In a moment the elderly female entered with a tray, on which was some bread and butter, a teapot and cup. The cup was of common blue earthenware, but the pot was of china, curiously fashioned, and seemingly of great antiquity. The old man poured me out a cupful of tea, and then, with the assistance of the woman, raised me higher, and propped me up with the pillows. I ate and drank; when the pot was emptied of its liquid (it did not contain much), I raised it up with my left hand to inspect it. The sides were covered with curious characters, seemingly hieroglyphics. After surveying them for some time, I replaced it upon the tray. " You seem fond of china," said I, to the old man, after the servant had retired with the breakfast things, and I had returned to my former posture; " you have china on the mantelpiece, and that was a remarkable teapot out of which I have just been drinking."

The old man fixed his eyes intently on me, and methought the expression of his countenance became yet more melancholy. " Yes," said he, at last, " I am fond of china—I have reason to be fond of china—but for china I should——" and here he sighed again.

" You value it for the quaintness and singularity of its form," said I ; " it appears to be less adapted for real use than our own pottery."

" I care little about its form," said the old man; " I care for it simply on account of——however, why talk to you on the subject which can have no possible interest to you? I expect the surgeon here presently."

" I do not like that surgeon at all," said I ; " how strangely he behaved last night, coming back, when I was just falling asleep, to ask me if I would sell my horse."

The old man smiled. " He has but one failing," said he, " an itch for horse-dealing; but for that he might be a much richer man than he is ; he is continually buying and exchanging horses, and generally finds himself a loser by his bargains : but he is a worthy creature, and skilful in his profession—it is well for you that you are under his care."

The old man then left me, and in about an hour returned

with the surgeon, who examined me and reported favour-
ably as to my case. He spoke to me with kindness and
feeling, and did not introduce the subject of the horse.
I asked him whether he thought I should be in time for
the fair. " I saw some people making their way thither
to-day," said he; " the fair lasts three weeks, and it has
just commenced. Yes, I think I may promise you that
you will be in time for the very heat of it. In a few days
you will be able to mount your saddle with your arm in a
sling, but you must by no means appear with your arm
in a sling at Horncastle, as people would think that your
horse had flung you, and that you wanted to dispose of
him because he was a vicious brute. You must, by all
means, drop the sling before you get to Horncastle."

For three days I kept my apartment by the advice of
the surgeon. I passed my time as I best could. Stretched
on my bed, I either abandoned myself to reflection, or
listened to the voices of the birds in the neighbouring
garden. Sometimes, as I lay awake at night, I would
endeavour to catch the tick of a clock, which methought
sounded from some distant part of the house.

The old man visited me twice or thrice every day to
inquire into my state. His words were few on these
occasions, and he did not stay long. Yet his voice and
his words were kind. What surprised me most in connection with this individual was, the delicacy of conduct
which he exhibited in not letting a word proceed from his
lips which could testify curiosity respecting who I was,
or whence I came. All he knew of me was, that I had
been flung from my horse on my way to a fair for the
purpose of disposing of the animal; and that I was now
his guest. I might be a common horse-dealer for what
he knew, yet I was treated by him with all the attention
which I could have expected, had I been an alderman of
Boston's heir, and known to him as such. The county
in which I am now, thought I at last, must be either
extraordinarily devoted to hospitality, or this old host of
mine must be an extraordinary individual. On the evening of the fourth day, feeling tired of my confinement, I
put my clothes on in the best manner I could, and left the
chamber. Descending a flight of stairs, I reached a kind
of quadrangle, from which branched two or three passages;
one of these I entered, which had a door at the farther

end, and one on each side; the one to the left standing
partly open, I entered it, and found myself in a middle-
sized room with a large window, or rather glass-door,
which looked into a garden, and which stood open. There
was nothing remarkable in this room, except a large
quantity of china. There was china on the mantelpiece
—china on two tables, and a small beaufet, which stood
opposite the glass-door, was covered with china—there
were cups, teapots, and vases of various forms, and on
all of them I observed characters—not a teapot, not a tea-
cup, not a vase of whatever form or size, but appeared
to possess hieroglyphics on some part or other. After
surveying these articles for some time with no little interest, I passed into the garden, in which there were small
parterres of flowers, and two or three trees, and which,
where the house did not abut, was bounded by a wall;
turning to the right by a walk by the side of a house, I
passed by a door—probably the one I had seen at the end
of the passage—and arrived at another window similar to
that through which I had come, and which also stood
open; I was about to pass through it, when I heard the
voice of my entertainer exclaiming, " Is that you? pray
come in."

I entered the room, which seemed to be a counterpart
of the one which I had just left. It was of the same size,
had the same kind of furniture, and appeared to be equally
well stocked with china; one prominent article it possessed, however, which the other room did not exhibit—
namely, a clock, which, with its pendulum moving tick-
a-tick, hung against the wall opposite to the door, the
sight of which made me conclude that the sound which
methought I had heard in the stillness of the night was
not an imaginary one. There it hung on the wall, with
its pendulum moving tick-a-tick. The old gentleman was
seated in an easy chair a little way into the room, having
the glass-door on his right hand. On a table before him
lay a large open volume, in which I observed Roman letters
as well as characters. A few inches beyond the book on
the table, covered all over with hieroglyphics, stood a
china vase. The eyes of the old man were fixed upon it.

" Sit down," said he, motioning me with his hand to
a stool close by, but without taking his eyes from the
vase.

" I can't make it out," said he, at last, removing his eyes from the vase, and leaning back on the chair, " I can't make it out."

" I wish I could assist you," said I.

" Assist me," said the old man, looking at me with a half smile.

" Yes," said I, " but I don't understand Chinese."

" I suppose not," said the old man, with another slight smile; " but—but——"

" Pray proceed," said I.

" I wished to ask you," said the old man, " how you knew that the characters on yon piece of crockery were Chinese; or, indeed, that there was such a language?"

" I knew the crockery was china," said I, " and naturally enough supposed what was written upon it to be Chinese; as for there being such a language—the English have a language, the French have a language, and why not the Chinese?"

" May I ask you a question?"

" As many as you like."

" Do you know any language besides English?"

" Yes," said I, " I know a little of two or three."

" May I ask their names?"

" Why not?" said I, " I know a little French."

" Anything else?"

" Yes, a little Welsh, and a little Haik."

" What is Haik?"

" Armenian."

" I am glad to see you in my house," said the old man, shaking me by the hand; " how singular that one coming as you did should know Armenian!"

" Not more singular," said I, " than that one living in such a place as this should know Chinese. How came you to acquire it?"

The old man looked at me, and sighed. " I beg pardon," said I, " for asking what is, perhaps, an impertinent question; I have not imitated your own delicacy; you have never asked me a question without first desiring permission, and here I have been days and nights in your house an intruder on your hospitality, and you have never so much as asked me who I am."

" In forbearing to do that," said the old man, " I merely obeyed the Chinese precept, ' Ask no questions of a guest;'

it is written on both sides of the teapot out of which you have had your tea."

"I wish I knew Chinese," said I. "Is it a difficult language to acquire?"

"I have reason to think so," said the old man. "I have been occupied upon it five-and-thirty years, and I am still very imperfectly acquainted with it; at least, I frequently find upon my crockery sentences the meaning of which to me is very dark, though it is true these sentences are mostly verses, which are, of course, more difficult to understand than mere prose."

"Are your Chinese studies," said I, "confined to crockery literature?"

"Entirely," said the old man; "I read nothing else."

"I have heard," said I, "that the Chinese have no letters, but that for every word they have a separate character—is it so?"

"For every word they have a particular character," said the old man; "though, to prevent confusion, they have arranged their words under two hundred and fourteen what we should call radicals, but which they call keys. As we arrange all our words in a dictionary under twenty-four letters, so do they arrange all their words, or characters, under two hundred and fourteen radical signs; the simplest radicals being the first, and the more complex the last."

"Does the Chinese resemble any of the European languages in words?" said I.

"I am scarcely competent to inform you," said the old man; "but I believe not."

"What does that character represent?" said I, pointing to one on the vase.

"A knife," said the old man, "that character is one of the simplest radicals or keys."

"And what is the sound of it?" said I.

"Tau," said the old man.

"Tau!" said I; "tau!"

"A strange word for a knife! is it not?" said the old man.

"Tawse!" said I; "tawse!"

"What is tawse?" said the old man.

"You were never at school at Edinburgh, I suppose?"

"Never," said the old man.

"That accounts for your not knowing the meaning of

tawse," said I; "had you received the rudiments of a classical education at the High School, you would have known the meaning of tawse full well. It is a leathern thong, with which refractory urchins are recalled to a sense of their duty by the dominie. Tau—tawse—how singular!"

"I cannot see what the two words have in common, except a slight agreement in sound."

"You will see the connection," said I, "when I inform you that the thong, from the middle to the bottom, is cut or slit into two or three parts, from which slits or cuts, unless I am very much mistaken, it derives its name—tawse, a thong with slits or cuts, used for chastising disorderly urchins at the High School, from the French tailler, to cut; evidently connected with the Chinese tau, a knife—how very extraordinary!"

CHAPTER XXXIII

Convalescence—The Surgeon's Bill—Letter of Recommendation—
Commencement of the Old Man's History.

Two days—three days passed away—and I still remained at the house of my hospitable entertainer; my bruised limb rapidly recovering the power of performing its functions. I passed my time agreeably enough, sometimes in my chamber, communing with my own thoughts; sometimes in the stable, attending to, and not unfrequently conversing with, my horse; and at meal-time—for I seldom saw him at any other—discoursing with the old gentleman, sometimes on the Chinese vocabulary, sometimes on Chinese syntax, and once or twice on English horseflesh; though on this latter subject, notwithstanding his descent from a race of horse-traders, he did not enter into with much alacrity. As a small requital for his kindness, I gave him one day, after dinner, unasked, a brief account of my history and pursuits. He listened with attention; and when it was concluded, thanked me for the confidence which I had reposed in him. "Such conduct," said he, "deserves a return. I will tell you my own history; it is brief, but may perhaps not prove uninteresting to you—

though the relation of it will give me some pain." "Pray, then, do not recite it," said I. "Yes," said the old man, "I will tell you, for I wish you to know it." He was about to begin, when he was interrupted by the arrival of the surgeon. The surgeon examined into the state of my bruised limb, and told me, what indeed I already well knew, that it was rapidly improving. "You will not even require a sling," said he, "to ride to Horncastle. When do you propose going?" he demanded. "When do you think I may venture?" I replied. "I think, if you are a tolerably good horseman, you may mount the day after to-morrow," answered the medical man. "By-the-bye, are you acquainted with anybody at Horncastle?" "With no living soul," I answered. "Then you would scarcely find stable-room for your horse. But I am happy to be able to assist you. I have a friend there who keeps a small inn, and who, during the time of the fair, keeps a stall vacant for any quadruped I may bring, until he knows whether I am coming or not. I will give you a letter to him, and he will see after the accommodation of your horse. To-morrow I will pay you a farewell visit, and bring you the letter." "Thank you," said I; "and do not forget to bring your bill." The surgeon looked at the old man, who gave him a peculiar nod. "Oh!" said he, in reply to me, "for the little service I have rendered you, I require no remuneration. You are in my friend's house, and he and I understand each other." "I never receive such favours," said I, "as you have rendered me, without remunerating them; therefore I shall expect your bill." "Oh! just as you please," said the surgeon; and shaking me by the hand more warmly than he had hitherto done, he took his leave.

On the evening of the next day, the last which I spent with my kind entertainer, I sat at tea with him in a little summer-house in his garden, partially shaded by the boughs of a large fig-tree. The surgeon had shortly before paid me his farewell visit, and had brought me the letter of introduction to his friend at Horncastle, and also his bill, which I found anything but extravagant. After we had each respectively drank the contents of two cups— and it may not be amiss here to inform the reader that though I took cream with my tea, as I always do when I can procure that addition, the old man, like most people bred up in the country, drank his without it—he thus addressed me :—" I am, as I told you on the night of your accident, the son of a breeder of horses, a respectable and honest man. When I was about twenty he died, leaving me, his only child, a comfortable property, consisting of about two hundred acres of land and some fifteen hundred pounds in money. My mother had died about three years previously. I felt the death of my mother keenly, but that of my father less than was my duty; indeed, truth compels me to acknowledge that I scarcely regretted his death. The cause of this want of proper filial feeling was the opposition which I had experienced from him in an affair which deeply concerned me. I had formed an attachment for a young female in the neighbourhood, who, though poor, was of highly respectable birth, her father having been a curate of the Established Church. She was, at the time of which I am speaking, an orphan, having lost both her parents, and supported herself by keeping a small school. My attachment was returned, and we had pledged our vows, but my father, who could not reconcile himself to her lack of fortune, forbade our marriage in the most positive terms. He was wrong, for she was a fortune in herself—amiable and accomplished. Oh! I cannot tell you all she was—" and here the old man drew his hand across his eyes. " By the death of my father, the only obstacle to our happiness appeared to be removed. We agreed, therefore, that our marriage should take place within the course of a year; and I forthwith commenced enlarging my house and getting my affairs in order. Having been left in the easy circumstances which I have described, I determined to follow no business, but to pass my life in a strictly domestic manner, and to be very, very happy. Amongst other property derived from my father were several horses, which I disposed of in this neighbourhood, with the exception of two remarkably fine ones, which I determined to take to the next fair at Horncastle, the only place where I expected to be able to obtain what I considered to be their full value. At length the time arrived for the commencement of the fair, which was within three months of the period which my beloved and myself had fixed upon for the celebration of our nuptials. To the fair I went, a couple of trusty men following me with the horses. I soon found a purchaser for the animals, a portly, plausible person, of about forty, dressed in a blue riding coat, brown top boots, and leather breeches. There was a strange-looking urchin with him, attired in nearly similar fashion, with a beam in one of his eyes, who called him father. The man paid me for the purchase in bank-notes—three fifty-pound notes for the two horses. As we were about to take leave of each other, he suddenly produced another fifty-pound note, in-quiring whether I could change it, complaining, at the same time, of the difficulty of procuring change in the fair. As I happened to have plenty of small money in my possession, and as I felt obliged to him for having pur-chased my horses at what I considered to be a good price, I informed him that I should be very happy to accommo-date him; so I changed him the note, and he, having taken possession of the horses, went his way, and I myself returned home.

" A month passed; during this time I paid away two of the notes which I had received at Horncastle from the dealer—one of them in my immediate neighbourhood, and the other at a town about fifteen miles distant, to which I had repaired for the purpose of purchasing some furni-ture. All things seemed to be going on most prosperously, and I felt quite happy, when one morning, as I was over-looking some workmen who were employed about my house, I was accosted by a constable, who informed me that he was sent to request my immediate appearance before a neighbouring bench of magistrates. Concluding that I was merely summoned on some unimportant busi-ness connected with the neighbourhood, I felt no surprise, and forthwith departed in company with the officer. The demeanour of the man upon the way struck me as some-what singular. I had frequently spoken to him before, and had always found him civil and respectful, but he was now reserved and sullen, and replied to two or three questions which I put to him in anything but a courteous manner. On arriving at the place where the magistrates were sitting—an inn at a small town about two miles distant—I found a more than usual number of people as-sembled, who appeared to be conversing with considerable eagerness. At sight of me they became silent, but crowded after me as I followed the man into the magistrates' room. There I found the tradesman to whom I had paid the note for the furniture at the town fifteen miles off in attendance, accompanied by an agent of the Bank of England; the former, it seems, had paid the note into a provincial bank, the proprietors of which, discovering it to be a forgery, had forthwith written up to the Bank of England, who had sent down their agent to investigate the matter. A third individual stood beside them—the person in my own immediate neighbourhood to whom I had paid the second note; this, by some means or other, before the coming down of the agent, had found its way to the same provincial bank, and also being pronounced a forgery, it had speedily been traced to the person to whom I had paid it. It was owing to the apparition of this second note that the agent had determined, without further inquiry, to cause me to be summoned before the rural tribunal.

"In a few words the magistrates' clerk gave me to understand the state of the case. I was filled with surprise and consternation. I knew myself to be perfectly innocent of any fraudulent intention, but at the time of which I am speaking it was a matter fraught with the greatest danger to be mixed up, however innocently, with the passing of false money. The law with respect to forgery was terribly severe, and the innocent as well as the guilty occasionally suffered. Of this I was not altogether ignorant; unfortunately, however, in my transactions with the stranger, the idea of false notes being offered to me, and my being brought into trouble by means of them, never entered my mind. Recovering myself a little, I stated that the notes in question were two of three notes which I had received at Horncastle, for a pair of horses, which it was well known I had carried thither.

"Thereupon, I produced from my pocket-book the third note, which was forthwith pronounced a forgery. I had scarcely produced the third note, when I remembered the one which I had changed for the Horncastle dealer, and with the remembrance came the almost certain conviction that it was also a forgery; I was tempted for a moment to produce it, and to explain the circumstance—would to God I had done so!—but shame at the idea of having been so wretchedly duped prevented me, and the opportunity was lost. I must confess that the agent of the bank behaved, upon the whole, in a very handsome manner; he said that as it was quite evident that I had disposed of certain horses at the fair, it was very probable that I might have received the notes in question in exchange for them, and that he was willing, as he had received a very excellent account of my general conduct, to press the matter no farther, that is, provided——" And here he stopped. Thereupon, one of the three magistrates, who were present, asked me whether I chanced to have any more of these spurious notes in my possession. He certainly had a right to ask the question; but there was something peculiar in his tone—insinuating suspicion. It is certainly difficult to judge of the motives which rule a person's conduct, but I cannot help imagining that he was somewhat influenced in his behaviour on that occasion, which was anything but friendly, by my having refused to sell him the horses at a price less than that which I expected to get at the fair; be this as it may, the question filled me with embarrassment, and I bitterly repented not having at first been more explicit. Thereupon the magistrate in the same kind of tone, demanded to see my pocket-book. I knew that to demur would be useless, and produced it, and therewith, amongst two or three small country notes, appeared the fourth which I had received from the Horncastle dealer. The agent took it up and examined it with attention. 'Well, is it a genuine note?' asked the magistrate. 'I am sorry to say that it is not,' said the agent; 'it is a forgery, like the other three.' The magistrate shrugged his shoulders, as indeed did several people in the room. 'A regular dealer in forged notes,' said a person close behind me; 'who would have thought it?'

"Seeing matters begin to look so serious, I aroused myself, and endeavoured to speak in my own behalf, giving a candid account of the manner in which I became possessed of the notes; but my explanation did not appear to meet much credit; the magistrate, to whom I have in particular alluded, asked, why I had not at once stated the fact of my having received a fourth note; and the agent, though in a very quiet tone, observed that he could not help thinking it somewhat strange that I should have changed a note of so much value for a perfect stranger, even supposing that he had purchased my horses, and had paid me their value in hard cash; and I noticed that he laid particular emphasis on the last words. I might have observed that I was an inexperienced young man, who, meaning no harm myself, suspected none in others, but I was confused, stunned, and my tongue seemed to cleave to the roof of my mouth. The men who had taken my horses to Horncastle, and for whom I had sent, as they lived close at hand, now arrived, but the evidence which they could give was anything but conclusive in my favour; they had seen me in company with an individual at Horncastle, to whom, by my orders, they had delivered certain horses, but they had seen no part of the money transaction; the fellow, whether from design or not, having taken me aside into a retired place, where he had paid me the three spurious notes, and induced me to change the fourth, which throughout the affair was what bore most materially against me. How matters might have terminated I do not know, I might have gone to prison, and I might have been—— Just then, when I most needed a friend, and least expected to find one, for though amongst those present there were several who were my neighbours, and who had professed friendship for me, none of them when they saw that I needed support and encouragement, came forward to yield me any, but, on the contrary, appeared by their looks to enjoy my terror and confusion—just then a friend entered the room in the person of the surgeon of the neighbourhood, the father of him who has attended you; he was not on very intimate terms with me, but he had occasionally spoken to me, and had attended my father in his dying illness, and chancing to hear that I was in trouble, he now hastened to assist me. After a short preamble, in which he apologized to the bench for interfering, he begged to be informed of the state of the case, whereupon the matter was laid before him in all its details. He was not slow in taking a fair view of it, and spoke well and eloquently in my behalf—insisting on the improbability that a person of my habits and position would be wilfully mixed up with a transaction like that of which it appeared I was suspected—adding, that as he was fully convinced of my innocence, he was ready to enter into any surety with respect to my appearance at any time to answer anything which might be laid to my charge. This last observation had particular effect, and as he was a person universally respected, both for his skill in his profession and his general demeanour, people began to think that a person in whom he took an interest could scarcely be concerned in anything criminal, and though my friend the magistrate—I call him so ironically —made two or three demurs, it was at last agreed between him and his brethren of the bench, that, for the present, I should be merely called upon to enter into my own recognizance for the sum of two hundred pounds, to appear whenever it should be deemed requisite to enter into any further investigation of the matter.

" So I was permitted to depart from the tribunal of petty justice without handcuffs, and uncollared by a constable; but people looked coldly and suspiciously upon me. The first thing I did was to hasten to the house of my beloved, in order to inform her of every circumstance attending the transaction. I found her, but how? A malicious female individual had hurried to her with a distorted tale, to the effect that I had been taken up as an utterer of forged notes; that an immense number had been found in my possession; that I was already committed, and that probably I should be executed. My affianced one tenderly loved me, and her constitution was delicate; fit succeeded fit; she broke a blood-vessel, and I found her deluged in blood; the surgeon had been sent for; he came and afforded her every possible relief. I was distracted; he bade me have hope, but I observed he looked very grave.

" By the skill of the surgeon, the poor girl was saved in the first instance from the arms of death, and for a few weeks she appeared to be rapidly recovering; by degrees, however, she became melancholy; a worm preyed upon her spirit; a slow fever took possession of her frame. I subsequently learned that the same malicious female who had first carried to her an exaggerated account of the affair, and who was a distant relative of her own, frequently visited her, and did all in her power to excite her fears with respect to its eventual termination. Time passed on in a very wretched manner. Our friend the surgeon showing to us both every mark of kindness and attention.

" It was owing to this excellent man that my innocence was eventually established. Having been called to a town on the borders of Yorkshire to a medical consultation, he chanced to be taking a glass of wine with the landlord of the inn at which he stopped, when the waiter brought in a note to be changed, saying ' That the Quaker gentleman, who had been for some days in the house, and was about to depart, had sent it to be changed, in order that he might pay his bill.' The landlord took the note, and looked at it. 'A fifty-pound bill,' said he; 'I don't like changing bills of that amount, lest they should prove bad ones; however, as it comes from a Quaker gentleman, I suppose it is all right.' The mention of a fifty-pound note aroused the attention of my friend, and he requested to be permitted to look at it; he had scarcely seen it, when he was convinced that it was one of the same description as those which had brought me into trouble, as it corresponded with them in two particular features, which the agent of the bank had pointed out to him and others as evidence of their spuriousness. My friend, without a moment's hesitation, informed the landlord that the note was a bad one, expressing at the same time a great wish to see the Quaker gentleman who wanted to have it changed. 'That you can easily do,' said the landlord, and forthwith conducted him into the common room, where he saw a respectable-looking man, dressed like a Quaker, and seemingly about sixty years of age.

"My friend, after a short apology, showed him the note which he held in his hand, stating that he had no doubt it was a spurious one, and begged to be informed where he had taken it, adding, that a particular friend of his was at present in trouble, owing to his having taken similar notes from a stranger at Horncastle; but that he hoped that he, the Quaker, could give information, by means of which the guilty party, or parties, could be arrested. At the mention of Horncastle, it appeared to my friend that the Quaker gave a slight start. At the conclusion of this speech, however, he answered, with great tranquillity, that he had received it in the way of business at ——, naming one of the principal towns in Yorkshire, from a very respectable person, whose name he was perfectly willing to communicate, and likewise his own, which he said was James, and that he was a merchant residing at Liverpool; that he would write to his friend at ——, requesting him to make inquiries on the subject; that just at that moment he was in a hurry to depart, having some particular business at a town about ten miles off, to go to which he had bespoken a post-chaise of the landlord; that with respect to the note, it was doubtless a very disagreeable thing to have a suspicious one in his possession, but that it would make little difference to him, as he had plenty of other money, and thereupon he pulled out a purse, containing various other notes, and some gold, observing, ' that his only motive for wishing to change the other note was a desire to be well provided with change;' and finally, that if they had any suspicion with respect to him, he was perfectly willing to leave the note in their possession till he should return, which he intended to do in about a fortnight. There was so much plausibility in the speech of the Quaker, and his appearance and behaviour were so perfectly respectable, that my friend felt almost ashamed of the suspicion which at first he had entertained of him, though, at the same time, he felt an unaccountable unwillingness to let the man depart without some further interrogation. The landlord, however, who did not wish to disoblige one who had been, and might probably be again, a profitable customer, declared that he was perfectly satisfied; and that he had no wish to detain the note, which he made no doubt the gentleman had received in the way of business, and that as the matter concerned him alone, he would leave it to him to make the necessary inquiries. ' Just as you please, friend,' said the Quaker, pocketing the suspicious note, ' I will now pay my bill.' Thereupon he discharged the bill with a five-pound note, which he begged the landlord to inspect carefully, and with two pieces of gold.

" The landlord had just taken the money, receipted the bill, and was bowing to his customer, when the door opened, and a lad, dressed in a kind of grey livery, appeared, and informed the Quaker that the chaise was ready. ' Is that boy your servant?' said the surgeon. ' He is, friend,' said the Quaker. ' Hast thou any reason for asking me that question?' ' And has he been long in your service?' ' Several years,' replied the Quaker, ' I took him into my house out of compassion, he being an orphan, but as the chaise is waiting, I will bid thee farewell.' ' I am afraid I must stop your journey for the present,' said the surgeon; ' that boy has exactly the same blemish in the eye which a boy had who was in company with the man at Horncastle, from whom my friend received the forged notes, and who there passed for his son.' ' I know nothing about that,' said the Quaker, ' but I am determined to be detained here no longer, after the satisfactory account which I have given as to the note's coming into my possession.' He then attempted to leave the room, but my friend detained him, a struggle ensued, during which a wig which the Quaker wore fell off, whereupon he instantly appeared to lose some twenty years of his age. ' Knock the fellow down, father,' said the boy, ' I'll help you.'

"And, forsooth, the pretended Quaker took the boy's advice, and knocked my friend down in a twinkling. The landlord, however, and waiter, seeing how matters stood, instantly laid hold of him; but there can be no doubt that he would have escaped from the whole three, had not certain guests who were in the house, hearing the noise, rushed in, and helped to secure him. The boy was true to his word, assisting him to the best of his ability, flinging himself between the legs of his father's assailants, causing several of them to stumble and fall. At length, the fellow was secured, and led before a magistrate; the boy, to whom he was heard to say something which nobody understood, and to whom, after the man's capture, no one paid much attention, was no more seen.

"The rest, as far as this man was concerned, may be told in a few words; nothing to criminate him was found on his person, but on his baggage being examined, a quantity of spurious notes were discovered. Much of his hardihood now forsook him, and in the hope of saving his life he made some very important disclosures; amongst other things, he confessed that it was he who had given me the notes in exchange for the horses, and also the note to be changed. He was subsequently tried on two indictments, in the second of which I appeared against him. He was condemned to die; but, in consideration of the disclosures he had made, his sentence was commuted to perpetual transportation.

"My innocence was thus perfectly established before the eyes of the world, and all my friends hastened to congratulate me. There was one who congratulated me more than all the rest——it was my beloved one, but——but——she was dying——"

Here the old man drew his hand before his eyes, and remained for some time without speaking; at length he removed his hand, and commenced again with a broken voice: " You will pardon me if I hurry over this part of my story, I am unable to dwell upon it. How dwell upon a period when I saw my only earthly treasure pine away gradually day by day, and knew that nothing could save her! She saw my agony, and did all she could to console me, saying that she was herself quite resigned. A little time before her death she expressed a wish that we should be united. I was too happy to comply with her request. We were united, I brought her to this house, where, in less than a week, she expired in my arms.''

CHAPTER XXXIV

The Old Man's Story continued—Misery in the Head—The Strange Marks—Tea-dealer from London—Difficulties of the Chinese Language.

AFTER another pause the old man once more resumed his narration :—'' If ever there was a man perfectly miserable it was myself, after the loss of that cherished woman. I sat solitary in the house, in which I had hoped in her company to realize the choicest earthly happiness, a prey to the bitterest reflections ; many people visited, and endeavoured to console me—amongst them was the clergyman of the parish, who begged me to be resigned, and told me that it was good to be afflicted. I bowed my head, but I could not help thinking how easy it must be for those who feel no affliction, to bid others to be resigned, and to talk of the benefit resulting from sorrow ; perhaps I should have paid more attention to his discourse than I did, provided he had been a person for whom it was possible to entertain much respect, but his own heart was known to be set on the things of this world.

'' Within a little time he had an opportunity, in his own case, of practising resignation, and of realizing the benefit of being afflicted. A merchant, to whom he had entrusted all his fortune, in the hope of a large interest, became suddenly a bankrupt, with scarcely any assets. I will not say that it was owing to this misfortune that the divine died in less than a month after its occurrence, but such was the fact. Amongst those who most frequently visited me was my friend the surgeon ; he did not confine himself to the common topics of consolation, but endeavoured to impress upon me the necessity of rousing myself, advising me to occupy my mind with some pursuit, particularly recommending agriculture; but agriculture possessed no interest for me, nor, indeed, any pursuit within my reach; my hopes of happiness had been blighted, and what cared I for anything? so at last he thought it best to leave me to myself, hoping that time would bring with it consolation; and I remained solitary in my house, waited upon by a male and a female servant. Oh, what dreary moments I passed! My only amusement—and it was a sad one—was to look at the things which once belonged to my beloved, and which were now in my possession. Oh, how fondly would I dwell upon them! There were some books; I cared not for books, but these had belonged to my beloved. Oh, how fondly did I dwell on them! Then there was her hat and bonnet—oh, me, how fondly did I gaze upon them! and after looking at her things for hours, I would sit and ruminate on the happiness I had lost. How I execrated the moment I had gone to the fair to sell horses! 'Would that I had never been to Horncastle to sell horses!' I would say; 'I might at this moment have been enjoying the company of my beloved, leading a happy, quiet, easy life, but for that fatal expedition;' that thought worked on my brain, till my brain seemed to turn round.

"One day I sat at the breakfast-table gazing vacantly around me, my mind was in a state of inexpressible misery; there was a whirl in my brain, probably like that which people feel who are rapidly going mad; this increased to such a degree that I felt giddiness coming upon me. To abate this feeling I no longer permitted my eyes to wander about, but fixed them upon an object on the table, and continued gazing at it for several minutes without knowing what it was; at length, the misery in my head was somewhat stilled, my lips moved, and I heard myself saying. 'What odd marks!' I had fastened my eyes on the side of a teapot, and by keeping them fixed upon it, had become aware of a fact that had escaped my notice before—namely, that there were marks upon it. I kept my eyes fixed upon them, and repeated at intervals, 'What strange marks!'— for I thought that looking upon the marks tended to abate the whirl in my head: I kept tracing the marks one after the other, and I observed that though they all bore a general resemblance to each other, they were all to a certain extent different. The smallest portion possible of curious interest had been awakened within me, and, at last, I asked myself, within my own mind, 'What motive could induce people to put such odd marks on their crockery? they were not pictures, they were not letters; what motive could people have for putting them there?' At last I removed my eyes from the teapot, and thought for a few moments about the marks; presently, however, I felt the whirl returning; the marks became almost effaced from my mind, and I was beginning to revert to my miserable ruminations, when suddenly methought I heard a voice say, 'The marks! the marks! cling to the marks? or——' So I fixed my eyes again upon the marks, inspecting them more attentively, if possible, than I had done before, and, at last, I came to the conclusion that they were not capricious or fanciful marks, but were arranged systematically; when I had gazed at them for a considerable time, I turned the teapot round, and on the other side I observed marks of a similar kind, which I soon discovered were identical with the ones I had been observing. All the marks were something alike, but all somewhat different, and on comparing them with each other, I was struck with the frequent occurrence of a mark crossing an upright line, or projecting from it, now on the right, now on the left side; and I said to myself, 'Why does this mark sometimes cross the upright line, and sometimes project?' and the more I thought on the matter, the less did I feel of the misery in my head.

"The things were at length removed, and I sat, as I had for some time past been wont to sit after my meals, silent and motionless; but in the present instance my mind was not entirely abandoned to the one mournful idea which had so long distressed it. It was, to a certain extent, occupied with the marks on the teapot; it is true that the mournful idea strove hard with the marks on the teapot for the mastery in my mind, and at last the painful idea drove the marks of the teapot out; they, however, would occasionally return and flit across my mind for a moment or two, and their coming was like a momentary relief from intense pain. I thought once or twice that I would have the teapot placed before me, that I might examine the marks at leisure, but I considered that it would be as well to defer the re-examination of the marks till the next morning; at that time I did not take tea of an evening. By deferring the examination thus, I had something to look forward to on the next morning. The day was a melancholy one, but it certainly was more tolerable to me than any of the others had been since the death of my beloved. As I lay awake that night I occasionally thought of the marks, and in my sleep methought I saw them upon the teapot vividly before me. On the morrow, I examined the marks again; how singular they looked! Surely they must mean something, and if so, what could they mean? and at last I thought within myself whether it would be possible for me to make out what they meant: that day I felt more relief than on the preceding one, and towards night I walked a little about.

"In about a week's time I received a visit from my friend the surgeon; after a little discourse, he told me that he perceived I was better than when he had last seen me, and asked me what I had been about; I told him that I had been principally occupied in considering certain marks which I had found on a teapot, and wondering what they could mean; he smiled at first, but instantly assuming a serious look, he asked to see the teapot. I produced it, and after having surveyed the marks with attention, he observed that they were highly curious, and also wondered what they meant. 'I strongly advise you,' said he, 'to attempt to make them out, and also to take moderate exercise, and to see after your concerns.' I followed his advice; every morning I studied the marks on the teapot, and in the course of the day took moderate exercise, and attended to little domestic matters, as became the master of a house.

"I subsequently learned that the surgeon, in advising me to study the marks, and endeavour to make out their meaning, merely hoped that by means of them my mind might by degrees be diverted from the mournful idea on which I had so long brooded. He was a man well skilled in his profession, but had read and thought very little on matters unconnected with it. He had no idea that the marks had any particular signification, or were anything else but common and fortuitous ones. That I became at all acquainted with their nature was owing to a ludicrous circumstance which I will now relate.

"One day, chancing to be at a neighbouring town, I

was struck with the appearance of a shop recently established. It had an immense bow-window, and every part of it, to which a brush could be applied, was painted in a gaudy flaming style. Large bowls of green and black tea were placed upon certain chests, which stood at the window. I stopped to look at them, such a display, whatever it may be at the present time, being, at the period of which I am speaking, quite uncommon in a country town. The tea, whether black or green, was very shining and inviting, and the bowls, of which there were three, standing on as many chests, were very grand and foreign looking. Two of these were white, with figures and trees painted upon them in blue; the other, which was the middlemost, had neither trees nor figures upon it, but, as I looked through the window, appeared to have on its sides the very same kind of marks which I had observed on the teapot at home; there were also marks on the tea-chests, somewhat similar, but much larger, and, apparently, not executed with so much care. ' Best teas direct from China,' said a voice close to my side; and looking round I saw a youngish man, with a frizzled head, flat face, and an immensely wide mouth, standing in his shirt-sleeves by the door. ' Direct from China,' said he; ' perhaps you will do me the favour to walk in and scent them?' ' I do not want any tea,' said I; ' I was only standing at the window examining those marks on the bowl and the chests. I have observed similar ones on a teapot at home.' ' Pray walk in, sir,' said the young fellow, extending his mouth till it reached nearly from ear to ear; ' pray walk in, and I shall be happy to give you any information respecting the manners and customs of the Chinese in my power.' Thereupon I followed him into his shop, where he began to harangue on the manners, customs, and peculiarities of the Chinese, especially their manner of preparing tea, not forgetting to tell me that the only genuine Chinese tea ever imported into England was to be found in his shop. ' With respect to those marks,' said he, ' on the bowl and chests, they are nothing more nor less than Chinese writing expressing something, though what I can't exactly tell you. Allow me to sell you this pound of tea,' he added, showing me a paper parcel. ' On the envelope there is a printed account of the Chinese system of writing, extracted from authors of the most established reputation. These things

I print, principally with the hope of, in some degree, removing the worse than Gothic ignorance prevalent amongst natives of these parts. I am from London myself. With respect to all that relates to the Chinese real imperial tea, I assure you sir, that——' Well, to make short of what you doubtless consider a very tiresome story, I purchased the tea and carried it home. The tea proved imperially bad, but the paper envelope really contained some information on the Chinese language and writing, amounting to about as much as you gained from me the other day. On learning that the marks on the teapot expressed words, I felt my interest with respect to them considerably increased, and returned to the task of inspecting them with greater zeal than before, hoping, by continually looking at them, to be able eventually to understand their meaning, in which hope you may easily believe I was disappointed, though my desire to understand what they represented continued on the increase. In this dilemma I determined to apply again to the shopkeeper from whom I bought the tea. I found him in rather low spirits, his shirt-sleeves were soiled, and his hair was out of curl. On my inquiring how he got on, he informed me that he intended speedily to leave, having received little or no encouragement, the people, in their Gothic ignorance, preferring to deal with an old-fashioned shopkeeper over the way, who, so far from possessing any acquaintance with the polity and institutions of the Chinese, did not, he believed, know that tea came from China. 'You are come for some more, I suppose?' said he. On receiving an answer in the negative he looked somewhat blank, but when I added that I came to consult with him as to the means which I must take in order to acquire the Chinese language he brightened up. 'You must get a grammar,' said he, rubbing his hands. 'Have you not one?' said I. 'No,' he replied, 'but any bookseller can procure you one.' As I was taking my departure, he told me that as he was about to leave the neighbourhood, the bowl at the window, which bore the inscription, besides some other pieces of porcelain of a similar description, were at my service, provided I chose to purchase them. I consented, and two or three days afterwards took from off his hands all the china in his possession which bore the inscriptions, paying what he demanded. Had I waited till the sale of his effects, which occurred within a few weeks, I could probably have procured it for a fifth part of the sum which I paid, the other pieces realizing very little. I did not, however, grudge the poor fellow what he got from me, as I considered myself to be somewhat in his debt for the information he had afforded me.

"As for the rest of my story, it may be briefly told. I followed the advice of the shopkeeper, and applied to a bookseller who wrote to his correspondent in London. After a long interval, I was informed that if I wished to learn Chinese, I must do so through the medium of French, there being neither Chinese grammar nor dictionary in our language. I was at first very much disheartened. I determined, however, at last to gratify my desire of learning Chinese, even at the expense of learning French. I procured the books, and in order to qualify myself to turn them to account, took lessons in French from a little Swiss, the usher of a neighbouring boarding-school. I was very stupid in acquiring French; perseverance, however, enabled me to acquire a knowledge sufficient for the object I had in view. In about two years I began to study Chinese by myself, through the medium of the French."

"Well," said I, "and how did you get on with the study of the Chinese?"

And then the old man proceeded to inform me how he got on with the study of Chinese, enumerated all the difficulties he had had to encounter; dilating upon his frequent despondency of mind, and occasionally his utter despair of ever mastering Chinese. He told me that more than once he had determined upon giving up the study, but when the misery in his head forthwith returned, to escape from which he had as often resumed it. It appeared, however, that ten years elapsed before he was able to use ten of the two hundred and fourteen keys, which serve to undo the locks of Chinese writing.

"And are you able at present to use the entire number?" I demanded.

"Yes," said the old man; "I can at present use the whole number. I know the key for every particular lock, though I frequently find the wards unwilling to give way."

"Has nothing particular occurred to you," said I, "during the time that you have been prosecuting your studies?"

"During the whole time in which I have been engaged in these studies," said the old man, "only one circumstance has occurred which requires any particular mention—the death of my old friend the surgeon—who was carried off suddenly by a fit of apoplexy. His death was a great shock to me, and for a time interrupted my studies. His son, however, who succeeded him, was very kind to me, and, in some degree, supplied his father's place; and I gradually returned to my Chinese locks and keys."

"And in applying keys to the Chinese locks you employ your time?"

"Yes," said the old man, "in making out the inscriptions on the various pieces of porcelain, which I have at different times procured, I pass my time. The first inscription which I translated was that on the teapot of my beloved."

"And how many other pieces of porcelain may you have at present in your possession?"

"About fifteen hundred."

"And how did you obtain them?" I demanded.

"Without much labour," said the old man, "in the neighbouring towns and villages—chiefly at auctions—of which, about twenty years ago, there were many in these parts."

"And may I ask your reasons for confining your studies entirely to the crockery literature of China, when you have all the rest at your disposal?"

"The inscriptions enable me to pass my time," said the old man; "what more would the whole literature of China do?"

"And from these inscriptions," said I, "what a book it is in your power to make, whenever so disposed. 'Translations from the crockery literature of China.' Such a book would be sure to take; even glorious John himself would not disdain to publish it." The old man smiled. "I have no desire for literary distinction," said he; "no ambition. My original wish was to pass my life in easy, quiet obscurity, with her whom I loved. I was disappointed in my wish; she was removed, who constituted my only felicity in this life; desolation came to my heart, and misery to my head. To escape from the latter I had recourse to Chinese. By degrees the misery left my head, but the desolation of the heart yet remains."

"Be of good cheer," said I; "through the instrumentality of this affliction you have learnt Chinese, and, in so doing, learnt to practise the duties of hospitality. Who but a man who could read Runes on a teapot, would have received an unfortunate wayfarer as you have received me?"

"Well," said the old man, "let us hope that all is for the best. I am by nature indolent, and, but for this affliction, should, perhaps, have hardly taken the trouble to do my duty to my fellow-creatures. I am very, very indolent," said he, slightly glancing towards the clock; "therefore let us hope that all is for the best; but, oh! these trials, they are very hard to bear."

CHAPTER XXXV

The Leave-taking—Spirit of the Hearth—What's o'Clock?

THE next morning, having breakfasted with my old friend, I went into the stable to make the necessary preparations for my departure; there, with the assistance of a stable lad, I cleaned and caparisoned my horse, and then, returning into the house, I made the old female attendant such a present as I deemed would be some compensation for the trouble I had caused. Hearing that the old gentleman was in his study, I repaired to him. "I am come to take leave of you," said I, "and to thank you for all the hospitality which I have received at your hands." The eyes of the old man were fixed steadfastly on the inscription which I had found him studying on a former occasion. "At length," he murmured to himself, "I have it —I think I have it;" and then, looking at me, he said, "So you are about to depart?"

"Yes," said I, "my horse will be at the front door in a few minutes; I am glad, however, before I go, to find that you have mastered the inscription."

"Yes," said the old man, "I believe I have mastered it; it seems to consist of some verses relating to the worship of the Spirit of the Hearth."

"What is the Spirit of the Hearth?" said I.

"One of the many demons which the Chinese worship,"

said the old man; "they do not worship one God, but many." And then the old man told me a great many highly-interesting particulars respecting the demon worship of the Chinese.

After the lapse of at least half an hour I said, "I must not linger here any longer, however willing. Horncastle is distant, and I wish to be there to-night. Pray can you inform me what's o'clock?"

The old man, rising, looked towards the clock which hung on the side of the room at his left hand, on the farther side of the table at which he was seated.

"I am rather short-sighted," said I, "and cannot distinguish the number, at that distance."

"It is ten o'clock," said the old man; "I believe somewhat past."

"A quarter, perhaps?"

"Yes," said the old man, "a quarter or——"

"Or?"

"Seven minutes, or ten minutes past ten."

"I do not understand you."

"Why, to tell you the truth," said the old man, with a smile, "there is one thing to the knowledge of which I could never exactly attain."

"Do you mean to say," said I, "that you do not know what's o'clock?"

"I can give a guess," said the old man, "to within a few minutes."

"But you cannot tell the exact moment?"

"No," said the old man.

"In the name of wonder," said I, "with that thing there on the wall continually ticking in your ear, how comes it that you do not know what's o'clock?"

"Why," said the old man, "I have contented myself with giving a tolerably good guess; to do more would have been too great trouble."

"But you have learnt Chinese," said I.

"Yes," said the old man, "I have learnt Chinese."

"Well," said I, "I really would counsel you to learn to know what's o'clock as soon as possible. Consider what a sad thing it would be to go out of the world not knowing what's o'clock. A millionth part of the trouble required to learn Chinese would, if employed, infallibly teach you to know what's o'clock."

"I had a motive for learning Chinese," said the old man, "the hope of appeasing the misery in my head. With respect to not knowing what's o'clock, I cannot see anything particularly sad in the matter. A man may get through the world very creditably without knowing what's o'clock. Yet, upon the whole, it is no bad thing to know what's o'clock—you, of course, do? It would be too good a joke if two people were to be together, one knowing Armenian and the other Chinese, and neither knowing what's o'clock. I'll now see you off."

CHAPTER XXXVI

Arrival at Horncastle—The Inn and Ostlers—The Garret—Figure of a Man with a Candle.

LEAVING the house of the old man who knew Chinese, but could not tell what was o'clock, I wended my way to Horncastle, which I reached in the evening of the same day, without having met any adventure on the way worthy of being marked down in this very remarkable history.

The town was a small one, seemingly ancient, and was crowded with people and horses. I proceeded, without delay, to the inn to which my friend the surgeon had directed me. "It is of no use coming here," said two or three ostlers, as I entered the yard—"all full—no room whatever;" whilst one added in an under tone, "That ere a'n't a bad-looking horse." "I want to see the master of this inn," said I, as I dismounted from the horse. "See the master," said an ostler—the same who had paid the negative kind of compliment to the horse—"a likely thing, truly; my master is drinking wine with some of the grand gentry, and can't be disturbed for the sake of the like of you." "I bring a letter to him," said I, pulling out the surgeon's epistle. "I wish you would deliver it to him," I added, offering a half-crown. "Oh, it's you, is it?" said the ostler, taking the letter and the half-crown; "my master will be right glad to see you; why, you ha'n't been here for many a year; I'll carry the note to him at once." And with these words he hurried into the house. "That's a nice horse, young man," said another ostler, "what will

you take for it?" to which interrogation I made no answer.
"If you wish to sell him," said the ostler, coming up to
me, and winking knowingly, "I think I and my partners
might offer you a summut under seventy pounds;" to
which kind and half-insinuated offer I made no reply, save
by winking in the same kind of knowing manner in which
I observed him wink. "Rather leary!" said a third
ostler. "Well, young man, perhaps you will drink to-
night with me and my partners, when we can talk the
matter over." Before I had time to answer, the landlord,
a well-dressed, good-looking man, made his appearance
with the ostler; he bore the letter in his hand. Without
glancing at me, he betook himself at once to consider the
horse, going round him, and observing every point with
the utmost minuteness. At last, having gone round the
horse three times, he stopped beside me, and keeping his
eyes on the horse, bent his head towards his right shoulder.
"That horse is worth some money," said he, turning towards me suddenly, and slightly touching me on the arm
with the letter which he held in his hand; to which observation I made no reply, save by bending my head towards
the right shoulder as I had seen him do. "The young
man is going to talk to me and my partners about it to-
night," said the ostler who had expressed an opinion that
he and his friends might offer me somewhat under seventy
pounds for the animal. "Pooh!" said the landlord, "the
young man knows what he is about; in the meantime lead
the horse to the reserved stall, and see well after him.
My friend," said he, taking me aside after the ostler
had led the animal away, "recommends you to me in the
strongest manner, on which account alone I take you and
your horse in. I need not advise you not to be taken in,
as I should say, by your look, that you are tolerably awake;
but there are queer hands at Horncastle at this time, and
those fellows of mine, you understand me——; but I have
a great deal to do at present, so you must excuse me."
And thereupon went into the house.

That same evening I was engaged at least two hours in
the stable, in rubbing the horse down, and preparing him
for the exhibition which I intended he should make in the
fair on the following day. The ostler, to whom I had
given the half-crown, occasionally assisted me, though he
was too much occupied by the horses of other guests to

devote any length of time to the service of mine; he more than once repeated to me his firm conviction that himself and partners could afford to offer me summut for the horse; and at a later hour when, in compliance with his invitation, I took a glass of summut with himself and partners, in a little room surrounded with corn-chests, on which we sat, both himself and partners endeavoured to impress upon me, chiefly by means of nods and winks, their conviction that they could afford to give me summut for the horse, provided I were disposed to sell him; in return for which intimation, with as many nods and winks as they had all collectively used, I endeavoured to impress upon them my conviction that I could get summut hand-somer in the fair than they might be disposed to offer me, seeing as how—which how I followed by a wink and a nod, which they seemed perfectly to understand, one or two of them declaring that if the case was so, it made a great deal of difference, and that they did not wish to be any hindrance to me, more particularly as it was quite clear I had been an ostler like themselves.

It was late at night when I began to think of retiring to rest. On inquiring if there was any place in which I could sleep, I was informed that there was a bed at my service, provided I chose to sleep in a two-bedded room, one of the beds of which was engaged by another gentleman. I expressed my satisfaction at this arrangement, and was conducted by a maid-servant up many pairs of stairs to a garret, in which were two small beds, in one of which she gave me to understand another gentleman slept; he had, however, not yet retired to rest; I asked who he was, but the maid-servant could give me no information about him, save that he was a highly respectable gentleman, and a friend of her master's. Presently, bidding me good night, she left me with a candle; and I, having undressed myself and extinguished the light, went to bed. Notwithstanding the noises which sounded from every part of the house, I was not slow in falling asleep, being thoroughly tired. I know not how long I might have been in bed, perhaps two hours, when I was partially awakened by a light shining upon my face, whereupon, unclosing my eyes, I perceived the figure of a man, with a candle in one hand, staring at my face, whilst with the other hand, he held back the curtain of the bed. As I have said before, I was only par-

tially awakened, my power of conception was consequently
very confused; it appeared to me, however, that the man
was dressed in a green coat; that he had curly brown or
black hair, and that there was something peculiar in his
look. Just as I was beginning to recollect myself, the
curtain dropped, and I heard, or thought I heard, a voice
say, "Don't know the cove." Then there was a rustling
like a person undressing, whereupon being satisfied that
it was my fellow-lodger, I dropped asleep, but was awakened again by a kind of heavy plunge upon the other bed,
which caused it to rock and creak, when I observed that
the light had been extinguished, probably blown out, if I
might judge from a rather disagreeable smell of burnt wick
which remained in the room, and which kept me awake
till I heard my companion breathing hard, when, turning
on the other side, I was again once more speedily in the
arms of slumber.

CHAPTER XXXVII

Horncastle Fair.

It had been my intention to be up and doing early on the
following morning, but my slumbers proved so profound,
that I did not wake until about eight; on arising, I again
found myself the sole occupant of the apartment, my more
alert companion having probably risen at a much earlier
hour. Having dressed myself, I descended, and going
to the stable, found my horse under the hands of my friend
the ostler, who was carefully rubbing him down. "There
a'n't a better horse in the fair," said he to me, "and as
you are one of us, and appear to be all right, I'll give you
a piece of advice—don't take less than a hundred and fifty
for him; if you mind your hits, you may get it, for I have
known two hundred given in this fair for one no better, if
so good." "Well," said I, "thank you for your advice,
which I will take, and, if successful, will give you ' summut ' handsome." "Thank you," said the ostler; "and
now let me ask whether you are up to all the ways of this
here place?" "I have never been here before," said I,
"but I have a pair of tolerably sharp eyes in my head."

" That I see you have," said the ostler, " but many a body, with as sharp a pair of eyes as yourn, has lost his horse in this fair, for want of having been here before, therefore," said he, " I'll give you a caution or two." Thereupon the ostler proceeded to give me at least half a dozen cautions, only two of which I shall relate to the reader :—the first, not to stop to listen to what any chance customer might have to say; and the last—the one on which he appeared to lay most stress—by no manner of means to permit a Yorkshire-man to get up into the saddle, " for," said he, " if you do, it is three to one that he rides off with the horse; he can't help it; trust a cat amongst cream, but never trust a York-shireman on the saddle of a good horse; by-the-by," he continued, " that saddle of yours is not a particularly good one, no more is the bridle. I tell you what, as you seem a decent kind of a young chap, I'll lend you a saddle and bridle of my master's, almost bran new; he won't object, I know, as you are a friend of his, only you must not forget your promise to come down with summut handsome after you have sold the animal."

After a slight breakfast I mounted the horse, which, decked out in his borrowed finery, really looked better by a large sum of money than on any former occasion. Making my way out of the yard of the inn, I was instantly in the principal street of the town, up and down which an immense number of horses were being exhibited, some led, and others with riders. " A wonderful small quantity of good horses in the fair this time !" I heard a stout jockey-looking individual say, who was staring up the street with his side towards me. " Halloo, young fellow !" said he, a few moments after I had passed, " whose horse is that? Stop ! I want to look at him !" Though confident that he was addressing himself to me, I took no notice, remembering the advice of the ostler, and proceeded up the street. My horse possessed a good walking step; but walking, as the reader knows, was not his best pace, which was the long trot, at which I could not well exercise him in the street, on account of the crowd of men and animals; however, as he walked along, I could easily perceive that he attracted no slight attention amongst those who, by their jockey dress and general appearance, I imagined to be connoisseurs; I heard various calls to stop, to none of which I paid the slightest attention. In a few minutes I found myself out of the town, when, turning round for the purpose of returning, I found I had been followed by several of the connoisseur-looking individuals, whom I had observed in the fair. " Now would be the time for a display," thought I; and looking around me I observed two five-barred gates, one on each side of the road, and fronting each other. Turning my horse's head to one, I pressed my heels to his sides, loosened the reins, and gave an encouraging cry, whereupon the animal cleared the gate in a twinkling. Before he had advanced ten yards in the field to which the gate opened, I had turned him round, and again giving him cry and rein, I caused him to leap back again into the road, and still allowing him head, I made him leap the other gate; and forthwith turning him round, I caused him to leap once more into the road, where he stood proudly tossing his head, as much as to say, " What more?" " A fine horse! a capital horse!" said several of the connoisseurs. " What do you ask for him?" " Too much for any of you to pay," said I. " A horse like this is intended for other kind of customers than any of you." " How do you know that?" said one; the very same person whom I had heard complaining in the street of the paucity of good horses in the fair. " Come, let us know what you ask for him?" " A hundred and fifty pounds!" said I; " neither more nor less." " Do you call that a great price?" said the man. " Why, I thought you would have asked double that amount! You do yourself injustice, young man." " Perhaps I do," said I, " but that's my affair; I do not choose to take more." " I wish you would let me get into the saddle," said the man; " the horse knows you, and therefore shows to more advantage; but I should like to see how he would move under me, who am a stranger. Will you let me get into the saddle, young man?" " No," said I; " I will not let you get into the saddle." " Why not?" said the man. " Lest you should be a Yorkshireman," said I; " and should run away with the horse." " Yorkshire?" said the man; " I am from Suffolk; silly Suffolk—so you need not be afraid of my running away with the horse." " Oh! if that's the case," said I, " I should be afraid that the horse would run away with you; so I will by no means let you mount." " Will you let me look in his mouth?" said the man. " If you please," said I; " but I tell you, he's apt to bite." "He can scarcely be a worse bite than his master," said the man, looking into the horse's mouth; "he's four off. I say, young man, will you warrant this horse?" "No," said I; "I never warrant horses; the horses that I ride can always warrant themselves." "I wish you would let me speak a word to you," said he. "Just come aside. It's a nice horse," said he, in a half whisper, after I had ridden a few paces aside with him. "It's a nice horse," said he, placing his hand upon the pommel of the saddle, and looking up in my face, "and I think I can find you a customer. If you would take a hundred, I think my lord would purchase it, for he has sent me about the fair to look him up a horse, by which he could hope to make an honest penny." "Well," said I, "and could he not make an honest penny, and yet give me the price I ask?" "Why," said the go-between, "a hundred and fifty pounds is as much as the animal is worth, or nearly so; and my lord, do you see——" "I see no reason at all," said I, "why I should sell the animal for less than he is worth, in order that his lordship may be benefited by him; so that if his lordship wants to make an honest penny, he must find some person who would consider the disadvantage of selling him a horse for less than it is worth, as counterbalanced by the honour of dealing with a lord, which I should never do; but I can't be wasting my time here. I am going back to the ——, where, if you, or any person, are desirous of purchasing the horse, you must come within the next half hour, or I shall probably not feel disposed to sell him at all." "Another word, young man," said the jockey; but without staying to hear what he had to say, I put the horse to his best trot, and re-entering the town, and threading my way as well as I could through the press, I returned to the yard of the inn, where, dismounting, I stood still, holding the horse by the bridle.

I had been standing in this manner about five minutes, when I saw the jockey enter the yard, accompanied by another individual. They advanced directly towards me. "Here is my lord come to look at the horse, young man," said the jockey. My lord, as the jockey called him, was a tall figure, of about five-and-thirty. He had on his head a hat somewhat rusty, and on his back a surtout of blue rather the worse for wear. His forehead, if not high,

was exceedingly narrow; his eyes were brown, with a rat-
like glare in them; the nose was rather long, and the
mouth very wide; the cheek-bones high, and the cheeks,
as to hue and consistency, exhibiting very much the appearance of a withered red apple; there was a gaunt expression of hunger in the whole countenance.   He had scarcely
glanced at the horse, when drawing in his cheeks, he thrust
out his lips very much after the manner of a baboon, when
he sees a piece of sugar held out towards him.   "Is this
horse yours?" said he, suddenly turning towards me, with
a kind of smirk.   "It's my horse," said I; "are you the
person who wishes to make an honest penny by it?"
"How!" said he, drawing up his head with a very con-
sequential look, and speaking with a very haughty tone,
"what do you mean?"   We looked at each other full in
the face; after a few moments, the muscles of the mouth
of him of the hungry look began to move violently, the
face was puckered into innumerable wrinkles, and the eyes
became half closed.   "Well," said I, "have you ever seen
me before?   I suppose you are asking yourself that question."   "Excuse me, sir," said he, dropping his lofty
look, and speaking in a very subdued and civil tone, "I
have never had the honour of seeing you before, that is "
—said he, slightly glancing at me again, and again moving
the muscles of his mouth, "no, I have never seen you
before," he added, making me a bow.   "I have never had
that pleasure; my business with you, at present, is to inquire the lowest price you are willing to take for this
horse.   My agent here informs me that you ask one hundred and fifty pounds, which I cannot think of giving—
the horse is a showy horse, but look, my dear sir, he has a
defect here, and there in his near fore leg I observe something which looks very like a splint—yes, upon my credit,"
said he, touching the animal, "he has a splint, or something which will end in one.   A hundred and fifty pounds,
sir! what could have induced you ever to ask anything like
that for this animal?   I protest that, in my time, I have
frequently bought a better for —— Who are you, sir?   I
am in treaty for this horse," said he to a man who had
come up whilst he was talking, and was now looking into
the horse's mouth.   "Who am I?" said the man, still
looking into the horse's mouth; "who am I? his lordship asks me.   Ah, I see, close on five," said he, releasing

the horse's jaws, and looking at me. This new comer was a thin, wiry-made individual, with wiry curling brown hair; his face was dark, and wore an arch and somewhat roguish expression; upon one of his eyes was a kind of speck or beam; he might be about forty, wore a green jockey coat, and held in his hand a black riding whip, with a knob of silver wire. As I gazed upon his countenance, it brought powerfully to my mind the face which, by the light of the candle, I had seen staring over me on the preceding night, when lying in bed and half asleep. Close beside him, and seemingly in his company, stood an exceedingly tall figure, that of a youth, seemingly about one-and-twenty, dressed in a handsome riding dress, and wearing on his head a singular hat, green in colour, and with a very high peak. "What do you ask for this horse?" said he of the green coat, winking at me with the eye which had a beam in it, whilst the other shone and sparkled like Mrs. Colonel W——'s Golconda diamond. "Who are you, sir, I demand once more?" said he of the hungry look. "Who am I? why, who should I be put Jack Dale, who buys horses for himself and other folk; I want one at present for this short young gentleman," said he, motioning with his finger to the gigantic youth. "Well, sir," said the other, "and what business have you to interfere between me and any purchase I may be disposed to make?" "Well, then," said the other, "be quick and purchase the horse, or, perhaps, I may." "Do you think I am to be dictated to by a fellow of your description?" said his lordship, "begone, or——" "What do you ask for this horse?" said the other to me, very coolly. "A hundred and fifty," said I. "I shouldn't mind giving it to you," said he. "You will do no such thing," said his lordship, speaking so fast that he almost stuttered. "Sir," said he to me, "I must give you what you ask; Symmonds, take possession of the animal for me," said he to the other jockey who attended him. "You will please to do no such thing without my consent," said I, "I have not sold him." "I have this moment told you that I will give you the price you demand," said his lordship; "is not that sufficient?" "No," said I, "there is a proper manner of doing everything—had you come forward in a manly and gentlemanly manner to purchase the horse, I should have been happy to sell him to you, but after all the fault you have found with him, I would not sell him to you at any price, so send your friend to find up another." "You behave in this manner, I suppose," said his lordship, "because this fellow has expressed a willingness to come to your terms. I would advise you to be cautious how you trust the animal in his hands; I think I have seen him before, and could tell you——" "What can you tell of me?" said the other, going up to him; "except that I have been a poor dicky-boy, and that now I am a dealer in horses, and that my father was lagged; that's all you could tell of me, and that I don't mind telling myself : but there are two things they can't say of me, they can't say that I am either a coward or a screw either, except so far as one who gets his bread by horses may be expected to be; and they can't say of me that I ever ate up an ice which a young woman was waiting for, or that I ever backed out of a fight. Horse!" said he, motioning with his finger tauntingly to the other; "what do you want with a horse, except to take the bread out of the mouth of a poor man—to-morrow is not the battle of Waterloo, so that you don't want to back out of danger, by pretending to have hurt yourself by falling from the creature's back, my lord of the white feather—come, none of your fierce looks—I am not afraid of you." In fact, the other had assumed an expression of the deadliest malice, his teeth were clenched, his lips quivered, and were quite pale; the rat-like eyes sparkled, and he made a half spring, à la rat, towards his adversary, who only laughed. Restraining himself, however, he suddenly turned to his understrapper, saying, "Symmonds, will you see me thus insulted? go and trounce this scoundrel; you can, I know." "Symmonds trounce me!" said the other, going up to the person addressed, and drawing his hand contemptuously over his face; "why, I beat Symmonds in this very yard in one round three years ago; didn't I, Symmonds?" said he to the understrapper, who held down his head, muttering, in a surly tone, "I didn't come here to fight; let every one take his own part." "That's right, Symmonds," said the other, "especially every one from whom there is nothing to be got. I would give you half-a-crown for all the trouble you have had, provided I were not afraid that my Lord Plume there would get it from you as soon as you leave the yard together. Come, take yourselves both off; there's nothing to be made here." Indeed, his lordship seemed to be of the same opinion, for after a further glance at the horse, a contemptuous look at me, and a scowl at the jockey, he turned on his heel, muttering something which sounded like fellows, and stalked out of the yard, followed by Symmonds.

"And now, young man," said the jockey, or whatever he was, turning to me with an arch leer, "I suppose I may consider myself as the purchaser of this here animal, for the use and behoof of this young gentleman?" making a sign with his head to the tall young man by his side. "By no means," said I, "I am utterly unacquainted with either of you, and before parting with the horse I must be satisfied as to the respectability of the purchaser." "Oh! as to that matter," said he, "I have plenty of vouchers for my respectability about me;" and thrusting his hand into his bosom below his waistcoat, he drew out a large bundle of notes. "These are the kind of things," said he, "which vouch best for a man's respectability." "Not always," said I; "indeed, sometimes these kind of things need vouchers for themselves." The man looked at me with a peculiar look. "Do you mean to say that these notes are not sufficient notes?" said he, "because if you do I shall take the liberty of thinking you are not over civil, and when I thinks a person is not over and above civil I sometimes takes off my coat; and when my coat is off——" "You sometimes knock people down," I added; "well, whether you knock me down or not, I beg leave to tell you that I am a stranger in this fair, and that I shall part with the horse to nobody who has no better guarantee for his respectability than a roll of bank-notes, which may be good or not for what I know, who am not a judge of such things." "Oh! if you are a stranger here," said the man, "as I believe you are, never having seen you here before except last night, when I think I saw you above stairs by the glimmer of a candle—I say, if you are a stranger, you are quite right to be cautious; queer things being done in this fair, as nobody knows better than myself," he added with a leer; "but I suppose if the landlord of the house vouches for me and my notes, you will have no objection to part with the horse to me?" "None whatever," said I, "and in the meantime the horse can return to the stable."

Thereupon I delivered the horse to my friend the ostler.

The landlord of the house on being questioned by me as to the character and condition of my new acquaintance, informed me that he was a respectable horsedealer, and an intimate friend of his, whereupon the purchase was soon brought to a satisfactory conclusion.

CHAPTER XXXVIII

High Dutch.

IT was evening: and myself and the two acquaintances I had made in the fair—namely, the jockey and the tall foreigner—sat in a large upstairs room, which looked into a court; we had dined with several people connected with the fair at a long *table d'hôte;* they had now departed, and we sat at a small side-table with wine and a candle before us; both my companions had pipes in their mouths —the jockey a common pipe, and the foreigner, one, the syphon of which, made of some kind of wood, was at least six feet long, and the bowl of which, made of a white kind of substance like porcelain, and capable of holding nearly an ounce of tobacco, rested on the ground. The jockey frequently emptied and replenished his glass; the foreigner sometimes raised his to his lips, for no other purpose seemingly than to moisten them, as he never drained his glass. As for myself, though I did not smoke, I had a glass before me, from which I sometimes took a sip. The room, notwithstanding the window was flung open, was in general so filled with smoke, chiefly that which was drawn from the huge bowl of the foreigner, that my companions and I were frequently concealed from each other's eyes. The conversation, which related entirely to the events of the fair, was carried on by the jockey and myself, the foreigner, who appeared to understand the greater part of what we said, occasionally putting in a few observations in broken English. At length the jockey, after the other had made some ineffectual attempts to express something intelligibly which he wished to say, observed, "Isn't it a pity that so fine a fellow as meinheer, and so clever a fellow too, as I believe him to be, is not a better master of our language?"

" Is the gentleman a German?" said I; " if so, I can interpret for him anything he wishes to say."

" The deuce you can," said the jockey, taking his pipe out of his mouth, and staring at me through the smoke.

" Ha! you speak German," vociferated the foreigner in that language. " By Isten, I am glad of it! I wanted to say——" And here he said in German what he wished to say, and which was of no great importance, and which I translated into English.

" Well, if you don't put me out," said the jockey; " what language is that—Dutch?"

" High Dutch," said I.

" High Dutch, and you speak High Dutch,—why, I had booked you for as great an ignoramus as myself, who can't write—no, nor distinguish in a book a great A from a bull's foot."

" A person may be a very clever man," said I—" no, not a clever man, for clever signifies clerkly, and a clever man one who is able to read and write, and entitled to the benefit of his clergy or clerkship; but a person may be a very acute person without being able to read or write. I never saw a more acute countenance than your own."

" No soft soap," said the jockey, " for I never uses any. However, thank you for your information; I have hitherto thought myself a'nition clever fellow, but from henceforth shall consider myself just the contrary, and only—what's the word?—confounded 'cute."

" Just so," said I.

" Well," said the jockey, " as you say you can speak High Dutch, I should like to hear you and master six foot six fire away at each other."

" I cannot speak German," said I, " but I can understand tolerably well what others say in it."

" Come no backing out," said the jockey, " let's hear you fire away for the glory of Old England."

" Then you are a German?" said I, in German to the foreigner.

" That will do," said the jockey, " keep it up."

" A German!" said the tall foreigner. " No, I thank God that I do not belong to the stupid sluggish Germanic race, but to a braver, taller, and handsomer people;" here taking the pipe out of his mouth, he stood up proudly erect, so that his head nearly touched the ceiling of the room, then reseating himself, and again putting the syphon to his lips, he added, " I am a Magyar."

" What is that?" said I.

The foreigner looked at me for a moment, somewhat contemptuously, through the smoke, then said, in a voice of thunder, "A Hungarian!"

" What a voice the chap has when he pleases!" interposed the jockey; " what is he saying?"

" Merely that he is a Hungarian," said I; but I added, " the conversation of this gentleman and myself in a language which you can't understand must be very tedious to you, we had better give it up."

" Keep on with it," said the jockey, " I shall go on listening very contentedly till I fall asleep, no bad thing to do at most times."

CHAPTER XXXIX

The Hungarian.

" THEN you are a countryman of Tekeli, and of the queen who made the celebrated water," said I, speaking to the Hungarian in German, which I was able to do tolerably well, owing to my having translated the Publisher's philosophy into that language, always provided I did not attempt to say much at a time.

Hungarian. Ah! you have heard of Tekeli, and of L'eau de la Reine d'Hongrie. How is that?

Myself. I have seen a play acted, founded on the exploits of Tekeli, and have read Pigault Le Brun's beautiful romance, entitled the " Barons of Felsheim," in which he is mentioned. As for the water, I have heard a lady, the wife of a master of mine, speak of it.

Hungarian. Was she handsome?

Myself. Very.

Hungarian. Did she possess the water?

Myself. I should say not; for I have heard her express a great curiosity about it.

Hungarian. Was she growing old?

Myself. Of course not; but why do you put all these questions?

Hungarian. Because the water is said to make people handsome, and above all, to restore to the aged the beauty of their youth. Well! Tekeli was my countryman, and I have the honour of having some of the blood of the Tekelis in my veins, but with respect to the queen, pardon me if I tell you that she was not an Hungarian; she was a Pole —Ersebet by name, daughter of Wladislaus Locticus King of Poland; she was the fourth spouse of Caroly the Second, King of the Magyar country, who married her in 1320. She was a great woman and celebrated politician, though at present chiefly known by her water.

Myself. How came she to invent it?

Hungarian. If her own account may be believed, she did not invent it. After her death, as I have read in Florentius of Buda, there was found a statement of the manner in which she came by it, written in her own hand, on a fly-leaf of her breviary, to the following effect :—Being afflicted with a grievous disorder at the age of seventy-two, she received the medicine which was called her water, from an old hermit whom she never saw before or afterwards ; it not only cured her, but restored to her all her former beauty, so that the King of Poland fell in love with her, and made her an offer of marriage, which she refused for the glory of God, from whose holy angel she believed she had received the water. The receipt for making it and directions for using it, were also found on the fly-leaf. The principal component parts were burnt wine and rose-mary, passed through an alembic; a drachm of it was to be taken once a week, " etelbenn vagy italbann," in the food or the drink, early in the morning, and the cheeks were to be moistened with it every day. The effects according to the statement, were wonderful—and perhaps they were upon the queen; but whether the water has been equally efficacious on other people, is a point which I cannot determine. I should wish to see some old woman who has been restored to youthful beauty by the use of L'eau de la Reine d'Hongrie.

Myself. Perhaps, if you did, the old gentlewoman would hardly be so ingenuous as the queen. But who are the Hungarians—descendants of Attila and his people?

The Hungarian shook his head, and gave me to understand that he did not believe that his nation were the descendants of Attila and his people, though he acknowledged that they were probably of the same race. Attila and his armies, he said, came and disappeared in a very mysterious manner, and that nothing could be said with positiveness about them; that the people now known as Magyars first made their appearance in Muscovy in the year 884, under the leadership of Almus, called so from Alom, which, in the Hungarian language, signifies a dream; his mother, before his birth, having dreamt that the child with which she was enceinte would be the father of a long succession of kings, which, in fact, was the case; that after beating the Russians he entered Hungary, and coming to a place called Ungvar, from which many people believed that modern Hungary derived its name, he captured it, and held in it a grand festival, which lasted four days, at the end of which time he resigned the leadership of the Magyars to his son Arpad. This Arpad and his Magyars utterly subdued Pannonia—that is, Hungary and Transylvania, wresting the government of it from the Sclavonian tribes who inhabited it, and settling down amongst them as conquerors! After giving me this information, the Hungarian exclaimed with much animation, —"A goodly country that which they had entered on, consisting of a plain surrounded by mountains, some of which intersect it here and there, with noble rapid rivers, the grandest of which is the mighty Dunau; a country with tiny volcanoes, casting up puffs of smoke and steam, and from which hot springs arise, good for the sick; with many fountains, some of which are so pleasant to the taste as to be preferred to wine; with a generous soil which, warmed by a beautiful sun, is able to produce corn, grapes, and even the Indian weed; in fact, one of the finest countries in the world, which even a Spaniard would pronounce to be nearly equal to Spain. Here they rested— meditating, however, fresh conquests. Oh, the Magyars soon showed themselves a mighty people. Besides Hungary and Transylvania, they subdued Bulgaria and Bosnia, and the land of Tot, now called Sclavonia. The generals of Zoltan, the son of Arpad, led troops of horsemen to the banks of the Rhine. One of them, at the head of a host, besieged Constantinople. It was then that Botond engaged in combat with a Greek of gigantic stature, who came out of the city and challenged the two best men in the Magyar army. 'I am the feeblest of the Magyars,' said Botond, ' but I will kill thee;' and he performed his word, having previously given a proof of the feebleness of his arm by striking his battle-axe through the brazen gate, making a hole so big that a child of five years old could walk through it.''

Myself. Of what religion were the old Hungarians?

Hungarian. They had some idea of a Supreme Being, whom they called Isten, which word is still used by the Magyars for God; but their chief devotion was directed to sorcerers and soothsayers, something like the Schamans of the Siberian steppes. They were converted to Christianity chiefly through the instrumentality of Istvan or Stephen, called after his death St. Istvan, who ascended the throne in the year one thousand. He was born in heathenesse, and his original name was Vojk : he was the first kiraly, or king of the Magyars. Their former leaders had been called fejedelmek, or dukes. The Magyar language has properly no term either for king or house. Kiraly is a word derived from the Sclaves; haz, or house, from the Germans, who first taught them to build houses, their original dwellings having been tilted waggons.

Myself. Many thanks for your account of the great men of your country.

Hungarian. The great men of my country! I have only told you of the—— Well, I acknowledge that Almus and Arpad were great men, but Hungary has produced many greater; I will not trouble you by recapitulating all, but there is one name I cannot forbear mentioning—but you have heard of it—even at Horncastle, the name of Hunyadi must be familiar.

Myself. It may be so, though I rather doubt it; but, however that may be, I confess my ignorance. I have never, until this moment, heard the name of Hunyadi.

Hungarian. Not of Hunyadi Janos, not of Hunyadi John—for the genius of our language compels us to put a man's Christian name after his other; perhaps you have heard of the name of Corvinus?

Myself. Yes, I have heard the name of Corvinus.

Hungarian. By my God, I am glad of it; I thought our hammer of destruction, our thunderbolt, whom the Greeks called Achilles, must be known to the people of Horncastle. Well, Hunyadi and Corvinus are the same.

Myself. Corvinus means the man of the crow, or raven.

I suppose that your John, when a boy, climbed up to a crow or a raven's nest, and stole the young; a bold feat, well befitting a young hero.

Hungarian. By Isten, you are an acute guesser; a robbery there was, but it was not Hunyadi who robbed the raven, but the raven who robbed Hunyadi.

Myself. How was that?

Hungarian. In this manner: Hunyadi, according to tradition, was the son of King Sigmond, by a peasant's daughter. The king saw and fell in love with her, whilst marching against the vaivode of Wallachia. He had some difficulty in persuading her to consent to his wishes, and she only yielded at last, on the king making her a solemn promise that, in the event of her becoming with child by him, he would handsomely provide for her and the infant. The king proceeded on his expedition; and on his returning in triumph from Wallachia, again saw the girl, who informed him that she was enceinte by him; the king was delighted with the intelligence, gave the girl money, and at the same time a ring, requesting her, if she brought forth a son, to bring the ring to Buda with the child, and present it to him. When her time was up, the peasant's daughter brought forth a fair son, who was baptized by the name of John. After some time the young woman communicated the whole affair to her elder brother, whose name was Gaspar, and begged him to convey her and the child to the king at Buda. The brother consented, and both set out, taking the child with them. On their way, the woman, wanting to wash her clothes, laid the child down, giving it the king's ring to play with. A raven, who saw the glittering ring, came flying, and plucking it out of the child's hand, carried it up into a tree; the child suddenly began to cry, and the mother, hearing it, left her washing, and running to the child, forthwith missed the ring, but hearing the raven croak in the tree, she lifted up her eyes, and saw it with the ring in its beak. The woman, in great terror, called her brother, and told him what had happened, adding that she durst not approach the king if the raven took away the ring. Gaspar, seizing his cross-bow and quiver, ran to the tree, where the raven was yet with the ring, and discharged an arrow at it, but, being in a great hurry, he missed it; with his second shot he was more lucky, for he hit the raven in the breast, which, together with the ring, fell to the ground. Taking up the ring, they went on their way, and shortly arrived at Buda. One day, as the king was walking after dinner in his outer hall, the woman appeared before him with the child, and, showing him the ring, said, " Mighty lord! behold this token! and take pity upon me and your own son." King Sigmond took the child and kissed it, and, after a pause, said to the mother, " You have done right in bringing me the boy; I will take care of you, and make him a nobleman." The king was as good as his word, he provided for the mother; caused the boy to be instructed in knightly exercises, and made him a present of the town of Hunyad, in Transylvania, on which account he was afterwards called Hunyadi, and gave him, as an armorial sign, a raven bearing a ring in his beak.

Such, oh young man of Horncastle! is the popular account of the birth of the great captain of Hungary, as related by Florentius of Buda. There are other accounts of his birth, which is, indeed, involved in much mystery, and of the reason of his being called Corvinus, but as this is the most pleasing, and is, upon the whole, founded on quite as good evidence as the others, I have selected it for recitation.

Myself. I heartily thank you; but you must tell me something more of Hunyadi. You call him your great captain; what did he do?

Hungarian. Do! what no other man of his day could have done. He broke the power of the Turk when he was coming to overwhelm Europe. From the blows inflicted by Hunyadi, the Turk never thoroughly recovered; he has been frequently worsted in latter times, but none but Hunyadi could have routed the armies of Amurath and Mahomed the Second.

Myself. How was it that he had an opportunity of displaying his military genius?

Hungarian. I can hardly tell you, but his valour soon made him famous; King Albert made him Ban of Szorenyi. He became eventually waivode of Transylvania, and governor of Hungary. His first grand action was the defeat of Bashaw Isack; and though himself surprised and routed at St. Imre, he speedily regained his prestige by defeating the Turks, with enormous slaughter, killing their leader, Mezerbeg; and subsequently, at the battle of the

Iron Gates, he destroyed ninety thousand Turks, sent by Amurath to avenge the late disgrace. It was then that the Greeks called him Achilles.

Myself. He was not always successful.

Hungarian. Who could be always successful against the early Turk? He was defeated in the battle in which King Vladislaus lost his life, but his victories outnumbered his defeats three-fold. His grandest victory—perhaps the grandest ever achieved by man—was over the terrible Mahomed the Second; who, after the taking of Constantinople in 1453, said, "One God in Heaven—one king on earth;" and marched to besiege Belgrade at the head of one hundred and fifty thousand men; swearing by the beard of the prophet, "That he would sup within it ere two months were elapsed." He brought with him dogs, to eat the bodies of the Christians whom he should take or slay; so says Florentius; hear what he also says : The Turk sat down before the town towards the end of June, 1454, covering the Dunau and Szava with ships : and on the 4th of July he began to cannonade Belgrade with cannons twenty-five feet long, whose roar could be heard at Szeged, a distance of twenty-four leagues, at which place Hunyadi had assembled his forces. Hunyadi had been able to raise only fifteen thousand of well-armed and disciplined men, though he had with him vast bands of people, who called themselves Soldiers of the Cross, but who consisted of inexperienced lads from school, peasants, and hermits, armed with swords, slings, and clubs. Hunyadi, undismayed by the great disparity between his forces and those of the Turk, advanced to relieve Belgrade, and encamped at Szalankemen with his army. There he saw at once, that his first step must be to attack the flotilla ; he therefore privately informed Szilagy, his wife's brother, who at that time defended Belgrade, that it was his intention to attack the ships of the Turks on the 14th day of July in front, and requested his co-operation in the rear. On the 14th came on the commencement of the great battle of Belgrade, between Hunyadi and the Turk. Many days it lasted.

Myself. Describe it.

Hungarian. I cannot. One has described it well—Florentius of Buda. I can only repeat a few of his words : —" On the appointed day, Hunyadi, with two hundred vessels, attacked the Turkish flotilla in front, whilst Szilagy, with forty vessels, filled with the men of Belgrade, assailed it in the rear; striving for the same object, they sunk many of the Turkish vessels, captured seventy-four, burnt many, and utterly annihilated the whole fleet. After this victory, Hunyadi, with his army, entered Belgrade, to the great joy of the Magyars. But though the force of Mahomed upon the water was destroyed, that upon the land remained entire; and with this, during six days and nights, he attacked the city without intermission, destroying its walls in many parts. His last and most desperate assault was made on the 21st day of July. Twice did the Turks gain possession of the outer town, and twice was it retaken with indescribable slaughter. The next day the combat raged without ceasing till mid-day, when the Turks were again beaten out of the town, and pursued by the Magyars to their camp. There the combat was renewed, both sides displaying the greatest obstinacy, until Mahomed received a great wound over his left eye. The Turks then, turning their faces, fled, leaving behind them three hundred cannon in the hands of the Christians, and more than twenty-four thousand slain on the field of battle."

Myself. After that battle, I suppose Hunyadi enjoyed his triumphs in peace?

Hungarian. In the deepest, for he shortly died. His great soul quitted his body, which was exhausted by almost superhuman exertions, on the 11th of August, 1456. Shortly before he died, according to Florentius, a comet appeared, sent, as it would seem, to announce his coming end. The whole Christian world mourned his loss. The Pope ordered the cardinals to perform a funeral ceremony at Rome in his honour. His great enemy himself grieved for him, and pronounced his finest eulogium. When Mahomed the Second heard of his death, he struck his head for some time against the ground without speaking. Suddenly he broke silence with these words, " Notwithstanding he was my enemy, yet do I bewail his loss; since the sun has shone in heaven, no Prince had ever yet such a man."

Myself. What was the name of his Prince?

Hungarian. Laszlo the Fifth; who, though under infinite obligations to Hunyadi, was anything but grateful to him; for he once consented to a plan which was laid to assassinate him, contrived by his mortal enemy Ulrik, Count of Cilejia; and after Hunyadi's death, caused his eldest son, Hunyadi Laszlo, to be executed on a false accusation, and imprisoned his younger son, Matyas, who, on the death of Laszlo, was elected by the Magyars to be their king, on the 24th of January, 1458.

Myself. Was this Matyas a good king?

Hungarian. Was Matyas Corvinus a good king? O young man of Horncastle! he was the best and greatest that ever Hungary possessed, and, after his father, the most renowned warrior,—some of our best laws were framed by him. It was he who organized the Hussar force, and it was he who took Vienna. Why does your Government always send fools to represent it at Vienna?

Myself. I really cannot say; but with respect to the Hussar force, is it of Hungarian origin?

Hungarian. Its name shows its origin. Huz, in Hungarian, is twenty and the Hussar force is so called because it is formed of twentieths. A law was issued by which it was ordered that every Hungarian nobleman, out of every twenty dependents, should produce a well-equipped horseman, and with him proceed to the field of battle.

Myself. Why did Matyas capture Venna?

Hungarian. Because the Emperor Frederick took part against him with the King of Poland, who claimed the kingdom of Hungary for his son, and had also assisted the Turk. He captured it in the year 1487, but did not survive his triumph long, expiring there in the year 1490. He was so veracious a man, that it was said of him, after his death. "Truth died with Matyas." It might be added that the glory of Hungary departed with him. I wish to say nothing more connected with Hungarian history.

Myself. Another word. Did Matyas leave a son?

Hungarian. A natural son, Hunyadi John, called so after the great man. He would have been universally acknowledged as King of Hungary but for the illegitimacy of his birth. As it was, Ulaszlo, the son of the King of Poland, afterwards called Ulaszlo the Second, who claimed Hungary as being descended from Albert, was nominated king by a great majority of the Magyar electors. Hunyadi John for some time disputed the throne with him; there was some bloodshed, but Hunyadi John eventually submitted, and became the faithful captain of Ulaszlo, notwithstanding that the Turk offered to assist him with an army of two hundred thousand men.

Myself. Go on.

Hungarian. To what? Tché Drak, to the Mohacs Veszedelem. Ulaszlo left a son, Lajos the Second, born without skin, as it is said, certainly without a head. He, contrary to the advice of all his wise counsellors,—and amongst them was Batory Stephen, who became eventually King of Poland—engaged, with twenty-five thousand men, at Mohacs, Soliman the Turk, who had an army of two hundred thousand. Drak! the Magyars were annihilated, King Lajos disappeared with his heavy horse and armour in a bog. We call that battle, which was fought on the 29th of August, 1526, the destruction of Mohacs, but it was the destruction of Hungary.

Myself. You have twice used the word drak, what is the meaning of it? Is it Hungarian?

Hungarian. No! it belongs to the mad Wallacks. They are a nation of madmen on the other side of Transylvania. Their country was formerly a fief of Hungary, like Moldavia, which is inhabited by the same race, who speak the same language and are equally mad.

Myself. What language do they speak?

Hungarian. A strange mixture of Latin and Sclavonian —they themselves being a mixed race of Romans and Sclavonians. Trajan sent certain legions to form military colonies in Dacia; and the present Wallacks and Moldavians are, to a certain extent, the descendants of the Roman soldiers, who married the women of the country. I say to a certain extent, for the Sclavonian element both in blood and language seems to prevail.

Myself. And what is drak?

Hungarian. Dragon; which the Wallacks use for "devil." The term is curious, as it shows that the old Romans looked upon the dragon as an infernal being.

Myself. You have been in Wallachia?

Hungarian. I have, and glad I was to get out of it. I hate the mad Wallacks.

Myself. Why do you call them mad?

Hungarian. They are always drinking or talking. I never saw a Wallachian eating or silent. They talk like madmen, and drink like madmen. In drinking they use

small phials, the contents of which they pour down their
throats. When I first went amongst them I thought the
whole nation was under a course of physic, but the terrible
jabber of their tongues soon undeceived me. Drak was
the first word I heard on entering Dacia, and the last when
I left it. The Moldaves, if possible, drink more, and talk
more than the Wallachians.

Myself. It is singular enough that the only Moldavian
I have known could not speak. I suppose he was born
dumb.

Hungarian. A Moldavian born dumb! Excuse me,
the thing is impossible,—all Moldavians are born talking!
I have known a Moldavian who could not speak, but he
was not born dumb. His master, an Armenian, snipped
off part of his tongue at Adrianople. He drove him mad
with his jabber. He is now in London, where his master
has a house. I have letters of credit on the house: the
clerk paid me money in London, the master was absent;
the money which you received for the horse belonged to
that house.

Myself. Another word with respect to Hungarian
history.

Hungarian. Drak! I wish to say nothing more about
Hungarian history.

Myself. The Turk, I suppose, after Mohacs, got poses-
sion of Hungary?

Hungarian. Not exactly. The Turk, upon the whole,
showed great moderation; not so the Austrian. Ferdinand the First claimed the crown of Hungary as being the
cousin of Maria, widow of Lajos; he found too many
disposed to support him. His claim, however, was resisted
by Zapolya John, a Hungarian magnate, who caused himself to be elected king. Hungary was for a long time
devastated by wars between the partisans of Zapolya and
Ferdinand. At last Zapolya called in the Turk. Soliman
behaved generously to him, and after his death befriended
his young son, and Isabella his queen; eventually the
Turks became masters of Transylvania and the greater part
of Hungary. They were not bad masters, and had many
friends in Hungary, especially amongst those of the reformed faith, to which I have myself the honour of belonging; those of the reformed faith found the Mufti more
tolerant than the Pope. Many Hungarians went with the

Turks to the siege of Vienna, whilst Tekeli and his horse-men guarded Hungary for them. A gallant enterprise that siege of Vienna, the last great effort of the Turk; it failed, and he speedily lost Hungary, but he did not sneak from Hungary like a frightened hound. His defence of Buda will not be soon forgotten, where Apty Basha, the gover-nor, died fighting like a lion in the breach. There's many a Hungarian would prefer Stamboul to Vienna. Why does your Government always send fools to represent it at Vienna?

Myself. I have already told you that I cannot say. What became of Tekeli?

Hungarian. When Hungary was lost he retired with the Turks into Turkey. Count Renoncourt, in his Memoirs, mentions having seen him at Adrianople. The Sultan, in consideration of the services which he had rendered to the Moslem in Hungary, made over the revenues of certain towns and districts for his subsistence. The count says that he always went armed to the teeth, and was always attended by a young female dressed in male attire, who had followed him in his wars, and had more than once saved his life. His end is wrapped in mystery, I—whose greatest boast, next to being a Hun-garian, is to be of his blood—know nothing of his end.

Myself. Allow me to ask who you are?

Hungarian. Egy szegeny Magyar Nemes ember, a poor Hungarian nobleman, son of one yet poorer. I was born in Transylvania, not far to the west of good Coloscvar. I served some time in the Austrian army as a noble Hussar, but am now equerry to a great nobleman, to whom I am distantly related. In his service I have travelled far and wide, buying horses. I have been in Russia and in Turkey, and am now at Horncastle, where I have had the satisfac-tion to meet with you, and to buy your horse, which is, in truth, a noble brute.

Myself. For a soldier and equerry you seem to know a great deal of the history of your country.

Hungarian. All I know is derived from Florentius of Buda, whom we call Budai Ferentz. He was professor of Greek and Latin at the Reformed College of Debreczen, where I was educated; he wrote a work entitled "Magyar Polgari Lexicon," Lives of Great Hungarian Citizens. He was dead before I was born, but I found his book, when

I was a child, in the solitary home of my father, which stood on the confines of a puszta, or wilderness, and that book I used to devour in winter nights when the winds were whistling around the house. Oh! how my blood used to glow at the descriptions of Magyar valour, and likewise of Turkish; for Florentius has always done justice to the Turk. Many a passage similar to this have I got by heart; it is connected with a battle on the plain of Rigo, which Hunyadi lost:—" The next day, which was Friday, as the two armies were drawn up in battle array, a Magyar hero riding forth, galloped up and down, challenging the Turks to single combat. Then came out to meet him the son of a renowned bashaw of Asia; rushing upon each other, both broke their lances, but the Magyar hero and his horse rolled over upon the ground, for the Turks had always the best horses." O young man of Horncastle! if ever you learn Hungarian—and learn it assuredly you will after what I have told you—read the book of Florentius of Buda, even if you go to Hungary to get it, for you will scarcely find it elsewhere, and even there with difficulty, for the book has been long out of print. It describes the actions of the great men of Hungary down to the middle of the sixteenth century; and besides being written in the purest Hungarian, has the merit of having for its author a professor of the Reformed College of Debreczen.

Myself. I will go to Hungary rather than not read it. I am glad that the Turk beat the Magyar. When I used to read the ballads of Spain I always sided with the Moor against the Christian.

Hungarian. It was a drawn fight after all, for the terrible horse of the Turk presently flung his own master, whereupon the two champions returned to their respective armies; but in the grand conflict which ensued, the Turks beat the Magyars, pursuing them till night, and striking them on the necks with their scymetars. The Turk is a noble fellow; I should wish to be a Turk, were I not a Magyar.

Myself. The Turk always keeps his word, I am told.

Hungarian. Which the Christian very seldom does, and even the Hungarian does not always. In 1444 Ulaszlo made, at Szeged, peace with Amurath for ten years, which he swore with an oath to keep, but at the instigation of the Pope Julian he broke it, and induced his great captain, Hunyadi John, to share in the perjury. The consequence was the battle of Varna, of the 10th of November, in which Hunyadi was routed, and Ulaszlo slain. Did you ever hear his epitaph? it is both solemn and edifying :—

> " Romulidæ Cannas ego Varnam clade notavi ;
> Discite mortales non temerare fidem :
> Me nisi Pontifices jussissent rumpere fœdus
> Non ferret Scythicum Pannonis ora jugum."

" Halloo!" said the jockey, starting up from a doze in which he had been indulging for the last hour, his head leaning upon his breast, " what is that? That's not high Dutch; I bargained for high Dutch, and I left you speaking high Dutch, as it sounded very much like the language of horses, as I have been told high Dutch does; but as for what you are speaking now, whatever you may call it, it sounds more like the language of another kind of animal. I suppose you want to insult me, because I was once a dicky-boy."

" Nothing of the kind," said I; " the gentleman was making a quotation in Latin."

" Latin, was it?" said the jockey; " that alters the case. Latin is genteel, and I have sent my eldest boy to an academy to learn it. Come, let us hear you fire away in Latin," he continued, proceeding to re-light his pipe, which, before going to sleep, he had laid on the table.

" If you wish to follow the discourse in Latin," said the Hungarian, in very bad English, " I can oblige you; I learned to speak very good Latin in the college of Debreczen."

" That's more," said I, " than I have done in the colleges where I have been; in any little conversation which we may yet have, I wish you would use German."

" Well," said the jockey, taking a whiff, " make your conversation as short as possible, whether in Latin or Dutch, for, to tell you the truth, I am rather tired of merely playing listener."

" You were saying you had been in Russia," said I; " I believe the Russians are part of the Sclavonian race."

Hungarian. Yes, part of the great Sclavonian family; one of the most numerous races in the world. The Russians themselves are very numerous; would that the Magyars could boast of the fifth part of their number!

Myself. What is the number of the Magyars?

Hungarian. Barely four millions. We came a tribe of Tartars into Europe, and settled down amongst Sclavonians, whom we conquered, but who never coalesced with us. The Austrian at present plays in Pannonia the Sclavonian against us, and us against the Sclavonian; but the downfall of the Austrian is at hand; they, like us, are not a numerous people.

Myself. Who will bring about his downfall?

Hungarian. The Russians. The Rysckie Tsar will lead his people forth, all the Sclavonians will join him, he will conquer all before him.

Myself. Are the Russians good soldiers?

Hungarian. They are stubborn and unflinching to an astonishing degree, and their fidelity to their Tsar is quite admirable. See how the Russians behaved at Plescova, in Livonia, in the old time, against our great Batory Stephen; they defended the place till it was a heap of rubbish, and mark how they behaved after they had been made prisoners. Stephen offered them two alternatives:—to enter into his service, in which they would have good pay, clothing, and fair treatment; or to be allowed to return to Russia. Without the slightest hesitation they, to a man, chose the latter, though well aware that their beloved Tsar, the cruel Ivan Basilowits, would put them all to death, amidst tortures the most horrible, for not doing what was impossible— preserving the town.

Myself. You speak Russian?

Hungarian. A little. I was born in the vicinity of a Sclavonian tribe; the servants of our house were Sclavonians, and I early acquired something of their language, which differs not much from that of Russia; when in that country I quickly understood what was said.

Myself. Have the Russians any literature?

Hungarian. Doubtless; but I am not acquainted with it, as I do not read their language; but I know something of their popular tales, to which I used to listen in their izbushkas; a principal personage in these is a creation quite original—called Baba Yaga.

Myself. Who is the Baba Yaga?

Hungarian. A female phantom, who is described as hurrying along the puszta, or steppe, in a mortar, pounding with a pestle at a tremendous rate, and leaving a long trace on the ground behind her with her tongue, which is three yards long, and with which she seizes any men and horses coming in her way, swallowing them down into her capacious belly. She has several daughters, very handsome, and with plenty of money; happy the young Mujik who catches and marries one of them, for they make excellent wives.

"Many thanks," said I, "for the information you have afforded me : this is rather poor wine," I observed, as I poured out a glass—" I suppose you have better wine in Hungary?"

"Yes, we have better wine in Hungary. First of all there is Tokay, the most celebrated in the world, though I confess I prefer the wine of Eger—Tokay is too sweet."

"Have you ever been at Tokay?"

"I have," said the Hungarian.

"What kind of place is Tokay?"

"A small town situated on the Tyzza, a rapid river descending from the north; the Tokay Mountain is just behind the town, which stands on the right bank. The top of the mountain is called Kopacs Teto, or the bald tip; the hill is so steep that during thunder-storms pieces frequently fall down upon the roofs of the houses. It was planted with vines by King Lajos, who ascended the throne in 1342. The best wine called Tokay is, however, not made at Tokay, but at Kassau, two leagues farther into the Carpathians, of which Tokay is a spur. If you wish to drink the best Tokay, you must go to Vienna, to which place all the prime is sent. For the third time I ask you, O young man of Horncastle! why does your Government always send fools to represent it at Vienna?"

"And for the third time I tell you, O son of Almus! that I cannot say; perhaps, however, to drink the sweet Tokay wine; fools, you know, always like sweet things."

"Good," said the Hungarian; "it must be so, and when I return to Hungary, I will state to my countrymen your explanation of a circumstance which has frequently caused them great perplexity. Oh! the English are a clever people, and have a deep meaning in all they do. What a vision of deep policy opens itself to my view! they do not send their fool to Vienna in order to gape at processions, and to bow and scrape at a base Papist court, but to drink at the great dinners the celebrated Tokay of Hungary, which the Hun-

garians, though they do not drink it, are very proud of,
and by doing so to intimate the sympathy which the English
entertain for their fellow religionists of Hungary. Oh!
the English are a deep people."

CHAPTER XL

The Horncastle Welcome—Tzernebock and Bielebock.

THE pipe of the Hungarian had, for some time past, exhibited considerable symptoms of exhaustion, little or no
ruttling having been heard in the tube, and scarcely a
particle of smoke, drawn through the syphon, having been
emitted from the lips of the possessor. He now rose from
his seat, and going to a corner of the room, placed his pipe
against the wall, then striding up and down the room, he
cracked his fingers several times, exclaiming, in a half-
musing manner, "Oh, the deep nation, which, in order to
display its sympathy for Hungary, sends its fool to
Vienna, to drink the sweet wine of Tokay!"

The jockey, having looked for some time at the tall
figure with evident approbation, winked at me with that
brilliant eye of his on which there was no speck, saying,
" Did you ever see a taller fellow?"

" Never," said I.

" Or a finer?"

" That's another question," said I, " which I am not so
willing to answer; however, as I am fond of truth, and
scorn to flatter, I will take the liberty of saying that I have
seen a finer."

" A finer! where?" said the jockey; whilst the Hungarian, who appeared to understand what we said, stood
still, and looked full at me.

" Amongst a strange set of people," said I, " whom, if
I were to name, you would, I dare say, only laugh at me."

" Who be they?" said the jockey. " Come, don't be
ashamed; I have occasionally kept queerish company
myself."

" The people whom we call gypsies," said I; " whom the
Germans call Zigeuner, and who call themselves Romany
chals."

"Zigeuner!" said the Hungarian; "by Isten! I do know those people."

"Romany chals!" said the jockey; "whew! I begin to smell a rat."

"What do you mean by smelling a rat?" said I.

"I'll bet a crown," said the jockey, "that you be the young chap what certain folks call 'the Romany Rye.'"

"Ah!" said I, "how came you to know that name?"

"Be not you he?" said the jockey.

"Why, I certainly have been called by that name."

"I could have sworn it," said the jockey; then rising from his chair, he laid his pipe on the table, took a large hand-bell which stood on the side-board, and going to the door, opened it, and commenced ringing in a most tremendous manner on the staircase. The noise presently brought up a waiter, to whom the jockey vociferated, "Go to your master, and tell him to send immediately three bottles of champagne, of the pink kind, mind you, which is twelve guineas a dozen;" the waiter hurried away, and the jockey resumed his seat and his pipe. I sat in silent astonishment until the waiter returned with a basket containing the wine, which, with three long glasses, he placed on the table. The jockey then got up, and going to a large bow-window at the end of the room, which looked into a court-yard, peeped out; then saying, "the coast is clear," he shut down the principal sash which was open for the sake of the air, and taking up a bottle of champagne, he placed another in the hands of the Hungarian, to whom he said something in private. The latter, who seemed to understand him, answered by a nod. The two then going to the end of the table fronting the window, and about eight paces from it, stood before it, holding the bottles by their necks; suddenly the jockey lifted up his arm. "Surely," said I, "you are not mad enough to fling that bottle through the window?" "Here's to the Romany Rye; here's to the sweet master," said the jockey, dashing the bottle through the pane in so neat a manner that scarcely a particle of glass fell into the room.

"Eljen edes csigany ur—eljen gul eray!" said the Hungarian, swinging round his bottle, and discharging it at the window; but, either not possessing the jockey's accuracy of aim, or reckless of the consequences, he flung his bottle so, that it struck against part of the wooden setting of the

panes, breaking along with the wood and itself three or four
panes to pieces. The crash was horrid, and wine and
particles of glass flew back into the room, to the no small
danger of its inmates. "What do you think of that?"
said the jockey; "were you ever so honoured before?"
"Honoured!" said I. "God preserve me in future from
such honour;" and I put my finger to my cheek, which
was slightly hurt by a particle of the glass. "That's the
way we of the cofrady honour great men at Horncastle,"
said the jockey. 'What, you are hurt! never mind; all the
better; your scratch shows that you are the body the compliment was paid to." "And what are you going to do
with the other bottle?" said I. "Do with it!" said the
jockey, "why, drink it, cosily and comfortably, whilst holding a little quiet talk. The Romany Rye at Horncastle,
what an idea!"

"And what will the master of the house say to all this
damage which you have caused him!"

"What will your master say, William?" said the jockey
to the waiter, who had witnessed the singular scene just
described without exhibiting the slightest mark of surprise.
William smiled, and slightly shrugging his shoulders, replied, "Very little, I dare say, sir; this a'n't the first time
your honour has done a thing of this kind." "Nor will it
be the first time that I shall have paid for it," said the
jockey; "well, I shall never have paid for a certain item
in the bill with more pleasure than I shall pay for it now.
Come, William, draw the cork, and let us taste the pink
champagne."

The waiter drew the cork, and filled the glasses with a
pinky liquor, which bubbled, hissed, and foamed. "How
do you like it?" said the jockey, after I had imitated the
example of my companions, by despatching my portion at
a draught.

"It is wonderful wine," said I; "I have never tasted
champagne before, though I have frequently heard it
praised; it more than answers my expectations; but, I
confess, I should not wish to be obliged to drink it every
day."

"Nor I," said the jockey, "for every-day drinking give
me a glass of old port, or——"

"Of hard old ale," I interposed, "which, according to
my mind, is better than all the wine in the world."

"Well said, Romany Rye," said the jockey, "just my own opinion; now, William, make yourself scarce."

The waiter withdrew, and I said to the jockey, "How did you become acquainted with the Romany chals?"

"I first became acquainted with them," said the jockey, "when I lived with old Fulcher the basketmaker, who took me up when I was adrift upon the world; I do not mean the present Fulcher, who is likewise called old Fulcher, but his father, who has been dead this many a year; while living with him in the caravan, I frequently met them in the green lanes, and of latter years I have had occasional dealings with them in the horse line."

"And the gypsies have mentioned me to you?" said I.

"Frequently," said the jockey, "and not only those of these parts; why, there's scarcely a part of England in which I have not heard the name of the Romany Rye mentioned by these people. The power you have over them is wonderful; that is, I should have thought it wonderful, had they not more than once told me the cause."

"And what is the cause?" said I, "for I am sure I do not know."

"The cause is this," said the jockey, "they never heard a bad word proceed from your mouth, and never knew you do a bad thing."

"They are a singular people," said I.

"And what a singular language they have got," said the jockey.

"Do you know it?" said I.

"Only a few words," said the jockey, "they were always chary in teaching me any."

"They were vary sherry to me too," said the Hungarian, speaking in broken English; "I only could learn from them half-a-dozen words, for example, gul eray, which, in the czigany of my country, means sweet gentleman; or edes ur in my own Magyar."

"Gudlo Rye, in the Romany of mine, means a sugar'd gentleman," said I; "then there are gypsies in your country?"

"Plenty," said the Hungarian, speaking German, "and in Russia and Turkey too; and wherever they are found, they are alike in their ways and language. Oh, they are a strange race, and how little known! I know little of them, but enough to say, that one horse-load of nonsense has been written about them; there is one Valter Scott——''

"Mind what you say about him," said I; "he is our grand authority in matters of philology and history."

"A pretty philologist," said the Hungarian," who makes the gypsies speak Roth-Welsch, the dialect of thieves; a pretty historian, who couples together Thor and Tzernebock."

"Where does he do that?" said I.

"In his conceited romance of 'Ivanhoe,' he couples Thor and Tzernebock together, and calls them gods of the heathen Saxons."

"Well," said I, "Thur or Thor was certainly a god of the heathen Saxons."

"True," said the Hungarian; "but why couple him with Tzernebock? Tzernebock was a word which your Valter had picked up somewhere without knowing the meaning. Tzernebock was no god of the Saxons, but one of the gods of the Sclaves, on the southern side of the Baltic. The Sclaves had two grand gods to whom they sacrificed, Tzernebock and Bielebock; that is, the black and white gods, who represented the powers of dark and light. They were overturned by Waldemar, the Dane, the great enemy of the Sclaves; the account of whose wars you will find in one fine old book, written by Saxo Gramaticus, which I read in the library of the college of Debreczen. The Sclaves, at one time, were masters of all the southern shore of the Baltic, where their descendants are still to be found, though they have lost their language, and call themselves Germans; but the word Zernevitz near Dantzic, still attests that the Sclavic language was once common in those parts. Zernevitz means the thing of blackness, as Tzernebock means the god of blackness. Prussia itself merely means, in Sclavish, Lower Russia. There is scarcely a race or language in the world more extended than the Sclavic. On the other side of the Dunau you will find the Sclaves and their language. Czernavoda is Sclavic, and means black water; in Turkish, kara su; even as Tzernebock means black god; and Belgrade, or Belograd, means the white town; even as Bielebock, or Bielebog, means the white god. Oh! he is one great ignorant, that Valter. He is going, they say, to write one history about Napoleon. I do hope that in his history he will couple his Thor and Tzernebock together. By my God! it would be good diversion that."

"Walter Scott appears to be no particular favourite of yours," said I.

"He is not," said the Hungarian; "I hate him for his slavish principles. He wishes to see absolute power restored in this country, and Popery also—and I hate him because——what do you think? In one of his novels, published a few months ago, he has the insolence to insult Hungary in the presence of one of her sons. He makes his great braggart, Cœur de Lion, fling a Magyar over his head. Ha! it was well for Richard that he never felt the gripe of a Hungarian. I wish the braggart could have felt the gripe of me, who am ' a' magyarok közt legkissebb,' the least among the Magyars. I do hate that Scott, and all his vile gang of Lowlanders and Highlanders. The black corps, the fekete regiment of Matyjas Hunyadi, was worth all the Scots, high or low, that ever pretended to be soldiers; and would have sent them all headlong into the Black Sea, had they dared to confront it on its shores; but why be angry with an ignorant, who couples together Thor and Tzernebock? Ha! Ha!"

"You have read his novels?" said I.

"Yes, I read them now and then. I do not speak much English, but I can read it well, and I have read some of his romances, and mean to read his ' Napoleon,' in the hope of finding Thor and Tzernebock coupled together in it, as in his high-flying ' Ivanhoe.' "

"Come," said the jockey, "no more Dutch, whether high or low. I am tired of it; unless we can have some English, I am off to bed."

"I should be very glad to hear some English," said I; "especially from your mouth. Several things which you have mentioned, have awakened my curiosity. Suppose you give us your history?"

"My history?" said the jockey. "A rum idea! however, lest conversation should lag, I'll give it you. First of all, however, a glass of champagne to each."

After we had each taken a glass of champagne, the jockey commenced his history.

CHAPTER XLI

The Jockey's Tale—Thieves' Latin—Liberties with Coin—The Smasher in Prison—Old Fulcher—Every One has His Gift—Fashion of the English.

"My grandfather was a shorter, and my father was a smasher; the one was scragg'd, and the other lagg'd."

I here interrupted the jockey by observing that his discourse was, for the greater part, unintelligible to me.

"I do not understand much English," said the Hungarian, who, having replenished and resumed his mighty pipe, was now smoking away; "but, by Isten, I believe it is the gibberish which that great ignorant Valther Scott puts into the mouths of the folks he calls gypsies."

"Something like it, I confess," said I, "though this sounds more genuine than his dialect, which he picked up out of the canting vocabulary at the end of the ' English Rogue,' a book which, however despised, was written by a remarkable genius. What do you call the speech you were using?" said I, addressing myself to the jockey.

"Latin," said the jockey, very coolly, "that is, that dialect of it which is used by the light-fingered gentry."

"He is right," said the Hungarian; "it is what the Germans call Roth-Welsch: they call it so because there are a great many Latin words in it, introduced by the priests, who, at the time of the Reformation, being too lazy to work and too stupid to preach, joined the bands of thieves and robbers who prowled about the country. Italy, as you are aware, is called by the Germans Welschland, or the land of the Welschers; and I may add that Wallachia derives its name from a colony of Welschers which Trajan sent there. Welsch and Wallack being one and the same word, and tantamount to Latin."

"I dare say you are right," said I; "but why was Italy termed Welschland?"

"I do not know," said the Hungarian.

"Then I think I can tell you," said I; "it was called so because the original inhabitants were a Cimbric tribe, who were called Gwyltiad, that is, a race of wild people, living in coverts, who were of the same blood, and spoke the same language as the present inhabitants of Wales. Welsh seems merely a modification of Gwyltiad. Pray continue your history," said I to the jockey, " only please to do so in a language which we can understand, and first of all interpret the sentence with which you began it."

" I told you that my grandfather was a shorter," said the jockey, by which is meant a gentleman who shortens or reduces the current coin of these realms, for which practice he was scragged, that is, hung by the scrag of the neck. And when I said that my father was a smasher, I meant one who passes forged notes, thereby doing his best to smash the Bank of England; by being lagged, I meant he was laid fast, that is, had a chain put round his leg and then transported."

" Your explanations are quite satisfactory," said I; " the three first words are metaphorical, and the fourth, lagged, is the old genuine Norse term, lagda, which signifies laid, whether in durance, or in bed, has nothing to do with the matter. What you have told me confirms me in an opinion which I have long entertained, that thieves' Latin is a strange mysterious speech, formed of metaphorical terms, and words derived from the various ancient languages. Pray tell me, now, how the gentleman, your grandfather, contrived to shorten the coin of these realms?"

" You shall hear," said the jockey; " but I have one thing to beg of you, which is, that when I have once begun my history you will not interrupt me with questions, I don't like them, they stops one, and puts one out of one's tale, and are not wanted; for anything which I think can't be understood, I should myself explain, without being asked. My grandfather reduced or shortened the coin of this country by three processes. By aquafortis, by clipping, and by filing. Filing and clipping he employed in reducing all sorts of coin, whether gold or silver; but aquafortis he used merely in reducing gold coin, whether guineas, jacob-uses, or Portugal pieces, otherwise called moidores, which were at one time as current as guineas. By laying a guinea in aquafortis for twelve hours, he could filch from it to the value of ninepence, and by letting it remain there for twenty-four to the value of eighteenpence, the aquafortis eating the gold away, and leaving it like a sediment in the vessel. He was generally satisfied with taking the value of ninepence from a guinea, of eighteenpence from a jaco-bus or moidore, or half-a-crown from a broad Spanish piece, whether he reduced them by aquafortis, filing, or clipping.

From a five-shilling piece, which is called a bull in Latin, because it is round like a bull's head, he would file or clip to the value of fivepence, and from lesser coin in proportion. He was connected with a numerous gang, or set, of people, who had given up their minds and talents entirely to shortening."

Here I interrupted the jockey. "How singular," said I, "is the fall and debasement of words; you talk of a gang, or set, of shorters; you are, perhaps, not aware that gang and set were, a thousand years ago, only connected with the great and Divine; they are ancient Norse words, which may be found in the heroic poems of the north, and in the Edda, a collection of mythologic and heroic songs. In these poems we read that such and such a king invaded Norway with a gang of heroes; or so and so, for example, Erik Bloodaxe, was admitted to the set of gods; but at present gang and set are merely applied to the vilest of the vile, and the lowest of the low,—we say a gang of thieves and shorters, or a set of authors. How touching is this debasement of words in the course of time; it puts me in mind of the decay of old houses and names. I have known a Mortimer who was a hedger and ditcher, a Berners who was born in a workhouse, and a descendant of the De Burghs, who bore the falcon, mending old kettles, and making horse and pony shoes in a dingle."

"Odd enough," said the jockey; "but you were saying you knew one Berners—man or woman? I would ask."

"A woman," said I.

"What might her Christian name be?" said the jockey.

"It is not to be mentioned lightly," said I, with a sigh.

"I shouldn't wonder if it were Isopel," said the jockey with an arch glance of his one brilliant eye.

"It was Isopel," said I; "did you know Isopel Berners?"

"Ay, and have reason to know her," said the jockey, putting his hand into his left waistcoat pocket, as if to feel for something, "for she gave me what I believe few men could do—a most confounded whopping. But now, Mr. Romany Rye, I have again to tell you that I don't like to be interrupted when I'm speaking, and to add that if you break in upon me a third time, you and I shall quarrel."

"Pray proceed with your story," said I; "I will not interrupt you again."

" Good !" said the jockey. " Where was I? Oh, with
a set of people who had given up their minds to shortening !
Reducing the coin, though rather a lucrative, was a very
dangerous trade. Coin filed felt rough to the touch; coin
clipped could be easily detected by the eye; and as for coin
reduced by aquafortis, it was generally so discoloured that,
unless a great deal of pains was used to polish it, people
were apt to stare at it in a strange manner, and to say,
' What have they been doing to this here gold?' My grandfather, as I have said before, was connected with a gang of
shorters, and sometimes shortened money, and at other
times passed off what had been shortened by other gentry.

" Passing off what had been shortened by others was his
ruin; for once, in trying to pass off a broad piece which had
been laid in aquafortis for four-and-twenty hours, and was
very black, not having been properly rectified, he was
stopped and searched, and other reduced coins being found
about him, and in his lodgings, he was committed to prison,
tried, and executed. He was offered his life, provided he
would betray his comrades; but he told the big-wigs, who
wanted him to do so, that he would see them farther first,
and died at Tyburn, amidst the cheers of the populace,
leaving my grandmother and father, to whom he had always
been a kind husband and parent—for, setting aside the
crime for which he suffered, he was a moral man; leaving
them, I say, to bewail his irreparable loss.

" 'Tis said that misfortune never comes alone; this is,
however, not always the case. Shortly after my grandfather's misfortune, as my grandmother and her son were
living in great misery in Spitalfields, her only relation—a
brother from whom she had been estranged some years,
on account of her marriage with my grandfather, who had
been in an inferior station to herself—died, leaving all his
property to her and the child. This property consisted of
a farm of about a hundred acres, with its stock, and some
money besides. My grandmother, who knew something of
business, instantly went into the country, where she farmed
the property for her own benefit and that of her son, to
whom she gave an education suitable to a person in his
condition, till he was old enough to manage the farm himself. Shortly after the young man came of age, my grandmother died, and my father, in about a year, married the
daughter of a farmer, from whom he expected some little

fortune, but who very much deceived him, becoming a bankrupt almost immediately after the marriage of his daughter, and himself and family going into the workhouse.

"My mother, however, made my father an excellent wife; and if my father in the long run did not do well it was no fault of hers. My father was not a bad man by nature, he was of an easy, generous temper, the most unfortunate temper, by the bye, for success in this life that any person can be possessed of, as those who have it are almost sure to be made dupes of by the designing. But, though easy and generous, he was anything but a fool; he had a quick and witty tongue of his own when he chose to exert it, and woe be to those who insulted him openly, for there was not a better boxer in the whole country round. My parents were married several years before I came into the world, who was their first and only child. I may be called an unfortunate creature; I was born with this beam or scale on my left eye, which does not allow me to see with it; and though I can see tolerably sharply with the other, indeed more than most people can with both of theirs, it is a great misfortune not to have two eyes like other people. Moreover, setting aside the affair of my eye, I had a very ugly countenance; my mouth being slightly wrung aside, and my complexion swarthy. In fact, I looked so queer that the gossips and neighbours, when they first saw me, swore I was a changeling—perhaps it would have been well if I had never been born; for my poor father, who had been particularly anxious to have a son, no sooner saw me than he turned away, went to the neighbouring town, and did not return for two days. I am by no means certain that I was not the cause of his ruin, for till I came into the world he was fond of his home, and attended much to business, but afterwards he went frequently into company, and did not seem to care much about his affairs : he was, how-ever, a kind man, and when his wife gave him advice never struck her, nor do I ever remember that he kicked me when I came in his way, or so much as cursed my ugly face, though it was easy to see that he didn't over-like me. When I was six years old I was sent to the village-school, where I was soon booked for a dunce, because the master found it impossible to teach me either to read or write. Before I had been at school two years, however, I had beaten boys four years older than myself, and could fling a stone with my left hand (for if I am right-eyed I am left-handed) higher and farther than any one in the parish. Moreover, no boy could equal me at riding, and no people ride so well or desperately as boys. I could ride a donkey—a thing far more difficult to ride than a horse—at full gallop over hedges and ditches, seated, or rather floating upon his hinder part,—so, though anything but clever, as this here Romany Rye would say, I was yet able to do things which few other people could do. By the time I was ten my father's affairs had got into a very desperate condition, for he had taken to gambling and horse-racing, and, being unsuccessful, had sold his stock, mortgaged his estate, and incurred very serious debts. The upshot was, that within a little time all he had was seized, himself imprisoned, and my mother and myself put into a cottage belonging to the parish, which, being very cold and damp, was the cause of her catching a fever, which speedily carried her off. I was then bound apprentice to a farmer, in whose service I underwent much coarse treatment, cold, and hunger.

" After lying in prison near two years, my father was liberated by an Act for the benefit of insolvent debtors; he was then lost sight of for some time; at last, however, he made his appearance in the neighbourhood dressed like a gentleman, and seemingly possessed of plenty of money. He came to see me, took me into a field, and asked me how I was getting on. I told him I was dreadfully used, and begged him to take me away with him; he refused, and told me to be satisfied with my condition, for that he could do nothing for me. I had a great love for my father, and likewise a great admiration for him on account of his character as a boxer, the only character which boys in general regard, so I wished much to be with him, independently of the dog's life I was leading where I was; I therefore said if he would not take me with him, I would follow him; he replied that I must do no such thing, for that if I did, it would be my ruin. I asked him what he meant, but he made no reply, only saying that he would go and speak to the farmer. Then taking me with him, he went to the farmer, and in a very civil manner said that he understood I had not been very kindly treated by him, but he hoped that in future I should be used better. The farmer answered in a surly tone, that I had been only too well treated, for that I was a worthless young scoundrel; high words ensued, and the farmer, forgetting the kind of man he had to deal with, checked him with my grandsire's misfortune, and said he deserved to be hanged like his father. In a moment my father knocked him down, and on his getting up, gave him a terrible beating, then taking me by the hand he hastened away; as we were going down a lane he said we were now both done for : ' I don't care a straw for that, father,' said I, ' provided I be with you.' My father took me to the neighbouring town, and going into the yard of a small inn, he ordered out a pony and light cart which belonged to him, then paying his bill, he told me to mount upon the seat, and getting up drove away like lightning; we drove for at least six hours without stopping, till we came to a cottage by the side of a heath; we put the pony and cart into a shed, and went into the cottage, my father unlocking the door with a key which he took out of his pocket; there was nobody in the cottage when we arrived, but shortly after there came a man and a woman, and then some more people, and by ten o'clock at night there were a dozen of us in the cottage. The people were companions of my father. My father began talking to them in Latin, but I did not understand much of the discourse, though I believe it was about myself, as their eyes were frequently turned to me. Some objections appeared to be made to what he said; however, all at last seemed to be settled, and we all sat down to some food. After that, all the people got up and went away, with the exception of the woman, who remained with my father and me. The next day my father also departed, leaving me with the woman, telling me before he went that she would teach me some things which it behoved me to know. I remained with her in the cottage upwards of a week; several of those who had been there coming and going. The woman, after making me take an oath to be faithful, told me that the people whom I had seen were a gang who got their livelihood by passing forged notes, and that my father was a principal man amongst them, adding, that I must do my best to assist them. I was a poor ignorant child at that time, and I made no objection, thinking that whatever my father did must be right; the woman then gave me some instructions in the smasher's dialect of the Latin language. I made great progress, because, for the first time in my life, I paid great attention to my lessons. At last my father returned, and, after some conversation with the woman, took me away in his cart. I shall be very short about what happened to my father and myself during two years. My father did his best to smash the Bank of England by passing forged notes, and I did my best to assist him. We attended races and fairs in all kinds of disguises; my father was a first-rate hand at a disguise, and could appear of all ages, from twenty to fourscore; he was, however, grabbed at last. He had said, as I have told you, that he should be my ruin, but I was the cause of his, and all owing to the misfortune of this here eye of mine. We came to this very place of Horncastle, where my father purchased two horses of a young man, paying for them with three forged notes, purporting to be Bank of Englanders of fifty pounds each, and got the young man to change another of the like amount; he at that time appeared as a respectable dealer, and I as his son, as I really was.

" As soon as we had got the horses, we conveyed them to one of the places of call belonging to our gang, of which there were several. There they were delivered into the hands of our companions, who speedily sold them in a distant part of the country. The sum which they fetched— for the gang kept very regular accounts—formed an important item on the next day of sharing, of which there were twelve in the year. The young man, whom my father had paid for the horses with his smashing notes, was soon in trouble about them, and ran some risk, as I heard, of being executed; but he bore a good character, told a plain story, and, above all, had friends, and was admitted to bail; to one of his friends he described my father and myself. This person happened to be at an inn in Yorkshire, where my father, disguised as a Quaker, attempted to pass a forged note. The note was shown to this individual, who pronounced it a forgery, it being exactly similar to those for which the young man had been in trouble, and which he had seen. My father, however, being supposed a respectable man, because he was dressed as a Quaker—the very reason, by the bye, why anybody who knew aught of the Quakers would have suspected him to be a rogue—would have been let go, had I not made my appearance, dressed as his footboy. The friend of the young man looked at my eye, and seized hold of my father, who made a desperate resistance, I assisting him, as in duty bound. Being, how-

ever, overpowered by numbers, he bade me by a look, and a
word or two in Latin, to make myself scarce. Though my
heart was fit to break, I obeyed my father, who was speedily
committed. I followed him to the county town in which he
was lodged, where shortly after I saw him tried, convicted,
and condemned. I then, having made friends with the
jailor's wife, visited him in his cell, where I found him very
much cast down. He said, that my mother had appeared to
him in a dream, and talked to him about a resurrection and
Christ Jesus; there was a Bible before him, and he told me
the chaplain had just been praying with him. He re-
proached himself much, saying, he was afraid he had been
my ruin, by teaching me bad habits. I told him not to say
any such thing, for that I had been the cause of his, owing
to the misfortune of my eye. He begged me to give over
all unlawful pursuits, saying, that if persisted in, they were
sure of bringing a person to destruction. I advised him to
try and make his escape, proposing, that when the turnkey
came to let me out, he should knock him down, and fight
his way out, offering to assist him; showing him a small
saw, with which one of our companions, who was in the
neighbourhood, had provided me, and with which he could
have cut through his fetters in five minutes; but he told me
he had no wish to escape, and was quite willing to die. I
was rather hard at that time; I am not very soft now; and
I felt rather ashamed of my father's want of what I called
spirit. He was not executed after all; for the chaplain, who
was connected with a great family, stood his friend, and got
his sentence commuted, as they call it, to transportation;
and in order to make the matter easy, he induced my father
to make some valuable disclosures with respect to the
smashers' system. I confess that I would have been hanged
before I would have done so, after having reaped the profit
of it; that is, I think so now, seated comfortably in my inn,
with my bottle of champagne before me. He, however,
did not show himself carrion; he would not betray his companions, who had behaved very handsomely to him, having
given the son of a lord, a great barrister, not a hundred-
pound forged bill, but a hundred hard guineas, to plead his
cause, and another ten, to induce him, after pleading, to
put his hand to his breast, and say, that, upon his honour,
he believed the prisoner at the bar to be an honest and
injured man. No; I am glad to be able to say, that my

father did not show himself exactly carrion, though I could almost have wished he had let himself—— However, I am here with my bottle of champagne and the Romany Rye, and he was in his cell, with bread and water and the prison chaplain. He took an affectionate leave of me before he was sent away, giving me three out of five guineas, all the money he had left. He was a kind man, but not exactly fitted to fill my grandfather's shoes. I afterwards learned that he died of fever, as he was being carried across the sea.

"During the 'sizes I had made acquaintance with old Fulcher. I was in the town on my father's account, and he was there on his son's, who, having committed a small larceny, was in trouble. Young Fulcher, however, unlike my father, got off, though he did not give the son of a lord a hundred guineas to speak for him, and ten more to pledge his sacred honour for his honesty, but gave Counsellor P—— one-and-twenty shillings to defend him, who so frightened the principal evidence, a plain honest farming-man, that he flatly contradicted what he had first said, and at last acknowledged himself to be all the rogues in the world, and, amongst other things, a perjured villain. Old Fulcher, before he left the town with his son,—and here it will be well to say that he and his son left it in a kind of triumph, the base drummer of a militia regiment, to whom they had given half-a-crown, beating his drum before them —old Fulcher, I say, asked me to go and visit him, telling me where, at such a time, I might find him and his caravan and family; offering, if I thought fit, to teach me basket-making: so, after my father had been sent off, I went and found up old Fulcher, and became his apprentice in the basket-making line. I stayed with him till the time of his death, which happened in about three months, travelling about with him and his family, and living in green lanes, where we saw gypsies and trampers, and all kinds of strange characters. Old Fulcher, besides being an industrious basket-maker, was an out-and-out thief, as was also his son, and, indeed, every member of his family. They used to make baskets during the day, and thieve during a great part of the night. I had not been with them twelve hours before old Fulcher told me that I must thieve as well as the rest. I demurred at first, for I remembered the fate of my father, and what he had told me about leaving off bad courses, but soon allowed myself to be over-persuaded; more especially as the first robbery I was asked to do was a fruit robbery. I was to go with young Fulcher, and steal some fine Morell cherries, which grew against a wall in a gentleman's garden; so young Fulcher and I went and stole the cherries, one half of which we ate, and gave the rest to the old man, who sold them to a fruiterer ten miles off from the place where we had stolen them. The next night old Fulcher took me out with himself. He was a great thief, though in a small way. He used to say, that they were fools, who did not always manage to keep the rope below their shoulders, by which he meant, that it was not advisable to commit a robbery, or do anything which could bring you to the gallows. He was all for petty larceny, and knew where to put his hand upon any little thing in England, which it was possible to steal. I submit it to the better judgment of the Romany Rye, who I see is a great hand for words and names, whether he ought not to have been called old Filcher, instead of Fulcher. I shan't give a regular account of the larcenies he committed during the short time I knew him, either alone by himself, or with me and his son. I shall merely relate the last.

" A melancholy gentleman, who lived a very solitary life, had a large carp in a shady pond in a meadow close to his house; he was exceedingly fond of it, and used to feed it with his own hand, the creature being so tame that it would put its snout out of the water to be fed when it was whistled to; feeding and looking at his carp were the only pleasures the poor melancholy gentleman possessed. Old Fulcher—being in the neighbourhood, and having an order from a fishmonger for a large fish, which was wanted at a great city dinner, at which His Majesty was to be present— swore he would steal the carp, and asked me to go with him. I had heard of the gentleman's fondness for his creature, and begged him to let it be, advising him to go and steal some other fish; but old Fulcher swore, and said he would have the carp, although its master should hang himself; I told him he might go by himself, but he took his son and stole the carp, which weighed seventeen pounds. Old Fulcher got thirty shillings for the carp, which I afterwards heard was much admired and relished by His Majesty. The master, however, of the carp, on losing his favourite, became more melancholy than ever, and in a little time hanged himself. 'What's sport for one, is death to another,' I once heard at the village-school read out of a copy-book.

"This was the last larceny old Fulcher ever committed. He could keep his neck always out of the noose, but he could not always keep his leg out of the trap. A few nights after, having removed to a distance, he went to an osier car in order to steal some osiers for his basket-making, for he never bought any. I followed a little way behind. Old Fulcher had frequently stolen osiers out of the car, whilst in the neighbourhood, but during his absence the property, of which the car was a part, had been let to a young gentleman, a great hand for preserving game. Old Fulcher had not got far into the car before he put his foot into a man-trap. Hearing old Fulcher shriek, I ran up, and found him in a dreadful condition. Putting a large stick which I carried into the jaws of the trap, I contrived to prize them open, and get old Fulcher's leg out, but the leg was broken. So I ran to the caravan, and told young Fulcher of what had happened, and he and I helped his father home. A doctor was sent for, who said that it was necessary to take the leg off, but old Fulcher, being very much afraid of pain, said it should not be taken off, and the doctor went away, but after some days, old Fulcher becoming worse, ordered the doctor to be sent for, who came and took off his leg, but it was then too late, mortification had come on, and in a little time old Fulcher died.

"Thus perished old Fulcher; he was succeeded in his business by his son, young Fulcher, who, immediately after the death of his father, was called old Fulcher, it being our English custom to call everybody old, as soon as their fathers are buried; young Fulcher—I mean he who had been called young, but was now old Fulcher—wanted me to go out and commit larcenies with him; but I told him that I would have nothing more to do with thieving, having seen the ill effects of it, and that I should leave them in the morning. Old Fulcher begged me to think better of it, and his mother joined with him. They offered, if I would stay, to give me Mary Fulcher as a mort, till she and I were old enough to be regularly married, she being the daughter of the one, and the sister of the other. I liked the girl very well, for she had always been civil to me, and had a fair complexion and nice red hair, both of which I like, being

a bit of a black myself; but I refused, being determined to
see something more of the world than I could hope to do
with the Fulchers, and, moreover, to live honestly, which
I could never do along with them. So the next morning I
left them : I was, as I said before, quite determined upon an
honest livelihood, and I soon found one. He is a great fool
who is ever dishonest in England. Any person who has
any natural gift, and everybody has some natural gift, is
sure of finding encouragement in this noble country of ours,
provided he will but exhibit it. I had not walked more than
three miles before I came to a wonderfully high church
steeple, which stood close by the road; I looked at the
steeple, and going to a heap of smooth pebbles which lay
by the roadside, I took up some, and then went into the
churchyard, and placing myself just below the tower, my
right foot resting on a ledge, about two foot from the
ground, I, with my left hand—being a left-handed person,
do you see—flung or chucked up a stone, which, lighting on
the top of the steeple, which was at least a hundred and
fifty feet high, did there remain. After repeating this feat
two or three times, I ' hulled ' up a stone, which went clean
over the tower, and then one, my right foot still on the
ledge, which rising at least five yards above the steeple,
did fall down just at my feet. Without knowing it, I was
showing off my gift to others besides myself, doing what,
perhaps, not five men in England could do. Two men, who
were passing by, stopped and looked at my proceedings,
and when I had done flinging came into the churchyard,
and, after paying me a compliment on what they had seen
me do, proposed that I should join company with them; I
asked them who they were, and they told me. The one was
Hopping Ned, and the other Biting Giles. Both had their
gifts, by which they got their livelihood; Ned could hop a
hundred yards with any man in England, and Giles could
lift up with his teeth any dresser or kitchen-table in the
country, and, standing erect, hold it dangling in his jaws.
There's many a big oak table and dresser in certain districts
of England, which bear the marks of Giles's teeth; and I
make no doubt that, a hundred or two years hence, there'll
be strange stories about those marks, and that people will
point them out as a proof that there were giants in bygone
time, and that many a dentist will moralize on the decays
which human teeth have undergone.

"They wanted me to go about with them, and exhibit my gift occasionally, as they did theirs, promising that the money that was got by the exhibitions should be honestly divided. I consented, and we set off together, and that evening coming to a village, and putting up at the ale-house, all the grand folks of the village being there smoking their pipes, we contrived to introduce the subject of hopping —the upshot being that Ned hopped against the school-master for a pound, and beat him hollow; shortly after, Giles, for a wager, took up the kitchen table in his jaws, though he had to pay a shilling to the landlady for the marks he left, whose grandchildren will perhaps get money by exhibiting them. As for myself, I did nothing that day, but the next, on which my companions did nothing, I showed off at hulling stones against a cripple, the crack man for stone-throwing, of a small town, a few miles farther on. Bets were made to the tune of some pounds; I contrived to beat the cripple, and just contrived; for to do him justice I must acknowledge he was a first-rate hand at stones, though he had a game hip, and went sideways; his head, when he walked—if his movements could be called walking—not being above three feet above the ground. So we travelled, I and my companions, showing off our gifts, Giles and I occasionally for a gathering, but Ned never hopping, unless against somebody for a wager. We lived honestly and comfortably, making no little money by our natural endowments, and were known over a great part of England as 'Hopping Ned,' 'Biting Giles,' and 'Hull over the Head Jack,' which was my name, it being the black-guard fashion of the English, do you see, to——"

Here I interrupted the jockey. "You may call it a black-guard fashion," said I, "and I dare say it is, or it would scarcely be English; but it is an immensely ancient one, and is handed down to us from our northern ancestry, espe-cially the Danes, who were in the habit of giving people surnames, or rather nicknames, from some quality of body or mind, but generally from some disadvantageous peculi-arity of feature; for there is no denying that the English, Norse, or whatever we may please to call them, are an envious, depreciatory set of people, who not only give their poor comrades contemptuous names, but their great people also. They didn't call you the matchless Hurler, because, by doing so, they would have paid you a compliment, but

Hull over the Head Jack, as much as to say that after all you were a scrub; so, in ancient time, instead of calling Regner the great conqueror, the Nation Tamer, they surnamed him Lodbrog, which signifies Rough or Hairy Breeks—lod or loddin signifying rough or hairy; and instead of complimenting Halgerdr, the wife of Gunnar of Hlitharend, the great champion of Iceland, upon her majestic presence, by calling her Halgerdr, the stately or tall; what must they do but term her Ha-brokr, or Highbreeks, it being the fashion in old times for Northern ladies to wear breeks, or breeches, which English ladies of the present day never think of doing; and just, as of old, they called Halgerdr Long-breeks, so this very day a fellow of Horncastle called, in my hearing, our noble-looking Hungarian friend here, Long-stockings. Oh, I could give you a hundred instances, both ancient and modern, of this unseemly propensity of our illustrious race, though I will only trouble you with a few more ancient ones; they not only nicknamed Regner, but his sons also, who were all kings, and distinguished men: one, whose name was Biorn, they nicknamed Ironsides; another, Sigurd, Snake in the Eye; another, White Sark, or White Shirt—I wonder they did not call him Dirty Shirt; and Ivarr, another, who was king of Northumberland, they called Bienlausi, or the Legless, because he was spindle-shanked, had no sap in his bones, and consequently no children. He was a great king, it is true, and very wise, nevertheless his blackguard countrymen, always averse, as their descendants are, to give credit to anybody, for any valuable quality or possession, must needs lay hold, do you see——"

But before I could say any more, the jockey, having laid down his pipe, rose, and having taken off his coat, advanced towards me.

CHAPTER XLII

A Short-tempered Person—Gravitation—The Best Endowment—Mary Fulcher—Fair Dealing—Horse-witchery—Darius and his Groom—The Jockey's Tricks—The Two Characters—The Jockey's Song.

THE jockey, having taken off his coat and advanced towards me, as I have stated in the preceding chapter, exclaimed, in an angry tone, " This is the third time you have interrupted me in my tale, Mr. Rye; I passed over the two first times with a simple warning, but you will now please to get up and give me the satisfaction of a man."

" I am really sorry," said I, " if I have given you offence, but you were talking of our English habits of bestowing nicknames, and I could not refrain from giving a few examples tending to prove what a very ancient habit it is."

" But you interrupted me," said the jockey, " and put me out of my tale, which you had no right to do; and as for your examples, how do you know that I wasn't going to give some as old or older than yourn? Now stand up, and I'll make an example of you."

" Well," said I, " I confess it was wrong in me to interrupt you, and I ask your pardon."

" That won't do," said the jockey, " asking pardon won't do."

" Oh," said I, getting up, " if asking pardon does not satisfy you, you are a different man from what I considered you."

But here the Hungarian, also getting up, interposed his tall form and pipe between us, saying in English, scarcely intelligible, " Let there be no dispute! As for myself, I am very much obliged to the young man of Horncastle for his interruption, though he has told me that one of his dirty townsmen called me ' Long-stocking.' By Isten! there is more learning in what he has just said than in all the verdammt English histories of Thor and Tzernebock I ever read."

" I care nothing for his learning," said the jockey. " I consider myself as good a man as he, for all his learning; so stand out of the way, Mr. Sixfooteleven, or——"

" I shall do no such thing," said the Hungarian. " I wonder you are not ashamed of yourself. You ask a young man to drink champagne with you, you make him dronk, he interrupt you with very good sense; he ask your pardon, yet you not——"

" Well," said the jockey, " I am satisfied. I am rather a short-tempered person, but I bear no malice. He is, as you say, drinking my wine, and has perhaps taken a drop too much, not being used to such high liquor; but one doesn't like to be put out of one's tale, more especially when one was about to moralize, do you see, oneself, and to show off what little learning one has. However, I bears no malice. Here is a hand to each of you; we'll take another glass each, and think no more about it."

The jockey having shaken both of our hands, and filled our glasses and his own with what champagne remained in the bottle, put on his coat, sat down, and resumed his pipe and story.

"Where was I? Oh, roaming about the country with Hopping Ned and Biting Giles. Those were happy days, and a merry and prosperous life we led. However, nothing continues under the sun in the same state in which it begins, and our firm was soon destined to undergo a change. We came to a village where there was a very high church steeple, and in a little time my comrades induced a crowd of people to go and see me display my gift by flinging stones above the heads of Matthew, Mark, Luke and John, who stood at the four corners on the top, carved in stone. The parson, seeing the crowd, came waddling out of his rectory to see what was going on. After I had flung up the stones, letting them fall just where I liked—and one, I remember, fell on the head of Mark, where I dare say it remains to the present day—the parson, who was one of the description of people called philosophers, held up his hand, and asked me to let the next stone I flung up fall upon it. He wished, do you see, to know with what weight the stone would fall down, and talked something about gravitation—a word which I could never understand to the present day, save that it turned out a grave matter to me. I, like a silly fellow myself, must needs consent, and, flinging the stone up to a vast height, contrived so that it fell into the parson's hand, which it cut dreadfully. The parson flew into a great rage, more particularly as everybody laughed at him, and, being a magistrate, ordered his clerk, who was likewise constable, to conduct me to prison as a rogue and vagabond, telling my comrades that if they did not take themselves off, he would serve them in the same manner. So Ned hopped off, and Giles ran after him, without making any gathering, and I was led to Bridewell, my mittimus following at the end of a week, the parson's hand not permitting him to write before that time. In the Bridewell I remained a month, when, being dismissed, I went in quest of my companions, whom, after some time, I found up, but they refused to keep my company any longer; telling me that I was a dangerous character, likely to bring them more trouble than profit; they had, moreover, filled up my place. Going into a cottage to ask for a drink of water, they saw a country fellow making faces to amuse his children; the faces were so wonderful that Hopping Ned and Biting Giles at once proposed taking him into partnership, and the man—who was a fellow not very fond of work—after a little entreaty, went away with them. I saw him exhibit his gift, and couldn't blame the others for preferring him to me; he was a proper ugly fellow at all times, but when he made faces his countenance was like nothing human. He was called Ugly Moses. I was so amazed at his faces, that though poor myself I gave him sixpence, which I have never grudged to this day, for I never saw anything like them. The firm throve wonderfully after he had been admitted into it. He died some little time ago, keeper of a public-house, which he had been enabled to take from the profits of his faces. A son of his, one of the children he was making faces to when my comrades entered his door, is at present a barrister, and a very rising one. He has his gift—he has not, it is true, the gift of the gab, but he has something better, he was born with a grin on his face, a quiet grin; he would not have done to grin through a collar like his father, and would never have been taken up by Hopping Ned and Biting Giles, but that grin of his caused him to be noticed by a much greater person than either; an attorney observing it took a liking to the lad, and pro-phesied that he would some day be heard of in the world; and in order to give him the first lift, took him into his office, at first to light fires and do such kind of work, and after a little time taught him to write, then promoted him to a desk, articled him afterwards, and being unmarried, and without children, left him what he had when he died. The young fellow, after practising at the law some time, went to the bar, where, in a few years, helped on by his grin, for he had nothing else to recommend him, he became, as I said before, a rising barrister. He comes our circuit, and I occasionally employ him, when I am obliged to go to law about such a thing as an unsound horse. He generally brings me through—or rather that grin of his does—and yet I don't like the fellow, confound him, but I'm an oddity—no, the one I like, and whom I generally employ, is a fellow quite different, a bluff sturdy dog, with no grin on his face, but with a look that seems to say I am an honest man, and what cares I for any one? And an honest man he is, and something more. I have known coves with a better gift of the gab, though not many, but he always speaks to the purpose, and understands law thoroughly; and that's not all. When at college, for he has been at college, he carried off everything before him as a Latiner, and was first-rate at a game they call matthew mattocks. I don't exactly know what it is, but I have heard that he who is first-rate at matthew mattocks is thought more of than if he were first-rate Latiner.

" Well, the chap that I'm talking about, not only came out first-rate Latiner, but first-rate at matthew mattocks too; doing, in fact, as I am told by those who knows, for I was never at college myself, what no one had ever done before. Well, he makes his appearance at our circuit, does very well, of course, but he has a somewhat high front, as becomes an honest man, and one who has beat every one at Latin and matthew mattocks; and one who can speak first-rate law and sense;—but see now, the cove with the grin, who has like myself never been at college; knows nothing of Latin, or matthew mattocks, and has no particular gift of the gab, has two briefs for his one, and I suppose very properly, for that grin of his curries favour with the juries; and mark me, that grin of his will enable him to beat the other in the long run. We all know what all barrister coves looks forward to—a seat on the hop sack. Well, I'll bet a bull to fivepence, that the grinner gets upon it, and the snarler doesn't; at any rate, that he gets there first. I calls my cove—for he is my cove—a snarler; because your first-rates at matthew mattocks are called snarlers, and for no other reason; for the chap, though with a high front, is a good chap, and once drank a glass of ale with me, after buying an animal out of my stable. I have often thought it a pity he wasn't born with a grin on his face like the son of Ugly *Moses*. It is true he would scarcely then have been an out and outer at Latin and matthew mattocks, but what need of either to a chap born with a grin? Talk of being born with a silver spoon in one's mouth! give me a cove born with a grin on his face —a much better endowment.

" I will now shorten my history as much as I can, for we have talked as much as folks do during a whole night in the Commons' House, though, of course, not with so much learning, or so much to the purpose, because—why? They are in the House of Commons, and we in a public room of an inn at Horncastle. The goodness of the ale, do ye see, never depending on what it is made of, oh, no! but on the fashion and appearance of the jug in which it is served up. After being turned out of the firm, I got my living in two or three honest ways, which I shall not trouble you with describing. I did not like any of them, however, as they did not exactly suit my humour; at last I found one which did. One Saturday afternoon, I chanced to be in the cattle-market of a place about eighty miles from here; there I won the favour of an old gentleman who sold dickeys. He had a very shabby squad of animals, without soul or spirit; nobody would buy them, till I leaped upon their hinder ends, and by merely wriggling in a particular manner, made them caper and bound so to people's liking, that in a few hours every one of them was sold at very sufficient prices. The old gentleman was so pleased with my skill, that he took me home with him, and in a very little time into partnership. It's a good thing to have a gift, but yet better to have two. I might have got a very decent livelihood by throwing stones, but I much question whether I should ever have attained to the position in society which I now occupy, but for my knowledge of animals. I lived very comfortably with the old gentleman till he died, which he did in about a fortnight after he had laid his old lady in the ground. Having no children, he left me what should remain after he had been buried decently, and the remainder was six dickeys and thirty shillings in silver. I remained in the dickey trade ten years, during which time I saved a hundred pounds. I then embarked in the horse line. One day, being in the ——— market on a Saturday, I saw Mary Fulcher with a halter round her neck, led about by a man, who offered to sell her for eighteen-pence. I took out the money forthwith and bought her; the man was her husband, a basket-maker, with whom she had lived several years without having any children; he was a drunken, quarrelsome fellow, and having had a dispute with her the day before, he determined to get rid of her, by putting a halter round her neck and leading her to the cattle-market, as if she were a mare, which he had, it seems, a right to do; all women being considered mares by old English law, and, indeed, still called mares in certain counties, where genuine old English is still preserved. That same afternoon, the man who had been her husband, having got drunk in a public-house, with the money which he had received for her, quarrelled with another man, and receiving a blow under the ear, fell upon the floor, and died of artiflex; and in less than three weeks I was married to Mary Fulcher, by virtue of regular bans. I am told she was legally my property by virtue of my having bought her with a halter round her neck; but, to tell you the truth, I think everybody should live by his trade, and I didn't wish to act shabbily towards our parson, who is a good fellow, and has certainly a right to his fees. A better wife than Mary Fulcher —I mean Mary Dale—no one ever had; she has borne me several children, and has at all times shown a willingness to oblige me, and to be my faithful wife. Amongst other things, I begged her to have done with her family, and I believe she has never spoken to them since.

" I have thriven very well in business, and my name is up as being a person who can be depended on, when folks treats me handsomely. I always make a point when a gentleman comes to me, and says, ' Mr. Dale,' or ' John,' for I have no objection to be called John by a gentleman— ' I wants a good horse, and am ready to pay a good price ' —I always makes a point, I say, to furnish him with an animal worth the money; but when I sees a fellow, whether he calls himself gentleman or not, wishing to circumvent me, what does I do? I doesn't quarrel with him; not I; but, letting him imagine he is taking me in, I contrives to sell him a screw for thirty pounds, not worth thirty shillings. All honest respectable people have at present great confidence in me, and frequently commissions me to buy them horses at great fairs like this.

" This short young gentleman was recommended to me by a great landed proprietor, to whom he bore letters of recommendation from some great prince in his own country, who had a long time ago been entertained at the house of the landed proprietor, and the consequence is, that I brings young six foot six to Horncastle, and purchases for him the horse of the Romany Rye. I don't do these kind things for nothing, it is true; that can't be expected; for every one must live by his trade; but, as I said before, when I am treated handsomely, I treat folks so. Honesty, I have discovered, as perhaps some other peole have, is by far the best policy; though, as I also said before, when I'm along with thieves, I can beat them at their own game. If I am obliged to do it, I can pass off the veriest screw as a flying drummedary, for even when I was a child I had found out by various means what may be done with animals. I wish now to ask a civil question, Mr. Romany Rye. Certain folks have told me that you are a horse witch; are you one, or are you not?"

"I, like yourself," said I, "know, to a certain extent, what may be done with animals."

"Then how would you, Mr. Romany Rye, pass off the veriest screw in the world for a flying drummedary?"

"By putting a small live eel down his throat; as long as the eel remained in his stomach, the horse would appear brisk and lively in a surprising degree."

"And how would you contrive to make a regular kicker and biter appear so tame and gentle, that any respectable fat old gentleman of sixty, who wanted an easy goer, would be glad to purchase him for fifty pounds?"

"By pouring down his throat four pints of generous old ale, which would make him so happy and comfortable, that he would not have the heart to kick or bite anybody, for a season at least."

"And where did you learn all this?" said the jockey.

"I have read about the eel in an old English book, and about the making drunk in a Spanish novel, and, singularly enough, I was told the same things by a wild blacksmith in Ireland. Now tell me, do you bewitch horses in this way?"

"I?" said the jockey; "mercy upon us! I wouldn't do such things for a hatful of money. No, no, preserve me from live eels and hocussing! And now let me ask you, how would you spirit a horse out of a field?"

"How would I spirit a horse out of a field?"

"Yes; supposing you were down in the world, and had determined on taking up the horse-stealing line of business."

"Why, I should—— But I tell you what, friend, I see you are trying to pump me, and I tell you plainly that I will hear something from you with respect to your art, before I tell you anything more. Now how would you whisper a horse out of a field, provided you were down in the world, and so forth?"

"Ah, ah, I see you are up to a game, Mr. Romany:

however, I am a gentleman in mind, if not by birth, and I scorn to do the unhandsome thing to anybody who has dealt fairly towards me. Now you told me something I didn't know, and I'll tell you something which perhaps you do know. I whispers a horse out of a field in this way : I have a mare in my stable; well, in the early season of the year I goes into my stable —— Well, I puts the sponge into a small bottle which I keeps corked. I takes my bottle in my hand, and goes into a field, suppose by night, where there is a very fine stag horse. I manage with great difficulty to get within ten yards of the horse, who stands staring at me just ready to run away. I then uncorks my bottle, presses my fore-finger to the sponge, and holds it out to the horse, the horse gives a sniff, then a start, and comes nearer. I corks up my bottle and puts it into my pocket. My business is done, for the next two hours the horse would follow me anywhere—the difficulty, indeed, would be to get rid of him. Now is that your way of doing business?"

" My way of doing business? Mercy upon us ! I wouldn't steal a horse in that way, or, indeed, in any way, for all the money in the world : however, let me tell you, for your comfort, that a trick somewhat similar is described in the history of Herodotus."

" In the history of Herod's ass !" said the jockey; " well, if I did write a book, it should be about something more genteel than a dickey."

" I did not say Herod's ass," said I, " but Herodotus, a very genteel writer, I assure you, who wrote a history about very genteel people, in a language no less genteel than Greek, more than two thousand years ago. There was a dispute as to who should be king amongst certain imperious chieftains. At last they agreed to obey him whose horse should neigh first on a certain day, in front of the royal palace, before the rising of the sun; for you must know that they did not worship the person who made the sun as we do, but the sun itself. So one of these chieftains, talking over the matter to his groom, and saying he wondered who would be king, the fellow said, ' Why you, master, or I don't know much about horses.' So the day before the day of trial, what does the groom do, but take his master's horse before the palace and introduce him to a mare in the stable, and then lead him forth again. Well, early the next day all the chieftains on their horses appeared in front of the palace before the dawn of day. Not a horse neighed but one, and that was the horse of him who had consulted with his groom, who, thinking of the animal within the stable, gave such a neigh that all the buildings rang. His rider was forthwith elected king, and a brave king he was. So this shows what seemingly wonderful things may be brought about by a little preparation."

"It doth," said the jockey; "what was the chap's name?"

"His name—his name—Darius Hystaspes."

"And the groom's?"

"I don't know."

"And he made a good king?"

"First-rate."

"Only think! well, if he made a good king, what a wonderful king the groom would have made, through whose knowledge of 'orses he was put on the throne. And now another question, Mr. Romany Rye, have you particular words which have power to soothe or aggravate horses?"

"You should ask me," said I, "whether I have horses that can be aggravated or soothed by particular words. No words have any particular power over horses or other animals who have never heard them before—how should they? But certain animals connect ideas of misery or enjoyment with particular words which they are acquainted with. I'll give you an example. I knew a cob in Ireland that could be driven to a state of kicking madness by a particular word, used by a particular person, in a particular tone; but that word was connected with a very painful operation which had been performed upon him by that individual, who had frequently employed it at a certain period whilst the animal had been under his treatment. The same cob could be soothed in a moment by another word, used by the same individual in a very different kind of tone; the word was deaghblasda, or sweet tasted. Some time after the operation, whilst the cob was yet under his hands, the fellow—who was what the Irish call a fairy smith—had done all he could to soothe the creature, and had at last succeeded by giving it gingerbread-buttons, of which the cob became passionately fond. Invariably, however, before giving it a button, he said, 'Deaghblasda,' with which word the cob by degrees associated an idea of unmixed enjoyment: so if he could rouse the cob to madness by the word which recalled the torture to its remembrance, he could as easily soothe it by the other word, which the cob knew would be instantly followed by the button, which the smith never failed to give him after using the word deaghblasda.''

'' There is nothing wonderful to be done,'' said the jockey, '' without a good deal of preparation, as I know myself. Folks stare and wonder at certain things which they would only laugh at if they knew how they were done; and to prove what I say is true, I will give you one or two examples. Can either of you lend me a handkerchief? That won't do,'' said he, as I presented him with a silk one. '' I wish for a delicate white handkerchief. That's just the kind of thing,'' said he, as the Hungarian offered him a fine white cambric handkerchief, beautifully worked with gold at the hems; '' now you shall see me set this handkerchief on fire.'' '' Don't let him do so by any means,'' said the Hungarian, speaking to me in German, '' it is the gift of a lady whom I highly admire, and I would not have it burnt for the world.'' '' He has no occasion to be under any apprehension,'' said the jockey, after I had interpreted to him what the Hungarian had said, '' I will restore it to him uninjured, or my name is not Jack Dale.'' Then sticking the handkerchief carelessly into the left side of his bosom, he took the candle, which by this time had burnt very low, and holding his head back, he applied the flame to the handkerchief, which instantly seemed to catch fire. '' What do you think of that?'' said he to the Hungarian. '' Why, that you have ruined me,'' said the latter. '' No harm done, I assure you,'' said the jockey, who presently, clapping his hand on his bosom, extinguished the fire, and returned the handkerchief to the Hungarian, asking him if it was burnt. '' I see no burn upon it,'' said the Hungarian; '' but in the name of Gott, how could you set it on fire without burning it?'' '' I never set it on fire at all,'' said the jockey; '' I set this on fire,'' showing us a piece of half-burnt calico. '' I placed this calico above it, and lighted not the handkerchief, but the rag. Now I will show you something else. I have a magic shilling in my pocket, which I can make run up along my arm. But, first of all, I would gladly know whether either of you can do the like.'' Thereupon the Hungarian and myself, putting our hands into our pockets, took out shillings, and endeavoured to make them run up our arms, but utterly failed; both shillings, after we had made two or three attempts, falling to the ground. " What noncomposses you both are," said the jockey; and placing a shilling on the end of the fingers of his right hand he made strange faces to it, drawing back his head, whereupon the shilling instantly began to run up his arm, occasionally hopping and jumping as if it were bewitched, always endeavouring to make towards the head of the jockey.

" How do I do that?" said he, addressing himself to me. " I really do not know," said I, ' unless it is by the motion of your arm.' " The motion of my nonsense," said the jockey, and, making a dreadful grimace, the shilling hopped upon his knee, and began to run up his thigh and to climb up his breast. " How is that done?" said he again. " By witchcraft, I suppose," said I. " There you are right," said the jockey; " by the witch-craft of one of Miss Berners' hairs; the end of one of her long hairs is tied to that shilling by means of a hole in it, and the other end goes round my neck by means of a loop; so that, when I draw back my head, the shilling follows it. I suppose you wish to know how I got the hair," said he, grinning at me. " I will tell you. I once, in the course of my ridings, saw Miss Berners beneath a hedge, combing out her long hair, and, being rather a modest kind of person, what must I do but get off my horse, tie him to a gate, go up to her, and endeavour to enter into conversation with her. After giving her the sele of the day, and complimenting her on her hair, I asked her to give me one of the threads; whereupon she gave me such a look, and, calling me fellow, told me to take myself off. ' I must have a hair first,' said I, making a snatch at one. I believe I hurt her; but, whether I did or not, up she started, and, though her hair was unbound, gave me the only drubbing I ever had in my life. Lor! how, with her right hand, she fibbed me whilst she held me round the neck with her left arm; I was soon glad to beg her pardon on my knees, which she gave me in a moment, when she saw me in that condition, being the most placable creature in the world, and not only her pardon, but one of the hairs which I longed for, which I put through a shilling, with which I have on evenings after fairs, like this, frequently worked what seemed to those who looked on downright witchcraft, but which is nothing more than pleasant deception. And now, Mr. Romany Rye, to testify my regard for you, I give you the shilling and the hair. I think you have a kind of respect for Miss Berners; but whether you have or not, keep them as long as you can, and whenever you look at them think of the finest woman in England, and of John Dale, the jockey of Horncastle. I believe I have told you my history,'" said he—" no, not quite; there is one circum-stance I had passed over. I told you that I have thriven very well in business, and so I have, upon the whole; at any rate, I find myself comfortably off now. I have horses, money, and owe nobody a groat; at any rate, nothing but what I could pay to-morrow. Yet I have had my dreary day, ay, after I had obtained what I call a station in the world. All of a sudden, about five years ago, everything seemed to go wrong with me—horses became sick or died, people who owed me money broke or ran away, my house caught fire, in fact, everything went against me; and not from any mismanagement of my own. I looked round for help, but—what do you think?—nobody would help me. Somehow or other it had got abroad that I was in difficulties, and everybody seemed disposed to avoid me, as if I had got the plague. Those who were always offer-ing me help when I wanted none, now, when they thought me in trouble, talked of arresting me. Yes; two par-ticular friends of mine, who had always been offering me their purses when my own was stuffed full, now talked of arresting me, though I only owed the scoundrels a hundred pounds each; and they would have done so, provided I had not paid them what I owed them; and how did I do that? Why, I was able to do it because I found a friend —and who was that friend? Why, a man who has since been hung, of whom everybody has heard, and of whom everybody for the next hundred years will occasionally talk.

" One day, whilst in trouble, I was visited by a person I had occasionally met at sporting-dinners. He came to look after a Suffolk Punch, the best horse, by the bye, that anybody can purchase to drive, it being the only animal of the horse kind in England that will pull twice at a dead weight. I told him that I had none at that time that I could recommend; in fact, that every horse in my stable was sick. He then invited me to dine with him at an inn close by, and I was glad to go with him, in the hope of getting rid of unpleasant thoughts. After dinner, during which he talked nothing but slang, observing I looked very melancholy, he asked me what was the matter with me, and I, my heart being opened by the wine he had made me drink, told him my circumstances without reserve. With an oath or two for not having treated him at first like a friend, he said he would soon set me all right; and pulling out two hundred pounds, told me to pay him when I could. I felt as I never felt before; however, I took his notes, paid my sneaks, and in less than three months was right again, and had returned him his money. On paying it to him, I said that I had now a Punch which would just suit him, saying that I would give it to him-- a free gift—for nothing. He swore at me; telling me to keep my Punch, for that he was suited already. I begged him to tell me how I could requite him for his kindness, whereupon, with the most dreadful oath I ever heard, he bade me come and see him hanged when his time was come. I wrung his hand, and told him I would, and I kept my word. The night before the day he was hanged at H——, I harnessed a Suffolk Punch to my light gig, the same Punch which I had offered to him, which I have ever since kept, and which brought me and this short young man to Horncastle, and in eleven hours I drove that Punch one hundred and ten miles. I arrived at H—— just in the nick of time. There was the ugly jail—the scaffold—and there upon it stood the only friend I ever had in the world. Driving my Punch, which was all in a foam, into the midst of the crowd, which made way for me as if it knew what I came for, I stood up in my gig, took off my hat, and shouted, ' God Almighty bless you, Jack !' The dying man turned his pale grim face towards me—for his face was always somewhat grim, do you see—nodded and said, or I thought I heard him say, ' All right, old chap.' The next moment—my eyes water. He had a high heart, got into a scrape whilst in the marines, lost his half-pay, took to the turf, ring, gambling, and at last cut the throat of a villain who had robbed him of nearly all he had. But he had good qualities, and I know for certain that he never did half the bad things laid to his charge; for example, he never bribed Tom Oliver to fight cross, as it was said he did on the day of the awful thunder-storm. Ned Flatnose fairly beat Tom

Oliver, for though Ned was not what's called a good fighter, he had a particular blow, which if he could put in he was sure to win. His right shoulder, do you see, was two inches farther back than it ought to have been, and consequently his right fist generally fell short; but if he could swing himself round, and put in a blow with that right arm, he could kill or take away the senses of anybody in the world. It was by putting in that blow in his second fight with Spring that he beat noble Tom. Spring beat him like a sack in the first battle, but in the second Ned Painter—for that was his real name—contrived to put in his blow, and took the senses out of Spring; and in like manner he took the senses out of Tom Oliver.

" Well, some are born to be hanged, and some are not; and many of those who are not hanged are much worse than those who are. Jack, with many a good quality, is hanged, whilst that fellow of a lord, who wanted to get the horse from you at about two-thirds of his value, without a single good quality in the world, is not hanged, and probably will remain so. You ask the reason why, perhaps. I'll tell you; the lack of a certain quality called courage, which Jack possessed in abundance, will preserve him; from the love which he bears his own neck he will do nothing which can bring him to the gallows. In my rough way I'll draw their characters from their childhood, and then ask whether Jack was not the best character of the two. Jack was a rough, audacious boy, fond of fighting, going a birds'-nesting, but I never heard he did anything particularly cruel save once, I believe, tying a canister to a butcher's dog's tail; whilst this fellow of a lord was by nature a savage beast, and when a boy would in winter pluck poor fowls naked, and set them running on the ice and in the snow, and was particularly fond of burning cats alive in the fire. Jack, when a lad, gets a commission on board a ship as an officer of horse marines, and in two or three engagements behaves quite up to the mark—at least of a marine; the marines having no particular character for courage, you know—never having run to the guns and fired them like madmen after the blue jackets had had more than enough. Oh, dear me, no ! My lord gets into the valorous British army, where cowardice—Oh, dear me ! —is a thing almost entirely unknown; and being on the field of Waterloo the day before the battle, falls off his horse, and, pretending to be hurt in the back, gets himself put on the sick list—a pretty excuse—hurting his back—for not being present at such a fight. Old Benbow, after part of both his legs had been shot away in a sea-fight, made the carpenter make him a cradle to hold his bloody stumps, and continued on deck, cheering his men till he died. Jack returns home, and gets into trouble, and having nothing to subsist by but his wits, gets his living by the ring and the turf, doing many an odd kind of thing, I dare say, but not half those laid to his charge. My lord does much the same without the excuse for doing so which Jack had, for he had plenty of means, is a leg, and a black, only in a more polished way, and with more cunning, and I may say success, having done many a rascally thing never laid to his charge. Jack at last cuts the throat of a villain who had cheated him of all he had in the world, and who, I am told, was in many points the counterpart of this screw and white feather, is taken up, tried, and executed; and certainly taking away a man's life is a dreadful thing; but is there nothing as bad? Whitefeather will cut no person's throat—I will not say who has cheated him, for, being a cheat himself, he will take good care that nobody cheats him, but he'll do something quite as bad; out of envy to a person who never injured him, and whom he hates for being more clever and respected than himself, he will do all he possibly can, by backbiting and every unfair means, to do that person a mortal injury. But Jack is hanged, and my lord it not. Is that right? My wife, Mary Fulcher—I beg her pardon, Mary Dale—who is a Methodist, and has heard the mighty preacher, Peter Williams, says some people are preserved from hanging by the grace of God. With her I differs, and says it is from want of courage. This Whitefeather, with one particle of Jack's courage, and with one tithe of his good qualities, would have been hanged long ago, for he has ten times Jack's malignity. Jack was hanged because, along with his bad qualities, he had courage and generosity; this fellow is not, because with all Jack's bad qualities, and many more, amongst which is cunning, he has neither courage nor generosity. Think of a fellow like that putting down two hundred pounds to relieve a distressed fellow-creature; why he would rob, but for the law and the fear it fills him with, a workhouse child of its breakfast,

as the saying is—and has been heard to say that he would
not trust his own father for sixpence, and he can't imagine
why such a thing as credit should be ever given. I never
heard a person give him a good word—stay, stay, yes! I
once heard an old parson, to whom I sold a Punch, say
that he had the art of receiving company gracefully and
dismissing them without refreshment. I don't wish to be
too hard with him, and so let him make the most of that
compliment. Well! he manages to get on, whilst Jack
is hanged; not quite enviably, however; he has had his
rubs, and pretty hard ones—everybody knows he slunk
from Waterloo, and occasionally checks him with so doing;
whilst he has been rejected by a woman—what a mortification to the low pride of which the scoundrel has plenty!
There's a song about both circumstances, which may, perhaps, ring in his ears on a dying bed. It's a funny kind
of song, set to the old tune of the Lord-Lieutenant or
Deputy, and with it I will conclude my discourse, for I
really think it's past one." The jockey then, with a very
tolerable voice, sung the following song :—

THE JOCKEY'S SONG.

Now list to a ditty both funny and true !—
　Merrily moves the dance along—
A ditty that tells of a coward and screw,
　My Lord-Lieutenant so free and young.

Sir Plume, though not liking a bullet at all,—
　Merrily moves the dance along—
Had yet resolution to go to a *ball,*
　My Lord-Lieutenant so free and young.

" Woulez wous danser, mademoiselle?"—
　Merrily moves the dance along ;—
Said she, " Sir, to dance I should like very well,"
　My Lord-Lieutenant so free and young.

They danc'd to the left, and they danc'd to the right,—
　Merrily moves the dance along ;—
And her troth the fair damsel bestow'd on the knight,
　My Lord-Lieutenant so free and young.

" Now what shall I fetch you, mademoiselle?"—
　Merrily moves the dance along ;—
Said she, " Sir, an ice I should like very well,"
　My Lord-Lieutenant so free and young.

But the ice, when he'd got it, he instantly ate,—
   Merrily moves the dance along ;—
Although his poor partner was all in a fret,
   My Lord-Lieutenant so free and young.

He ate up the ice like a prudent young lord,—
   Merrily moves the dance along ;—
For he saw 't was the very last ice on the board,—
   My Lord-Lieutenant so free and young.

" Now, when shall we marry?" the gentleman cried ;—
   Merrily moves the dance along ;—
" Sir, get you to Jordan," the damsel replied,
   My Lord-Lieutenant so free and young.

" I never will wed with the pitiful elf "—
   Merrily moves the dance along—
" Who ate up the ice which I wanted myself,"
   My Lord-Lieutenant so free and young.

" I'd pardon your backing from red Waterloo,"—
   Merrily moves the dance along—
" But I never will wed with a coward and screw,"
   My Lord-Lieutenant so free and young.

CHAPTER XLIII

The Church.

THE next morning I began to think of departing; I had
sewed up the money which I had received for the horse in
a portion of my clothing, where I entertained no fears for
its safety, with the exception of a small sum in notes,
gold, and silver, which I carried in my pocket. Ere departing, however, I determined to stroll about and examine
the town, and observe more particularly the homours of
the fair than I had hitherto an opportunity of doing. The
town, when I examined it, offered no object worthy of attention but its church—an edifice of some antiquity; under
the guidance of an old man, who officiated as sexton, I
inspected its interior attentively, occasionally conversing
with my guide, who, however, seemed much more disposed
to talk about horses than the church. " No good horses
in the fair this time, measter," said he; " none but one
brought hither by a chap whom nobody knows, and bought
by a foreigneering man, who came here with Jack Dale.

The horse fetched a good swinging price, which is said, however, to be much less than its worth; for the horse is a regular clipper; not such a one, 'tis said, has been seen in the fair for several summers. Lord Whitefeather says that he believes the fellow who brought him to be a highwayman, and talks of having him taken up, but Lord Whitefeather is only in a rage because he could not get him for himself. The chap would not sell it to un; Lord Screw wanted to beat him down, and the chap took huff, said he wouldn't sell it to him at no price, and accepted the offer of the foreigneering man, or of Jack, who was his 'terpreter, and who scorned to higgle about such a hanimal, because Jack is a gentleman, though bred a dickey-boy, whilst t'other, though bred a lord, is a screw and a whitefeather. Every one says the cove was right, and I says so too; I likes spirit, and if the cove were here, and in your place, measter, I would invite him to drink a pint of beer. Good horses are scarce now, measter, ay, and so are good men, quite a different set from what there were when I was young; that was the time for men and horses. Lord bless you, I know all the breeders about here; they are not a bad set, and they breed a very fairish set of horses, but they are not like what their fathers were, nor are their horses like their fathers' horses. Now there is Mr. —— the great breeder, a very fairish man, with very fairish horses; but, Lord bless you, he's nothing to what his father was, nor his steeds to his father's; I ought to know, for I was at the school here with his father, and afterwards for many a year helped him to get up his horses; that was when I was young, measter—those were the days. You look at that monument, measter," said he, as I stopped and looked attentively at a monument on the southern side of the church near the altar; "that was put up for a rector of this church, who lived a long time ago, in Oliver's time, and was ill-treated and imprisoned by Oliver and his men; you will see all about it on the monument. There was a grand battle fought nigh this place, between Oliver's men and the Royal party, and the Royal party had the worst of it, as I'm told they generally had; and Oliver's men came into the town, and did a great deal of damage, and illtreated the people. I can't remember anything about the matter myself, for it happened just one hundred years before I was born, but my father was ac-

quainted with an old countryman, who lived not many
miles from here, who said he remembered perfectly well
the day of the battle; that he was a boy at the time, and
was working in a field near the place where the battle was
fought; and heard shouting, and noise of firearms, and
also the sound of several balls, which fell in the field near
him. Come this way, measter, and I will show you some
remains of that day's field." Leaving the monument, on
which was inscribed an account of the life and sufferings
of the Royalist Rector of Horncastle, I followed the sexton
to the western end of the church, where, hanging against
the wall, were a number of scythes stuck in the ends of
poles. "Those are the weapons, measter," said the
sexton, "which the great people put into the hands of the
country folks, in order that they might use them against
Oliver's men; ugly weapons enough; however, Oliver's
men won, and Sir Jacob Ashley and his party were beat.
And a rare time Oliver and his men had of it, till Oliver
died, when the other party got the better, not by fighting,
'tis said, but through a General Monk, who turned sides.
Ah, the old fellow that my father knew, said he well
remembered the time when General Monk went over and
proclaimed Charles the Second. Bonfires were lighted
everywhere, oxen roasted, and beer drunk by pailfuls;
the country folks were drunk with joy, and something
else; sung scurvy songs about Oliver to the tune of
Barney Banks, and pelted his men, wherever they found
them, with stones and dirt." "The more ungrateful
scoundrels they," said I. "Oliver and his men fought
the battle of English independence against a wretched king
and corrupt lords. Had I been living at the time, I should
have been proud to be a trooper of Oliver." "You would,
measter, would you? Well, I never quarrels with the
opinions of people who come to look at the church, and
certainly independence is a fine thing. I like to see a
chap of an independent spirit, and if I were now to see
the cove that refused to sell his horse to my Lord Screw and
Whitefeather, and let Jack Dale have him, I would offer
to treat him to a pint of beer—e'es, I would, verily. Well,
measter, you have now seen the church, and all there's
in it worth seeing—so I'll just lock up, and go and finish
digging the grave I was about when you came, after which
I must go into the fair to see how matters are going on.

Thank ye, measter," said he, as I put something into his hand; " thank ye kindly; 'tis not every one who gives me a shilling now-a-days who comes to see the church, but times are very different from what they were when I was young; I was not sexton then, but something better; helped Mr. —— with his horses, and got many a broad crown. Those were the days, measter, both for men and horses— and I say, measter, if men and horses were so much better when I was young than they are now, what, I wonder, must they have been in the time of Oliver and his men?"

CHAPTER XLIV

An Old Acquaintance.

LEAVING the church, I strolled through the fair, looking at the horses, listening to the chaffering of the buyers and sellers, and occasionally putting in a word of my own, which was not always received with much deference; suddenly, however, on a whisper arising that I was the young cove who had brought the wonderful horse to the fair which Jack Dale had bought for the foreigneering man, I found myself an object of the greatest attention; those who had before replied with stuff! and nonsense! to what I said, now listened with the greatest eagerness to any nonsense I wished to utter, and I did not fail to utter a great deal; presently, however, becoming disgusted with the beings about me, I forced my way, not very civilly, through my crowd of admirers; and passing through an alley and a back street, at last reached an outskirt of the fair, where no person appeared to know me. Here I stood, looking vacantly on what was going on, musing on the strange infatuation of my species, who judge of a person's words, not from their intrinsic merit, but from the opinion— generally an erroneous one—which they have formed of the person. From this reverie I was roused by certain words which sounded near me, uttered in a strange tone, and in a strange cadence—the words were, " them that finds, wins; and them that can't find, loses." Turning my eyes in the direction from which the words proceeded, I saw six or seven people, apparently all countrymen, gathered round a person standing behind a tall white table of very small compass. "What!" said I, "the thimble-engro of —— Fair here at Horncastle." Advancing nearer, however, I perceived that though the present person was a thimble-engro, he was a very different one from my old acquaintance of —— Fair. The present one was a fellow about half-a-foot taller than the other. He had a long, haggard, wild face, and was dressed in a kind of jacket, something like that of a soldier, with dirty hempen trousers, and with a foreign-looking peaked hat on his head. He spoke with an accent evidently Irish, and occasionally changed the usual thimble formule, "them that finds wins, and them that can't—och, sure!—they loses;" saying also frequently, "your honour," instead of "my lord." I observed, on drawing nearer, that he handled the pea and thimble with some awkwardness, like that which might be expected from a novice in the trade. He contrived, however, to win several shillings, for he did not seem to play for gold, from "their honours." Awkward, as he was, he evidently did his best, and never flung a chance away by permitting any one to win. He had just won three shillings from a farmer, who, incensed at his loss, was calling him a confounded cheat, and saying that he would play no more, when up came my friend of the preceding day, Jack, the jockey. This worthy, after looking at the thimble-man a moment or two, with a peculiarly crafty glance, cried out, as he clapped down a shilling on the table, "I will stand you, old fellow!" "Them that finds wins; and them that can't—och, sure!—they loses," said the thimble-man. The game commenced, and Jack took up the thimble without finding the pea; another shilling was produced, and lost in the same manner; "this is slow work," said Jack, banging down a guinea on the table; "can you cover that, old fellow?" The man of the thimble looked at the gold, and then at him who produced it, and scratched his head. "Come, cover that, or I shall be off," said the jockey. "Och, sure, my lord!—no, I mean your honour—no, sure, your lordship," said the other, "if I covers it at all, it must be with silver, for divil a bit of gold have I by me." "Well, then, produce the value in silver," said the jockey, "and do it quickly, for I can't be staying here all day." The thimble-man hesitated, looked at Jack with a dubious look, then at the gold, and then scratched his head. There was now a laugh amongst the surrounders, which evidently nettled the fellow, who forthwith thrust his hand into his pocket, and pulling out all his silver treasure, just contrived to place the value of the guinea on the table. "Them that finds wins, and them that can't find—*loses*," interrupted Jack, lifting up a thimble, out of which rolled a pea. "There, paddy, what do you think of that?" said he, seizing the heap of silver with one hand, whilst he pocketed the guinea with the other. The thimble-engro stood, for some time, like one transfixed, his eyes glaring wildly, now at the table, and now at his successful customers; at last he said, "Arrah, sure, master!—no, I manes my lord—you are not going to ruin a poor boy!" "Ruin you!" said the other; "what! by winning a guinea's change? a pretty small dodger you—if you have not sufficient capital, why do you engage in so deep a trade as thimbling? come, will you stand another game?" "Och, sure, master, no! the twenty shillings and one which you have cheated me of were all I had in the world." "Cheated you," said Jack, "say that again, and I will knock you down." "Arrah! sure, master, you knows that the pea under the thimble was not mine; here is mine, master; now give me back my money." "A likely thing," said Jack; "no, no, I know a trick worth two or three of that; whether the pea was yours or mine, you will never have your twenty shillings and one again; and if I have ruined you, all the better; I'd gladly ruin all such villains as you, who ruin poor men with your dirty tricks, whom you would knock down and rob on the road, if you had but courage; not that I mean to keep your shillings, with the exception of the two you cheated from me, which I'll keep. A scramble, boys! a scramble!" said he, flinging up all the silver into the air, with the exception of the two shillings; and a scramble there instantly was, between the rustics who had lost their money and the urchins who came running up; the poor thimble-engro tried likewise to have his share; and though he flung himself down, in order to join more effectually in the scramble, he was unable to obtain a single sixpence; and having in his rage given some of his fellow-scramblers a cuff or two, he was set upon by the boys and country fellows, and compelled to make an inglorious retreat with his table, which had been flung down in the

scuffle, and had one of its legs broken. As he retired, the
rabble hooted, and Jack, holding up in derision the pea
with which he had out-manœuvred him, exclaimed, " I
always carry this in my pocket in order to be a match for
vagabonds like you."

The tumult over, Jack gone, and the rabble dispersed,
I followed the discomfited adventurer at a distance, who,
leaving the town, went slowly on, carrying his dilapidated
piece of furniture; till coming to an old wall by the roadside, he placed it on the ground, and sat down, seemingly
in deep despondency, holding his thumb to his mouth.
Going nearly up to him, I stood still, whereupon he looked
up, and perceiving I was looking steadfastly at him, he
said, in an angry tone, " Arrah! what for are you staring
at me so? By my shoul, I think you are one of the thaives
who are after robbing me. I think I saw you among them,
and if I were only sure of it, I would take the liberty of
trying to give you a big bating." " You have had enough
of trying to give people a beating," said I; "you had
better be taking your table to some skilful carpenter to get
it repaired. He will do it for sixpence." " Divil a sixpence did you and your thaives leave me," said he; " and
if you do not take yourself off, joy, I will be breaking your
ugly head with the foot of it." " Arrah, Murtagh!" said
I, " would ye be breaking the head of your friend and
scholar, to whom you taught the blessed tongue of Oilien
nan Naomha, in exchange for a pack of cards?" Murtagh,
for he it was, gazed at me for a moment with a bewildered
look; then, with a gleam of intelligence in his eye, he said,
" Shorsha! no, it can't be—yes, by my faith it is!" Then,
springing up, and seizing me by the hand, he said, " Yes,
by the powers, sure enough it is Shorsha agra! Arrah,
Shorsha! where have you been this many a day? Sure,
you are not one of the spalpeens who are after robbing
me?" " Not I," I replied, " but I saw all that happened.
Come, you must not take matters so to heart; cheer up;
such things will happen in connection with the trade you
have taken up." " Sorrow befall the trade, and the thief
who taught it me," said Murtagh; " and yet the trade is
not a bad one, if I only knew more of it, and had some one
to help and back me. Och! the idea of being cheated and
bamboozled by that one-eyed thief in the horseman's
dress." " Let bygones be bygones, Murtagh," said I;

"it is no use grieving for the past; sit down, and let us have a little pleasant gossip. Arrah, Murtagh! when I saw you sitting under the wall, with your thumb to your mouth, it brought to my mind tales which you used to tell me all about Finn-ma-Coul. You have not forgotten Finn-ma-Coul, Murtagh, and how he sucked wisdom out of his thumb." "Sorrow a bit have I forgot about him, Shorsha," said Murtagh, as we sat down together, "nor what you yourself told me about the snake. Arrah, Shorsha! what ye told me about the snake, bates anything I ever told you about Finn. Ochone, Shorsha! perhaps you will be telling me about the snake once more? I think the tale would do me good, and I have need of comfort, God knows, ochone!" Seeing Murtagh in such a distressed plight, I forthwith told him over again the tale of the snake, in precisely the same words as I have related it in the first part of this history. After which, I said, "Now, Murtagh, tit for tat; ye will be telling me one of the old stories of Finn-ma-Coul." "Och, Shorsha! I haven't heart enough," said Murtagh. "Thank you for your tale, but it makes me weep; it brings to my mind Dungarvon times of old—I mean the times we were at school together." "Cheer up, man," said I, "and let's have the story, and let it be about Ma-Coul and the salmon and his thumb." "Arrah, Shorsha! I can't. Well, to oblige you, I'll give it you. Well, you know Ma-Coul was an exposed child, and came floating over the salt sea in a chest which was cast ashore at Veintry Bay. In the corner of that bay was a castle, where dwelt a giant and his wife, very respectable and decent people, and this giant, taking his morning walk along the bay, came to the place where the child had been cast ashore in his box. Well, the giant looked at the child, and being filled with compassion for his exposed state, took the child up in his box, and carried him home to his castle, where he and his wife, being dacent respectable people, as I telled ye before, fostered the child and took care of him, till he became old enough to go out to service and gain his livelihood, when they bound him out apprentice to another giant, who lived in a castle up the country, at some distance from the bay.

"This giant, whose name was Darmod David Odeen, was not a respectable person at all, but a big old vagabond. He was twice the size of the other giant, who, though

bigger than any man, was not a big giant; for, as there
are great and small men, so there are great and small
giants—I mean some are small when compared with the
others. Well, Finn served this giant a considerable time,
doing all kinds of hard and unreasonable service for him,
and receiving all kinds of hard words, and many a hard
knock and kick to boot—sorrow befall the old vagabond
who could thus ill-treat a helpless foundling. It chanced
that one day the giant caught a salmon, near a salmon-leap
upon his estate—for, though a big ould blackguard, he
was a person of considerable landed property, and high
sheriff for the county Cork. Well, the giant brings home
the salmon by the gills, and delivers it to Finn, telling him
to roast it for the giant's dinner; 'but take care, ye young
blackguard,' he added, 'that in roasting it—and I expect
ye to roast it well—you do not let a blister come upon its
nice satin skin, for if ye do, I will cut the head off your
shoulders.' 'Well,' thinks Finn, 'this is a hard task;
however, as I have done many hard tasks for him, I will
try and do this too, though I was never set to do anything
yet half so difficult.' So he prepared his fire, and put his
gridiron upon it, and lays the salmon fairly and softly upon
the gridiron, and then he roasts it, turning it from one side
to the other just in the nick of time, before the soft satin
skin could be blistered. However, on turning it over the
eleventh time—and twelve would have settled the business
—he found he had delayed a little bit of time too long in
turning it over, and that there was a small, tiny blister on
the soft outer skin. Well, Finn was in a mighty panic,
remembering the threats of the ould giant; however, he did
not lose heart, but clapped his thumb upon the blister in
order to smooth it down. Now the salmon, Shorsha, was
nearly done, and the flesh thoroughly hot, so Finn's thumb
was scalt, and he, clapping it to his mouth, sucked it, in
order to draw out the pain, and in a moment—hubbuboo!
—became imbued with all the wisdom of the world.

Myself. Stop, Murtagh! stop!

Murtagh. All the witchcraft, Shorsha.

Myself. How wonderful!

Murtagh. Was it not, Shorsha? The salmon, do you
see, was a fairy salmon.

Myself. What a strange coincidence!

Murtagh. A what, Shorsha?

Myself. Why, that the very same tale should be told of Finn-ma-Coul, which is related of Sigurd Fafnisbane.

"What thief was that, Shorsha?"

"Thief! 'Tis true, he took the treasure of Fafnir. Sigurd was the hero of the North, Murtagh, even as Finn is the great hero of Ireland. He, too, according to one account, was an exposed child, and came floating in a casket to a wild shore, where he was suckled by a hind, and afterwards found and fostered by Mimir, a fairy blacksmith; he, too, sucked wisdom from a burn. According to the Edda, he burnt his finger whilst feeling of the heart of Fafnir, which he was roasting, and putting it into his mouth in order to suck out the pain, became imbued with all the wisdom of the world, the knowledge of the language of birds, and what not. I have heard you tell the tale of Finn a dozen times in the blessed days of old, but its identity with the tale of Sigurd never occurred to me till now. It is true, when I knew you of old, I had never read the tale of Sigurd, and have since almost dismissed matters of Ireland from my mind; but as soon as you told me again about Finn's burning his finger, the coincidence struck me. I say, Murtagh, the Irish owe much to the Danes——"

"Devil a bit, Shorsha, do they owe to the thaives, except many a bloody bating and plundering, which they never paid them back. Och, Shorsha! you, edicated in ould Ireland, to say that the Irish owes anything good to the plundering villains—the Siol Loughlin."

"They owe them half their traditions, Murtagh, and amongst others, Finn-ma-Coul and the burnt finger; and if ever I publish the Loughlin songs, I'll tell the world so."

"But, Shorsha, the world will never believe ye—to say nothing of the Irish part of it."

"Then the world, Murtagh—to say nothing of the Irish part of it—will be a fool, even as I have often thought it; the grand thing, Murtagh, is to be able to believe oneself, and respect oneself. How few whom the world believes believe and respect themselves."

"Och, Shorsha! shall I go on with the tale of Finn?"

"I'd rather you should not, Murtagh; I know all about it already."

"Then why did you bother me to tell it at first, Shorsha? Och, it was doing my ownself good, and making me forget my own sorrowful state, when ye interrupted me with your

thaives of Danes! Och, Shorsha! let me tell you how
Finn, by means of sucking his thumb, and the witchcraft
he imbibed from it, contrived to pull off the arm of the ould
wagabone, Darmod David Odeen, whilst shaking hands
with him—for Finn could do no feat of strength without
sucking his thumb, Shorsha, as Conan the Bald told the
son of Oisin in the song which I used to sing ye in Dungarvon times of old;" and here Murtagh repeated certain
Irish words to the following effect :—

> " O little the foolish words I heed
> O Oisin's son, from thy lips which come ;
> No strength were in Finn for valorous deed,
> Unless to the gristle he suck'd his thumb."

" Enough is as good as a feast, Murtagh, I am no longer
in the cue for Finn. I would rather hear your own history. Now tell us, man, all that has happened to ye since
Dungarvon times of old?"

" Och, Shorsha, it would be merely bringing all my
sorrows back upon me!"

" Well, if I know all your sorrows, perhaps I shall be
able to find a help for them. I owe you much, Murtagh;
you taught me Irish, and I will do all I can to help you."

" Why, then, Shorsha, I'll tell ye my history. Here
goes!"

CHAPTER XLV

Murtagh's Tale.

" WELL, Shorsha, about a year and a half after you left
us—and a sorrowful hour for us it was when ye left us,
losing, as we did, your funny stories of your snake—and
the battles of your military—they sent me to Paris and
Salamanca, in order to make a saggart of me."

" Pray excuse me," said I, " for interrupting you, but
what kind of place is Salamanca?"

" Divil a bit did I ever see of it, Shorsha!"

" Then why did ye say ye were sent there? Well,
what kind of place is Paris? Not that I care much about
Paris."

" Sorrow a bit did I ever see of either them, Shorsha,

for no one sent me to either. When we says at home a person is going to Paris and Salamanca, it manes that he is going abroad to study to be a saggart, whether he goes to them places or not. No, I never saw either—bad luck to them—I was shipped away from Cork up the straits to a place called Leghorn, from which I was sent to ―― to a religious house, where I was to be instructed in saggart- ing till they had made me fit to cut a dacent figure in Ireland. We had a long and tedious voyage, Shorsha; not so tedious, however, as it would have been had I been fool enough to lave your pack of cards behind me, as the thaif, my brother Denis, wanted to persuade me to do, in order that he might play with them himself. With the cards I managed to have many a nice game with the sailors, winning from them ha'pennies and sixpences until the cap- tain said I was ruining his men, and keeping them from their duty; and, being a heretic and a Dutchman, swore that unless I gave over he would tie me up to the mast and give me a round dozen. This threat obliged me to be more on my guard, though I occasionally contrived to get a game at night, and to win sixpennies and ha'pennies.

"We reached Leghorn at last, and glad I was to leave the ship and the master, who gave me a kick as I was getting over the side, bad luck to the dirty heretic for kicking a son of the church, for I have always been a true son of the church, Shorsha, and never quarrelled with it unless it interfered with me in my playing at cards. I left Leghorn with certain muleteers, with whom I played at cards at the baiting-houses, and who speedily won from me all the ha'pennies and sixpences I had won from the sailors. I got my money's worth, however, for I learnt from the muleteers all kind of quaint tricks upon the cards, which I knew nothing of before; so I did not grudge them what they chated me of, and when we parted we did so in kindness on both sides. On getting to ―― I was received into the religious house for Irishes. It was the Irish house, Shorsha, into which I was taken, for I do not wish ye to suppose that I was in the English religious house which there is in that city, in which a purty set are educated, and in which purty doings are going on if all tales be true.

"In this Irish house I commenced my studies, learning to sing and to read the Latin prayers of the church. 'Faith,

Shorsha, many's the sorrowful day I passed in that house learning the prayers and litanies, being half-starved, with no earthly diversion at all, at all; until I took the cards out of my chest and began instructing in card-playing the chum which I had with me in my cell; then I had plenty of diversion along with him during the times when I was not engaged in singing, and chanting, and saying the prayers of the church; there was, however, some drawback in playing with my chum, for though he was very clever in learning, divil a sixpence had he to play with, in which respect he was like myself, the master who taught him, who had lost all my money to the muleteers who taught me the tricks upon the cards; by degrees, however, it began to be noised about the religious house that Murtagh, from Hibrodary,[1] had a pack of cards with which he played with his chum in the cell; whereupon other scholars of the religious house came to me, some to be taught and others to play, so with some I played, and others I taught, but neither to those who could play, or to those who could not, did I teach the elegant tricks which I learnt from the muleteers. Well, the scholars came to me for the sake of the cards, and the porter and cook of the religious house, who could both play very well, came also; at last I became tired of playing for nothing, so I borrowed a few bits of silver from the cook, and played against the porter, and by means of my tricks I won money from the porter, and then I paid the cook the bits of silver which I had borrowed of him; and played with him, and won a little of his money, which I let him win back again, as I had lived long enough in a religious house to know that it is dangerous to take money from the cook. In a little time, Shorsha, there was scarcely anything going on in the house but card-playing; the almoner played with me, and so did the sub-rector, and I won money from both; not too much, however, lest they should tell the rector, who had the character of a very austere man, and of being a bit of a saint; however, the thief of a porter, whose money I had won, informed the rector of what was going on, and one day the rector sent for me into his private apartment, and gave me so long and pious a lecture upon the heinous sin of card-playing, that I thought I should sink into the ground; after about half-an-hour's inveighing against card-playing, he

[1] Tipperary.

began to soften his tone, and with a long sigh told me
that at one time of his life he had been a young man himself, and had occasionally used the cards; he then began
to ask me some questions about card-playing, which
questions I afterwards found were to pump from me what
I knew about the science.   After a time he asked me
whether I had got my cards with me, and on my telling
him I had, he expressed a wish to see them, whereupon I
took the pack out of my pocket, and showed it to him;
he looked at it very attentively, and at last, giving another
deep sigh, he said, that though he was nearly weaned from
the vanities of the world, he had still an inclination to see
whether he had entirely lost the little skill which at one
time he possessed.   When I heard him speak in this
manner, I told him that if his reverence was inclined for
a game of cards, I should be very happy to play one with
him; scarcely had I uttered these words than he gave a
third sigh, and looked so very much like a saint that I
was afraid he was going to excommunicate me.   Nothing
of the kind, however, for presently he gets up and locks
the door, then sitting down at the table, he motioned me
to do the same, which I did, and in five minutes we were
playing at cards, his reverence and myself.

" I soon found that his reverence knew quite as much
about card-playing as I did.   Divil a trick was there connected with cards that his reverence did not seem awake
to.   As, however, we were not playing for money, this
circumstance did not give me much uneasiness; so we
played game after game for two hours, when his reverence, having business, told me I might go, so I took up
my cards, make my obedience, and left him.   The next
day I had other games with him, and so on for a very
long time, still playing for nothing.   At last his reverence
grew tired of playing for nothing, and proposed that we
should play for money.   Now, I had no desire to play
with his reverence for money, as I knew that doing so
would bring on a quarrel.   As long as we were playing
for nothing, I could afford to let his reverence use what
tricks he pleased; but if we played for money, I couldn't
do so.   If he played his tricks, I must play mine, and
use every advantage to save my money; and there was
one I possessed which his reverence did not.   The cards
being my own, I had put some delicate little marks on

the trump cards, just at the edges, so that when I dealt, by means of a little sleight of hand, I could deal myself any trump card I pleased. But I wished, as I said before, to have no dealings for money with his reverence, knowing that he was master in the house, and that he could lead me a dog of a life if I offended him, either by winning his money, or not letting him win mine. So I told him I had no money to play with, but the ould thief knew better; he knew that I was every day winning money from the scholars, and the sub-rector, and the other people of the house, and the ould thaif had determined to let me go on in that way winning money, and then by means of his tricks, which he thought I dare not resent, to win from me all my earnings—in a word, Shorsha, to let me fill myself like a sponge, and then squeeze me for his own advantage. So he made me play with him, and in less than three days came on the quarrel; his reverence chated me, and I chated his reverence; the ould thaif knew every trick that I knew, and one or two more; but in daling out the cards I nicked his reverence; scarcely a trump did I ever give him, Shorsha, and won his money purty freely. Och, it was a purty quarrel! All the delicate names in the ' Newgate Calendar,' if ye ever heard of such a book; all the hang-dog names in the Newgate histories, and the lives of Irish rogues, did we call each other—his reverence and I ! Suddenly, however, putting out his hand, he seized the cards, saying, ' I will examine these cards, ye cheating scoundrel ! for I believe there are dirty marks on them, which ye have made in order to know the winning cards.' ' Give me back my pack,' said I, ' or m'anam on Dioul if I be not the death of ye !' His reverence, however, clapped the cards into his pocket, and made the best of his way to the door, I hanging upon him. He was a gross, fat man, but, like most fat men, deadly strong, so he forced his way to the door, and, opening it, flung himself out, with me still holding on him like a terrier dog on a big fat pig ; then he shouts for help, and in a little time I was secured and thrust into a lock-up room, where I was left to myself. Here was a purty alteration. Yesterday I was the idol of the religious house, thought more on than his reverence, every one paying me court and wurtship, and wanting to play cards with me, and to learn my tricks, and fed, moreover, on the tidbits of the table; and to-day I was in a cell, nobody coming to look at me but the blackguard porter who had charge of me, my cards taken from me, and with nothing but bread and water to live upon. Time passed dreary enough for a month, at the end of which time his reverence came to me, leaving the porter just outside the door in order to come to his help should I be violent; and then he read me a very purty lecture on my conduct, saying I had turned the religious house topsy-turvy, and corrupted the scholars, and that I was the cheat of the world, for that on inspecting the pack he had discovered the dirty marks which I had made upon the trump cards for to know them by. He said a great deal more to me, which is not worth relating, and ended by telling me that he intended to let me out of confinement next day, but that if ever I misconducted myself any more, he would clap me in again for the rest of my life. I had a good mind to call him an ould thaif, but the hope of getting out made me hold my tongue, and the next day I was let out; and need enough I had to be let out, for what with being alone, and living on bread and water, I was becoming frighted, or, as the doctors call it, narvous. But when I was out —oh, what a change I found in the religious house! no card-playing, for it had been forbidden to the scholars, and there was now nothing going on but reading and singing; divil a merry visage to be seen, but plenty of prim airs and graces; but the case of the scholars, though bad enough, was not half so bad as mine, for they could spake to each other, whereas I could not have a word of conversation, for the ould thaif of a rector had ordered them to send me to 'Coventry,' telling them that I was a gambling cheat, with morals bad enough to corrupt a horse regiment; and whereas they were allowed to divert themselves with going out, I was kept reading and singing from morn till night. The only soul who was willing to exchange a word with me was the cook, and sometimes he and I had a little bit of discourse in a corner, and we condoled with each other, for he liked the change in the religious house almost as little as myself; but he told me that, for all the change below stairs, there was still card-playing on above, for that the ould thaif of a rector, and the sub-rector, and the almoner played at cards together, and that the rector won money from the others—

the almoner had told him so—and, moreover, that the rector was the thaif of the world, and had once been kicked out of a club-house at Dublin for cheating at cards, and after that circumstance had apparently reformed and lived decently till the time when I came to the religious house with my pack, but that the sight of that had brought him back to his ould gambling. He told the cook, moreover, that the rector frequently went out at night to the houses of the great clergy and cheated at cards.

"In this melancholy state, with respect to myself, things continued a long time, when suddenly there was a report that his Holiness the Pope intended to pay a visit to the religious house in order to examine into its discipline. When I heard this I was glad, for I determined after the Pope had done what he had come to do, to fall upon my knees before him, and make a regular complaint of the treatment I had received, to tell him of the cheating at cards of the rector, and to beg him to make the ould thaif give me back my pack again. So the day of the visit came, and his Holiness made his appearance with his attendants, and, having looked over the religious house, he went into the rector's room with the rector, the sub-rector, and the almoner. I intended to have waited until his Holiness came out, but finding he stayed a long time I thought I would e'en go into him, so I went up to the door without anybody observing me—his attendants being walking about the corridor—and opening it I slipped in, and there what do you think I saw? Why, his Holiness the Pope, and his reverence the rector, and the sub-rector, and the almoner seated at cards; and the ould thaif of a rector was dealing out the cards which ye had given me, Shorsha, to his Holiness the Pope, the sub-rector, the almoner, and himself."

In this part of his history I interrupted Murtagh, saying that I was afraid he was telling untruths, and that it was highly improbable that the Pope would leave the Vatican to play cards with Irish at their religious house, and that I was sure, if on his, Murtagh's authority, I were to tell the world so, the world would never believe it.

"Then the world, Shorsha, would be a fool, even as you were just now saying you had frequently believed it to be; the grand thing, Shorsha, is to be able to believe oneself; if ye can do that, it matters very little whether

the world believe ye or no. But a purty thing for you
and the world to stickle at the Pope's playing at cards at
a religious house of Irish; och! if I were to tell you
and the world, what the Pope has been sometimes at, at
the religious house of English thaives, I would excuse
you and the world for turning up your eyes. However,
I wish to say nothing against the Pope. I am a son of
the church, and if the Pope don't interfere with my cards,
divil a bit will I have to say against him; but I saw the
Pope playing, or about to play, with the pack which had
been taken from me, and when I told the Pope, the Pope
did not—— Ye had better let me go on with my history,
Shorsha; whether you or the world believe it or not,
I am sure it is quite as true as your tale of the snake, or
saying that Finn got his burnt finger from the thaives of
Loughlin; and whatever you may say, I am sure the world
will think so too."

I apologized to Murtagh for interrupting him, and telling him that his history, whether true or not, was infinitely
diverting, begged him to continue it.

CHAPTER XLVI

Murtagh's Story continued—The Priest, Exorcist, and Thimble-
engro—How to Check a Rebellion.

"I was telling ye, Shorsha, when ye interrupted me, that
I found the Pope, the rector, the sub-rector, and the
almoner seated at the table, the rector with my pack of
cards in his hands, about to deal out to the Pope and the
rest, not forgetting himself, for whom he intended all the
trump-cards, no doubt. No sooner did they perceive me
than they seemed taken all aback; but the rector, suddenly
starting up with the cards in his hand, asked me what I
did there, threatening to have me well disciplined if I did
not go about my business; 'I am come for my pack,' said
I, 'ye ould thaif, and to tell his Holiness how I have been
treated by ye;' then going down on my knees before his
Holiness, I said, 'Arrah, now, your Holiness! will ye not
see justice done to a poor boy who has been sadly misused?
The pack of cards which that old ruffian has in his hand

are my cards, which he has taken from me, in order to chate with. Arrah! don't play with him, your Holiness, for he'll only chate ye—there are dirty marks upon the cards which bear the trumps, put there in order to know them by; and the ould thaif in daling out will give himself all the good cards, and chate ye of the last farthing in your pocket; so let them be taken from him, your Holiness, and given back to me; and order him to lave the room, and then, if your Holiness be for an honest game, don't think I am the boy to baulk ye. I'll take the old ruffian's place, and play with ye till evening, and all night besides, and divil an advantage will I take of the dirty marks, though I know them all, having placed them on the cards myself.' I was going on in this way when the ould thaif of a rector, flinging down the cards, made at me as if to kick me out of the room, whereupon I started up and said, 'If ye are for kicking, sure two can play at that;' and then I kicked at his rever-ence, and his reverence at me, and there was a regular scrimmage between us, which frightened the Pope, who, getting up, said some words which I did not understand, but which the cook afterwards told me were, 'English extravagance, and this is the second edition;' for it seems that, a little time before, his Holiness had been frightened in St. Peter's Church by the servant of an English family, which those thaives of the English religious house had been endeavouring to bring over to the Catholic faith, and who didn't approve of their being converted. Och! his Holiness did us all sore injustice to call us English, and to confound our house with the other; for however dirty our house might be, our house was a clane house compared with the English house, and we honest people compared with those English thaives. Well, his Holiness was frighted, and the almoner ran out, and brought in his Holiness's attendants, and they laid hold of me, but I struggled hard, and said, 'I will not go without my pack; arrah, your Holiness! make them give me my pack, which Shorsha gave me in Dun-garvon times of old;' but my struggles were of no use. I was pulled away and put out in the ould dungeon, and his Holiness went away sore frighted, crossing himself much, and never returned again.

"In the old dungeon I was fastened to the wall by a chain, and there I was disciplined once every other day for the first three weeks, and then I was left to myself, and my chain, and hunger; and there I sat in the dungeon, sometimes screeching, sometimes hallooing, for I soon became frighted, having nothing in the cell to divert me. At last the cook found his way to me by stealth, and comforted me a little, bringing me tidbits out of the kitchen; and he visited me again and again—not often, however, for he dare only come when he could steal away the key from the custody of the thaif of a porter. I was three years in the dungeon, and should have gone mad but for the cook, and his words of comfort, and his tidbits, and nice books which he brought me out of the library, which were the 'Calendars of Newgate,' and the 'Lives of Irish Rogues and Raparees,' the only English books in the library. However, at the end of three years, the ould thaif of a rector, wishing to look at them books, missed them from the library, and made a perquisition about them, and the thaif of a porter said that he shouldn't wonder if I had them; saying that he had once seen me reading; and then the rector came with others to my cell, and took my books from me, from under my straw, and asked me how I came by them; and on my refusal to tell, they disciplined me again till the blood ran down my back; and making more perquisition they at last accused the cook of having carried the books to me, and not denying, he was given warning to leave next day, but he left that night, and took me away with him; for he stole the key, and came to me and cut my chain through, and then he and I escaped from the religious house through a window—the cook with a bundle, containing what things he had. No sooner had we got out than the honest cook gave me a little bit of money and a loaf, and told me to follow a way which he pointed out, which he said would lead to the sea; and then, having embraced me after the Italian way, he left me, and I never saw him again. So I followed the way which the cook pointed out, and in two days reached a seaport called Chiviter Vik, terribly foot-foundered, and there I met a sailor who spoke Irish, and who belonged to a vessel just ready to sail for France; and the sailor took me on board his vessel, and said I was his brother, and the captain gave me a passage to a place in France called Marseilles; and when I got there, the captain and sailor got a little money for me and a passport, and I travelled across the country towards a place they directed me to called Bayonne, from which they said I might, perhaps, get to Ireland. Coming, however, to a place called Pau, all my money being gone, I enlisted into a regiment called the Army of the Faith, which was going into Spain, for the King of Spain had been dethroned and imprisoned by his own subjects, as perhaps you may have heard; and the King of France, who was his cousin, was sending an army to help him, under the command of his own son, whom the English called Prince Hilt, because when he was told that he was appointed to the command, he clapped his hand on the hilt of his sword. So I enlisted into the regiment of the Faith, which was made up of Spaniards, many of them priests who had run out of Spain, and broken Germans, and foot-foundered Irish, like myself. It was said to be a blackguard regiment, that same regiment of the Faith; but, 'faith, I saw nothing blackguardly going on in it, for you would hardly reckon card-playing and dominoes, and pitch and toss blackguardly, and I saw nothing else in it. There was one thing in it which I disliked—the priests drawing their Spanish knives occasionally, when they lost their money. After we had been some time at Pau, the army of the Faith was sent across the mountains into Spain, as the vanguard of the French; and no sooner did the Spaniards see the Faith than they made a dash at it, and the Faith ran away, myself along with it, and got behind the French army, which told it to keep there, and the Faith did so, and followed the French army, which soon scattered the Spaniards, and in the end placed the king on his throne again. When the war was over the Faith was disbanded; some of the foreigners, however, amongst whom I was one, were put into a Guard regiment, and there I continued for more than a year.

" One day, being at a place called the Escurial, I took stock, as the tradesmen say, and found I possessed the sum of eighty dollars won by playing at cards, for though I could not play so well with the foreign cards as with the pack you gave me, Shorsha, I had yet contrived to win money from the priests and soldiers of the Faith. Finding myself possessed of such a capital, I determined to leave the service, and to make the best of my way to Ireland; so I deserted, but coming in an evil hour to a place they calls Torre Lodones, I found the priest playing at cards with his parishioners. The sight of the cards made me stop, and then, fool like, notwithstanding the treasure I had about me, I must wish to play, so not being able to speak their language, I made signs to them to let me play, and the priest and his thaives consented willingly; so I sat down to cards with the priest and two of his parishioners, and in a little time had won plenty of their money, but I had better never have done any such thing, for suddenly the priest and all his parishioners set upon me and bate me, and took from me all I had, and cast me out of the village more dead than alive. Och! it's a bad village that, and if I had known what it was I would have avoided it, or run straight through it, though I saw all the card-playing in the world going on in it. There is a proverb about it, as I was afterwards told, old as the time of the Moors, which holds good to the present day—it is, that in Torre Lodones there are twenty-four housekeepers, and twenty-five thieves, maning that all the people are thaives, and the clergyman to boot, who is not reckoned a housekeeper; and troth I found the clergyman the greatest thaif of the lot. After being cast out of that village I travelled for nearly a month, subsisting by begging tolerably well, for though most of the Spanish are thaives, they are rather charitable; but though charitable thaives they do not like their own being taken from them without leave being asked, as I found to my cost; for on my entering a garden near Seville, without leave, to take an orange, the labourer came running up and struck me to the ground with a hatchet, giving me a big wound in the arm. I fainted with loss of blood, and on reviving I found myself in a hospital at Seville, to which the labourer and the people of the village had taken me. I should have died of starvation in that hospital had not some English people heard of me and come to see me; they tended me with food till I was cured, and then paid my passage on board a ship to London, to which place the ship carried me.

"And now I was in London with five shillings in my pocket—all I had in the world—and that did not last for long; and when it was gone I begged in the streets, but I did not get much by that, except a month's hard labour in the correction-house; and when I came out I knew not what to do, but thought I would take a walk in the country, for it was spring-time, and the weather was fine, so I took a walk about seven miles from London, and came to a place where a great fair was being held; and there I begged, but got nothing but a halfpenny, and was thinking of going farther, when I saw a man with a table, like that of mine, playing with thimbles, as you saw me. I looked at the play, and saw him win money, and run away, and hunted by constables more than once. I kept following the man, and at last entered into conversation with him; and learning from him that he was in want of a companion to help him, I offered to help him if he would pay me; he looked at me from top to toe, and did not wish at first to have anything to do with me, as he said my appearance was against me. 'Faith, Shorsha, he had better have looked at home, for his appearance was not much in his favour: he looked very much like a Jew, Shorsha. However, he at last agreed to take me to be his companion, or bonnet as he called it; and I was to keep a look-out, and let him know when constables were coming, and to spake a good word for him occasionally, whilst he was chating folks with his thimbles and his pea. So I became his bonnet, and assisted him in the fair, and in many other fairs beside; but I did not like my occupation much, or rather my master, who, though not a big man, was a big thaif, and an unkind one, for do all I could I could never give him pleasure; and he was continually calling me fool and bogtrotter, and twitting me because I could not learn his thaives' Latin, and discourse with him in it, and comparing me with another acquaintance, or bit of a pal of his, whom he said he had parted with in the fair, and of whom he was fond of saying all kinds of wonderful things, amongst others, that he knew the grammar of all tongues. At last, wearied with being twitted by him with not being able to learn his thaives' Greek, I proposed that I should teach him Irish, that we should spake it together when we had anything to say in secret. To that he consented willingly; but, och! a purty hand he made with Irish, 'faith, not much better than I did with his thaives' Hebrew. Then my turn came, and I twitted him nicely with dulness, and compared him with a pal that I had in ould Ireland, in Dungarvon times of yore, to whom I teached Irish, telling him that he was the broth of a boy, and not only knew the grammar of all human tongues, but the dialects of the snakes besides; in fact, I tould him all about your own sweet self, Shorsha, and many a dispute and quarrel had we together about our pals, which was the cleverest fellow, his or mine.

" Well, after having been wid him about two months, I quitted him without noise, taking away one of his tables, and some peas and thimbles; and that I did with a safe conscience, for he paid me nothing, and was not over free with the meat and the drink, though I must say of him that he was a clever fellow, and perfect master of his trade, by which he made a power of money, and bating his not being able to learn Irish, and a certain Jewish lisp which he had, a great master of his tongue, of which he was very proud; so much so, that he once told me that when he had saved a certain sum of money he meant to leave off the thimbling business, and enter Parliament; into which, he said, he could get at any time, through the interest of a friend of his, a Tory Peer—my Lord Whitefeather, with whom, he said, he had occasionally done business. With the table, and other things which I had taken, I commenced trade on my own account, having contrived to learn a few of his tricks. My only capital was the change for half-a-guinea, which he had once let fall, and which I picked up, which was all I could ever get from him : for it was impossible to stale any money from him, he was so awake, being up to all the tricks of thaives, having followed the diving trade, as he called it, for a considerable time. My wish was to make enough by my table to enable me to return with credit to ould Ireland, where I had no doubt of being able to get myself ordained as priest; and, in troth, notwithstanding I was a beginner, and without any companion to help me, I did tolerably well, getting my meat and drink, and increasing my small capital, till I came to this unlucky place of Horncastle, where I was utterly ruined by the thaif in the rider's dress. And now, Shorsha, I am after telling you my history; perhaps you will now be telling me something about yourself?"

I told Murtagh all about myself that I deemed necessary to relate, and then asked him what he intended to do; he repeated that he was utterly ruined, and that he had no prospect before him but starving, or making away with himself. I inquired " How much would take him to Ireland, and establish him there with credit." " Five pounds," he answered, adding, " but who in the world would be fool enough to lend me five pounds, unless it be yourself, Shorsha, who, may be, have not got it; for when you told me about yourself, you made no boast of the state of your affairs." " I am not very rich," I replied, "but I think I can accommodate you with what you want. I consider myself under great obligations to you, Murtagh; it was you who instructed me in the language of Oilein nan Naomha, which has been the foundation of all my acquisitions in philology; without you, I should not have been what I am —Lavengro! which signifies a philologist. Here is the money, Murtagh," said I, putting my hand into my pocket, and taking out five pounds, "much good may it do you." He took the money, stared at it, and then at me—"And you mane to give me this, Shorsha?" "It is no longer mine to give," said I; "it is yours." "And you give it me for the gratitude you bear me?" "Yes," said I, "and for Dungarvon times of old." "Well, Shorsha," said he, "you are a broth of a boy, and I'll take your benefaction— five pounds! och, Jasus!" He then put the money in his pocket, and springing up, waved his hat three times, uttering some old Irish cry; then, sitting down, he took my hand, and said, "Sure, Shorsha, I'll be going thither; and when I get there, it is turning over another leaf I will be; I have learnt a thing or two abroad; I will become a priest; that's the trade, Shorsha! and I will cry out for repale; that's the cry, Shorsha! and I'll be a fool no longer." "And what will you do with your table?" said I. "'Faith, I'll be taking it with me, Shorsha; and when I gets to Ireland, I'll get it mended, and I will keep it in the house which I shall have; and when I looks upon it, I will be thinking of all I have undergone." "You had better leave it behind you," said I; "if you take it with you, you will, perhaps, take up the thimble trade again before you get to Ireland, and lose the money I am after giving you." "No fear of that, Shorsha; never will I play on that table again, Shorsha, till I get it mended, which shall not be till I am a priest, and have a house in which to place it."

Murtagh and I then went into the town, where we had some refreshment together, and then parted on our several ways. I heard nothing of him for nearly a quarter of a century, when a person who knew him well, coming from Ireland, and staying at my humble house, told me a great deal about him. He reached Ireland in safety, soon reconciled himself with his Church, and was ordained a priest; in the priestly office he acquitted himself in a way very satisfactory, upon the whole, to his superiors, having, as he frequently said, learned wisdom abroad. The Popish Church never fails to turn to account any particular gift which its servants may possess; and discovering soon that Murtagh was endowed with considerable manual dexterity—proof of which he frequently gave at cards, and at a singular game which he occasionally played at thimbles—it selected him as a very fit person to play the part of exorcist; and accordingly he travelled through a great part of Ireland, casting out devils from people possessed, which he afterwards exhibited, sometimes in the shape of rabbits, and occasionally birds and fishes. There is a holy island in a lake in Ireland, to which the people resort at a particular season of the year. Here Murtagh frequently attended, and it was here that he performed a cure which will cause his name long to be remembered in Ireland, delivering a possessed woman of two demons, which he brandished aloft in his hands, in the shape of two large eels, and subsequently hurled into the lake, amidst the shouts of an enthusiastic multitude. Besides playing the part of an exorcist, he acted that of a politician with considerable success; he attached himself to the party of the sire of agitation—" the man of paunch," and preached and hallooed for repeal with the loudest and best, as long as repeal was the cry; as soon, however, as the Whigs attained the helm of Government, and the greater part of the loaves and fishes—more politely termed the patronage of Ireland —was placed at the disposition of the priesthood, the tone of Murtagh, like that of the rest of his brother saggarts, was considerably softened; he even went so far as to declare that politics were not altogether consistent with sacerdotal duty; and resuming his exorcisms, which he had for some time abandoned, he went to the Isle of Holiness, and delivered a possessed woman of six demons in the shape of white mice. He, however, again resumed the political mantle in the year 1848, during the short period of the rebellion of the so-called Young Irelanders. The priests, though they apparently sided with this party, did not approve of it, as it was chiefly formed of ardent young men, fond of what they termed liberty, and by no means admirers of priestly domination, being mostly Protestants. Just before the outbreak of this rebellion, it was determined between the priests and the ——, that this party should be rendered comparatively innocuous by being deprived of the sinews of war—in other words, certain sums of money which they had raised for their enterprise. Murtagh was deemed the best qualified person in Ireland to be entrusted with the delicate office of getting their money from them. Having received his instructions, he invited the leaders to his parsonage amongst the mountains, under pretence of deliberating with them about what was to be done. They arrived there just before nightfall, dressed in red, yellow, and green, the colours so dear to enthusiastic Irishmen; Murtagh received them with great apparent cordiality, and entered into a long discourse with them, promising them the assistance of himself and order, and received from them a profusion of thanks. After a time Murtagh, observing, in a jocular tone, that consulting was dull work, proposed a game of cards, and the leaders, though somewhat surprised, assenting, he went to a closet, and taking out a pack of cards, laid it upon the table; it was a strange dirty pack, and exhibited every mark of having seen very long service. On one of its guests making some remarks on the " ancientness " of its appearance, Murtagh observed that there was a very wonderful history attached to that pack; it had been presented to him, he said, by a young gentleman, a disciple of his, to whom, in Dungarvon times of yore, he had taught the Irish language, and of whom he related some very extraordinary things; he added that he, Murtagh, had taken it to ——, where it had once the happiness of being in the hands of the Holy Father; by a great misfortune, he did not say what, he had lost possession of it, and had returned without it, but had some time since recovered it; a nephew of his, who was being educated at —— for a priest, having found it in a nook of the college, and sent it to him.

Murtagh and the leaders then played various games with this pack, more especially one called by the initiated " blind hookey," the result being that at the end of about two hours the leaders found they had lost one-half of their funds; they now looked serious, and talked of leaving the house, but Murtagh begging them to stay to supper, they consented. After supper, at which the guests drank rather freely, Murtagh said that, as he had not the least wish to win their money, he intended to give them their revenge; he would not play at cards with them, he added, but at a funny game of thimbles, at which they would be sure of winning back their own; then going out, he brought in a table, tall and narrow, on which placing certain thimbles and a pea, he proposed that they should stake whatever they pleased on the almost certainty of finding the pea under the thimbles. The leaders, after some hesitation, consented, and were at first eminently successful, winning back the greater part of what they had lost; after some time, however, Fortune, or rather Murtagh, turned against them, and then, instead of leaving off, they doubled and trebled their stakes, and continued doing so until they had lost nearly the whole of their funds. Quite furious, they now swore that Murtagh had cheated them, and insisted on having their property restored to them. Murtagh, without a word of reply, went to the door, and shouting into the passage something in Irish, the room was instantly filled with bog-trotters, each at least six feet high, with a stout shillelah in his hand. Murtagh then turning to his guests, asked them what they meant by insulting an anointed priest; telling them that it was not for the likes of them to avenge the wrongs of Ireland. " I have been clane mistaken in the whole of ye," said he, " I supposed ye Irish, but have found, to my sorrow, that ye are nothing of the kind; purty fellows to pretend to be Irish, when there is not a word of Irish on the tongue of any of ye, divil a ha'porth; the illigant young gentleman to whom I taught Irish, in Dungarvon times of old, though not born in Ireland, has more Irish in him than any ten of ye. He is the boy to avenge the wrongs of Ireland, if ever foreigner is to do it." Then saying something to the bog-trotters, they instantly cleared the room of the young Irelanders, who retired sadly disconcerted; nevertheless, being very silly young fellows, they hoisted the standard of rebellion; few, however, joining them, partly because they had no money, and partly because the priests abused them with might and main, their rebellion ended in a lamentable manner; themselves being seized and tried, and though convicted, not deemed of sufficient importance to be sent to the scaffold, where they might have had the satisfaction of saying—

" Dulce et decorum est pro patria mori."

My visitor, after saying that of the money won, Murtagh retained a considerable portion, that a part went to the hierarchy for what were called church purposes, and that

the —— took the remainder, which it employed in establishing a newspaper, in which the private characters of the
worthiest and most loyal Protestants in Ireland were tra-
duced and vilified, concluded his account by observing, that
it was the common belief that Murtagh, having by his services, ecclesiastical and political, acquired the confidence
of the priesthood and favour of the Government, would, on
the first vacancy, be appointed to the high office of Popish
Primate of Ireland.

CHAPTER XLVII

Departure from Horncastle—Recruiting Sergeant—Kauloes and
Lolloes.

LEAVING Horncastle I bent my steps in the direction of the
east. I walked at a brisk rate, and late in the evening
reached a large town, situate at the entrance of an extensive
firth, or arm of the sea, which prevented my farther progress eastward. Sleeping that night in the suburbs of the
town, I departed early next morning in the direction of the
south. A walk of about twenty miles brought me to another
large town, situated on a river, where I again turned towards the east. At the end of the town I was accosted
by a fiery-faced individual, somewhat under the middle size,
dressed as a recruiting sergeant.

"Young man," said the recruiting sergeant, "you are
just the kind of person to serve the Honourable East India
Company."

"I had rather the Honourable Company should serve
me," said I.

"Of course, young man. Well, the Honourable East
India Company shall serve you—that's reasonable. Here,
take this shilling; 'tis service-money. The Honourable
Company engages to serve you, and you the Honourable
Company; both parties shall be thus served; that's just
and reasonable."

"And what must I do for the Company?"

"Only go to India; that's all."

"And what should I do in India?"

"Fight, my brave boy! fight, my youthful hero!"

" What kind of country is India?"

" The finest country in the world ! Rivers, bigger than the Ouse. Hills, higher than anything near Spalding ! Trees—you never saw such trees ! Fruits—you never saw such fruits !"

" And the people—what kind of folk are they?"

" Pah ! Kauloes—blacks—a set of rascals not worth regarding."

" Kauloes !" said I ; " blacks !"

" Yes," said the recruiting sergeant ; " and they call us lolloes, which, in their beastly gibberish, means red."

" Lolloes !" said I ; " reds !"

" Yes," said the recruiting sergeant, " kauloes and lolloes ; and all the lolloes have to do is to kick and cut down the kauloes, and take from them their rupees, which mean silver money. Why do you stare so?"

" Why," said I, " this is the very language of Mr. Petulengro."

" Mr. Pet——?"

" Yes," said I, " and Tawno Chikno."

" Tawno Chik——? I say, young fellow, I don't like your way of speaking ; no, nor your way of looking. You are mad, sir ; you are mad ; and what's this? Why, your hair is grey ! You won't do for the Honourable Company —they like red. I'm glad I didn't give you the shilling. Good day to you."

" I shouldn't wonder," said I, as I proceeded rapidly along a broad causeway, in the direction of the east, " if Mr. Petulengro and Tawno Chikno came originally from India. I think I'll go there."

APPENDIX

CHAPTER I

A Word for Lavengro.

LAVENGRO is the history up to a certain period of one of rather a peculiar mind and system of nerves, with an exterior shy and cold, under which lurk much curiosity, especially with regard to what is wild and extraordinary, a considerable quantity of energy and industry, and an unconquerable love of independence. It narrates his earliest dreams and feelings, dwells with minuteness on the ways, words, and characters of his father, mother, and brother, lingers on the occasional resting-places of his wandering half military childhood, describes the gradual hardening of his bodily frame by robust exercises, his successive struggles, after his family and himself have settled down in a small local capital, to obtain knowledge of every kind, but more particularly philological lore; his visits to the tent of the Romany chal, and the parlour of the Anglo-German philosopher; the effect produced upon his character by his flinging himself into contact with people all widely differing from each other, but all extraordinary; his reluctance to settle down to the ordinary pursuits of life; his struggles after moral truth; his glimpses of God and the obscuration of the Divine Being, to his mind's eye; and his being cast upon the world of London by the death of his father, at the age of nineteen. In the world within a world, the world of London, it shows him playing his part for some time as he best can, in the capacity of a writer for reviews and magazines, and describes what he saw and underwent whilst labouring in that capacity; it represents him, however, as never forgetting that he is the son of a brave but poor gentleman, and that if he is a hack author, he is likewise a scholar. It shows him doing no dishonourable jobs, and proves that if he occasionally associates with low characters, he does so chiefly to gratify the curiosity of a scholar. In his conversations with the apple-woman of London

Bridge, the scholar is ever apparent, so again in his acquaintance with the man of the table, for the book is no raker up of the uncleanness of London, and if it gives what at first sight appears refuse, it invariably shows that a pearl of some kind, generally a philological one, is contained amongst it; it shows its hero always accompanied by his love of independence, scorning in the greatest poverty to receive favours from anybody, and describes him finally rescuing himself from peculiarly miserable circumstances by writing a book, an original book, within a week, even as Johnson is said to have written his " Rasselas," and Beckford his " Vathek," and tells how, leaving London, he betakes himself to the roads and fields.

In the country it shows him leading a life of roving adventure, becoming tinker, gypsy, postillion, ostler; associating with various kinds of people, chiefly of the lower classes, whose ways and habits are described; but, though leading this erratic life, we gather from the book that his habits are neither vulgar nor vicious, that he still follows to a certain extent his favourite pursuits, hunting after strange characters, or analyzing strange words and names. At the conclusion of the last chapter, which terminates the first part of the history, it hints that he is about to quit his native land on a grand philological expedition.

Those who read this book with attention—and the author begs to observe that it would be of little utility to read it hurriedly—may derive much information with respect to matters of philology and literature; it will be found treating of most of the principal languages from Ireland to China, and of the literature which they contain; and it is particularly minute with regard to the ways, manners, and speech of the English section of the most extraordinary and mysterious clan or tribe of people to be found in the whole world —the children of Roma. But it contains matters of much more importance than anything in connection with philology, and the literature and manners of nations. Perhaps no work was ever offered to the public in which the kindness and providence of God have been set forth by more striking examples, or the machinations of priestcraft been more truly and lucidly exposed, or the dangers which result to a nation when it abandons itself to effeminacy, and a rage for what is novel and fashionable, than the present.

With respect to the kindness and providence of God, are

they not exemplified in the case of the old apple-woman and her son? These are beings in many points bad, but with warm affections, who, after an agonizing separation, are restored to each other, but not until the hearts of both are changed and purified by the influence of affliction. Are they not exemplified in the case of the rich gentleman, who touches objects in order to avert the evil chance? This being has great gifts and many amiable qualities, but does not everybody see that his besetting sin is selfishness? He fixes his mind on certain objects, and takes inordinate interest in them, because they are his own, and those very objects, through the providence of God, which is kindness in disguise, become snakes and scorpions to whip him. Tired of various pursuits, he at last becomes an author, and publishes a book, which is very much admired, and which he loves with his usual inordinate affection; the book, consequently, becomes a viper to him, and at last he flings it aside and begins another; the book, however, is not flung aside by the world, who are benefited by it, deriving pleasure and knowledge from it : so the man who merely wrote to gratify self, has already done good to others, and got himself an honourable name. But God will not allow that man to put that book under his head and use it as a pillow : the book has become a viper to him, he has banished it, and is about another, which he finishes and gives to the world; it is a better book than the first, and every one is delighted with it; but it proves to the writer a scorpion, because he loves it with inordinate affection; but it was good for the world that he produced this book, which stung him as a scorpion. Yes; and good for himself, for the labour of writing it amused him, and perhaps prevented him from dying of apoplexy; but the book is banished, and another is begun, and herein, again, is the providence of God manifested; the man has the power of producing still, and God determines that he shall give to the world what remains in his brain, which he would not do, had he been satisfied with the second work; he would have gone to sleep upon that as he would upon the first, for the man is selfish and lazy. In his account of what he suffered during the composition of this work, his besetting sin of selfishness is manifest enough; the work on which he is engaged occupies his every thought; it is his idol, his deity, it shall be all his own, he won't borrow a thought from any one else, and he is so afraid lest, when he publishes it, that it should be thought that he had borrowed from any one, that he is continually touching objects, his nervous system, owing to his extreme selfishness, having become partly deranged. He is left touching, in order to banish the evil chance from his book, his deity. No more of his history is given; but does the reader think that God will permit that man to go to sleep on his third book, however extraordinary it may be? Assuredly not. God will not permit that man to rest till he has cured him to a certain extent of his selfishness, which has, however, hitherto been very useful to the world.

Then, again, in the tale of Peter Williams, is not the hand of Providence to be seen? This person commits a sin in his childhood, utters words of blasphemy, the remembrance of which, in after life, preying upon his imagination, unfits him for quiet pursuits, to which he seems to have been naturally inclined; but for the remembrance of that sin, he would have been Peter Williams the quiet and respectable Welsh farmer, somewhat fond of reading the ancient literature of his country in winter evenings, after his work was done. God, however, was aware that there was something in Peter Williams to entitle him to assume a higher calling; he therefore permits this sin, which, though a childish affair, was yet a sin, and committed deliberately, to prey upon his mind till he becomes at last an instrument in the hand of God, a humble Paul, the great preacher, Peter Williams, who, though he considers himself a reprobate and a castaway, instead of having recourse to drinking in mad desperation, as many do who consider themselves reprobates, goes about Wales and England preaching the word of God, dilating on his power and majesty, and visiting the sick and afflicted, until God sees fit to restore to him his peace of mind; which he does not do, however, until that mind is in a proper condition to receive peace, till it has been purified by the pain of the one idea which has so long been permitted to riot in his brain; which pain, however, an angel, in the shape of a gentle faithful wife, had occasionally alleviated; for God is merciful even in the blows which He bestoweth, and will not permit any one to be tempted beyond the measure which he can support. And here it will be as well for the reader to ponder upon the means by which the Welsh preacher is relieved from his mental misery : he is not relieved by a text from the Bible, by the words of consolation and wisdom addressed to him by his angel-minded wife, nor by the preaching of one yet more eloquent than himself; but by a quotation made by Lavengro from the life of Mary Flanders, cut-purse and prostitute, which life Lavengro had been in the habit of reading at the stall of his old friend the apple-woman, on London Bridge, who had herself been very much addicted to the perusal of it, though without any profit whatever. Should the reader be dissatisfied with the manner in which Peter Williams is made to find relief, the author would wish to answer, that the Almighty frequently accomplishes his purposes by means which appear very singular to the eyes of men, and at the same time to observe that the manner in which that relief is obtained, is calculated to read a lesson to the proud, fanciful, and squeamish, who are ever in a fidget lest they should be thought to mix with low society, or to bestow a moment's attention on publications which are not what is called of a perfectly unobjectionable character. Had not Lavengro formed the acquaintance of the apple-woman on London Bridge, he would not have had an opportunity of reading the life of Mary Flanders; and, consequently, of storing in a memory, which never forgets anything, a passage which contained a balm for the agonized mind of poor Peter Williams. The best medicines are not always found in the finest shops. Suppose, for example, if, instead of going to London Bridge to read, he had gone to Albemarle Street, and had received from the proprietors of the literary establishment in that very fashionable street, permission to read the publications on the tables of the saloons there, does the reader think he would have met any balm in those publications for the case of Peter Williams? does the reader suppose that he would have found Mary Flanders there? He would certainly have found that highly unobjectionable publication, " Rasselas," and the " Spectator," or " Lives of Royal and Illustrious Personages," but, of a surety, no Mary Flanders; so when Lavengro met with Peter Williams, he would have been unprovided with a balm to cure his ulcerated mind, and have parted from him in a way not quite so satisfactory as the manner in which he took his leave of him; for it is certain that he might have read " Rasselas," and all other unexceptionable works to be found in the library of Albemarle Street, over and over again, before he would have found any cure in them for the case of Peter Williams. Therefore the author requests the reader to drop any squeamish nonsense he may wish to utter about Mary Flanders, and the manner in which Peter Williams was cured.

And now with respect to the old man who knew Chinese, but could not tell what was o'clock. This individual was a man whose natural powers would have been utterly buried and lost beneath a mountain of sloth and laziness, had not God determined otherwise. He had in his early years chalked out for himself a plan of life in which he had his own ease and self-indulgence solely in view; he had no particular bad passions to gratify, he only wished to live a happy quiet life, just as if the business of this mighty world could be carried on by innocent people fond of ease or quiet, or that Providence would permit innocent quiet drones to occupy any portion of the earth and to cumber it. God had at any rate decreed that this man should not cumber it as a drone. He brings a certain affliction upon him, the agony of which produces that terrible whirling of the brain which, unless it is stopped in time, produces madness; he suffers indescribable misery for a period, until one morning his attention is arrested, and his curiosity is aroused, by certain Chinese letters on a teapot; his curiosity increases more and more, and, of course, in proportion as his curiosity is increased with respect to the Chinese marks, the misery in his brain, produced by his mental affliction, decreases. He sets about learning Chinese, and after the lapse of many years, during which his mind subsides into a certain state of tranquillity, he acquires sufficient knowledge of Chinese to be able to translate with ease the inscriptions to be found on its singular crockery. Yes, the laziest of human beings, through the Providence of God, a being too of rather inferior capacity, acquires the written part of a language so difficult that, as Lavengro said on a former occasion, none but the cleverest people in Europe, the French, are able to acquire it. But God did not intend that man should merely acquire Chinese. He intended that he should be of use to his species, and by the instrumentality of the first Chinese inscription which he trans-

lates, the one which first arrested his curiosity, he is
taught the duty of hospitality; yes, by means of an inscription in the language of a people, who have scarcely
an idea of hospitality themselves, God causes the slothful
man to play a useful and beneficent part in the world,
relieving distressed wanderers, and, amongst others,
Lavengro himself. But a striking indication of the man's
surprising sloth is still apparent in what he omits to do;
he has learnt Chinese, the most difficult of languages, and
he practises acts of hospitality, because he believes himself enjoined to do so by the Chinese inscription, but he
cannot tell the hour of the day by the clock within his
house; he can get on, he thinks, very well without being
able to do so; therefore from this one omission, it is easy
to come to a conclusion as to what a sluggard's part the
man would have played in life, but for the dispensation
of Providence; nothing but extreme agony could have induced such a man to do anything useful. He still continues, with all he has acquired, with all his usefulness,
and with all his innocence of character, without any proper
sense of religion, though he has attained a rather
advanced age. If it be observed, that this want of religion is a great defect in the story, the author begs leave
to observe that he cannot help it. Lavengro relates the
lives of people so far as they were placed before him, but
no further. It was certainly a great defect in so good a
man to be without religion; it was likewise a great defect
in so learned a man not to be able to tell what was o'clock.
It is probable that God, in his loving kindness, will not
permit that man to go out of the world without religion;
who knows but some powerful minister of the church
full of zeal for the glory of God, will illume that man's
dark mind; perhaps some clergyman will come to the
parish who will visit him and teach him his duty to his
God. Yes, it is very probable that such a man, before
he dies, will have been made to love his God; whether he
will ever learn to know what's o'clock is another matter.
It is probable that he will go out of the world without
knowing what's o'clock. It is not so necessary to be
able to tell the time of day by the clock as to know one's
God through His inspired word; a man cannot get to
heaven without religion, but a man can get there very
comfortably without knowing what's o'clock.

But, above all, the care and providence of God are manifested in the case of Lavengro himself, by the manner in which he is enabled to make his way in the world up to a certain period, without falling a prey either to vice or poverty. In his history, there is a wonderful illustration of part of the text, quoted by his mother, " I have been young, but now am old, yet never saw I the righteous forsaken, or his seed begging his bread.'' He is the son of good and honourable parents, but at the critical period of life, that of entering into the world, he finds himself without any earthly friend to help him, yet he manages to make his way; he does not become a Captain in the Life Guards, it is true, nor does he get into Parliament, nor does the last volume conclude in the most satisfactory and unobjectionable manner, by his marrying a dowager countess, as that wise man Addison did, or by his settling down as a great country gentleman, perfectly happy and contented, like the very moral Roderick Random, or the equally estimable Peregrine Pickle; he is hack author, gypsy, tinker, and postillion, yet, upon the whole, he seems to be quite as happy as the younger sons of most earls, to have as high feelings of honour; and when the reader loses sight of him, he has money in his pocket honestly acquired, to enable him to commence a journey quite as laudable as those which the younger sons of earls generally undertake. Surely all this is a manifestation of the kindness and providence of God: and yet he is not a religious person; up to the time when the reader loses sight of him, he is decidedly not a religious person; he has glimpses, it is true, of that God who does not forsake him, but he prays very seldom, is not fond of going to church; and, though he admires Tate and Brady's version of the Psalms, his admiration is rather caused by the beautiful poetry which that version contains than the religion; yet his tale is not finished—like the tale of the gentleman who touched objects, and that of the old man who knew Chinese without knowing what was o'clock; perhaps, like them, he is destined to become religious, and to have, instead of occasional glimpses, frequent and distinct views of his God; yet, though he may become religious, it is hardly to be expected that he will become a very precise and straightlaced person; it is probable that he will retain, with his scholarship, something of his gypsyism, his predilection for the hammer and tongs, and perhaps some inclination to put on certain gloves, not white kid, with any friend who may be inclined for a little old English diversion, and a readiness to take a glass of ale, with plenty of malt in it, and as little hop as may well be—ale at least two years old—with the aforesaid friend, when the diversion is over; for, as it is the belief of the writer that a person may get to heaven very comfortably without knowing what's o'clock, so it is his belief that he will not be refused admission there, because to the last he has been fond of healthy and invigorating exercises, and felt a willingness to partake of any of the good things which it pleases the Almighty to put within the reach of his children during their sojourn upon earth.

CHAPTER II
On Priestcraft.

THE writer will now say a few words about priestcraft, and the machinations of Rome, and will afterwards say something about himself, and his motives for writing against them.

With respect to Rome, and her machinations, much valuable information can be obtained from particular parts of Lavengro, and its sequel. Shortly before the time when the hero of the book is launched into the world, the Popish agitation in England had commenced. The Popish propaganda had determined to make a grand attempt on England; Popish priests were scattered over the land, doing the best they could to make converts to the old superstition. With the plans of Rome, and her hopes, and the reasons on which those hopes are grounded, the hero of the book becomes acquainted, during an expedition which he makes into the country, from certain conversations which he holds with a priest in a dingle, in which the hero had taken up his residence; he likewise learns from the same person much of the secret history of the Roman See, and many matters connected with the origin and progress of the Popish superstition. The individual with whom he holds these conversations is a learned, intelligent, but highly-unprincipled person, of a character however very common amongst the priests of Rome, who in general are people void of all religion, and who, notwithstanding they are tied to Rome by a band which they have neither the power nor wish to break, turn her and her practices, over their cups with their confidential associates, to a ridicule only exceeded by that to which they turn those who become the dupes of their mistress and themselves.

It is now necessary that the writer should say something with respect to himself, and his motives for waging war against Rome. First of all, with respect to himself, he wishes to state, that to the very last moment of his life, he will do and say all that in his power may be to hold up to contempt and execration the priestcraft and practices of Rome; there is, perhaps, no person better acquainted than himself, not even among the choicest spirits of the priesthood, with the origin and history of Popery. From what he saw and heard of Popery in England, at a very early period of his life, his curiosity was aroused, and he spared himself no trouble, either by travel or study, to make himself well acquainted with it in all its phases, the result being a hatred of it, which he hopes and trusts he shall retain till the moment when his spirit quits the body. Popery is the great lie of the world; a source from which more misery and social degradation have flowed upon the human race, than from all the other sources from which those evils come. It is the oldest of all superstitions; and though in Europe it assumes the name of Christianity, it existed and flourished amidst the Himalayan hills at least two thousand years before the real Christ was born in Bethlehem of Judea; in a word, it is Buddhism; and let those who may be disposed to doubt this assertion, compare the Popery of Rome, and the superstitious practices of its followers, with the doings of the priests who surround the grand Lama; and the mouthings, bellowing, turnings round, and, above all, the penances of the followers of Buddh with those of Roman devotees. But he is not going to dwell here on this point; it is dwelt upon at tolerable length in the text, and has likewise been handled with extraordinary power by the pen of the gifted but irreligious Volney; moreover, the *élite* of the Roman priesthood are perfectly well aware that their system is nothing but Buddhism under a slight disguise, and the European world in general has entertained for some time past an inkling of the fact.

And now a few words with respect to the motives of the writer for expressing a hatred for Rome.

This expressed abhorrence of the author for Rome might be entitled to little regard, provided it were possible to attribute it to any self-interested motive. There have been professed enemies of Rome, or of this or that system; but their professed enmity may frequently be traced to some cause which does them little credit; but the writer of these lines has no motive, and can have no motive, for his enmity to Rome, save the abhorrence of an honest heart for what is false, base, and cruel. A certain clergyman wrote with much heat against the Papists in the time of —— who was known to favour the Papists, but was not expected to continue long in office, and whose supposed successor, the person, indeed, who did succeed him, was thought to be hostile to the Papists. This divine, who obtained a rich benefice from the successor of —— who during ——'s time had always opposed him in everything he proposed to do, and who, of course, during that time affected to be very inimical to Popery—this divine might well be suspected of having a motive equally creditable for writing against the Papists, as that which induced him to write for them, as soon as his patron, who eventually did something more for him, had espoused their cause; but what motive, save an honest one, can the present writer have, for expressing an abhorrence of Popery? He is no clergyman, and consequently can expect neither benefices nor bishoprics, supposing it were the fashion of the present, or likely to be the fashion of any future administration, to reward clergymen with benefices or bishoprics, who, in the defence of the religion of their country write, or shall write, against Popery, and not to reward those who write, or shall write, in favour of it, and all its nonsense and abominations.

" But if not a clergyman, he is the servant of a certain society, which has the overthrow of Popery in view, and therefore," etc. This assertion, which has been frequently made, is incorrect, even as those who have made it probably knew it to be. He is the servant of no society whatever. He eats his own bread, and is one of the very few men in England who are independent in every sense of the word.

It is true he went to Spain with the colours of that society on his hat—oh! the blood glows in his veins! oh! the marrow awakes in his old bones when he thinks of what he accomplished in Spain in the cause of religion and civilization with the colours of that society in his hat, and its weapon in his hand, even the sword of the word of God; how with that weapon he hewed left and right, making the priests fly before him, and run away squeaking: "Vaya! que demonio es este!" Ay, and when he thinks of the plenty of Bible swords which he left behind him, destined to prove, and which have already proved, pretty calthrops in the heels of Popery. "Halloo! Batuschca," he exclaimed the other night, on reading an article in a newspaper; "what do you think of the present doings in Spain? Your old friend the zingaro, the gitano who rode about Spain, to say nothing of Galicia, with the Greek Buchini behind him as his squire, had a hand in bringing them about; there are many brave Spaniards connected with the present movement who took Bibles from his hands, and read them and profited by them, learning from the inspired page the duties of one man towards another, and the real value of a priesthood and their head, who set at nought the word of God, and think only of their own temporal interests; ay, and who learned Gitano—their own Gitano—from the lips of the London Caloró, and also songs in the said Gitano, very fit to dumbfounder your semi-Buddhist priests when they attempt to bewilder people's minds with their school-logic and pseudo-ecclesiastical nonsense, songs such as—

"Un Erajai
Sinaba chibando un sermon——."

—But with that society he has long since ceased to have any connection; he bade it adieu with feelings of love and admiration more than fourteen years ago; so, in continuing to assault Popery, no hopes of interest founded on that society can sway his mind—interest! who, with worldly interest in view, would ever have anything to do with that society? It is poor and supported, like its founder Christ, by poor people; and so far from having political influence, it is in such disfavour, and has ever been, with the dastardly great, to whom the government of England has for many years past been confided, that they having borne its colours only for a month would be sufficient to exclude any man, whatever his talents, his learning, or his courage may be, from the slightest chance of being permitted to serve his country either for fee, or without. A fellow who unites in himself the bankrupt trader, the broken author, or rather book-maker, and the laughed-down single speech spouter of the House of Commons, may look forward, always supposing that at one time he has been a foaming radical, to the government of an important colony. Ay, an ancient fox who has lost his tail may, provided he has a score of radical friends, who will swear that he can bark Chinese, though Chinese is not barked but sung, be forced upon a Chinese colony, though it is well known that to have lost one's tail is considered by the Chinese in general as an irreparable infamy, whilst to have been once connected with a certain society, to which, to its honour be it said, all the radical party are vehemently hostile, would be quite sufficient to keep any one not only from a government, but something much less, even though he could translate the rhymed " Sessions of Hariri," and were versed, still retaining his tail, in the two languages in which Kien-Loung wrote his Eulogium on Moukden, that piece which, translated by Amyot, the learned Jesuit, won the applause of the celebrated Voltaire.

No! were the author influenced by hopes of fee or reward, he would, instead of writing against Popery, write for it; all the trumpery titled—he will not call them great again—would then be for him, and their masters the radicals, with their hosts of newspapers, would be for him, more especially if he would commence maligning the society whose colours he had once on his hat—a society which, as the priest says in the text, is one of the very few Protestant institutions for which the Popish Church entertains any fear, and consequently respect, as it respects nothing which it does not fear. The writer said that certain " rulers " would never forgive him for having been connected with that society; he went perhaps too far in saying "never." It is probable that they would take him into favour on one condition, which is, that he should turn his pen and his voice against that society; such a mark "of a better way of thinking" would perhaps induce them to give him a government, nearly as good as that which they gave to a certain ancient radical fox at the intercession of his radical friends (who were bound to keep him from the pauper's kennel), after he had promised to foam, bark, and snarl at corruption no more; he might even entertain hopes of succeeding, nay, of superseding, the ancient creature in his government; but even were he as badly off as he is well off, he would do no such thing. He would rather exist on crusts and water; he has often done so, and been happy; nay, he would rather starve than be a rogue— for even the feeling of starvation is happiness compared with what he feels who knows himself to be a rogue, provided he has any feeling at all. What is the use of a mitre or knighthood to a man who has betrayed his principles? What is the use of a gilt collar, nay, even of a pair of scarlet breeches, to a fox who has lost his tail? Oh! the horror which haunts the mind of a fox who has lost his tail; and with reason, for his very mate loathes him, and more especially if, like himself, she has lost her brush. Oh! the horror which haunts the mind of the two-legged rogue who has parted with his principles, or those which he professed—for what? We'll suppose a government. What's the use of a government, if the next day after you have received it, you are obliged for very shame to scurry off to it with the hoot of every honest man sounding in your ears?

> "Lightly liar leaped and away ran."
>
> PIERS PLOWMAN.

But bigotry, it has been said, makes the author write against Popery; and thorough-going bigotry, indeed, will make a person say or do anything. But the writer is a very pretty bigot truly! Where will the public find traces of bigotry in anything he has written? He has written against Rome with all his heart, with all his mind, with all his soul, and with all his strength; but as a person may be quite honest, and speak and write against Rome, in like manner he may speak and write against her, and be quite free from bigotry; though it is impossible for any one but a bigot or a bad man to write or speak in her praise; her doctrines, actions, and machinations being what they are.

Bigotry! The author was born, and has always continued in the wrong church for bigotry, the quiet, unpretending Church of England; a church which, had it been a bigoted church, and not long suffering almost to a fault, might with its opportunities, as the priest says in the text, have stood in a very different position from that which it occupies at present. No! let those who are in search of bigotry, seek for it in a church very different from the inoffensive Church of England, which never encourages cruelty or calumny. Let them seek for it amongst the members of the Church of Rome, and more especially amongst those who have renegaded to it. There is nothing, however false and horrible, which a pervert to Rome will not say for his church, and which his priests will not encourage him in saying; and there is nothing, however horrible—the more horrible indeed and revolting to human nature, the more eager he would be to do it—which he will not do for it, and which his priests will not encourage him in doing.

Of the readiness which converts to Popery exhibit to sacrifice all the ties of blood and affection on the shrine of their newly-adopted religion, there is a curious illustration in the work of Luigi Pulci. This man, who was born at Florence in the year 1432, and who was deeply versed in the Bible, composed a poem, called the "Morgante Maggiore," which he recited at the table of Lorenzo de Medici, the great patron of Italian genius. It is a mock-heroic and religious poem, in which the legends of knight-errantry, and of the Popish Church, are turned to unbounded ridicule. The pretended hero of it is a converted giant, called Morgante; though his adventures do not occupy the twentieth part of the poem, the principal personages being Charlemagne, Orlando, and his cousin Rinaldo of Montalban. Morgante has two brothers, both of them giants, and in the first canto of the poem, Morgante is represented with his brothers as carrying on a feud with the abbot and monks of a certain convent, built upon the confines of heathenesse; the giants being in the habit of flinging down stones, or rather huge rocks, on the convent. Orlando, however, who is banished from the court of Charlemagne, arriving at the convent, undertakes

to destroy them, and, accordingly, kills Passamonte and
Alabastro, and converts Morgante, whose mind had been
previously softened by a vision, in which the "Blessed
Virgin" figures. No sooner is he converted than, as a
sign of his penitence, what does he do, but hastens and
cuts off the hands of his two brothers, saying—

> "Io vo' tagliar le mani a tutti quanti
> E porterolle a que' monaci santi."

And he does cut off the hands of his brethren, and carries
them to the abbot, who blesses him for so doing. Pulci
here is holding up to ridicule and execration the horrid
butchery or betrayal of friends by popish converts, and the
encouragement they receive from the priest. No sooner
is a person converted to Popery, than his principal thought
is how he can bring the hands and feet of his brethren,
however harmless they may be, and different from the
giants, to the "holy priests," who, if he manages to do so,
never fail to praise him, saying to the miserable wretch,
as the abbot said to Morgante :—

> "Tu sarai or perfetto e vero amico
> A Cristo, quanto tu gli eri nemico."

Can the English public deny the justice of Pulci's illustration, after something which it has lately witnessed? [1]
Has it not seen equivalents for the hands and feet of
brothers carried by popish perverts to the "holy priests,"
and has it not seen the manner in which the offering has
been received? Let those who are in quest of bigotry
seek for it among the perverts to Rome, and not amongst
those who, born in the pale of the Church of England,
have always continued in it.

[1] This was written in 1854.

CHAPTER III

On Foreign Nonsense.

WITH respect to the third point, various lessons which the book reads to the nation at large, and which it would be well for the nation to ponder and profit by.

There are many species of nonsense to which the nation is much addicted, and of which the perusal of Lavengro ought to give them a wholesome shame. First of all, with respect to the foreign nonsense so prevalent now in England. The hero is a scholar; but, though possessed of a great many tongues, he affects to be neither Frenchman, nor German, nor this or that foreigner; he is one who loves his country, and the language and literature of his country, and speaks up for each and all when there is occasion to do so. Now what is the case with nine out of ten amongst those of the English who study foreign languages? No sooner have they picked up a smattering of this or that speech than they begin to abuse their own country, and everything connected with it, more especially its language. This is particularly the case with those who call themselves German students. It is said, and the writer believes with truth, that when a woman falls in love with a particularly ugly fellow, she squeezes him with ten times more zest than she would a handsome one, if captivated by him. So it is with these German students; no sooner have they taken German in hand than there is nothing like German. Oh, the dear delightful German! How proud I am that it is now my own, and that its divine literature is within my reach! And all this whilst mumbling the most uncouth speech, and crunching the most crabbed literature in Europe. The writer is not an exclusive admirer of everything English; he does not advise his country people never to go abroad, never to study foreign languages, and he does not wish to persuade them that there is nothing beautiful or valuable in foreign literature; he only wishes that they would not make themselves fools with respect to foreign people, foreign languages or reading; that if they chance to have been in Spain, and have picked up a little Spanish, they would not affect the airs of Spaniards; that if males they would not make Tom-fools of themselves by sticking cigars into their mouths, dressing themselves in zamarras, and saying, carajo![1] and if females that they would not make zanies of themselves by sticking cigars into their mouths, flinging mantillas over their heads, and by saying carai, and perhaps carajo too; or if they have been in France or Italy, and have picked up a little French or Italian, they would not affect to be French or Italians; and particularly, after having been a month or two in Germany, or picked up a little German in England, they would not make themselves foolish about everything German, as the Anglo-German in the book does—a real character, the founder of the Anglo-German school in England, and the cleverest Englishman who ever talked or wrote encomiastic nonsense about Germany and the Germans. Of all infatuations connected with what is foreign, the infatuation about everything that is German, to a certain extent prevalent in England, is assuredly the most ridiculous. One can find something like a palliation for people making themselves somewhat foolish about particular languages, literatures, and people. The Spanish certainly is a noble language, and there is something wild and captivating in the Spanish character, and its literature contains the grand book of the world. French is a manly language. The French are the great martial people in the world; and French literature is admirable in many respects. Italian is a sweet language, and of beautiful simplicity—its literature perhaps the first in the world. The Italians!—wonderful men have sprung up in Italy. Italy is not merely famous for painters, poets, musicians, singers, and linguists—the greatest linguist the world ever saw, the late Cardinal Mezzofanti, was an Italian; but it is celebrated for men—men emphatically speaking: Columbus was an Italian, Alexander Farnese was an Italian, so was the mightiest of the mighty, Napoleon Bonaparte;—but the German language, German literature, and the Germans! The writer has already stated his opinion with respect to German; he does not speak from ignorance or prejudice; he has heard German spoken, and many other languages. German literature! He does not speak from ignorance, he has read that and many a literature, and he repeats—— However, he acknowledges that there is one fine poem in the German language, that

[1] An obscene oath.

poem is the " Oberon;" a poem, by the bye, ignored by the Germans—a speaking fact—and of course, by the Anglo-Germanists. The Germans! he has been amongst them, and amongst many other nations, and confesses that his opinion of the Germans, as men, is a very low one. Germany, it is true, has produced one very great man, the monk who fought the Pope, and nearly knocked him down; but this man his countrymen—a telling fact— affect to despise, and, of course, the Anglo-Germanists: the father of Anglo-Germanism was very fond of inveighing against Luther.

The madness, or rather foolery, of the English for foreign customs, dresses, and languages, is not an affair of to-day, or yesterday—it is of very ancient date, and was very properly exposed nearly three centuries ago by one Andrew Borde, who under the picture of a " Naked man, with a pair of shears in one hand, and a roll of cloth in the other," [1] inserted the following lines along with others :—

> " I am an Englishman, and naked I stand here,
> Musing in my mind what garment I shall weare ;
> For now I will weare this, and now I will weare that,
> Now I will weare, I cannot tell what.
> All new fashions be pleasant to mee,
> I will have them, whether I thrive or thee ;
> What do I care if all the world me fail?
> I will have a garment reach to my taile ;
> Then am I a minion, for I wear the new guise.
> The next yeare after I hope to be wise,
> Not only in wearing my gorgeous array,
> For I will go to learning a whole summer's day ;
> I will learn Latine, Hebrew, Greek, and French,
> And I will learn Dutch, sitting on my bench.
> I had no peere if to myself I were true,
> Because I am not so, divers times do I rue.
> Yet I lacke nothing, I have all things at will
> If I were wise and would hold myself still,
> And meddle with no matters but to me pertaining,
> But ever to be true to God and my king.
> But I have such matters rowling in my pate,
> That I will and do—I cannot tell what," etc.

[1] See "Muses' Library," pp. 86, 87. London, 1738.

CHAPTER IV

On Gentility Nonsense—Illustrations of Gentility.

WHAT is gentility? People in different stations in England—entertain different ideas of what is genteel,[1] but it
must be something gorgeous, glittering, or tawdry, to be
considered genteel by any of them. The beau-ideal of the
English aristocracy, of course with some exceptions, is
some young fellow with an imperial title, a military personage of course, for what is military is so particularly
genteel, with flaming epaulets, a cocked hat and plume,
a prancing charger, and a band of fellows called generals
and colonels, with flaming epaulets, cocked hats and
plumes, and prancing chargers vapouring behind him. It
was but lately that the daughter of an English marquis
was heard to say, that the sole remaining wish of her
heart—she had known misfortunes, and was not far from
fifty—was to be introduced to—whom? The Emperor of
Austria! The sole remaining wish of the heart of one
who ought to have been thinking of the grave and judgment, was to be introduced to the miscreant who had

[1] Genteel with them seems to be synonymous with Gentile and
Gentoo; if so, the manner in which it has been applied for ages
ceases to surprise, for genteel is heathenish. Ideas of barbaric
pearl and gold, glittering armour, plumes, tortures, blood-shedding,
and lust, should always be connected with it. Wace, in his grand
Norman poem, calls the Baron genteel :—

        " La furent li gentil Baron," etc.

And he certainly could not have applied the word better than to the
strong Norman thief, armed cap-à-pie, without one particle of truth
or generosity; for a person to be a pink of gentility, that is
heathenism, should have no such feelings; and, indeed, the admirers
of gentility seldom or never associate any such feelings with it. It
was from the Norman, the worst of all robbers and miscreants,
who built strong castles, garrisoned them with devils, and tore out
poor wretches' eyes, as the Saxon Chronicle says, that the English
got their detestable word genteel. What could ever have made the
English such admirers of gentility, it would be difficult to say : for,
during three hundred years, they suffered enough by it. Their
genteel Norman landlords were their scourgers, their torturers, the
plunderers of their homes, the dishonourers of their wives, and the
deflowerers of their daughters. Perhaps, after all, fear is at the root
of the English veneration for gentility.

caused the blood of noble Hungarian females to be whipped out of their shoulders, for no other crime than devotion to their country, and its tall and heroic sons. The middle classes—of course there are some exceptions—admire the aristocracy, and consider them pinks, the aristocracy who admire the Emperor of Austria, and adored the Emperor of Russia, till he became old, ugly, and unfortunate, when their adoration instantly terminated; for what is more ungenteel than age, ugliness, and misfortune! The beau-ideal with those of the lower classes, with peasants and mechanics, is some flourishing railroad contractor : look, for example, how they worship Mr. Flamson. This person makes his grand début in the year 'thirty-nine, at a public meeting in the principal room of a country inn. He has come into the neighbourhood with the character of a man worth a million pounds, who is to make everybody's fortune; at this time, however, he is not worth a shilling of his own, though he flashes about dexterously three or four thousand pounds, part of which sum he has obtained by specious pretences, and part from certain individuals who are his confederates. But in the year 'forty-nine, he is really in possession of the fortune which he and his agents pretended to be worth ten years before—he is worth a million pounds. By what means has he come by them? By railroad contracts, for which he takes care to be paid in hard cash before he attempts to perform them, and to carry out which he makes use of the sweat and blood of wretches who, since their organization, have introduced crimes and language into England to which it was previously almost a stranger—by purchasing, with paper, shares by hundreds in the schemes to execute which he contracts, and which are his own devising; which shares he sells as soon as they are at a high premium, to which they are speedily forced by means of paragraphs, inserted by himself and agents, in newspapers devoted to his interest, utterly reckless of the terrible depreciation to which they are almost instantly subjected. But he is worth a million pounds, there can be no doubt of the fact—he has not made people's fortunes, at least those whose fortunes it was said he would make; he has made them away; but his own he has made, emphatically made it; he is worth a million pounds. Hurrah for the millionnaire! The clown who views the pandemonium of red brick which he has built on the estate which he has purchased in the neighbourhood of the place of his grand début, in which every species of architecture, Greek, Indian, and Chinese, is employed in caricature—who hears of the grand entertainment he gives at Christmas in the principal dining-room, the hundred wax-candles, the waggon-load of plate, and the ocean of wine which form parts of it, and above all the two ostrich poults, one at the head, and the other at the foot of the table, exclaims, "Well! if he a'n't bang up, I don't know who be; why he beats my lord hollow!" The mechanic of the borough town, who sees him dashing through the streets in an open landau, drawn by four milk-white horses, amidst his attendant out-riders; his wife, a monster of a woman, by his side, stout as the wife of Tamerlane, who weighed twenty stone, and bedizened out like her whose person shone with the jewels of plundered Persia, stares with silent wonder, and at last exclaims "That's the man for my vote!" You tell the clown that the man of the mansion has contributed enormously to corrupt the rural innocence of England; you point to an incipient branch railroad, from around which the accents of Gomorrah are sounding, and beg him to listen for a moment, and then close his ears. Hodge scratches his head and says, "Well, I have nothing to say to that; all I know is, that he is bang up, and I wish I were he;" perhaps he will add—a Hodge has been known to add—"He has been kind enough to put my son on that very railroad; 'tis true the company is somewhat queer, and the work rather killing, but he gets there half-a-crown a day, whereas from the farmers he would only get eighteen-pence." You remind the mechanic that the man in the landau has been the ruin of thousands and you mention people whom he himself knows, people in various grades of life, widows and orphans amongst them, whose little all has been dissipated, and whom he has reduced to beggary by inducing them to become sharers in his delusive schemes. But the mechanic says, "Well, the more fools they to let themselves be robbed. But I don't call that kind of thing robbery, I merely call it out-witting; and everybody in this free country has a right to outwit others if he can. What a turn-out he has!" One was once heard to add, "I never saw a more genteel-looking man in all my life except one, and that was a gentleman's walley, who was much like him. It is true that he is rather under-sized, but then madam, you know, makes up for all.''

CHAPTER V

Subject of Gentility continued.

IN the last chapter have been exhibited specimens of gentility, so considered by different classes; by one class power, youth, and epaulets are considered the ne plus ultra of gentility; by another class pride, stateliness, and title; by another, wealth and flaming tawdriness. But what constitutes a gentleman? It is easy to say at once what constitutes a gentleman, and there are no distinctions in what is gentlemanly,[1] as there are in what is genteel. The characteristics of a gentleman are high feeling—a determination never to take a cowardly advantage of another—a liberal education—absence of narrow views—generosity and courage, propriety of behaviour. Now a person may be genteel according to one or another of the three standards described above, and not possess one of the characteristics of a gentleman. Is the emperor a gentleman, with spatters of blood on his clothes, scourged from the backs of noble Hungarian women? Are the aristocracy gentlefolks, who admire him? Is Mr. Flamson a gentleman, although he has a million pounds? No! cowardly miscreants, admirers of cowardly miscreants, and people who make a million pounds by means compared with which those employed to make fortunes by the getters up of the South Sea Bubble might be called honest dealing, are decidedly not gentlefolks. Now as it is clearly demonstrable that a person may be perfectly genteel according to some standard or other, and yet be no gentleman, so it is demonstrable that a person may have no pretensions to

1 Gentle and gentlemanly may be derived from the same root as genteel; but nothing can be more distinct from the mere genteel, than the ideas which enlightened minds associate with these words. Gentle and gentlemanly mean something kind and genial; genteel, that which is glittering or gaudy. A person can be a gentleman in rags, but nobody can be genteel.

gentility, and yet be a gentleman. For example, there is Lavengro! Would the admirers of the emperor, or the admirers of those who admire the emperor, or the admirers of Mr. Flamson, call him genteel? and gentility with them is everything! Assuredly they would not; and assuredly they would consider him respectively as a being to be shunned, despised, or hooted. Genteel! Why at one time he is a hack author—writes reviewals for eighteen-pence a page—edits a Newgate chronicle. At another he wanders the country with a face grimy from occasionally mending kettles; and there is no evidence that his clothes are not seedy and torn, and his shoes down at the heel; but by what process of reasoning will they prove that he is no gentleman? Is he not learned? Has he not gener-osity and courage? Whilst a hack author, does he pawn the books entrusted to him to review? Does he break his word to his publisher? Does he write begging letters? Does he get clothes or lodgings without paying for them? Again, whilst a wanderer, does he insult helpless women on the road with loose proposals or ribald discourse? Does he take what is not his own from the hedges? Does he play on the fiddle, or make faces in public-houses, in order to obtain pence or beer? or does he call for liquor, swallow it, and then say to a widowed landlady, "Mis-tress, I have no brass?" In a word, what vice and crime does he perpetrate—what low acts does he commit? There-fore, with his endowments, who will venture to say that he is no gentleman?—unless it be an admirer of Mr. Flamson—a clown—who will, perhaps, shout—"I say he is no gentleman; for who can be a gentleman who keeps no gig?"

The indifference exhibited by Lavengro for what is merely genteel, compared with his solicitude never to in-fringe the strict laws of honour, should read a salutary lesson. The generality of his countrymen are far more careful not to transgress the customs of what they call gentility, than to violate the laws of honour or morality. They will shrink from carrying their own carpet-bag, and from speaking to a person in seedy raiment, whilst to matters of much higher importance they are shamelessly indifferent. Not so Lavengro; he will do anything that he deems convenient, or which strikes his fancy, provided it does not outrage decency, or is unallied to profligacy; is not ashamed to speak to a beggar in rags, and will associate with anybody, provided he can gratify a laudable curiosity. He has no abstract love for what is low, or what the world calls low. He sees that many things which the world looks down upon are valuable, so he prizes much which the world condemns; he sees that many things which the world admires are contemptible, so he despises much which the world does not; but when the world prizes what is really excellent, he does not contemn it, because the world regards it. If he learns Irish, which all the world scoffs at, he likewise learns Italian, which all the world melts at. If he learns Gypsy, the language of the tattered tent, he likewise learns Greek, the language of the college-hall. If he learns smithery, he also learns——ah! what does he learn to set against smithery?—the law? No; he does not learn the law, which, by the way, is not very genteel. Swimming? Yes, he learns to swim. Swimming, however, is not genteel; and the world—at least the genteel part of it—acts very wisely in setting its face against it; for to swim you must be naked, and how would many a genteel person look without his clothes? Come, he learns horsemanship; a very genteel accomplishment, which every genteel person would gladly possess, though not all genteel people do.

Again as to associates: if he holds communion when a boy with Murtagh, the scarecrow of an Irish academy, he associates in after life with Francis Ardry, a rich and talented young Irish gentleman about town. If he accepts an invitation from Mr. Petulengro to his tent, he has no objection to go home with a rich genius to dinner; who then will say that he prizes a thing or a person because they are ungenteel? That he is not ready to take up with everything that is ungenteel he gives a proof, when he refuses, though on the brink of starvation, to become bonnet to the thimble-man, an office, which, though profitable, is positively ungenteel. Ah! but some sticker-up for gentility will exclaim, "The hero did not refuse this office from an insurmountable dislike to its ungentility, but merely from a feeling of principle." Well! the writer is not fond of argument, and he will admit that such was the case; he admits that it was a love of principle, rather than an over-regard for gentility, which prevented the hero from accepting, when on the brink of starvation, an ungenteel though lucrative office, an office which, the writer begs leave to observe, many a person with a great regard for gentility, and no particular regard for principle, would in a similar strait have accepted; for when did a mere love for gentility keep a person from being a dirty scoundrel, when the alternatives were " either be a dirty scoundrel or starve?" One thing, however, is certain, which is, that Lavengro did not accept the office, which if a love for what is low had been his ruling passion he certainly would have done; consequently, he refuses to do one thing which no genteel person would willingly do, even as he does many things which every genteel person would gladly do, for example, speaks Italian, rides on horseback, associates with a fashionable young man, dines with a rich genius, et cetera. Yet—and it cannot be minced—he and gentility with regard to many things are at strange divergency; he shrinks from many things at which gentility placidly hums a tune, or approvingly simpers, and does some things at which gentility positively shrinks. He will not run into debt for clothes or lodgings, which he might do without any scandal to gentility; he will not receive money from Francis Ardry, and go to Brighton with the sister of Annette Le Noir, though there is nothing ungenteel in borrowing money from a friend, even when you never intend to repay him, and something poignantly genteel in going to a watering-place with a gay young Frenchwoman; but he has no objection, after raising twenty pounds by the sale of that extraordinary work " Joseph Sell," to set off into the country, mend kettles under hedge-rows, and make pony and donkey shoes in a dingle. Here, perhaps, some plain, well-meaning person will cry—and with much apparent justice—how can the writer justify him in this act? What motive, save a love for what is low, could induce him to do such a thing? Would the writer have everybody who is in need of recreation go into the country, mend kettles under hedges, and make pony shoes in dingles? To such an observation the writer would answer, that Lavengro had an excellent motive in doing what he did, but that the writer is not so unreasonable as to wish everybody to do the same. It is not everybody who can mend kettles. It is not everybody who is in similar circumstances to those in which Lavengro was. Lavengro flies from London and hack authorship, and takes to the roads from fear of consumption; it is expensive to put up at inns, and even at public-houses, and Lavengro has not much money; so he buys a tinker's cart and apparatus, and sets up as tinker, and subsequently as blacksmith; a person living in a tent, or in anything else, must do something or go mad; Lavengro had a mind, as he himself well knew, with some slight tendency to madness, and had he not employed himself, he must have gone wild; so to employ himself he drew upon one of his resources, the only one available at the time. Authorship had nearly killed him, he was sick of reading, and had besides no books; but he possessed the rudiments of an art akin to tinkering; he knew something of smithery, having served a kind of apprenticeship in Ireland to a fairy smith; so he draws upon his smithery to enable him to acquire tinkering, he speedily acquires that craft, even as he had speedily acquired Welsh, owing to its connection with Irish, which language he possessed; and with tinkering he amuses himself until he lays it aside to resume smithery. A man who has an innocent resource, has quite as much right to draw upon it in need, as he has upon a banker in whose hands he has placed a sum; Lavengro turns to advantage, under particular circumstances, a certain resource which he has, but people who are not so forlorn as Lavengro, and have not served the same apprenticeship which he had, are not advised to follow his example. Surely he was better employed in plying the trades of tinker and smith than in having recourse to vice, in running after milk-maids, for example. Running after milk-maids is by no means an ungenteel rural diversion; but let any one ask some respectable casuist (the Bishop of London for example), whether Lavengro was not far better employed, when in the country, at tinkering and smithery than he would have been in running after all the milk-maids in Cheshire, though tinkering is in general considered a very ungenteel employment, and smithery little better, notwithstanding that an Orcadian poet, who wrote in Norse about eight hundred years ago, reckons the latter among nine noble arts which he possessed, naming it along with playing at chess, on the harp, and ravelling runes, or as the original has it, " treading runes "—that is, compressing them into a small compass by mingling one letter with another, even as the Turkish caligraphists ravel the Arabic letters, more especially those who write talismans.

" Nine arts have I, all noble;
    I play at chess so free,
At ravelling runes I'm ready,
    At books and smithery;
I'm skilled o'er ice at skimming
    On skates, I shoot and row,
And few at harping match me,
    Or minstrelsy, I trow."

But though Lavengro takes up smithery, which, though
the Orcadian ranks it with chess-playing and harping, is
certainly somewhat of a grimy art, there can be no doubt
that, had he been wealthy and not so forlorn as he was, he
would have turned to many things, honourable, of course,
in preference. He has no objection to ride a fine horse
when he has the opportunity : he has his day-dream of
making a fortune of two hundred thousand pounds by
becoming a merchant and doing business after the Armenian fashion; and there can be no doubt that he would
have been glad to wear fine clothes, provided he had had
sufficient funds to authorize him in wearing them. For
the sake of wandering the country and plying the hammer
and tongs, he would not have refused a commission in the
service of that illustrious monarch George the Fourth, provided he had thought that he could live on his pay, and not
be forced to run in debt to tradesmen, without any hope of
paying them, for clothes and luxuries, as many highly
genteel officers in that honourable service were in the habit
of doing. For the sake of tinkering, he would certainly
not have refused a secretaryship of an embassy to Persia,
in which he might have turned his acquaintance with Per-
sian, Arabic, and the Lord only knows what other languages, to account. He took to tinkering and smithery,
because no better employments were at his command. No
war is waged in the book against rank, wealth, fine clothes,
or dignified employments; it is shown, however, that a
person may be a gentleman and a scholar without them.
Rank, wealth, fine clothes, and dignified employments, are
no doubt very fine things, but they are merely externals,
they do not make a gentleman, they add external grace
and dignity to the gentleman and scholar, but they make
neither; and is it not better to be a gentleman without
them than not a gentleman with them? Is not Lavengro,
when he leaves London on foot with twenty pounds in his
pocket, entitled to more respect than Mr. Flamson flaming

in his coach with a million? And is not even the honest
jockey at Horncastle, who offers a fair price to Lavengro
for his horse, entitled to more than the scoundrel lord, who
attempts to cheat him of one-fourth of its value?

Millions, however, seem to think otherwise, by their
servile adoration of people whom without rank, wealth,
and fine clothes they would consider infamous, but whom
possessed of rank, wealth, and glittering habiliments they
seem to admire all the more for their profligacy and crimes.
Does not a blood-spot, or a lust-spot, on the clothes of a
blooming emperor, give a kind of zest to the genteel young
god? Do not the pride, superciliousness, and selfishness
of a certain aristocracy make it all the more regarded by
its worshippers? and do not the clownish and gutter-blood
admirers of Mr. Flamson like him all the more because
they are conscious that he is a knave? If such is the case
—and, alas! is it not the case?—they cannot be too frequently told that fine clothes, wealth, and titles adorn a
person in proportion as he adorns them; that if worn by the
magnanimous and good they are ornaments indeed, but if
by the vile and profligate they are merely san benitos, and
only serve to make their infamy doubly apparent; and that
a person in seedy raiment and tattered hat, possessed of
courage, kindness, and virtue, is entitled to more respect
from those to whom his virtues are manifested than any
cruel profligate emperor, selfish aristocrat, or knavish
millionaire in the world.

The writer has no intention of saying that all in England
are affected with the absurd mania for gentility; nor is
such a statement made in the book; it is shown therein that
individuals of certain classes can prize a gentleman, notwithstanding seedy raiment, dusty shoes or tattered hat,—
for example, the young Irishman, the rich genius, the
postillion, and his employer. Again, when the life of the
hero is given to the world, amidst the howl about its low-
ness and vulgarity, raised by the servile crew whom its
independence of sentiment has stung, more than one
powerful voice has been heard testifying approbation of its
learning and the purity of its morality. That there is some
salt in England, minds not swayed by mere externals, he
is fully convinced; if he were not, he would spare himself
the trouble of writing; but to the fact that the generality
of his countrymen are basely grovelling before the shrine

of what they are pleased to call gentility, he cannot shut his eyes.

Oh! what a clever person that Cockney was, who, travelling in the Aberdeen railroad carriage, after edifying the company with his remarks on various subjects, gave it as his opinion that Lieutenant P—— would, in future, be shunned by all respectable society! And what a simple person that elderly gentleman was, who, abruptly starting, asked in rather an authoritative voice, "and why should Lieutenant P—— be shunned by respectable society?" and who, after entering into what was said to be a masterly analysis of the entire evidence of the case, concluded by stating, "that having been accustomed to all kinds of evidence all his life, he had never known a case in which the accused had obtained a more complete and triumphant justification than Lieutenant P—— had done in the late trial."

Now the Cockney, who is said to have been a very foppish Cockney, was perfectly right in what he said, and therein manifested a knowledge of the English mind and character, and likewise of the modern English language, to which his catechist, who, it seems, was a distinguished member of the Scottish bar, could lay no pretensions. The Cockney knew what the Lord of Session knew not, that the British public is gentility crazy, and he knew, moreover, that gentility and respectability are synonymous. No one in England is genteel or respectable that is "looked at," who is the victim of oppression; he may be pitied for a time, but when did not pity terminate in contempt? A poor, harmless young officer—but why enter into the details of the infamous case? they are but too well known, and if ever cruelty, pride, and cowardice, and things much worse than even cruelty, cowardice, and pride were brought to light, and, at the same time, countenanced, they were in that case. What availed the triumphant justification of the poor victim? There was at first a roar of indignation against his oppressors, but how long did it last? He had been turned out of the service, they remained in it with their red coats and epaulets; he was merely the son of a man who had rendered good service to his country, they were, for the most part, highly connected—they were in the extremest degree genteel, he quite the reverse; so the nation wavered, considered, thought the genteel side was the safest after all,

and then with the cry of, " Oh ! there is nothing like gentility," ratted bodily. Newspaper and public turned against
the victim, scouted him, apologized for the—what should
they be called?—who were not only admitted into the most
respectable society, but courted to come, the spots not
merely of wine on their military clothes, giving them a kind
of poignancy. But there is a God in heaven; the British
glories are tarnished—Providence has never smiled on
British arms since that case—oh! Balaklava! thy name
interpreted is net of fishes, and well dost thou deserve that
name. How many a scarlet golden fish has of late perished
in the mud amidst thee, cursing the genteel service, and
the genteel leader which brought him to such a doom.

Whether the rage for gentility is most prevalent amongst
the upper, middle, or lower classes it is difficult to say; the
priest in the text seems to think that it is exhibited in the
most decided manner in the middle class; it is the writer's
opinion, however, that in no class is it more strongly de-
veloped than in the lower : what they call being well-born
goes a great way amongst them, but the possession of
money much farther, whence Mr. Flamson's influence over
them. Their rage against, and scorn for, any person who
by his courage and talents has advanced himself in life, and
still remains poor, are indescribable; " he is no better than
ourselves," they say, " why should he be above us?"—for
they have no conception that anybody has a right to ascend-
ency over themselves except by birth or money. This feeling amongst the vulgar has been, to a certain extent, the
bane of two services, naval and military. The writer does
not make this assertion rashly; he observed this feeling at
work in the army when a child, and he has good reason for
believing that it was as strongly at work in the navy at the
same time, and is still as prevalent in both. Why are not
brave men raised from the ranks? is frequently the cry;
why are not brave sailors promoted? The Lord help brave
soldiers and sailors who are promoted; they have less to
undergo from the high airs of their brother officers, and
those are hard enough to endure, than from the insolence
of the men. Soldiers and sailors promoted to command
are said to be in general tyrants; in nine cases out of ten,
when they are tyrants, they have been obliged to have
recourse to extreme severity in order to protect themselves
from the insolence and mutinous spirit of the men,—" He

is no better than ourselves : shoot him, bayonet him, or fling him overboard !'' they say of some obnoxious individual raised above them by his merit. Soldiers and sailors, in general, will bear any amount of tyranny from a lordly sot, or the son of a man who has '' plenty of brass ''—their own term—but will mutiny against the just orders of a skilful and brave officer who '' is no better than themselves.'' There was the affair of the '' Bounty,'' for example : Bligh was one of the best seamen that ever trod deck, and one of the bravest of men ; proofs of his seamanship he gave by steering, amidst dreadful weather, a deeply-laden boat for nearly four thousand miles over an almost unknown ocean—of his bravery, at the fight of Copenhagen, one of the most desperate ever fought, of which after Nelson he was the hero : he was, moreover, not an unkind man ; but the crew of the '' Bounty '' mutinied against him, and set him half naked in an open boat, with certain of his men who remained faithful to him, and ran away with the ship. Their principal motive for doing so was an idea, whether true or groundless the writer cannot say, that Bligh was '' no better than themselves;'' he was certainly neither a lord's illegitimate, nor possessed of twenty thousand pounds. The writer knows what he is writing about, having been acquainted in his early years with an individual who was turned adrift with Bligh, and who died about the year '22, a lieutenant in the navy, in a provincial town in which the writer was brought up. The ringleaders in the mutiny were two scoundrels, Christian and Young, who had great influence with the crew, because they were genteelly connected. Bligh, after leaving the '' Bounty,'' had considerable difficulty in managing the men who had shared his fate, because they considered themselves '' as good men as he,'' notwithstanding, that to his conduct and seamanship they had alone to look, under Heaven, for salvation from the ghastly perils that surrounded them. Bligh himself, in his journal, alludes to this feeling. Once, when he and his companions landed on a desert island, one of them said, with a mutinous look, that he considered himself '' as good a man as he;'' Bligh, seizing a cutlass, called upon him to take another and defend himself, whereupon the man said that Bligh was going to kill him, and made all manner of concessions ; now why did this fellow consider himself as good a man as

Bligh? Was he as good a seaman? no, nor a tenth part as good. As brave a man? no, nor a tenth part as brave; and of these facts he was perfectly well aware, but bravery and seamanship stood for nothing with him, as they still stand with thousands of his class; Bligh was not genteel by birth or money, therefore Bligh was no better than himself. Had Bligh, before he sailed, got a twenty-thousand pound prize in the lottery, he would have experienced no insolence from this fellow, for there would have been no mutiny in the " Bounty." " He is our betters," the crew would have said, " and it is our duty to obey him."

The wonderful power of gentility in England is exemplified in nothing more than in what it is producing amongst Jews, Gypsies, and Quakers. It is breaking up their venerable communities. All the better, some one will say. Alas! alas! It is making the wealthy Jews forsake the synagogue for the opera-house, or the gentility chapel, in which a disciple of Mr. Platitude, in a white surplice, preaches a sermon at noon-day from a desk, on each side of which is a flaming taper. It is making them abandon their ancient literature, their " Mischna," their " Gemara," their " Zohar," for gentility novels, " The Young Duke," the most unexceptionably genteel book ever written, being the principal favourite. It makes the young Jew ashamed of the young Jewess, it makes her ashamed of the young Jew. The young Jew marries an opera-dancer, or if the dancer will not have him, as is frequently the case, the cast-off Miss of the Honourable Spencer So-and-so. It makes the young Jewess accept the honourable offer of a cashiered lieutenant of the Bengal Native Infantry; or, if such a person does not come forward, the dishonourable offer of a cornet of a regiment of crack hussars. It makes poor Jews, male and female, forsake the synagogue for the sixpenny theatre or penny hop; the Jew to take up with an Irish female of loose character, and the Jewess with a musician of the Guards, or the Tipperary servant of Captain Mulligan. With respect to the gypsies, it is making the women what they never were before—harlots; and the men what they never were before—careless fathers and husbands. It has made the daughter of Ursula the chaste take up with the base drummer of a wild-beast show. It makes Gorgiko Brown, the gypsy man, leave his tent and his old wife, of an evening, and thrust himself into society which could

well dispense with him. "Brother," said Mr. Petulengro
to the Romany Rye, after telling him many things connected with the decadence of gypsyism, "there is one
Gorgiko Brown, who, with a face as black as a tea-kettle,
wishes to be mistaken for a Christian tradesman; he goes
into the parlour of a third-rate inn of an evening, calls for
rum and water, and attempts to enter into conversation with
the company about politics and business; the company
flout him and give him the cold shoulder, or perhaps complain to the landlord, who comes and asks him what business he has in the parlour, telling him if he wants to drink
to go into the tap-room, and perhaps collars him and
kicks him out, provided he refuses to move." With
respect to the Quakers, it makes the young people like the
young Jews, crazy after gentility diversions, worship, marriages, or connections, and makes old Pease do what it
makes Gorgiko Brown do, thrust himself into society which
could well dispense with him, and out of which he is not
kicked, because unlike the gypsy he is not poor. The
writer would say much more on these points, but want of
room prevents him; he must therefore request the reader
to have patience until he can lay before the world a
pamphlet, which he has been long meditating, to be entitled
"Remarks on the strikingly similar Effects which a Love
for Gentility has produced, and is producing, amongst Jews,
Gypsies, and Quakers."

The Priest in the book has much to say on the subject
of this gentility-nonsense; no person can possibly despise
it more thoroughly than that very remarkable individual
seems to do, yet he hails its prevalence with pleasure,
knowing the benefits which will result from it to the church
of which he is the sneering slave. "The English are mad
after gentility," says he; "well, all the better for us; their
religion for a long time past has been a plain and simple
one, and consequently by no means genteel; they'll quit it
for ours, which is the perfection of what they admire; with
which Templars, Hospitalers, mitred abbots, Gothic abbeys,
long-drawn aisles, golden censers, incense, et cetera, are
connected; nothing, or next to nothing, of Christ, it is true,
but weighed in the balance against gentility, where will
Christianity be? why, kicking against the beam—ho! ho!"
And in connection with the gentility-nonsense, he expatiates
largely, and with much contempt, on a species of literature

by which the interests of his church in England have been very much advanced—all genuine priests have a thorough contempt for everything which tends to advance the interests of their church—this literature is made up of pseudo Jacobitism, Charlie o'er the waterism, or nonsense about Charlie o'er the water. And the writer will now take the liberty of saying a few words about it on his own account.

CHAPTER VI

On Scotch Gentility-Nonsense—Charlie o'er the Waterism.

OF the literature just alluded to Scott was the inventor. It is founded on the fortunes and misfortunes of the Stuart family, of which Scott was the zealous defender and apologist, doing all that in his power lay to represent the members of it as noble, chivalrous, high-minded, unfortunate princes; though, perhaps, of all the royal families that ever existed upon the earth, this family was the worst. It was unfortunate enough, it is true; but it owed its misfortunes entirely to its crimes, viciousness, bad faith, and cowardice. Nothing will be said of it here until it made its appearance in England to occupy the English throne.

The first of the family which we have to do with, James, was a dirty, cowardly miscreant, of whom the less said the better. His son, Charles the First, was a tyrant—exceedingly cruel and revengeful, but weak and dastardly; he caused a poor fellow to be hanged in London, who was not his subject, because he had heard that the unfortunate creature had once bitten his own glove at Cadiz, in Spain, at the mention of his name; and he permitted his own bull-dog, Strafford, to be executed by his own enemies, though the only crime of Strafford was, that he had barked furiously at those enemies, and had worried two or three of them, when Charles shouted, " Fetch 'em." He was a bitter, but yet a despicable enemy, and the coldest and most worthless of friends; for though he always hoped to be able, some time or other, to hang his enemies, he was always ready to curry favour with them, more especially if he could do so at the expense of his friends. He was the haughtiest, yet

meanest of mankind. He once caned a young nobleman
for appearing before him in the drawing-room not dressed
exactly according to the court etiquette; yet he conde-
scended to flatter and compliment him who, from principle,
was his bitterest enemy, namely, Harrison, when the re-
publican colonel was conducting him as a prisoner to London. His bad faith was notorious; it was from abhorrence
of the first public instance which he gave of his bad faith,
his breaking his word to the Infanta of Spain, that the
poor Hiberno-Spaniard bit his glove at Cadiz; and it was
his notorious bad faith which eventually cost him his head;
for the Republicans would gladly have spared him, provided
they could put the slightest confidence in any promise, however solemn, which he might have made to them. Of them,
it would be difficult to say whether they most hated or despised him. Religion he had none. One day he favoured
Popery; the next, on hearing certain clamours of the people,
he sent his wife's domestics back packing to France, because they were Papists. Papists, however, should make
him a saint, for he was certainly the cause of the taking of
Rochelle.

His son, Charles the Second, though he passed his youth
in the school of adversity, learned no other lesson from it
than the following one—take care of yourself, and never do
an action, either good or bad, which is likely to bring you
into any great difficulty; and this maxim he acted up to
as soon as he came to the throne. He was a Papist, but
took especial care not to acknowledge his religion, at which
he frequently scoffed, till just before his last gasp, when
he knew that he could lose nothing, and hoped to gain
everything by it. He was always in want of money, but
took care not to tax the country beyond all endurable
bounds; preferring to such a bold and dangerous course,
to become the pensioner of Louis, to whom, in return for
his gold, he sacrificed the honour and interests of Britain.
He was too lazy and sensual to delight in playing the part
of a tyrant himself; but he never checked tyranny in others
save in one instance. He permitted beastly butchers to
commit unmentionable horrors on the feeble, unarmed, and
disunited Covenanters of Scotland, but checked them when
they would fain have endeavoured to play the same game
on the numerous united, dogged, and warlike Independents
of England. To show his filial piety, he bade the hangman

dishonour the corpses of some of his father's judges, before
whom, when alive, he ran like a screaming hare; but permitted those who had lost their all in supporting his father's
cause, to pine in misery and want. He would give to a
painted harlot a thousand pounds for a loathsome embrace,
and to a player or buffoon a hundred for a trumpery pun,
but would refuse a penny to the widow or orphan of an old
Royalist soldier. He was the personification of selfishness;
and as he loved and cared for no one, so did no one love or
care for him. So little had he gained the respect or affection of those who surrounded him, that after his body had
undergone an after-death examination, parts of it were
thrown down the sinks of the palace, to become eventually
the prey of the swine and ducks of Westminster.

His brother, who succeeded him, James the Second, was
a Papist, but sufficiently honest to acknowledge his Popery,
but upon the whole, he was a poor creature; though a tyrant,
he was cowardly, had he not been a coward he would never
have lost his throne. There were plenty of lovers of tyranny
in England who would have stood by him, provided he
would have stood by them, and would, though not Papists,
have encouraged him in his attempt to bring back England
beneath the sway of Rome, and perhaps would eventually
have become Papists themselves; but the nation raising a
cry against him, and his son-in-law, the Prince of Orange,
invading the country, he forsook his friends, of whom he
had a host, but for whom he cared little—left his throne,
for which he cared a great deal—and Popery in England,
for which he cared yet more, to their fate, and escaped to
France, from whence, after taking a little heart, he repaired
to Ireland, where he was speedily joined by a gallant army
of Papists whom he basely abandoned at the Boyne, running
away in a most lamentable condition, at the time when by
showing a little courage he might have enabled them to
conquer. This worthy, in his last will, bequeathed his heart
to England—his right arm to Scotland—and his bowels to
Ireland. What the English and Scotch said to their respective bequests is not known, but it is certain that an old
Irish priest, supposed to have been a great-grand-uncle of
the present Reverend Father Murtagh, on hearing of the
bequest to Ireland, fell into a great passion, and having
been brought up at " Paris and Salamanca," expressed his
indignation in the following strain :—" Malditas sean tus

tripas ! teniamos bastante del olor de tus tripas al tiempo de tu nuida dela batalla del Boyne !"

His son, generally called the Old Pretender, though born in England, was carried in his infancy to France, where he was brought up in the strictest principles of Popery, which principles, however, did not prevent him becoming (when did they ever prevent any one?) a worthless and profligate scoundrel; there are some doubts as to the reality of his being a son of James, which doubts are probably unfounded, the grand proof of his legitimacy being the thorough baseness of his character. It was said of his father that he could speak well, and it may be said of him that he could write well, the only thing he could do which was worth doing, always supposing that there is any merit in being able to write. He was of a mean appearance, and, like his father, pusillanimous to a degree. The meanness of his appearance disgusted, and his pusillanimity discouraged the Scotch when he made his apearance amongst them in the year 1715, some time after the standard of rebellion had been hoisted by Mar. He only stayed a short time in Scotland, and then, seized with panic, retreated to France, leaving his friends to shift for themselves as they best could. He died a pensioner of the Pope.

The son of this man, Charles Edward, of whom so much in later years has been said and written, was a worthless ignorant youth, and a profligate and illiterate old man. When young, the best that can be said of him is, that he had occasionally springs of courage, invariably at the wrong time and place, which merely served to lead his friends into inextricable difficulties. When old, he was loathsome and contemptible to both friend and foe. His wife loathed him, and for the most terrible of reasons; she did not pollute his couch, for to do that was impossible—he had made it so vile; but she betrayed it, inviting to it not only Alfieri the Filthy, but the coarsest grooms. Doctor King, the warmest and almost last adherent of his family, said, that there was not a vice or crime of which he was not guilty; as for his foes, they scorned to harm him even when in their power. In the year 1745 he came down from the Highlands of Scotland, which had long been a focus of rebellion. He was attended by certain clans of the Highlands, desperadoes used to free-bootery from their infancy, and, consequently, to the use of arms, and possessed of a

certain species of discipline; with these he defeated at
Prestonpans a body of men called soldiers, but who were
in reality peasants and artizans, levied about a month
before, without discipline or confidence in each other, and
who were miserably massacred by the Highland army; he
subsequently invaded England, nearly destitute of regular
soldiers, and penetrated as far as Derby, from which place
he retreated on learning that regular forces which had
been hastily recalled from Flanders were coming against
him, with the Duke of Cumberland at their head; he was
pursued, and his rearguard overtaken and defeated by the
dragoons of the duke at Clifton, from which place the rebels
retreated in great confusion across the Eden into Scotland,
where they commenced dancing Highland reels and strathspeys on the bank of the river, for joy at their escape,
whilst a number of wretched girls, paramours of some of
them, were perishing in the waters of the swollen river in
an attempt to follow them; they themselves passed over by
eighties and by hundreds, arm in arm, for mutual safety,
without the loss of a man, but they left the poor paramours
to shift for themselves, nor did any of these canny people
after passing the stream dash back to rescue a single female
life,—no, they were too well employed upon the bank in
dancing strathspeys to the tune of "Charlie o'er the
water." It was, indeed, Charlie o'er the water, and canny
Highlanders o'er the water, but where were the poor prosti-
tutes meantime? *In the water.*

The Jacobite farce, or tragedy, was speedily brought to
a close by the battle of Culloden; there did Charlie wish
himself back again o'er the water, exhibiting the most un-
mistakable signs of pusillanimity; there were the clans cut
to pieces, at least those who could be brought to the charge,
and there fell Giles Mac Bean, or as he was called in Gaelic,
Giliosa Mac Beathan, a kind of giant, six feet four inches
and a quarter high, "than whom," as his wife said in a
coronach she made upon him, "no man who stood at
Cuiloitr was taller"—Giles Mac Bean the Major of the clan
Cattan—a great drinker—a great fisher—a great shooter,
and the champion of the Highland host.

The last of the Stuarts was a cardinal.

Such were the Stuarts, such their miserable history.
They were dead and buried in every sense of the word until
Scott resuscitated them—how? by the power of fine writing

and by calling to his aid that strange divinity, gentility. He wrote splendid novels about the Stuarts, in which he represents them as unlike what they really were as the graceful and beautiful papillon is unlike the hideous and filthy worm. In a word, he made them genteel, and that was enough to give them paramount sway over the minds of the British people. The public became Stuart-mad, and everybody, specially the women, said, " What a pity it was that we hadn't a Stuart to govern." All parties, Whig, Tory, or Radical, became Jacobite at heart, and admirers of absolute power. The Whigs talked about the liberty of the subject, and the Radicals about the rights of man still, but neither party cared a straw for what it talked about, and mentally swore that, as soon as by means of such stuff they could get places, and fill their pockets, they would be as Jacobite as the Jacobs themselves. As for Tories, no great change in them was necessary; everything favouring absolutism and slavery being congenial to them. So the whole nation, that is, the reading part of the nation, with some exceptions, for thank God there has always been some salt in England, went over the water to Charlie. But going over to Charlie was not enough, they must, or at least a considerable part of them, go over to Rome too, or have a hankering to do so. As the Priest sarcastically observes in the text, " As all the Jacobs were Papists, so the good folks who through Scott's novels admire the Jacobs must be Papists too." An idea got about that the religion of such genteel people as the Stuarts must be the climax of gentility, and that idea was quite sufficient. Only let a thing, whether temporal or spiritual, be considered genteel in England, and if it be not followed it is strange indeed; so Scott's writings not only made the greater part of the nation Jacobite, but Popish.

Here some people will exclaim—whose opinions remain sound and uncontaminated—what you say is perhaps true with respect to the Jacobite nonsense at present so prevalent being derived from Scott's novels, but the Popish nonsense, which people of the genteeler classes are so fond of, is derived from Oxford. We sent our sons to Oxford nice honest lads, educated in the principles of the Church of England, and at the end of the first term they came home puppies, talking Popish nonsense, which they had learned from the pedants to whose care we had entrusted them;

ay, not only Popery but Jacobitism, which they hardly carried with them from home, for we never heard them talking Jacobitism before they had been at Oxford; but now their conversation is a farrago of Popish and Jacobite stuff—" Complines and Claverse." Now, what these honest folks say is, to a certain extent, founded on fact; the Popery which has overflowed the land during the last fourteen or fifteen years, has come immediately from Oxford, and likewise some of the Jacobitism, Popish and Jacobite nonsense, and little or nothing else, having been taught at Oxford for about that number of years. But whence did the pedants get the Popish nonsense with which they have corrupted youth? Why, from the same quarter from which they got the Jacobite nonsense with which they have inoculated those lads who were not inoculated with it before— Scott's novels. Jacobitism and Laudism, a kind of half Popery, had at one time been very prevalent at Oxford, but both had been long consigned to oblivion there, and people at Oxford cared as little about Laud as they did about the Pretender. Both were dead and buried there, as everywhere else, till Scott called them out of their graves, when the pedants of Oxford hailed both—ay, and the Pope, too, as soon as Scott had made the old fellow fascinating, through particular novels, more especially the " Monastery " and " Abbot." Then the quiet, respectable, honourable Church of England would no longer do for the pedants of Oxford; they must belong to a more genteel church— they were ashamed at first to be downright Romans—so they would be Lauds. The pale-looking, but exceedingly genteel non-juring clergyman in Waverley was a Laud; but they soon became tired of being Lauds, for Laud's Church, gew-gawish and idolatrous as it was, was not sufficiently tinselly and idolatrous for them, so they must be Popes, but in a sneaking way, still calling themselves Church-of-England men, in order to batten on the bounty of the church which they were betraying, and likewise have opportunities of corrupting such lads as might still resort to Oxford with principles uncontaminated.

So the respectable people, whose opinions are still sound, are, to a certain extent, right when they say that the tide of Popery, which has flowed over the land, has come from Oxford. It did come immediately from Oxford, but how did it get to Oxford? Why, from Scott's novels. Oh!

that sermon which was the first manifestation of Oxford feeling, preached at Oxford some time in the year '38 by a divine of a weak and confused intellect, in which Popery was mixed up with Jacobitism! The present writer remembers perfectly well, on reading some extracts from it at the time in a newspaper, on the top of a coach, exclaiming—" Why, the simpleton has been pilfering from Walter Scott's novels !"

O Oxford pedants ! Oxford pedants ! ye whose politics and religion are both derived from Scott's novels ! what a pity it is that some lad of honest parents, whose mind ye are endeavouring to stultify with your nonsense about " Complines and Claverse," has not the spirit to start up and cry, " Confound your gibberish ! I'll have none of it. Hurrah for the Church, and the principles of my *father !*"

CHAPTER VII

Same Subject continued.

Now what could have induced Scott to write novels tending to make people Papists and Jacobites, and in love with arbitrary power? Did he think that Christianity was a gaudy mummery? He did not, he could not, for he had read the Bible ; yet was he fond of gaudy mummeries, fond of talking about them. Did he believe that the Stuarts were a good family, and fit to govern a country like Britain? He knew that they were a vicious, worthless crew, and that Britain was a degraded country as long as they swayed the sceptre ; but for those facts he cared nothing, they governed in a way which he liked, for he had an abstract love of despotism, and an abhorrence of everything savouring of freedom and the rights of man in general. His favourite political picture was a joking, profligate, careless king, nominally absolute—the heads of great houses paying court to, but in reality governing, that king, whilst revelling with him on the plunder of a nation, and a set of crouching, grovelling vassals (the literal meaning of vassal is a wretch), who, after allowing themselves to be horsewhipped, would take a bone if flung to them, and be grateful ; so that in love with mummery, though he knew what Christianity was, no wonder he admired such a church as that of Rome, and that which Laud set up; and by nature formed to be the holder of the candle to ancient worm-eaten and profligate families, no wonder that all his sympathies were with the Stuarts and their dissipated insolent party, and all his hatred directed against those who endeavoured to check them in their proceedings, and to raise the generality of mankind something above a state of vassalage, that is, wretchedness. Those who were born great, were, if he could have had his will, always to remain great, however worthless their characters. Those who were born low, were always to remain so, however great their talents; though, if that rule were carried out, where would he have been himself?

In the book which he called the "History of Napoleon Bonaparte," in which he plays the sycophant to all the legitimate crowned heads in Europe, whatever their crimes, vices, or miserable imbecilities, he, in his abhorrence of everything low which by its own vigour makes itself illustrious, calls Murat of the sabre the son of a pastry-cook, of a Marseilleise pastry-cook. It is a pity that people who give themselves hoity-toity airs—and the Scotch in general are wonderfully addicted to giving themselves hoity-toity airs, and checking people better than themselves with their birth [1] and their country—it is a great pity that such people do not look at home—son of a pastry-cook, of a Marseilleise pastry-cook! Well, and what was Scott himself? Why, son of a pettifogger, of an Edinburgh pettifogger. "Oh, but Scott was descended from the old cow-stealers of Buccleuch, and therefore——" descended from old cow-stealers, was he? Well, had he nothing to boast of beyond such a pedigree, he would have lived and died the son of a pettifogger, and been forgotten, and deservedly so; but he

[1] The writer has been checked in print by the Scotch with being a Norfolk man. Surely, surely, these latter times have not been exactly the ones in which it was expedient for Scotchmen to check the children of any county in England with the place of their birth, more especially those who have had the honour of being born in Norfolk—times in which British fleets, commanded by Scotchmen, have returned laden with anything but laurels from foreign shores. It would have been well for Britain had she had the old Norfolk man to dispatch to the Baltic or the Black sea, lately, instead of Scotch admirals.

possessed talents, and by his talents rose like Murat, and like him will be remembered for his talents alone, and deservedly so. " Yes, but Murat was still the son of a pastrycook, and though he was certainly good at the sabre, and cut his way to a throne, still——" Lord! what fools there are in the world; but as no one can be thought anything of in this world without a pedigree, the writer will now give a pedigree for Murat, of a very different character from the cow-stealing one of Scott, but such a one as the proudest he might not disdain to claim. Scott was descended from the old cow-stealers of Buccleuch—was he? Good! and Murat was descended from the old Moors of Spain, from the Abencerages (sons of the saddle) of Granada. The name Murat is Arabic, and is the same as Murad (Le Desiré, or the wished-for one). Scott in his genteel Life of Bonaparte, says that " when Murat was in Egypt, the similarity between the name of the celebrated Mameluke Mourad and that of Bonaparte's Meilleur Sabreur was remarked, and became the subject of jest amongst the comrades of the gallant Frenchman." But the writer of the novel of Bonaparte did not know that the names were one and the same. Now which was the best pedigree, that of the son of the pastry-cook, or that of the son of the pettifogger? Which was the best blood? Let us observe the workings of the two bloods. He who had the blood of the " sons of the saddle " in him, became the wonderful cavalier of the most wonderful host that ever went forth to conquest, won for himself a crown, and died the death of a soldier, leaving behind him a son, only inferior to himself in strength, in prowess, and in horsemanship. The descendant of the cow-stealer became a poet, a novel writer, the panegyrist of great folk and genteel people; became insolvent because, though an author, he deemed it ungenteel to be mixed up with the business part of the authorship; died paralytic and broken-hearted because he could no longer give entertainments to great folks, leaving behind him, amongst other children, who were never heard of, a son, who, through his father's interest, had become lieutenant-colonel in a genteel cavalry regiment. A son who was ashamed of his father because his father was an author; a son who—paugh—why ask which was the best blood?

So, owing to his rage for gentility, Scott must needs

become the apologist of the Stuarts and their party; but God made this man pay dearly for taking the part of the wicked against the good; for lauding up to the skies the miscreants and robbers, and calumniating the noble spirits of Britain, the salt of England, and his own country.   As God had driven the Stuarts from their throne, and their followers from their estates, making them vagabonds and beggars on the face of the earth, taking from them all that they cared for, so did that same God, who knows perfectly well how and where to strike, deprive the apologist of that wretched crew of all that rendered life pleasant in his eyes, the lack of which paralyzed him in body and mind, rendered him pitiable to others, loathsome to himself,—so much so, that he once said, " Where is the beggar who would change places with me, notwithstanding all my fame?" Ah ! God knows perfectly well how to strike. He permitted him to retain all his literary fame to the very last—his literary fame for which he cared nothing; but what became of the sweetness of life, his fine house, his grand company, and his entertainments? The grand house ceased to be his; he was only permitted to live in it on sufferance, and whatever grandeur it might still retain, it soon became as desolate a looking house as any misanthrope could wish to see— where were the grand entertainments and the grand company? there are no grand entertainments where there is no money; no lords and ladies where there are no entertainments—and there lay the poor lodger in the desolate house, groaning on a bed no longer his, smitten by the hand of God in the part where he was most vulnerable. Of what use telling such a man to take comfort, for he had written the " Minstrel " and " Rob Roy,"—telling him to think of his literary fame? Literary fame, indeed ! he wanted back his lost gentility :—

" Retain my altar,
I care nothing for it—but, oh ! touch not my *beard*."
                                    PORNY's *War of the Gods*.

He dies, his children die too, and then comes the crowning judgment of God on what remains of his race and the house which he had built. He was not a Papist himself, nor did he wish any one belonging to him to be Popish, for he had read enough of the Bible to know that no one can be saved through Popery, yet had he a sneaking affection for it, and

would at times in an underhand manner, give it a good
word both in writing and discourse, because it was a gaudy
kind of worship, and ignorance and vassalage prevailed so
long as it flourished—but he certainly did not wish any
of his people to become Papists, nor the house which he had
built to become a Popish house, though the very name he
gave it savoured of Popery; but Popery becomes fashionable through his novels and poems—the only one that remains of his race, a female grandchild, marries a person
who, following the fashion, becomes a Papist, and makes
her a Papist too. Money abounds with the husband, who
buys the house, and then the house becomes the rankest
Popish house in Britain. A superstitious person might
almost imagine that one of the old Scottish Covenanters,
whilst the grand house was being built from the profits
resulting from the sale of writings favouring Popery and
persecution, and calumniatory of Scotland's saints and mar-
tyrs, had risen from the grave, and banned Scott, his race,
and his house, by reading a certain psalm.

In saying what he has said about Scott, the author has
not been influenced by any feeling of malice or ill-will, but
simply by a regard for truth, and a desire to point out to
his countrymen the harm which has resulted from the
perusal of his works;—he is not one of those who would
depreciate the talents of Scott—he admires his talents, both
as a prose writer and a poet; as a poet especially he admires
him, and believes him to have been by far the greatest, with
perhaps the exception of Mickiewicz, who only wrote for
unfortunate Poland, that Europe has given birth to during
the last hundred years. As a prose writer he admires him
less, it is true, but his admiration for him in that capacity
is very high, and he only laments that he prostituted his
talents to the cause of the Stuarts and gentility. What
book of fiction of the present century can you read twice,
with the exception of "Waverley" and "Rob Roy?"
There is "Pelham," it is true, which the writer of these
lines has seen a Jewess reading in the steppe of Debreczin,
and which a young Prussian Baron, a great traveller, whom
he met at Constantinople in '44 told him he always carried
in his valise. And, in conclusion, he will say, in order to
show the opinion which he entertains of the power of Scott
as a writer, that he did for the sceptre of the wretched Pretender what all the kings of Europe could not do for his

body—placed it on the throne of these realms; and for Popery, what Popes and Cardinals strove in vain to do for three centuries—brought back its mummeries and nonsense into the temples of the British Isles.

Scott during his lifetime had a crowd of imitators, who, whether they wrote history so called—poetry so called—or novels—nobody would call a book a novel if he could call it anything else—wrote Charlie o'er the water nonsense; and now that he has been dead nearly a quarter of a century, there are others daily springing up who are striving to imitate Scott in his Charlie o'er the water nonsense—for nonsense it is, even when flowing from his pen. They, too, must write Jacobite histories, Jacobite songs, and Jacobite novels, and much the same figure as the scoundrel menials in the comedy cut when personating their masters, and retailing their masters' conversation, do they cut as Walter Scotts. In their histories, they too talk about the Prince and Glenfinnan, and the pibroch; and in their songs about "Claverse" and "Bonny Dundee." But though they may be Scots, they are not Walter Scotts. But it is perhaps chiefly in the novel that you see the veritable hog in armour; the time of the novel is of course the '15 or '45; the hero a Jacobite, and connected with one or other of the enterprises of those periods; and the author, to show how unprejudiced he is, and what *original* views he takes of subjects, must needs speak up for Popery, whenever he has occasion to mention it; though, with all his originality, when he brings his hero and the vagabonds with which he is concerned before a barricadoed house, belonging to the Whigs, he can make them get into it by no other method than that which Scott makes his rioters employ to get into the Tolbooth, *burning down* the door.

To express the more than utter foolishness of this latter Charlie o'er the water nonsense, whether in rhyme or prose, there is but one word, and that word a Scotch word. Scotch, the sorriest of jargons, compared with which even Roth Welsch is dignified and expressive, has yet one word to express what would be inexpressible by any word or combination of words in any language, or in any other jargon in the world; and very properly; for as the nonsense is properly Scotch, so should the word be Scotch which expresses it—that word is "fushionless," pronounced *fooshionless;* and when the writer has called the

nonsense fooshionless—and he does call it fooshionless—
he has nothing more to say, but leaves the nonsense to its
fate.

CHAPTER VIII

On Canting Nonsense.

THE writer now wishes to say something on the subject of
canting nonsense, of which there is a great deal in England.
There are various cants in England, amongst which is the
religious cant. He is not going to discuss the subject of
religious cant : lest, however, he should be misunderstood,
he begs leave to repeat that he is a sincere member of the
Church of England, in which he believes there is more
religion, and consequently less cant, than in any other
church in the world; nor is he going to discuss many other
cants; he shall content himself with saying something about
two—the temperance cant and the unmanly cant. Temperance canters say that " it is unlawful to drink a glass of
ale." Unmanly canters say that " it is unlawful to use
one's fists." The writer begs leave to tell both these
species of canters that they do not speak words of truth.

It is very lawful to take a cup of ale, or wine, for the
purpose of cheering or invigorating yourself when you are
faint and down-hearted; and likewise to give a cup of ale
or wine to others when they are in a similar condition. The
Holy Scripture sayeth nothing to the contrary, but rather
encourageth people in so doing by the text, " Wine maketh
glad the heart of man." But it is not lawful to intoxicate
yourself with frequent cups of ale or wine, nor to make
others intoxicated, nor does the Holy Scripture say it is.
The Holy Scripture no more says that it is lawful to intoxicate yourself or others, than it says that it is unlawful to
take a cup of ale or wine yourself, or to give one to others.
Noah is not commended in the Scripture for making himself
drunken on the wine he brewed. Nor is it said that the
Saviour, when he supplied the guests with first-rate wine
at the marriage-feast, told them to make themselves drunk
upon it. He is said to have supplied them with first-rate
wine, but He doubtless left the quantity which each should

drink to each party's reason and discretion. When you set
a good dinner before your guests, you do not expect that
they should gorge themselves with the victuals you set
before them. Wine may be abused, and so may a leg of
mutton.

Second. It is lawful for any one to use his fists in his
own defence, or in the defence of others, provided they
can't help themselves; but it is not lawful to use them for
purposes of tyranny or brutality. If you are attacked by
a ruffian, as the elderly individual in Lavengro is in the inn-
yard, it is quite lawful, if you can, to give him as good a
thrashing as the elderly individual gave the brutal coachman; and if you see a helpless woman—perhaps your own
sister—set upon by a drunken lord, a drunken coachman,
or a drunken coalheaver, or a brute of any description, either
drunk or sober, it is not only lawful but laudable, to give
them, if you can, a good drubbing; but it is not lawful
because you have a strong pair of fists, and know how to
use them, to go swaggering through a fair, jostling against
unoffending individuals; should you do so, you would be
served quite right if you were to get a drubbing, more particularly if you were served out by some one less strong, but
more skilful than yourself—even as the coachman was
served out by a pupil of the immortal Broughton—sixty
years old, it is true, but possessed of Broughton's guard
and chop. Moses is not blamed in the Scripture for taking
part with the oppressed, and killing an Egyptian persecutor.
We are not told how Moses killed the Egyptian; but it is
quite as creditable to Moses to suppose that he killed the
Egyptian by giving him a buffet under the left ear, as by
stabbing him with a knife. It is true that the Saviour in
the New Testament tells His disciples to turn the left cheek
to be smitten, after they had received a blow on the right;
but He was speaking to people divinely inspired, or whom
He intended divinely to inspire—people selected by God for
a particular purpose. He likewise tells these people to part
with various articles of raiment when asked for them, and
to go a-travelling without money, and take no thought of
the morrow. Are those exhortations carried out by very
good people in the present day? Do Quakers, when smitten
on the right cheek, turn the left to the smiter? When asked
for their coat, do they say, " Friend, take my shirt also?"
Has the Dean of Salisbury no purse? Does the Archbishop

of Canterbury go to an inn, run up a reckoning, and then say to his landlady, "Mistress, I have no coin?" Assuredly the Dean has a purse, and a tolerably well-filled one; and, assuredly, the Archbishop, on departing from an inn, not only settles his reckoning, but leaves something handsome for the servants, and does not say that he is forbidden by the gospel to pay for what he has eaten, or the trouble he has given, as a certain Spanish cavalier said he was forbidden by the statutes of chivalry. Now, to take the part of yourself, or the part of the oppressed, with your fists, is quite as lawful in the present day as it is to refuse your coat and shirt also to any vagabond who may ask for them, and not to refuse to pay for supper, bed, and breakfast, at the Feathers, or any other inn, after you have had the benefit of all three.

The conduct of Lavengro with respect to drink may, upon the whole, serve as a model. He is no drunkard, nor is he fond of intoxicating other people; yet when the horrors are upon him he has no objection to go to a public-house and call for a pint of ale, nor does he shrink from recommending ale to others when they are faint and downcast. In one instance, it is true, he does what cannot be exactly justified; he encourages the Priest in the dingle, in more instances than one, in drinking more hollands and water than is consistent with decorum. He has a motive indeed in doing so; a desire to learn from the knave in his cups the plans and hopes of the Propaganda of Rome. Such conduct, however, was inconsistent with strict fair dealing and openness; and the author advises all those whose consciences never reproach them for a single unfair or covert act committed by them, to abuse him heartily for administering hollands and water to the Priest of Rome. In that instance the hero is certainly wrong; yet in all other cases with regard to drink, he is manifestly right. To tell people that they are never to drink a glass of ale or wine themselves, or to give one to others, is cant; and the writer has no toleration for cant of any description. Some cants are not dangerous; but the writer believes that a more dangerous cant than the temperance cant, or as it is generally called, teetotalism, is scarcely to be found. The writer is willing to believe that it originated with well meaning, though weak people; but there can be no doubt that it was quickly turned to account

by people who were neither well meaning nor weak. Let
the reader note particularly the purpose to which this cry
has been turned in America; the land, indeed, par excellence, of humbug and humbug cries. It is there continually
in the mouth of the most violent political party, and is made
an instrument of almost unexampled persecution. The
writer would say more on the temperance cant, both in
England and America, but want of space prevents him.
There is one point on which he cannot avoid making a few
brief remarks—that is, the inconsistent conduct of its
apostles in general. The teetotal apostle says, it is a dreadful thing to be drunk. So it is, teetotaller; but if so, why
do you get drunk? I get drunk? Yes, unhappy man, why
do you get drunk on smoke and passion? Why are your
garments impregnated with the odour of the Indian weed?
Why is there a pipe or a cigar always in your mouth?
Why is your language more dreadful than that of a Pois-
sarde? Tobacco-smoke is more deleterious than ale, teetotaller; bile more potent than brandy. You are fond of
telling your hearers what an awful thing it is to die drunken.
So it is, teetotaller. Then take good care that you do not
die with smoke and passion, drunken, and with temperance
language on your lips; that is, abuse and calumny against
all those who differ from you. One word of sense you have
been heard to say, which is, that spirits may be taken as
a medicine. Now you are in a fever of passion, teetotaller;
so, pray take this tumbler of brandy; take it on the
homœopathic principle, that heat is to be expelled by heat.
You are in a temperance fury, so swallow the contents of
this tumbler, and it will, perhaps, cure you. You look at
the glass wistfully—you occasionally take a glass medicin-
ally—and it is probable you do. Take one now. Consider
what a dreadful thing it would be to die passion drunk; to
appear before your Maker with *in*temperate language on
your lips. That's right! You don't seem to wince at the
brandy. That's right!—well done! All down in two pulls.
Now you look like a reasonable being!

If the conduct of Lavengro with regard to drink is open
to little censure, assuredly the use which he makes of his
fists is entitled to none at all. Because he has a pair of
tolerably strong fists, and knows to a certain extent how
to use them, is he a swaggerer or oppressor? To what ill
account does he turn them? Who more quiet, gentle, and

inoffensive than he? He beats off a ruffian who attacks him in a dingle; has a kind of friendly tuzzle with Mr. Petulengro, and behold the extent of his fistic exploits.

Ay, but he associates with prize-fighters; and that very fellow, Petulengro, is a prize-fighter, and has fought for a stake in a ring. Well, and if he had not associated with prize-fighters, how could he have used his fists? Oh, anybody can use his fists in his own defence, without being taught by prize-fighters. Can they? Then why does not the Italian, or Spaniard, or Affghan use his fists when insulted or outraged, instead of having recourse to the weapons which he has recourse to? Nobody can use his fists without being taught the use of them by those who have themselves been taught, no more than any one can "whiffle" without being taught by a master of the art. Now let any man of the present day try to whiffle. Would not any one who wished to whiffle have to go to a master of the art? Assuredly! but where would he find one at the present day? The last of the whifflers hanged himself about a fortnight ago on a bell-rope in a church steeple of "the old town," from pure grief that there was no further demand for the exhibition of his art, there being no demand for whiffling since the discontinuation of Guildhall banquets. Whiffling is lost. The old chap left his sword behind him; let any one take up the old chap's sword and try to whiffle. Now much the same hand as he would make who should take up the whiffler's sword and try to whiffle, would he who should try to use his fists who had never had the advantage of a master. Let no one think that men use their fists naturally in their own disputes—men have naturally recourse to any other thing to defend themselves or to offend others; they fly to the stick, to the stone, to the murderous and cowardly knife, or to abuse as cowardly as the knife, and occasionally more murderous. Now which is best when you hate a person, or have a pique against a person, to clench your fist and say "Come on," or to have recourse to the stone, the knife, or murderous calumny? The use of the fist is almost lost in England. Yet are the people better than they were when they knew how to use their fists? The writer believes not. A fisty combat is at present a great rarity, but the use of the knife, the noose, and of poison, to say nothing of calumny, are of more frequent occurrence in England than perhaps in any country in Europe. Is polite taste better than when it could bear the details of a fight? The writer believes not. Two men cannot meet in a ring to settle a dispute in a manly manner without some trumpery local newspaper letting loose a volley of abuse against "the disgraceful exhibition," in which abuse it is sure to be sanctioned by its dainty readers; whereas some murderous horror, the discovery for example of the mangled remains of a woman in some obscure den, is greedily seized hold of by the moral journal, and dressed up for its readers, who luxuriate and gloat upon the ghastly dish. Now, the writer of Lavengro has no sympathy with those who would shrink from striking a blow, but would not shrink from the use of poison or calumny; and his taste has little in common with that which cannot tolerate the hardy details of a prize-fight, but which luxuriates on descriptions of the murder dens of modern England. But prize-fighters and pugilists are blackguards, a reviewer has said; and blackguards they would be provided they employed their skill and their prowess for purposes of brutality and oppression; but prize-fighters and pugilists are seldom friends to brutality and oppression; and which is the blackguard, the writer would ask, he who uses his fists to take his own part, or instructs others to use theirs for the same purpose, or the being who from envy and malice, or at the bidding of a malicious scoundrel, endeavours by calumny, falsehood, and misrepresentation to impede the efforts of lonely and unprotected genius?

One word more about the race, all but extinct, of the people opprobriously called prize-fighters. Some of them have been as noble, kindly men as the world ever produced. Can the rolls of the English aristocracy exhibit names belonging to more noble, more heroic men than those who were called respectively Pearce, Cribb, and Spring? Did ever one of the English aristocracy contract the seeds of fatal consumption by rushing up the stairs of a burning edifice, even to the topmost garret, and rescuing a woman from seemingly inevitable destruction? The writer says no. A woman was rescued from the top of a burning house; but the man who rescued her was no aristocrat; it was Pearce, not Percy, who ran up the burning stairs. Did ever one of those glittering ones save a fainting female from the libidinous rage of six ruffians? The writer believes not. A woman was rescued from the libidinous fury of six monsters on —— Down ; but the man who rescued her was no aristocrat ; it was Pearce not Paulet, who rescued the woman, and thrashed my lord's six gamekeepers—Pearce, whose equal never was, and probably never will be, found in sturdy combat. Are there any of the aristocracy of whom it can be said that they never did a cowardly, cruel, or mean action, and that they invariably took the part of the unfortunate and weak against cruelty and oppression ? As much can be said of Cribb, of Spring, and the other ; but where is the aristocrat of whom as much can be said ? Wellington ? Wellington indeed ! a skilful general, and a good man of valour, it is true, but with that cant word of " duty " continually on his lips, did he rescue Ney from his butchers ? Did he lend a helping hand to Warner ?

In conclusion, the writer would advise those of his country-folks who read his book to have nothing to do with the two kinds of canting nonsense described above, but in their progress through life to enjoy as well as they can, but always with moderation, the good things of this world, to put confidence in God, to be as independent as possible, and to take their own parts. If they are low-spirited, let them not make themselves foolish by putting on sackcloth, drinking water, or chewing ashes, but let them take wholesome exercise, and eat the most generous food they can get, taking up and reading occasionally, not the lives of Ignatius Loyola and Francis Spira, but something more agreeable ; for example, the life and adventures of Mr. Duncan Campbell, the deaf and dumb gentleman ; the travels of Captain Falconer in America, and the journal of John Randall, who went to Virginia and married an Indian wife ; not forgetting, amidst their eating and drinking, their walks over heaths, and by the sea-side, and their agreeable literature, to be charitable to the poor, to read the Psalms and to go to church twice on a Sunday. In their dealings with people, to be courteous to everybody, as Lavengro was, but always independent like him ; and if people meddle with them, to give them as good as they bring, even as he and Isopel Berners were in the habit of doing ; and it will be as well for him to observe that he by no means advises women to be too womanly, but bearing the conduct of Isopel Berners in mind, to take their own parts, and if anybody strikes them, to strike again.

Beating of women by the lords of the creation has become

very prevalent in England since pugilism has been discountenanced. Now the writer strongly advises any woman who is struck by a ruffian to strike him again; or if she cannot clench her fists, and he advises all women in these singular times to learn to clench their fists, to go at him with tooth and nail, and not to be afraid of the result, for any fellow who is dastard enough to strike a woman, would allow himself to be beaten by a woman, were she to make at him in self-defence, even if, instead of possessing the stately height and athletic proportions of the aforesaid Isopel, she were as diminutive in stature, and had a hand as delicate, and foot as small, as a certain royal lady, who was some time ago assaulted by a fellow upwards of six feet high, whom the writer has no doubt she could have beaten had she thought proper to go at him. Such is the deliberate advice of the author to his countrymen and women—advice in which he believes there is nothing unscriptural or repugnant to common sense.

The writer is perfectly well aware that, by the plain language which he has used in speaking of the various kinds of nonsense prevalent in England, he shall make himself a multitude of enemies; but he is not going to conceal the truth or to tamper with nonsense, from the fear of provoking hostility. He has a duty to perform and he will perform it resolutely; he is the person who carried the Bible to Spain; and as resolutely as he spoke in Spain against the superstitions of Spain, will he speak in England against the nonsense of his own native land. He is not one of those who, before they sit down to write a book, say to themselves, what cry shall we take up? what principles shall we advocate? what principles shall we abuse? before we put pen to paper we must find out what cry is the loudest, what principle has the most advocates, otherwise, after having written our book, we may find ourselves on the weaker side.

A sailor of the " Bounty," waked from his sleep by the noise of the mutiny, lay still in his hammock for some time, quite undecided whether to take part with the captain or to join the mutineers. " I must mind what I do," said he to himself, " lest, in the end, I find myself on the weaker side;" finally, on hearing that the mutineers were successful, he went on deck, and seeing Bligh pinioned to the mast, he put his fist to his nose, and otherwise insulted him. Now, there are many writers of the present day whose conduct is very similar to that of the sailor. They lie listening in their corners till they have ascertained which principle has most advocates; then, presently, they make their appearance on the deck of the world with their book; if truth has been victorious, then has truth the hurrah! but if truth is pinioned against the mast, then is their fist thrust against the nose of truth, and their gibe and their insult spirted in her face. The strongest party had the sailor, and the strongest party has almost invariably the writer of the present day.

CHAPTER IX

Pseudo-Critics.

A CERTAIN set of individuals calling themselves critics have attacked Lavengro with much virulence and malice. If what they call criticism had been founded on truth, the author would have had nothing to say. The book contains plenty of blemishes, some of them, by the bye, wilful ones, as the writer will presently show; not one of these, however, has been detected and pointed out; but the best passages in the book, indeed whatever was calculated to make the book valuable, have been assailed with abuse and misrepresentation. The duty of the true critic is to play the part of a leech, and not of a viper. Upon true and upon malignant criticism there is an excellent fable by the Spaniard Iriarte. The viper says to the leech, " Why do people invite your bite, and flee from mine?" " Because," says the leech, " people receive health from my bite, and poison from yours." " There is as much difference," says the clever Spaniard," between true and malignant criticism, as between poison and medicine." Certainly a great many meritorious writers have allowed themselves to be poisoned by malignant criticism; the writer, however, is not one of those who allow themselves to be poisoned by pseudo-critics; no! no! he will rather hold them up by their tails, and show the creatures wriggling, blood and foam streaming from their broken jaws. First of all, however, he will notice one of their objections. " The book isn't true," say they. Now one of the principal reasons with those that have attacked Lavengro for their abuse of it is, that it is particularly true in one instance, namely, that it exposes their own nonsense, their love of humbug, their slavishness, their dressings, their goings out, their scraping and bowing to great people; it is the showing up of " gentility-nonsense " in Lavengro that has been one principal reason for raising the above cry; for in Lavengro is denounced the besetting folly of the English people, a folly which those who call themselves guardians of the public taste are far from being above. " We can't abide anything that isn't true !" they exclaim. Can't they? Then why are they so enraptured with any fiction that is adapted to purposes of humbug, which tends to make them satisfied with their own proceedings, with their own nonsense, which does not tell them to reform, to become more alive to their own failings, and less sensitive about the tyrannical goings on of the masters, and the degraded condition, the sufferings, and the trials of the serfs in the star Jupiter? Had Lavengro, instead of being the work of an independent mind, been written in order to further any of the thousand and one cants, and species of nonsense prevalent in England, the author would have heard much less about its not being true, both from public detractors and private censurers.

" But Lavengro pretends to be an autobiography," say the critics; and here the writer begs leave to observe, that it would be well for people who profess to have a regard for truth, not to exhibit in every assertion which they make a most profligate disregard of it; this assertion of theirs is a falsehood, and they know it to be a falsehood. In the preface Lavengro is stated to be a dream; and the writer takes this opportunity of stating that he never said it was an autobiography; never authorized any person to say that it was one; and that he has in innumerable instances declared in public and private, both before and after the work was published, that it was not what is generally termed an autobiography : but a set of people who pretend to write criticisms on books, hating the author for various reasons, —amongst others, because, having the proper pride of a gentleman and a scholar, he did not, in the year '43, choose to permit himself to be exhibited and made a zany of in London, and especially because he will neither associate

with, nor curry favour with, them who are neither gentle·
men nor scholars,—attack his book with abuse and calumny.
He is, perhaps, condescending too much when he takes
any notice of such people; as, however, the English public
is wonderfully led by cries and shouts, and generally ready
to take part against any person who is either unwilling or
unable to defend himself, he deems it advisable not to be
altogether quiet with those who assail him. The best way
to deal with vipers is to tear out their teeth; and the best
way to deal with pseudo-critics is to deprive them of their
poison-bag, which is easily done by exposing their ignorance. The writer knew perfectly well the description of
people with whom he would have to do, he therefore very
quietly prepared a stratagem, by means of which he could
at any time exhibit them, powerless and helpless, in his
hand. Critics, when they review books, ought to have a
competent knowledge of the subjects which those books
discuss.

Lavengro is a philological book, a poem if you choose
to call it so. Now, what a fine triumph it would have been
for those who wished to vilify the book and its author, provided they could have detected the latter tripping in his
philology—they might have instantly said that he was an
ignorant pretender to philology—they laughed at the idea
of his taking up a viper by its tail, a trick which hundreds
of country urchins do every September, but they were silent
about the really wonderful part of the book, the philological
matter—they thought philology was his stronghold, and
that it would be useless to attack him there; they of course
would give him no credit as a philologist, for anything like
fair treatment towards him was not to be expected at their
hands, but they were afraid to attack his philology—yet
that was the point, and the only point in which they might
have attacked him successfully; he was vulnerable there.
How was this? Why, in order to have an opportunity of
holding up pseudo-critics by the tails, he wilfully spelt
various foreign words wrong—Welsh words, and even
Italian words—did they detect these mis-spellings? not one
of them, even as he knew they would not, and he now
taunts them with ignorance; and the power of taunting
them with ignorance is the punishment which he designed
for them—a power which they might but for their ignorance
have used against him. The writer besides knowing some-

thing of Italian and Welsh, knows a little of Armenian language and literature; but who knowing anything of the Armenian language, unless he had an end in view, would say, that the word sea in Armenian is anything like the word tide in English? The word for sea in Armenian is dzow, a word connected with the Tebetian word for water, and the Chinese shuy, and the Turkish su, signifying the same thing; but where is the resemblance between dzow and tide? Again, the word for bread in ancient Armenian is hats; yet the Armenian on London Bridge is made to say zhats, which is not the nominative of the Armenian noun for bread, but the accusative: now, critics, ravening against a man because he is a gentleman and a scholar, and has not only the power but also the courage to write original works, why did you not discover that weak point? Why, because you were ignorant, so here ye are held up! Moreover, who with a name commencing with Z, ever wrote fables in Armenian? There are two writers of fables in Armenian—Varthan and Koscht, and illustrious writers they are, one in the simple, and the other in the ornate style of Armenian composition, but neither of their names begins with a Z. Oh, what a precious opportunity ye lost, ye ravening crew, of convicting the poor, half-starved, friendless boy of the book, of ignorance or misrepresentation, by asking who with a name beginning with Z ever wrote fables in Armenian; but ye couldn't help yourselves, ye are duncie. We duncie! Ay, duncie. So here ye are held up by the tails, blood and foam streaming from your jaws.

The writer wishes to ask here, what do you think of all this, Messieurs les Critiques? Were ye ever served so before? But don't you richly deserve it? Haven't you been for years past bullying and insulting everybody whom you deemed weak, and currying favour with everybody whom you thought strong? "*We* approve of this. We disapprove of that. Oh, this will never do. These are fine lines!" The lines perhaps some horrid sycophantic rubbish addressed to Wellington, or Lord So-and-so. To have your ignorance thus exposed, to be shown up in this manner, and by whom? A gypsy! Ay, a gypsy was the very right person to do it. But is it not galling, after all?

"Ah, but *we* don't understand Armenian, it cannot be expected that *we* should understand Armenian, or Welsh, or —— Hey, what's this? The mighty *we* not understand

Armenian or Welsh, or —— Then why does the mighty *we* pretend to review a book like Lavengro? From the arrogance with which it continually delivers itself, one would think that the mighty *we* is omniscient; that it understands every language; is versed in every literature; yet the mighty *we* does not even know the word for bread in Armenian. It knows bread well enough by name in England, and frequently bread in England only by its name, but the truth is, that the mighty *we*, with all its pretension, is in general a very sorry creature, who, instead of saying nous disons, should rather say nous dis : Porny in his " Guerre des Dieux," very profanely makes the three in one say, Je faisons; now, Lavengro, who is anything but profane, would suggest that critics, especially magazine and Sunday newspaper critics, should commence with nous dis, as the first word would be significant of the conceit and assumption of the critic, and the second of the extent of the critic's information. The *we* says its say, but when fawning sycophancy or vulgar abuse are taken from that say, what remains? Why a blank, a void like Ginnungagap.

As the writer, of his own accord, has exposed some of the blemishes of his book—a task, which a competent critic ought to have done—he will now point out two or three of its merits, which any critic, not altogether blinded with ignorance, might have done, or not replete with gall and envy would have been glad to do. The book has the merit of communicating a fact connected with physiology, which in all the pages of the multitude of books was never previously mentioned—the mysterious practice of touching objects to baffle the evil chance. The miserable detractor will, of course, instantly begin to rave about such a habit being common : well and good; but was it ever before described in print, or all connected with it dissected? He may then vociferate something about Johnson having touched :—the writer cares not whether Johnson, who, by the bye, during the last twenty or thirty years, owing to people having become ultra Tory mad from reading Scott's novels and the " Quarterly Review," has been a mighty favourite, especially with some who were in the habit of calling him a half crazy old fool—touched, or whether he did or not; but he asks where did Johnson ever describe the feelings which induced him to perform the magic touch, even supposing that he did perform it? Again, the history gives an account of a certain book called the " Sleeping Bard," the most remarkable prose work of the most difficult language but one, of modern Europe,—a book, for a notice of which, he believes, one might turn over in vain the pages of any review printed in England, or, indeed, elsewhere.— So here are two facts, one literary and the other physiological, for which any candid critic was bound to thank the author, even as in Romany Rye there is a fact connected with Iro Norman Myth, for the disclosing of which, any person who pretends to have a regard for literature is bound to thank him, namely, that the mysterious Finn or Fingal of " Ossian's Poems " is one and the same person as the Sigurd Fofnisbane of the Edda and the Wilkina, and the Siegfried Horn of the Lay of the Niebelungs.

The writer might here conclude, and, he believes, most triumphantly; as, however, he is in the cue for writing, which he seldom is, he will for his own gratification, and for the sake of others, dropping metaphors about vipers and serpents, show up in particular two or three sets or cliques of people, who, he is happy to say, have been particularly virulent against him and his work, for nothing indeed could have given him greater mortification than their praise.

In the first place, he wishes to dispose of certain individuals who call themselves men of wit and fashion—about town— who he is told have abused his book " vaustly "— their own word. These people paint their cheeks, wear white kid gloves, and dabble in literature, or what they conceive to be literature. For abuse from such people, the writer was prepared. Does any one imagine that the writer was not well aware, before he published his book, that, whenever he gave it to the world, he should be attacked by every literary coxcomb in England who had influence enough to procure the insertion of a scurrilous article in a magazine or newspaper ! He has been in Spain, and has seen how invariably the mule attacks the horse; now why does the mule attack the horse? Why, because the latter carries about with him that which the envious hermaphrodite does not possess.

They consider, forsooth, that his book is low—but he is not going to waste words about them—one or two of whom, he is told, have written very duncie books about Spain, and are highly enraged with him, because certain books which he wrote about Spain were not considered duncie. No, he is not going to waste words upon them, for verily he dislikes their company, and so he'll pass them by, and proceed to others.

The Scotch Charlie o'er the water people have been very loud in the abuse of Lavengro—this again might be expected; the sarcasms of the Priest about the Charlie o'er the water nonsense of course stung them. Oh! it is one of the claims which Lavengro has to respect, that it is the first, if not the only work, in which that nonsense is, to a certain extent, exposed. Two or three of their remarks on passages of Lavengro, he will reproduce and laugh at. Of course your Charlie o'er the water people are genteel exceedingly, and cannot abide anything low. Gypsyism they think is particularly low, and the use of gypsy words in literature beneath its gentility; so they object to gypsy words being used in Lavengro where gypsies are introduced speaking—"What is Romany forsooth?" say they. Very good! And what is Scotch? has not the public been nauseated with Scotch for the last thirty years? "Ay, but Scotch is not"—the writer believes he knows much better than the Scotch what Scotch is and what it is not; he has told them before what it is, a very sorry jargon. He will now tell them what it is not—a sister or an immediate daughter of the Sanscrit, which Romany is. "Ay, but the Scotch are"—foxes, foxes, nothing else than foxes, even like the gypsies—the difference between the gypsy and Scotch fox being that the first is wild, with a mighty brush, the other a sneak with a gilt collar and without a tail.

A Charlie o'er the water person attempts to be witty, because the writer has said that perhaps a certain old Edinburgh High-School porter, of the name of Boee, was perhaps of the same blood as a certain Bui, a Northern Kemp who distinguished himself at the battle of Horinger Bay. A pretty matter, forsooth, to excite the ridicule of a Scotchman! Why, is there a beggar or trumpery fellow in Scotland, who does not pretend to be somebody, or related to somebody? Is not every Scotchman descended from some king, kemp, or cow-stealer of old, by his own account at least? Why, the writer would even go so far as to bet a trifle that the poor creature, who ridicules Boee's supposed ancestry, has one of his own, at least as grand and as apocryphal as old Boee's of the High School.

The same Charlie o'er the water person is mightily indignant that Lavengro should have spoken disrespectfully of William Wallace; Lavengro, when he speaks of that personage, being a child of about ten years old, and repeating merely what he had heard. All the Scotch, by the bye, for a great many years past, have been great admirers of William Wallace, particularly the Charlie o'er the water people, who in their nonsense-verses about Charlie generally contrive to bring in the name of William, Willie, or Wullie Wallace. The writer begs leave to say that he by no means wishes to bear hard against William Wallace, but he cannot help asking why, if William, Willie, or Wullie Wallace was such a particularly nice person, did his brother Scots betray him to a certain renowned southern warrior, called Edward Longshanks, who caused him to be hanged and cut into four in London, and his quarters to be placed over the gates of certain towns? They got gold, it is true, and titles, very nice things, no doubt; but, surely, the life of a patriot is better than all the gold and titles in the world—at least Lavengro thinks so—but Lavengro has lived more with gypsies than Scotchmen, and gypsies do not betray their brothers. It would be some time before a gypsy would hand over his brother to the harum-beck, even supposing you would not only make him a king, but a justice of the peace, and not only give him the world, but the best farm on the Holkham estate; but gypsies are wild foxes, and there is certainly a wonderful difference between the way of thinking of the wild fox who retains his brush, and that of the scurvy kennel creature who has lost his tail.

Ah! but thousands of Scotch, and particularly the Charlie o'er the water people, will say, "We didn't sell Willie Wallace, it was our forbears who sold Willie Wallace——If Edward Longshanks had asked us to sell Wullie Wallace, we would soon have shown him that——" Lord better ye, ye poor trumpery set of creatures, ye would not have acted a bit better than your forefathers; remember how ye have ever treated the few amongst ye who, though born in the kennel, have shown something of the spirit of the wood. Many of ye are still alive who delivered over men, quite as honest and patriotic as William Wallace, into the hands of an English minister, to be chained and transported for merely venturing to speak and write in the cause of humanity, at the time when

Europe was beginning to fling off the chains imposed by kings and priests. And it is not so very long since Burns, to whom ye are now building up obelisks rather higher than he deserves, was permitted by his countrymen to die in poverty and misery, because he would not join with them in songs of adulation to kings and the trumpery great. So say not that ye would have acted with respect to William Wallace one whit better than your fathers—and you in particular, ye children of Charlie, whom do ye write nonsense-verses about ? A family of dastard despots, who did their best, during a century and more, to tread out the few sparks of independent feeling still glowing in Scotland—but enough has been said about ye.

Amongst those who have been prodigal in abuse and defamation of Lavengro, have been your modern Radicals, and particularly a set of people who filled the country with noise against the King and Queen, Wellington, and the Tories, in '32. About these people the writer will presently have occasion to say a good deal, and also of real Radicals. As, however, it may be supposed that he is one of those who delight to play the sycophant to kings and queens, to curry favour with Tories, and to bepraise Wellington, he begs leave to state that such is not the case.

About kings and queens he has nothing to say; about Tories, simply that he believes them to be a bad set; about Wellington, however, it will be necessary for him to say a good deal, of mixed import, as he will subsequently frequently have occasion to mention him in connection with what he has to say about pseudo-Radicals.

CHAPTER X

Pseudo-Radicals.

ABOUT Wellington, then, he says, that he believes him at the present day to be infinitely overrated. But there certainly was a time when he was shamefully underrated. Now what time was that? Why the time of pseudo-Radicalism, par excellence, from '20 to '32. Oh, the abuse that was heaped on Wellington by those who traded in Radical cant—your newspaper editors and review writers! and how he was sneered at then by your Whigs, and how faintly supported he was by your Tories, who were half ashamed of him; for your Tories, though capital fellows as followers, when you want nobody to back you, are the faintest creatures in the world when you cry in your agony, " Come and help me!" Oh, assuredly Wellington was infamously used at that time, especially by your traders in Radicalism, who howled at and hooted him; said he had every vice—was no general—was beaten at Waterloo—was a poltroon—moreover a poor illiterate creature, who could scarcely read or write; nay, a principal Radical paper said boldly he could not read, and devised an ingenious plan for teaching Wellington how to read. Now this was too bad; and the writer, being a lover of justice, frequently spoke up for Wellington, saying, that as for vice, he was not worse than his neighbours; that he was brave; that he won the fight at Waterloo, from a half-dead man, it is true, but that he did win it. Also, that he believed he had read " Rules for the Manual and Platoon Exercises " to some purpose; moreover, that he was sure he could write, for that he the writer had once written to Wellington, and had received an answer from him; nay, the writer once went so far as to strike a blow for Wellington; for the last time he used his fists was upon a Radical sub-editor, who was mobbing Wellington in the street, from behind a rank of grimy fellows; but though the writer spoke up for Wellington to a certain extent when he was shamefully underrated, and once struck a blow for him when he was about being hustled, he is not going to join in the loathsome sycophantic nonsense which it has been the fashion to use with respect to Wellington these last twenty years. Now what have those years been to England! Why the years of ultra-gentility, everybody in England having gone gentility mad during the last twenty years, and no people more so than your pseudo-Radicals. Wellington was turned out, and your Whigs and Radicals got in, and then commenced the period of ultra-gentility in England. The Whigs and Radicals only hated Wellington as long as the patronage of the country was in his hands, none of which they were tolerably sure he would bestow on them; but no sooner did they get it into their own, than they forthwith became admirers of

Wellington. And why? Because he was a duke, petted
at Windsor and by foreign princes, and a very genteel
personage. Formerly many of your Whigs and Radicals
had scarcely a decent coat on their backs; but now the
plunder of the country was at their disposal, and they had
as good a chance of being genteel as any people. So they
were willing to worship Wellington because he was very
genteel, and could not keep the plunder of the country
out of their hands. And Wellington has been worshipped,
and prettily so, during the last fifteen or twenty years.
He is now a noble fine-hearted creature; the greatest
general the world ever produced; the bravest of men; and
—and—mercy upon us! the greatest of military writers!
Now the present writer will not join in such sycophancy.
As he was not afraid to take the part of Wellington when
he was scurvily used by all parties, and when it was
dangerous to take his part, so he is not afraid to speak
the naked truth about Wellington in these days, when
it is dangerous to say anything about him but what is
sycophantically laudatory. He said in '32, that as to vice,
Wellington was not worse than his neighbours; but he is
not going to say, in '54, that Wellington was a noble-
hearted fellow; for he believes that a more cold-hearted
individual never existed. His conduct to Warner, the
poor Vaudois, and Marshal Ney, showed that. He said,
in '32, that he was a good general and a brave man; but
he is not going, in '54, to say that he was the best general,
or the bravest man the world ever saw. England has
produced a better general—France two or three—both
countries many braver men. The son of the Norfolk
clergyman was a brave man; Marshal Ney was a braver
man. Oh, that battle of Copenhagen! Oh, that covering
the retreat of the Grand Army! And though he said in '32
that he could write, he is not going to say in '54 that he
is the best of all military writers. On the contrary, he
does not hesitate to say that any Commentary of Julius
Cæsar, or any chapter in Justinus, more especially the one
about the Parthians, is worth the ten volumes of Wellington's Despatches; though he has no doubt that, by saying
so, he shall especially rouse the indignation of a certain
newspaper, at present one of the most genteel journals
imaginable—with a slight tendency to Liberalism, it is
true, but perfectly genteel—which is nevertheless the very

one which, in '32, swore bodily that Wellington could neither read nor write, and devised an ingenious plan for teaching him how to read.

Now, after the above statement, no one will venture to say, if the writer should be disposed to bear hard upon Radicals, that he would be influenced by a desire to pay court to princes, or to curry favour with Tories, or from being a blind admirer of the Duke of Wellington; but the writer is not going to declaim against Radicals, that is, real Republicans, or their principles; upon the whole, he is something of an admirer of both. The writer has always had as much admiration for everything that is real and honest as he has had contempt for the opposite. Now real Republicanism is certainly a very fine thing, a much finer thing than Toryism, a system of common robbery, which is nevertheless far better than Whiggism [1]—a compound of petty larceny, popular instruction, and receiving of stolen goods. Yes, real Republicanism is certainly a very fine thing, and your real Radicals and Republicans are certainly very fine fellows, or rather were fine fellows, for the Lord only knows where to find them at the present day—the writer does not. If he did, he would at any time go five miles to invite one of them to dinner, even supposing that he had to go to a workhouse in order to find the person he wished to invite. Amongst the real Radicals of

[1] As the present work will come out in the midst of a vehement political contest, people may be led to suppose that the above was written expressly for the time. The writer therefore begs to state that it was written in the year 1854. He cannot help adding that he is neither Whig, Tory, nor Radical, and cares not a straw what party governs England, provided it is governed well. But he has no hopes of good government from the Whigs. It is true that amongst them there is one very great man, Lord Palmerston, who is indeed the sword and buckler, the chariots and the horses of the party; but it is impossible for his lordship to govern well with such colleagues as he has—colleagues which have been forced upon him by family influence, and who are continually pestering him into measures anything but conducive to the country's honour and interest. If Palmerston would govern well, he must get rid of them; but from that step, with all his courage and all his greatness, he will shrink. Yet how proper and easy a step it would be! He could easily get better, but scarcely worse, associates. They appear to have one object in view, and only one—jobbery. It was chiefly owing to a most flagitious piece of jobbery, which one of his lordship's principal colleagues sanctioned and promoted, that his lordship experienced his late parliamentary disasters.

England, those who flourished from the year '16 to '20, there were certainly extraordinary characters, men partially insane, perhaps, but honest and brave—they did not make a market of the principles which they professed, and never intended to do so; they believed in them, and were willing to risk their lives in endeavouring to carry them out. The writer wishes to speak in particular of two of these men, both of whom perished on the scaffold—their names were Thistlewood and Ings. Thistlewood, the best known of them, was a brave soldier, and had served with distinction as an officer in the French service; he was one of the excellent swordsmen of Europe; had fought several duels in France, where it is no child's play to fight a duel; but had never unsheathed his sword for single combat, but in defence of the feeble and insulted—he was kind and open-hearted, but of too great simplicity; he had once ten thousand pounds left him, all of which he lent to a friend, who disappeared and never returned a penny. Ings was an uneducated man, of very low stature, but amazing strength and resolution; he was a kind husband and father, and though a humble butcher, the name he bore was one of the royal names of the heathen Anglo-Saxons. These two men, along with five others, were executed, and their heads hacked off, for levying war against George the Fourth; the whole seven dying in a manner which extorted cheers from the populace; the most of then uttering philosophical or patriotic sayings. Thistlewood, who was, perhaps, the most calm and collected of all, just before he was turned off, said, "We are now going to discover the great secret." Ings, the moment before he was choked, was singing "Scots wha ha' wi' Wallace bled." Now there was no humbug about those men, nor about many more of the same time and of the same principles. They might be deluded about Republicanism, as Algernon Sidney was, and as Brutus was, but they were as honest and brave as either Brutus or Sidney; and as willing to die for their principles. But the Radicals who succeeded them were beings of a very different description; they jobbed and traded in Republicanism, and either parted with it, or at the present day are eager to part with it for a consideration. In order to get the Whigs into power, and themselves places, they brought the country by their inflammatory language to the verge of a revolution, and were the cause that many perished on the scaffold; by their incendiary harangues and newspaper articles they caused the Bristol conflagration, for which six poor creatures were executed; they encouraged the mob to pillage, pull down and burn, and then rushing into garrets looked on. Thistlewood tells the mob the Tower is a second Bastile; let it be pulled down. A mob tries to pull down the Tower; but Thistlewood is at the head of that mob; he is not peeping from a garret on Tower Hill like Gulliver at Lisbon. Thistlewood and Ings say to twenty ragged individuals, Liverpool and Castlereagh are two satellites of despotism; it would be highly desirable to put them out of the way. And a certain number of ragged individuals are surprised in a stable in Cato Street, making preparations to put Castlereagh and Liverpool out of the way, and are fired upon with muskets by Grenadiers, and are hacked at with cutlasses by Bow Street runners; but the twain who encouraged those ragged individuals to meet in Cato Street are not far off, they are not on the other side of the river, in the Borough, for example, in some garret or obscure cellar. The very first to confront the Guards and runners are Thistlewood and Ings; Thistlewood whips his long thin rapier through Smithers' lungs, and Ings makes a dash at Fitzclarence with his butcher's knife. Oh, there was something in those fellows! honesty and courage—but can as much be said for the inciters of the troubles of '32? No; they egged on poor ignorant mechanics and rustics, and got them hanged for pulling down and burning, whilst the highest pitch to which their own daring ever mounted was to mob Wellington as he passed in the streets.

Now, these people were humbugs, which Thistlewood and Ings were not. They raved and foamed against kings, queens, Wellington, the aristocracy, and what not, till they had got the Whigs into power, with whom they were in secret alliance, and with whom they afterwards openly joined in a system of robbery and corruption, more flagitious than the old Tory one, because there was more cant about it; for themselves they got consulships, commissionerships, and in some instances governments; for their sons clerkships in public offices; and there you may see those sons with the never-failing badge of the low scoundrel-puppy, the gilt chain at the waistcoat pocket;

and there you may hear and see them using the languishing tones, and employing the airs and graces which wenches use and employ, who, without being in the family way, wish to make their keepers believe that they are in the family way. Assuredly great is the cleverness of your Radicals of '32, in providing for themselves and their families. Yet, clever as they are, there is one thing they cannot do—they get governments for themselves, commissionerships for their brothers, clerkships for their sons, but there is one thing beyond their craft—they cannot get husbands for their daughters, who, too ugly for marriage, and with their heads filled with the nonsense they have imbibed from gentility-novels, go over from Socinus to the Pope, becoming sisters in fusty convents, or having heard a few sermons in Mr. Platitude's "chapelle," seek for admission at the establishment of mother S——, who, after employing them for a time in various menial offices, and making them pluck off their eyebrows hair by hair, generally dismisses them on the plea of sluttishness; whereupon they return to their papas to eat the bread of the country, with the comfortable prospect of eating it still in the shape of a pension after their sires are dead. Papa (ex uno disce omnes) living as quietly as he can; not exactly enviably, it is true, being now and then seen to cast an uneasy and furtive glance behind, even as an animal is wont, who has lost by some mischance a very slight appendage; as quietly however as he can, and as dignifiedly, a great admirer of every genteel thing and genteel personage, the Duke in particular, whose "Despatches," bound in red morocco, you will find on his table. A disliker of coarse expressions, and extremes of every kind, with a perfect horror for revolutions and attempts to revolutionize, exclaiming now and then, as a shriek escapes from whipped and bleeding Hungary, a groan from gasping Poland, and a half-stifled curse from down-trodden but scowling Italy, "Confound the revolutionary canaille, why can't it be quiet!" in a word, putting one in mind of the parvenu in the "Walpurgis Nacht." The writer is no admirer of Göthe, but the idea of that parvenu was certainly a good one. Yes, putting one in mind of the individual who says—

"Wir waren wahrlich auch nicht dumm,
Und thaten oft was wir nicht sollten;

Doch jetzo kehrt sich alles um und um,
  Und eben da wir's fest erhalten wollten."

We were no fools, as every one discern'd,
  And stopp'd at nought our projects in fulfilling;
But now the world seems topsy-turvy turn'd,
  To keep it quiet just when we were willing.

Now, this class of individuals entertain a mortal hatred for Lavengro and its writer, and never lose an opportunity of vituperating both. It is true that such hatred is by no means surprising. There is certainly a great deal of difference between Lavengro and their own sons; the one thinking of independence and philology, whilst he is clinking away at kettles, and hammering horse-shoes in dingles; the others stuck up at public offices with gilt chains at their waistcoat-pockets, and giving themselves the airs and graces of females of a certain description. And there certainly *is* a great deal of difference between the author of Lavengro and themselves—he retaining his principles and his brush; they with scarlet breeches on, it is true, but without their Republicanism, and their tails. Oh, the writer can well afford to be vituperated by your pseudo-Radicals of '32!

Some time ago the writer was set upon by an old Radical and his wife; but the matter is too rich not to require a chapter to itself.

CHAPTER XI

The Old Radical.

" This very dirty man, with his very dirty face,
  Would do any dirty act, which would get him a place."

SOME time ago the writer was set upon by an old Radical and his wife; but before he relates the manner in which they set upon him, it will be as well to enter upon a few particulars tending to elucidate their reasons for so doing.

The writer had just entered into his eighteenth year, when he met at the table of a certain Anglo-Germanist an individual, apparently somewhat under thirty, of middle stature, a thin and weaselly figure, a sallow complexion, a certain obliquity of vision, and a large pair of spectacles. This person, who had lately come from abroad, and had published a volume of translations, had attracted some slight notice in the literary world, and was looked upon as a kind of lion in a small provincial capital. After dinner he argued a great deal, spoke vehemently against the church, and uttered the most desperate Radicalism that was perhaps ever heard, saying, he hoped that in a short time there would not be a king or queen in Europe, and inveighing bitterly against the English aristocracy, and against the Duke of Wellington in particular, whom he said, if he himself was ever president of an English republic—an event which he seemed to think by no means improbable—he would hang for certain infamous acts of profligacy and bloodshed which he had perpetrated in Spain. Being informed that the writer was something of a philologist, to which character the individual in question laid great pretensions, he came and sat down by him, and talked about languages and literature. The writer, who was only a boy, was a little frightened at first, but, not wishing to appear a child of absolute ignorance, he summoned what little learning he had, and began to blunder out something about the Celtic languages and literature, and asked the Lion who he conceived Finn-Ma-Coul to be? and whether he did not consider the " Ode to the Fox," by Red Rhys of Eryry, to be a masterpiece of pleasantry? Receiving no answer to these questions from the Lion, who, singular enough, would frequently, when the writer put a question to him, look across the table, and flatly contradict some one who was talking to some other person, the writer dropped the Celtic languages and literature, and asked him whether he did not think it a funny thing that Temugin, generally called Genghis Khan, should have married the daughter of Prester John?[1] The Lion, after giving a side-glance at the writer through his left spectacle glass, seemed about to reply, but was unfortunately prevented, being seized with an irresistible impulse to contradict a respectable doctor of medicine, who was engaged in conversation with the master of the house at the upper and farther end of the table, the writer

[1] A fact.

being a poor ignorant lad, sitting of course at the bottom.
The doctor, who had served in the Peninsula, having
observed that Ferdinand the Seventh was not quite so
bad as had been represented, the Lion vociferated that he
was ten times worse, and that he hoped to see him and the
Duke of Wellington hanged together. The doctor, who,
being a Welshman, was somewhat of a warm temper,
growing rather red, said that at any rate he had been informed that Ferdinand the Seventh knew sometimes how
to behave himself like a gentleman—this brought on a long
dispute, which terminated rather abruptly. The Lion having observed that the doctor must not talk about Spanish
matters with one who had visited every part of Spain,
the doctor bowed, and said he was right, for that he believed no people in general possessed such accurate information about countries as those who had travelled them
as bagmen. On the Lion asking the doctor what he
meant, the Welshman, whose under jaw began to move
violently, replied, that he meant what he said. Here the
matter ended, for the Lion, turning from him, looked at
the writer. The writer, imagining that his own conversation hitherto had been too trivial and common-place for
the Lion to consider worth his while to take much notice
of it, determined to assume a little higher ground, and
after repeating a few verses of the Koran, and gabbling
a little Arabic, asked the Lion what he considered to be
the difference between the Hegira and the Christian era,
adding, that he thought the general computation was in
error by about one year; and being a particularly modest
person, chiefly, he believes, owing to his having been at
school in Ireland, absolutely blushed at finding that the
Lion returned not a word in answer. "What a wonderful
individual I am seated by," thought he, "to whom Arabic
seems a vulgar speech, and a question about the Hegira
not worthy of an answer!" not reflecting that as lions
come from the Sahara, they have quite enough of Arabic
at home, and that the question about the Hegira was
rather mal à propos to one used to prey on the flesh of
hadjis. "Now I only wish he would vouchsafe me a
little of his learning," thought the boy to himself, and in
this wish he was at last gratified; for the Lion, after asking him whether he was acquainted at all with the Sclavonian languages, and being informed that he was not,

absolutely dumb-foundered him by a display of Sclavonian erudition.

Years rolled by—the writer was a good deal about, sometimes in London, sometimes in the country, sometimes abroad; in London he occasionally met the man of the spectacles, who was always very civil to him, and, indeed, cultivated his acquaintance. The writer thought it rather odd that, after he himself had become acquainted with the Sclavonian languages and literature, the man of the spectacles talked little or nothing about them. In a little time, however, the matter ceased to cause him the slightest surprise, for he had discovered a key to the mystery. In the mean time the man of spectacles was busy enough; he speculated in commerce, failed, and paid his creditors twenty pennies in the pound; published translations, of which the public at length became heartily tired; having, indeed, got an inkling of the manner in which those translations were got up. He managed, however, to ride out many a storm, having one trusty sheet-anchor —Radicalism. This he turned to the best advantage— writing pamphlets and articles in reviews, all in the Radical interest, and for which he was paid out of the Radical fund; which articles and pamphlets, when Toryism seemed to reel on its last legs, exhibited a slight tendency to Whiggism. Nevertheless, his abhorrence of desertion of principle was so great in the time of the Duke of Wellington's administration, that when S—— left the Whigs and went over, he told the writer, who was about that time engaged with him in a literary undertaking, that the said S—— was a fellow with a character so infamous, that any honest man would rather that you spit in his face than insult his ears with the mention of the name of S——.

The literary project having come to nothing,—in which, by the bye, the writer was to have all the labour, and his friend all the credit, provided any credit should accrue from it,—the writer did not see the latter for some years, during which time considerable political changes took place; the Tories were driven from, and the Whigs placed in, office, both events being brought about by the Radicals coalescing with the Whigs, over whom they possessed great influence for the services which they had rendered. When the writer next visited his friend, he found him very much altered; his opinions were by no means so exalted as they had been—he was not disposed even to be rancorous against the Duke of Wellington, saying that there were worse men than he, and giving him some credit as a general; a hankering after gentility seeming to pervade the whole family, father and sons, wife and daughters, all of whom talked about genteel diversions—gentility novels, and even seemed to look with favour on High Churchism, having in former years, to all appearance, been bigoted Dissenters. In a little time the writer went abroad; as, indeed, did his friend; not, however, like the writer, at his own expense, but at that of the country—the Whigs having given him a travelling appointment, which he held for some years, during which he received upwards of twelve thousand pounds of the money of the country, for services which will, perhaps, be found inscribed on certain tablets, when another Astolfo shall visit the moon. This appointment, however, he lost on the Tories resuming power—when the writer found him almost as Radical and patriotic as ever, just engaged in trying to get into Parliament, into which he got by the assistance of his Radical friends, who, in conjunction with the Whigs, were just getting up a crusade against the Tories, which they intended should be a conclusive one.

A little time after the publication of "The Bible in Spain," the Tories being still in power, this individual, full of the most disinterested friendship for the author, was particularly anxious that he should be presented with an official situation, in a certain region a great many miles off. "You are the only person for that appointment," said he; "you understand a great deal about the country, and are better acquainted with the two languages spoken there than any one in England. Now I love my country, and have, moreover, a great regard for you, and as I am in Parliament, and have frequent opportunities of speaking to the Ministry, I shall take care to tell them how desirable it would be to secure your services. It is true they are Tories, but I think that even Tories would give up their habitual love of jobbery in a case like yours, and for once show themselves disposed to be honest men and gentlemen; indeed, I have no doubt they will, for having so deservedly an infamous character, they would be glad to get themselves a little credit, by a presentation which could not possibly be traced to jobbery or favouritism."

The writer begged his friend to give himself no trouble about the matter, as he was not desirous of the appointment, being in tolerably easy circumstances, and willing to take some rest after a life of labour. All, however, that he could say was of no use, his friend indignantly observing, that the matter ought to be taken entirely out of his hands, and the appointment thrust upon him for the credit of the country. " But may not many people be far more worthy of the appointment than myself?" said the writer. " Where?" said the friendly Radical. " If you don't get it, it will be made a job of, given to the son of some steward, or, perhaps, to some quack who has done dirty work; I tell you what, I shall ask it for you, in spite of you; I shall, indeed !" and his eyes flashed with friendly and patriotic fervour through the large pair of spectacles which he wore.

And, in fact, it would appear that the honest and friendly patriot put his threat into execution. " I have spoken," said he, " more than once to this and that individual in Parliament, and everybody seems to think that the appointment should be given to you. Nay, that you should be forced to accept it. I intend next to speak to Lord A——" And so he did, at least it would appear so. On the writer calling upon him one evening, about a week afterwards, in order to take leave of him, as the writer was about to take a long journey for the sake of his health, his friend no sooner saw him than he started up in a violent fit of agitation, and glancing about the room, in which there were several people, amongst others two Whig members of Parliament, said, " I am glad you are come, I was just speaking about you. This," said he, addressing the two members, " is so and so, the author of so and so, the well-known philologist; as I was telling you, I spoke to Lord A—— this day about him, and said that he ought forthwith to have the head appointment in —— and what did the fellow say? Why, that there was no necessity for such an appointment at all, and if there were, why——and then he hummed and ha'd. Yes," said he, looking at the writer, " he did indeed. What a scandal ! what an infamy ! But I see how it will be, it will be a job. The place will be given to some son of a steward or to some quack, as I said before. Oh, these Tories ! Well, if this does not make one——" Here he stopped short, crunched his teeth, and looked the image of desperation.

Seeing the poor man in this distressed condition, the writer begged him to be comforted, and not to take the matter so much to heart; but the indignant Radical took the matter very much to heart, and refused all comfort whatever, bouncing about the room, and, whilst his spectacles flashed in the light of four spermaceti candles, exclaiming, " It will be a job—a Tory job ! I see it all, I see it all, I see it all !"

And a job it proved, and a very pretty job, but no Tory job. Shortly afterwards the Tories were out, and the Whigs were in. From that time the writer heard not a word about the injustice done to the country in not presenting him with the appointment to——; the Radical, however, was busy enough to obtain the appointment, not for the writer, but for himself, and eventually succeeded, partly through Radical influence, and partly through that of a certain Whig lord, for whom the Radical had done, on a particular occasion, work of a particular kind. So, though the place was given to a quack, and the whole affair a very pretty job, it was one in which the Tories had certainly no hand.

In the meanwhile, however, the friendly Radical did not drop the writer. Oh, no ! On various occasions he obtained from the writer all the information about the country in question, and was particularly anxious to obtain from the writer, and eventually did obtain, a copy of a work written in the court language of that country, edited by the writer, a language exceedingly difficult, which the writer, at the expense of a considerable portion of his eyesight, had acquired, at least as far as by the eyesight it could be acquired. What use the writer's friend made of the knowledge he had gained from him, and what use he made of the book, the writer can only guess; but he has little doubt that when the question of sending a person to —— was mooted in a Parliamentary Committee—which it was at the instigation of the writer's friend—the Radical on being examined about the country, gave the information which he had obtained from the writer as his own, and flashed the book and its singular characters in the eyes of the Committee; and then of course his Radical friends would instantly say, " This is the man !

there is no one like him. See what information he possesses; and see that book written by himself in the court language of Serendib. This is the only man to send there. What a glory, what a triumph it would be to Britain, to send out a man so deeply versed in the mysterious lore of—— as our illustrious countryman; a person who with his knowledge could beat with their own weapons the wise men of —— Is such an opportunity to be lost? Oh, no! surely not; if it is, it will be an eternal disgrace to England, and the world will see that Whigs are no better than Tories.''

Let no one think the writer uncharitable in these suppositions. The writer is only too well acquainted with the antecedents of the individual, to entertain much doubt that he would shrink from any such conduct, provided he thought that his temporal interest would be forwarded by it. The writer is aware of more than one instance in which he has passed off the literature of friendless young men for his own, after making them a slight pecuniary compensation and deforming what was originally excellent by interpolations of his own. This was his especial practice with regard to translation, of which he would fain be esteemed the king. This Radical literato is slightly acquainted with four or five of the easier dialects of Europe, on the strength of which knowledge he would fain pass for a universal linguist, publishing translations of pieces originally written in various difficult languages; which translations, however, were either made by himself from literal renderings done for him into French or German, or had been made from the originals into English, by friendless young men, and then deformed by his alterations.

Well, the Radical got the appointment, and the writer certainly did not grudge it him. He, of course, was aware that his friend had behaved in a very base manner towards him, but he bore him no ill-will, and invariably when he heard him spoken against, which was frequently the case, took his part when no other person would; indeed, he could well afford to bear him no ill-will. He had never sought for the appointment, nor wished for it, nor, indeed, ever believed himself to be qualified for it. He was conscious, it is true, that he was not altogether unacquainted with the language and literature of the country with which

the appointment was connected. He was likewise aware
that he was not altogether deficient in courage and in
propriety of behaviour. He knew that his appearance was
not particularly against him; his face not being like that
of a convicted pickpocket, nor his gait resembling that of
a fox who has lost his tail; yet he never believed himself
adapted for the appointment, being aware that he had no
aptitude for the doing of dirty work, if called to do it, nor
pliancy which would enable him to submit to scurvy treatment, whether he did dirty work or not—requisites, at the
time of which he is speaking, indispensable in every British
official; requisites, by the bye, which his friend the Radical
possessed in a high degree; but though he bore no ill-
will towards his friend, his friend bore anything but good-
will towards him; for from the moment that he had
obtained the appointment for himself, his mind was filled
with the most bitter malignity against the writer, and
naturally enough; for no one ever yet behaved in a base
manner towards another, without forthwith conceiving a
mortal hatred against him. You wrong another, know
yourself to have acted basely, and are enraged, not against
yourself—for no one hates himself—but against the innocent cause of your baseness; reasoning very plausibly,
" But for that fellow, I should never have been base; for
had he not existed I could not have been so, at any rate
against him;" and this hatred is all the more bitter, when
you reflect that you have been needlessly base.

Whilst the Tories are in power the writer's friend, of
his own accord, raves against the Tories because they do
not give the writer a certain appointment, and makes, or
says he makes, desperate exertions to make them do so;
but no sooner are the Tories out, with whom he has no influence, and the Whigs in, with whom he, or rather his
party, has influence, than he gets the place for himself,
though, according to his own expressed opinion—an
opinion with which the writer does not, and never did,
concur—the writer was the only person competent to hold
it. Now had he, without saying a word to the writer, or
about the writer with respect to the employment, got the
place for himself when he had an opportunity, knowing,
as he very well knew, himself to be utterly unqualified for
it, the transaction, though a piece of jobbery, would not

have merited the title of a base transaction; as the matter
stands, however, who can avoid calling the whole affair
not only a piece of—come, come, out with the word—
scoundrelism on the part of the writer's friend, but a most
curious piece of uncalled-for scoundrelism? and who, with
any knowledge of fallen human nature, can wonder at the
writer's friend entertaining towards him a considerable
portion of gall and malignity?

This feeling on the part of the writer's friend was wonderfully increased by the appearance of Lavengro, many
passages of which the Radical in his foreign appointment
applied to himself and family—one or two of his children
having gone over to Popery, the rest become members of
Mr. Platitude's chapel, and the minds of all being filled
with ultra notions of gentility.

The writer, hearing that his old friend had returned to
England, to apply, he believes, for an increase of salary,
and for a title, called upon him, unwillingly, it is true, for
he had no wish to see a person for whom, though he bore
him no ill-will, he could not avoid feeling a considerable
portion of contempt; the truth is, that his sole object in
calling was to endeavour to get back a piece of literary
property which his friend had obtained from him many
years previously, and which, though he had frequently
applied for it, he never could get back. Well, the writer
called; he did not get his property, which, indeed, he had
scarcely time to press for, being almost instantly attacked
by his good friend and his wife—yes, it was then that the
author was set upon by an old Radical and his wife—the
wife, who looked the very image of shame and malignity,
did not say much, it is true, but encouraged her husband in all he said. Both of their own accord introduced
the subject of Lavengro. The Radical called the writer
a grumbler, just as if there had ever been a greater grumbler than himself until, by the means above described, he
had obtained a place : he said that the book contained a
melancholy view of human nature—just as if anybody
could look in his face without having a melancholy view of
human nature. On the writer quietly observing that the
book contained an exposition of his principles, the pseudo-
Radical replied, that he cared nothing for his principles—
which was probably true, it not being likely that he would

care for another person's principles after having shown so thorough a disregard for his own. The writer said that the book, of course, would give offence to humbugs; the Radical then demanded whether he thought him a humbug?—the wretched wife was the Radical's protection, even as he knew she would be; it was on her account that the writer did not kick his good friend; as it was, he looked at him in the face and thought to himself, " How is it possible I should think you a humbug, when only last night I was taking your part in a company in which everybody called you a humbug?"

The Radical, probably observing something in the writer's eye which he did not like, became all on a sudden abjectly submissive, and, professing the highest admiration for the writer, begged him to visit him in his government; this the writer promised faithfully to do, and he takes the present opportunity of performing his promise.

This is one of the pseudo-Radical calumniators of Lavengro and its author; were the writer on his deathbed he would lay his hand on his heart and say, that he does not believe that there is one trait of exaggeration in the portrait which he has drawn. This is one of the pseudo-Radical calumniators of Lavengro and its author; and this is one of the genus, who, after having railed against jobbery for perhaps a quarter of a century, at present batten on large official salaries which they do not earn. England is a great country, and her interests require that she should have many a well-paid official both at home and abroad; but will England long continue a great country if the care of her interests, both at home and abroad, is in many instances intrusted to beings like him described above, whose only recommendation for an official appointment was that he was deeply versed in the secrets of his party and of the Whigs?

Before he concludes, the writer will take the liberty of saying of Lavengro that it is a book written for the express purpose of inculcating virtue, love of country, learning, manly pursuits, and genuine religion, for example, that of the Church of England, and for awakening a contempt for nonsense of every kind, and a hatred for priestcraft, more especially that of Rome.

And in conclusion, with respect to many passages of his book in which he has expressed himself in terms neither measured nor mealy, he will beg leave to observe, in the words of a great poet, who lived a profligate life, it is true, but who died a sincere penitent—thanks, after God, to good Bishop Burnet—

> " All this with indignation I have hurl'd
> At the pretending part of this proud world,
> Who, swollen with selfish vanity, devise
> False freedoms, formal cheats, and holy lies,
> Over their fellow fools to tyrannize."
>
> ROCHESTER.

THE END

INDEX

Index   397